The
Williamson
Effect

Edited by

Roger Zelazny

The
Williamson
Effect

A Tom Doherty Associates Book
New York

TOR®

THE WILLIAMSON EFFECT

Story notes by James Frenkel

A Tor Book
Published by Tom Doherty Associates, Inc.
175 Fifth Avenue
New York, NY 10010

Tor Books on the World Wide Web:
http://www.tor.com

Tor® is a registered trademark of Tom Doherty Associates, Inc.

Design by Lynn Newmark

Library of Congress Cataloging-in-Publication Data

The Williamson effect / edited by Roger Zelazny.—1st ed.
    p.   cm.
  "A Tom Doherty Associates book."
  ISBN 0-312-85748-9
  1. Science fiction, American.   2. Williamson, Jack, 1908–   —
Influence.   3. Williamson, Jack, 1908–   —Fiction.   I. Zelazny,
Roger.
PS648.S3W55   1996
813'.087208—dc20   95-53150
                                                            CIP

First Edition: May 1996

Printed in the United States of America

0 9 8 7 6 5 4 3 2 1

Roger Zelazny, winner of six Hugo and three Nebula awards and the editor of this collection, died of cancer on June 14, 1995. Before his death, he had completed the majority of the editorial work for *The Williamson Effect*. In keeping with the tradition Roger had established as editor for other collections, Jim Frenkel provided short introductions for each story. Jane Lindskold assisted with tying up loose ends and coordinating the collection for publication.

Acknowledgments

This page and the following constitute an extension of the copyright page.

The Publisher would like to acknowledge the following parties for their cooperation in the production of this book:

"A World in Love with Change" is copyright ©1996 by David Brin. Published by arrangement with the author.

"The Mayor of Mare Tranq" is copyright ©1996 by Frederik Pohl. Published by arrangement with the author.

"Before the Legion" is copyright ©1996 by Paul Dellinger. Published by arrangement with the author.

Contents

The
Williamson
Effect

Introduction

A World in Love with Change

David Brin

There is a legend.

It tells how once a clever Yankee trader routed a Chinese wizard in a business deal. Soon, the Oriental enchanter regretted the transaction. Watching furiously as his treasure was rowed out to a waiting Clipper ship, the fuming magician vowed revenge on the clever merchant. He gathered all the dwindling power-manna of his region, and while the merchant was still in range to hear, the wizard hurled his mightiest spell.

"For ten generations shall this fate befall you . . . and not only you, but your nation and all your people.

"May you live in interesting times!"

It is a traditional curse and one with fearsome implications to any Chinese. For during their long millennia of history, it has nearly always been better to endure boring placidity and sameness than the event-filled times that concern record-keepers—floods, wars, famines, and civic unrest—the very things the wizard now wished on his enemy's home and kin.

But magic has strange traits. It is neither as democratic as a bullet nor as dispassionate as a bomb. The subjective power of a spell depends as much on the mental state of the recipient as on the one who casts it. In this case, the victim was American, an explorer. And though fluent in Chinese, our merchant captain did not quite perceive the magician's words the way they were meant.

"May you live in interesting times!"

On hearing this, the surprised Yankee blinked a few times at the wizard on the dock. Then he smiled broadly and replied—

"Gee . . . thanks!"

Jack Williamson is no Yankee trader, but he might have been. His life is one long tale of hoodwinking fate, of turning adversity into advantage, and, above all, changing the world through the sheer magic of his perceptions. By seeing the universe in a new way—and conveying his vision through science fiction—Williamson helped break some of the old spells that held human beings enthralled for so long. Traditions of static sameness. The old fear of innovation.

He helped make the world we live in. A world in love with change.

That is hardly a destiny anyone might have predicted for John Stewart Williamson, when he was born in Bisbee, Arizona, in April, 1908. At just six weeks of age, his parents took him by

wagon and then mule-back to a threadbare ranch, high in the
Sierra Madre mountains of Sonora, Mexico—only the latest in a
series of hopeful family migrations that had drawn the Williamson clan onward throughout the period known as the Wild
West. With each failed venture the final option had always been
to pack up and try somewhere else, until, when Jack was seven
years old, the clan finally stopped their covered wagon near Portales, New Mexico, where Jack lives to this day.

He often cites Walter Prescott Webb's famous appraisal of
the American psyche—that it was forged by the Great Frontier.
Early in this century, pundits were predicting that American
character would change once the last open spaces were fenced.
They said the nation's mood of expansive optimism, of hope and
endless opportunity, could not survive once people lacked a
place to run to. A place for dreams to go.

Jack always agreed with this assessment. But then, who says
the frontier is gone? Who says it ever has to go away?

Born into a hard life, bullied by other children and ever-
lonely in his poverty, young Jack Williamson cast around for his
own borderlands, eventually finding them in both science and
science fiction. Held up against the backdrop of his wooden
shack, the lurid cover of a pulpy 1927 issue of Hugo Gernsback's
Amazing Stories seemed to frame the outlines of a doorway. A door
Jack shouldered open with all the spirit he could muster.

In those days, the written word was like a lifeline. It told of
faraway goings-on. Of flying machines and great wars, of tower-
ing buildings and experiments with that fabric of matter. It
hinted of new ways to look at time and space. Not far from
where Jack lived, Goddard was beginning the Age of the Rocket.
(Some years later, the same region would flare with a false
atomic dawn.)

Nearly all past civilizations seem to have shared a deep, archetypal belief that there was once a Golden Age—a shining time when people were better, knew more, and were closer to the gods . . . heights from which we fell and can never aspire again. Under such a world-view, Truth could only be found in a tribe's oldest text, and change is regarded, at best, with deep suspicion.

Amazing Stories was one vehicle proselytizing a *new* faith—a heretical creed that dared to put a golden age not in some pined-for past, but in the future; something difficult to attain, but worth striving for, achievable not through prayer alone, but mostly by hard work and vision. Naturally, this heresy was not well-regarded by society's guardians. At one point, a psychiatrist offered to *cure* Jack of the affliction of writing science fiction. But the addiction is a hard one to give up. Jack Williamson was never cured, never drawn back to the old creed.

We fellow heretics can be deeply thankful for that.

It is a strange belief system, this *zeitgeist* that I call the Dogma of Otherness. By its rule, enthusiasm and eccentricity are *virtues*, while any degree of fanaticism is apostasy. In the 1950s, when certain science fiction editors and authors began touting pseudo-Freudian cure-alls, psychic star drives and cynical religions, Jack Williamson was among those who told the truth about attractive myths—that wish fulfillment is fine on the pages of an adventure story. Our metaphors can express wonder, danger, and a vast universe of possibilities. But in real life it is the give-and-take of skeptical enquiry that drives the honest human quest for wisdom. Science fiction has no altars, nor priests or gurus . . . though we do have a saint or two.

I devoured my own share of science fiction during a lonely youth, often without bothering to note the authors on the cover. Later I learned, to my amazement, that the creator of the pulpy, fun *Legion of Space* series was the same man who penned *The Trial of Terra,* one of the most deeply moving books ever to muse on humanity's long, hard climb out of ignorance. On reflection, I saw how much Williams's unforgettable character, Giles Habibula, owed to Shakespeare's Falstaff, and how Habibula in turn inspired Poul Anderson's unforgettable Nicholas Van Rijn . . . a continuity of homage that continues to this day. (My own Pedro Manella would have been a poor shadow of himself without such inspiration.)

Although his roots sink deeply into an Eastern New Mexico oasis, where he was long a beloved professor of English and Linguistics, Jack Williamson always loved to travel—from an early, Twain-like trip down the Mississippi in a small boat with Edmond Hamilton to later expeditions in China, Russia, and Egypt with his wife, Blanche. Were all those space adventures just a way to go sightseeing where his body could not go? In taking readers to a Dyson Sphere, or the Oort Cloud, or the gritty Mars of his recent novel, *Beachhead,* Jack always seems to be saying— this isn't just a fantasy. This is a might-be!

Might-bes can be frightening. The best often are. *With Folded Hands* enabled Jack to present one of the most chilling explorations of a human future ever penned. One in which our creations betray us by doing exactly what they had been told. Rejecting the clichéd villains that fill most recent movies and thrillers— typically blood-soaked and bent on doing harm—Jack instead crafted the humanoids, virtually omnipotent robot beings whose sole objective is to serve humankind, cherishing and keeping us from harm, preventing us from engaging in any risky pastime, even unsupervised sex. This was not the first time a writer portrayed people oppressed by their creations. Nor did Jack invent the phrase "Be careful what you wish for." But in the literal-

minded humanoids, he conveyed with brilliant originality a danger we may someday face, when our servants turn on us, programmed with nothing but kindness.

Other ideas have poured across Williamson pages. Explorations in linguistics, early depictions of organ transplantation
(and associated crime), and the original notion that we may
someday send machines to the stars—programmed to con-
struct human colonists at the end of their long voyage. All the
way up to the recent Mars Movement of the early nineties,
Jack has been attuned to the latest trends, pitching his own
contributions alongside those of much younger writers. In collaboration with Frederik Pohl and others, he continues to blaze
new trails. Beyond being chosen as the second-ever Grand
Master of Science Fiction by the Science Fiction Writers of
America, Jack's honors include a Hugo Award for best non-fic-
tion work, his fascinating autobiography, *Wonder's Child: My Life
in Science Fiction.*

No one could list all the creative people whose careers were
influenced by science fiction, particularly the writings of Jack
Williamson. Among the better known names is Carl Sagan,
whose recent book, *A Pale Blue Dot,* devotes page after page to
discussing the influence of Jack's work in directing his thoughts
outward, toward a new frontier.

Perhaps one of Jack's greatest contributions will have been
his work in legitimizing the field he loves. Of course science fiction never needed the approval of stodgy academics in order to
become the most vibrant form of popular literature. But it is satisfying at last to see many universities recognize this with courses
and programs in science fiction. Working alongside James Gunn
and others, Jack was a pioneer in overcoming smug campus attitudes, patiently gathering the resources needed by researchers
and teachers who yearned to explore this literature of the new

frontier. For these and other lifetime efforts, a newly discovered asteroid was named Jackwilliamson 1994. A twinkling memento —one that Jack would love to see melted down someday, and turned into wondrous things.

For those of us lucky enough to know him, Jack Williamson is most cherished as friend and role model. In a world thick with self-righteousness and egotism, where individuality is extolled above manners or citizenship, Jack has shown generations of new writers that one needn't be insolent in order to be noticed. Vanity is a tempting impediment that helps no one to be great. In his gentle modesty and calm persistence, Jack Williamson lives the word *gentleman*. He sets an example for those who all too often get caught up in the momentum of our own ideas, so trans-fixed by the sound of our own voices that we forget to listen.

Jack's friends often jest that he'll likely outlive us all. But the joke has a fringe of respectful wonder. For nothing seems impos-sible where Jack Williamson is concerned. His work, spanning most of the century, has inspired countless minds away from ni-hilism and despair, to veer toward science and wonder. If anyone helped make this civilization—if anyone deserves to see where it finally winds up taking us—it is this man.

Jack Williamson has always believed in a world in love with change.

Here, to start off this *festschrift* with proper verve and enthusiasm, is a wonderful alternate history story by a Williamson collaborator and science fiction great. One of mankind's oldest dreams is of going into space. The protagonist of this clever yarn should be familiar, since he is Jack Williamson himself. I like to think Jack would enjoy the alternate fate that unfolds in the following tale.

The Mayor of Mare Tranq

Frederik Pohl

The incident that changed young Johnny Williamson's life took place in Arizona, in the year of 1916. If it had just rained a little more in that bad, dry year, Johnny's father, Sam Williamson, might have made a go of the farm. But it didn't. The soil dried. The seedlings withered. The crop would not be made. Sam let the dust flow through his fingers and made his decision: dryland farming was too chancy to feed a family; something had to be done.

His first thought was to move on to some more hospitable area, Texas or maybe even Old Mexico, where it did sometimes rain. But he didn't have to. His neighbor, the Republican party boss of the county, made him an offer: he would give Sam a job in his general store if only Sam would put his name in as a candidate for the Congress of the United States. That wasn't meant as a serious prospect for a career in government. The boss only wanted a name to put before the voters in order to complete the ticket, with no real chance of being elected. Big Bill Bronck, the Democratic incumbent, was well known to be unbeatable in any election. However, Fate intervened. The day before the election Big Bill Bronck was shot to death in the parlor of a county-seat brothel, and when the votes were counted Sam Williamson, with his wife and children, was on his way to the capital.

The city of Washington, D.C., was a marvel to Sam's boys, young Johnny and his brother Jim. They had never been in a big city before. The storefront moving-picture shows, the clanging trolley cars in the streets, the hordes of people rushing about on their business—the boys blossomed there. It wasn't all to their good. The city was a lot more fun than school, and, sadly, they both developed a talent for playing hookey in order to explore the wonders of the metropolis. Happily, that didn't much matter, because they were both bright enough to breeze through their classes in grammar and high school. When Johnny was eighteen years old he graduated from high school as valedictorian of his class . . . the week before his father died.

That was a terrible blow to the family. They were left with no reason to stay in Washington, and only a Congressman's pension to feed the young family. Johnny's mother decided their best bet was to head west for Texas, where cousins had land outside of Dallas and ranch living was cheap. That didn't solve Johnny's problem. He was ready for college, but where was the tuition money to come from? However, in the event that problem was no problem. Representative Bob Blakeless of Ohio, formerly Sam Williamson's closest associate on the Fish, Game and

Poultry Subcommittee, was ready and willing to give his late colleague's boy a Congressional appointment to any service school he chose, and young Johnny selected the U.S. Military Academy at West Point.

At the Academy Johnny stopped playing hookey. He thrived at the Point. He paid attention to his studies, lived by the cadet code, and walked off his demerits until he stopped getting them. He turned out to be a first-rate cadet. When he graduated, fifth in his class, he was privileged to pick his own branch of Army service, and what he chose was the fledgling Army Air Corps.

Those were bad years economically. The stock market had collapsed and the country was groaning under the weight of the Great Depression. Money was scarce everywhere, even for the military, and the equipment of the Army Air Corps showed it. The slow, cranky biplanes the Corps was flying belonged to another, obsolete generation; every airman knew that the sleek new planes the Germans and the English were practicing with across the Atlantic could outfly and outfight any of them. Accidents were frequent and often terminal, but Second Lieutenant Williamson was lucky . . . and skilled, too. He took to flying like a duck to water. He became an instructor, then a check pilot for the new P-36s that were coming in, and then war broke out in Europe. Pearl Harbor changed everything—for Williamson as well as for everyone else. He was one of the first fighter pilots sent to North Africa and quickly showed he was one of the best. The ten-year lieutenant became a captain, then a major commanding a squadron. He had four clusters to his Air Medal and his confirmed kills amounted to eleven by the time of V-J Day. He was one of the few urged to stay on when most of the Army, Navy and Marine Corps were demobbing. By the time he reached his twenty-year retirement he was a full colonel . . . and possessed by a new ambition.

John had been in London at the time of the V-2s. He had
sneaked across the Channel to Peenemunde to see the place
where those rockets came from, and he had been struck by the
thought that those same rockets could take something—maybe
even someone—into space, and he wished with all his heart for
that to happen. To *him.* So, now a civilian, he went to work for an
aerospace company in Texas, doing his best to make sure that if
ever someone tried to make that great leap into the unknown
there would be machines available to make it work.

He thrilled when the new President, John Fitzgerald
Kennedy, made his speech about putting men on the Moon. It
was his chance. Slim, yes, but a lot better than no chance at all,
and so Williamson instantly began calling in old favors. His former seconds-in-command were now colonels and generals; he
begged them to help get him into the space program. And they
tried. They really tried. They pulled all the strings they could for
their old boss, but time was against them. Col. John Stewart Williamson (Retd.) was fifty-three on the day when Kennedy made
his historic speech . . . and that was simply Too Old.

His dream was over. His prospects of getting into space were
exactly zero . . . that is, they were until the events of November
1963.

What brought John Williamson into the city that day was his
brother's little son, Gary. The boy was as dedicated to the idea of
space travel as his uncle, and a devoted admirer of the President
who was going to make it real. What Gary Williamson wanted,
more than anything else, was to see his hero and maybe even
take some pictures of him with his new movie camera.

By the time they got to a point where the Presidential procession was going to pass all the good places were taken, but

John Williamson was up to that challenge. There was a kind of a
warehouse building by the side of the road, apparently unoccupied at the moment. Williamson tried doors until he found one
that would open, and he and the boy climbed stairs to look out
on the street. They found a good window at once, but there was
a tree that seemed to be in the way. Williamson left the boy
there and scouted some of the other rooms . . . and, in the third
one, was startled to see a scruffy man with a rifle glaring angrily
down at the street.

It could have been something innocent. It could even have
been (Williamson thought later) a Dallas detective in plain
clothes, guarding the route of the procession. He didn't stop to
think of any of those possibilities. Reflexes took over. He
charged the man, knocked the rifle out the window, overpow-
ered the would-be assassin and was sitting on his chest when a
pair of actual Dallas cops, alerted by the sight of the rifle falling
out of the window, came pounding up the stairs to take charge.

That night Williamson and his nephew were called to see the
President on Air Force One. Mrs. Kennedy was there, looking
sweet and appealing in her pink suit and pink pillbox hat; so were
Texas Governor John Connally and his wife; so were a couple of
Secret Service men, amiably but carefully watching every move
Williamson and the boy made. The President got up from his
overstuffed chair, grimacing with some sort of pain in his back,
and extended a hand to Williamson. "Colonel Williamson," he
said, "they tell me you're the one who took out this fellow—"

"Oswald," his wife supplied. "His name is Lee Harvey Oswald."

"Yes, Oswald. I don't know what kind of a shot he was. My
Secret Service friends here tell me that we would have been a
pretty tough target to hit—"

"A damn impossible target," Governor Connally grumbled, and the First Lady said sweetly:

"Oh, not *impossible*. I'm glad we didn't have to find out."

"But anyway," the President said, "it looks like you just might have saved my life and maybe Jackie's, too. I owe you, Colonel. Is there something I can do for you?"

"I want to go to the Moon," Williamson said promptly.

Kennedy grinned. "Can't blame you there; so do I. Well, put in your application and we'll—"

"I did," Williamson interrupted. "They turned me down. They said I was too old. But I have eighteen hundred hours, mostly in P-38s and P-51s but some jets, too. I believe I can handle a spacecraft whenever there's one to handle, and I know I can pass any physical they can give me."

The President looked at him thoughtfully. "I bet you could, at that. All right. Put in your application again . . . and this time, write on the bottom that you have an age waiver officially granted by the President of the United States."

Williamson did pass the physical. Williamson did excel in astronaut training. Williamson was the second one of the Mercury Eight to make a suborbital flight, and when the Apollo program reached the point of actually doing what President Kennedy had promised and putting a man on the surface of the Moon, Colonel John Stewart Williamson was one of the three men strapped into the capsule as the giant Saturn-V lifted off from Cape Canaveral.

He was not, however, one of the landers. Williamson's job was to remain in the orbiter while Armstrong and Aldrin rode the lunar landing capsule down to the surface. It wasn't perfect. He would have preferred to be in on the actual descent. But it was one hell of a lot better than anything else around, and he accepted the assignment with grace and pleasure . . . until the moment when the capsule was scheduled to take off again for orbital rendezvous.

For all those hours of waiting in the orbiter while Armstrong and Aldrin capered around the lunar surface in their ungainly suits, John Williamson had worn around his neck a leather strap that held a small volume with complete, preplanned instructions for actions he should take in every possible emergency. *Almost* every possible emergency, anyway. There was one exception.

At the planned moment of liftoff Williamson was over the horizon in his orbit, out of sight of the landing area in Mare Tranquilitatis. He could neither see the capsule nor hear their transmissions to Mike Collins at Earth Control at that second. He didn't know what had happened until he rounded the curve of the Moon, and by the time he could pick up their messages the situation had become critical. "—tipping too far," said Buzz Aldrin's voice from the surface. "Try again!" urged the voice from Earth Control. "Can't," said Aldrin despairingly. "Looks like the soil's a little soft under that leg. We're tipping already from the vibration. If we go to full burn we'll just tip this beast over on its side."

That was when Williamson cut in. "You can't get lift?" he demanded unbelievingly.

" 'Fraid not, Johnny," said Aldrin. "We're stuck. Say good-bye to everybody for us when you get back."

And that was the one contingency for which Williamson had no instructions. In the event that the lunar module was unable to lift off there was no way for the orbiter to come down to their rescue. And so the book did not say what to do, because in that case there was simply nothing to be done.

Or at least nothing that the people who wrote the book had been able to foresee.

* * *

Colonel John Stewart Williamson, on the other hand, was not in the habit of doing nothing. He was a pilot. Stuff happened, but no matter how bad things looked there was always something you could try—right up to the moment when you crashed or died, and that was all she wrote. But until that moment came you never gave up.

So he did three more lunar orbits, keeping his camera on the landing module in its drunken, half-toppled posture every minute he was above the horizon, knowing that all around the world there were two billion people—now two and a half billion— now maybe three, as new ones heard what was going on and tuned in—billions of Earth's people, all watching the terrible scene on the lunar surface. Williamson's heart was heavy, but his mind was still racing. And when at last he started the burn that would lift him out of lunar orbit and start him on the long, slow fall toward reentry he got on the radio again. "Earth Control, Earth Control," he said into his microphone, "Earth Control, don't stand around with your thumbs up your asses, start figuring out what you're going to do for these guys."

The time it took for an answer was longer than the normal couple of seconds transit-time delay. Then Mike Collins, the Boston controller, said, "Hey, Johnny, cut that out! The whole world's listening to you. Don't get their hopes up when you know we can't do a thing."

"I say again, Earth Control," Williamson snapped, "you don't want to waste any more time talking about what you can't do. You *have* to do something. You don't want to let them die there!"

The next pause was longer, and when the voice came on it wasn't Mike Collins, it was the Director himself, and savage. "Colonel Williamson, have you gone out of your tree? We can't rescue them! They're well and truly stuck!"

"Who said rescue? Just keep them *alive*! There are two more lunar modules and three Apollos at the Cape right now, and enough Saturn Fives to lift them. All right, you can't send another crew down until you figure out what went wrong. But you can send a goddam *capsule* down—crewless, on automatic—and load it with air and water—lots of it, because you don't have to bother filling the tank with return fuel—and keep them going for a couple of weeks—until you send another one down—and another, and another until you figure out how to get them home. You can do that, all right. The only thing you *can't* do is let them die there!"

Would NASA have listened to what Williamson was saying if half the world hadn't heard it at the same time? Perhaps it would have. But also, perhaps not. Perhaps organization and precedent would have carried the day, and the proposal been turned over to an assessment committee. And only then, a week or month later, would a decision have been made—to abandon the pair on the Moon to preserve the project's orderly schedule, or perhaps even to do what Williamson urged . . . though by then Armstrong and Aldrin would, of course, be dead.

That didn't happen. Neither the controllers in Boston nor their masters in Washington had the choice. Within minutes the phone lines to NASA were hot with loud-talking citizens demanding that the space agency send immediate help to the stranded astronauts—and so were the lines to the White House, and to both houses of Congress, and to every newspaper and broadcasting station, too, and not just in the United States. The whole world was crying out to save the astronauts, and within the hour the order went out to start preflighting the next Moonbound Apollo.

*   *   *

And, of course, the rest is history. On any clear night when the
Moon is at quarter everyone in the world can see the diamond-
dust lights of the community in Mare Tranq, and everyone
knows how it got there. How twelve separate missions brought
air, food and water down to Mare Tranquilitatis. How on the
seventh mission Colonel Williamson himself piloted the module
down to the surface to become the third man on the Moon . . .
and to stay. How by the time all the design flaws in the landing
struts had been identified and fixed there was such a wealth of
matériel clustered around the original landing site—"The Earth-
light Trailer Park," one astronaut dubbed it—that it had become
a de facto lunar outpost, and before long a priceless resource.
The next step in space travel was clearly the stars. The way to
get there was clearly by nuclear-fusion propulsion, fueled by
helium-4 . . . and where else in the solar system was there a richer
store of He-4 than the masses the solar wind had sown into the
lunar soil, atom by atom, over the four-and-a-half-billion-year
life of the Sun?

     And then there was no question of who was the right person
to head it . . . and so John Stewart Williamson became the first,
and so far the only, loved and honored Mayor of Mare Tranq.

Jack Williamson:
THE MAN THEY NAMED THE ASTEROID AFTER

In the summer of 1939, when I first met Professor John Stewart Williamson, he wasn't either a professor or even a Ph.D. yet—had had to drop out of college without a degree for a while because he couldn't afford to go on— but I was almightily impressed with the man all the same. Jack Williamson had already had a profound effect on my life. It was his *Amazing Stories* serial, *The Stone from the Green Star*, that had converted me from second-hand-store buyer to newsstand customer. When I read the story's first installment in a previously-owned copy of the magazine, I couldn't wait for the next part to arrive in the second-hand store. It wrecked my finances for a week, but I walked right up to the stand and bought my first mint copy of an sf magazine to find out how it came out. (Jack now says that he's not particularly proud of that story; in fact, it's just about the only one of his longer pieces that he has never allowed to come out in book form. But I was only eleven at the time, and what did I know?)

That was in 1931. Eight years later, when Jack turned up in New York City and we did meet, I was older and considerably more sophisticated, but still vastly impressed. A few years after that, a war having come along, I was at the Air Force weather school at Chanute Field, Illinois, and so was Jack; later still, that war over, I was running a literary agency in New York City and Jack became one of my star clients. By then it was pretty clear to me that Jack Williamson had become inextricably entangled in my life . . . and, you know?, I wouldn't have it any other way.

Jack Williamson and I have been friends ever since. More than that, we've been colleagues and collaborators as well: agent/client, editor/contributor, most of all co-authors of—let's see—oh, I think by now we're up to a total of ten science fiction novels. That says a lot right there, for literary collaboration isn't for everybody. I've done rather a lot of it over the years, with mixed results. More than once the outcomes have been less than entirely satisfying, and there have been times when the collaborative process itself can best be described as pure misery.

That isn't what it has been like with Jack Williamson. In more than forty years we've never had a cross word over what we were writing together, and not very many for any other reason, either. I can't take the credit for that. I have to admit that belongs to Jack, who is—among many other admirable traits—close to qualifying as the very best-natured human being it has ever been my good fortune to meet.

Curiously, we never set out to collaborate on novels. Jack had generally preferred to do his writing on his own; I had done more of that kind of literary pairing at one time or another, especially in my early days as a beginning writer, but had more or less decided against doing much more of it. But around 1950, when I was acting as Jack's literary agent, I was happy to find that the markets were hungry for his stories, but somewhat depressed by the fact that I was selling them faster than he could write them. In an effort to increase his production I asked if he had any unfinished manuscripts lying around. He had. By return mail he sent along several hundred pages of undersea adventures that he'd begun some time earlier, had tried to develop in several ways and, at the last, had bogged down on completely. I thought the fragments were far too good to throw away; since Jack himself had abandoned them I proposed that he let me try my hand at whipping them into shape. He agreed, and out of that came the three novels of *The Undersea Trilogy*.

A few years later Jack found himself at the same dead end on some stories that had to do with exploration of Fred Hoyle's "steady-state" universe. That was a really neat cosmological theory, giving scope for some marvelously colorful astronomical settings which Jack had described in lovely, lavish detail; Hoyle's notion proposed that the universe had neither beginning nor end but was just *there*, and moreover was continually expanding as new matter and new space were spontaneously created out of nothingness. Unfortunately, the theory was revealed to be wrong when a couple of neighbors of mine in New Jersey discovered the low-temperature microwave radiation left over from the Big Bang; that irreparably shot down Hoyle's model, because it meant the universe did definitely have at least a beginning. But while the steady-state theory was still a possibility Jack invited me to take my own crack at those lovely fragments, and that became the three books of *The Starchild Trilogy*.

By then it had become clear that we enjoyed working together, and so we wrote another batch of books, this time with forethought and deliberate design. I mean, a *lot* of forethought. Before Jack and I began a new book it was our practice to bounce ideas back and forth for months, sometimes a year or more. Because we live a couple of thousand miles apart (and because I am so unregenerate as to refuse to have anything to do with e-mail or the computer nets in general) we do our preliminary discussion by ordinary, old-fashioned letter mail. Extensively. I'm pretty sure that if you stacked all the correspondence that went into any of our books next to the book manuscript itself, the correspondence pile would be a good deal the taller.

What gets us started on a story idea? Usually it's something scientific. Jack is as addicted a fan of science as I am — we've spent a lot of time together checking out places like Stonehenge, and the Sandia National Laboratories, and panda breeding stations and ancient hydrological works in China; we both belong to a clutch of scientific organizations and take pleasure in reading their journals, and so it happens, now and then, that some new notion in science begins to suggest story possibilities to us. Freeman Dyson's idea that a truly technologically advanced society would enclose its star to trap energy for their purposes led us to *Farthest Star* and *Wall Around a Star*; the tectonics of the mid-ocean ridges and the discovery of odd forms of deep-sea life to *Land's End*; Stephen Hawking's *A Brief History of Time*, with its gaudy visions of serial universes linked together like sausages on a string, to *The Singers of Time*. (That was originally intended to be called *The Turtles of Time*, but at the last minute the publishers got cold feet, fearing confusion with the Teenage Mutant Ninja Turtles, who were making themselves felt around that time.)

I've been talking about Jack solely in his incarnation as a writer, but of course that doesn't do the man justice. He did eventually manage to go back to school, got his bachelor's and his master's and ultimately his Ph.D.; whereupon he launched a highly productive second (and concurrent) career as a college professor at Eastern New Mexico University. (He's nominally retired now, as a distinguished professor emeritus; but of course he goes right on teaching new classes every year anyway.)

Among the other subjects Jack taught at ENMU was a course in science fiction, which led him to conduct the first census of sf classes in American schools, which made possible the formation of the Science Fiction Research Association, the academic wing of the field. He also found time, somewhere along the line, to serve two terms as president of our trade union, the Science Fiction Writers of America. He is, of course, officially a Grand Master, and so recognized by the members of SFWA; and, more than that, when the astronomers were looking for an appropriate name for an asteroid they, quite rightly, could think of nothing better than to name it after him.

All of which is part of the evidence which leads me to believe that this man can do anything . . . which, in turn, is what inspired this little story of something that (in the real world) Jack has not actually done . . . yet.

—Frederik Pohl

Perhaps the most beloved character created by Jack Williamson in his long and fruitful career is the rascally scoundrel Giles Habibula, based, by Jack's own admission, on William Shakespeare's Falstaff. Habibula's life prior to his well-chronicled escapades with the Legion of Space is shrouded in mystery. Here is one scenario that comes to us from the uncertain future, as divined by a faithful follower of the Legion.

Before the Legion

Paul Dellinger

It is not an easy thing I do now, nor something I do lightly. Poor old Giles Habibula has never been one to stir around in the bleached bones and musty skeletons of the past, lad—never even to my closest comrades, Jay Kalam, himself the commander of the Legion of Space, or Hal Samdu, his strong right arm. . . .

But for you, Chan Derron—for the grandson whose kinship I discovered so fortuitously during our pursuit of the fearful Basilisk and his mortal threat to the entire system—aye, for your eyes and ears only, I leave this recording, trusting to the discretion of an aging legionnaire's only blood relation to keep the blessed contents within the family, so to speak.

*   *   *

Old Giles must look back almost fifty years, lad—aye, before our encounters with the frightful Medusae or the evil Cometeers, back to when some of our planets were still wild frontier worlds, and the Legion's foothold upon them tenuous at best. I was to become one of those legionnaires myself, lad, although not of my own choosing. For poor aging Giles Habibula was then in the bloom of hot-blooded youth, and had shaken off the dust of old Earth and its smothering robot servants hustling about to serve and obey and protect us all from harm, and from precious life itself, to my way of thinking. I sought adventure and fortune first as an asterite, a rock rat scratching a living in high vaccuum from the rich ores of the belt—then to terraformed Mars, where excavating jobs were as plentiful as the treasures discovered by the first expedition in those buried meteor fields in the Martian highlands. And finally to Venus and its two-month days and nights. . . .

But young Giles soon learned that there were better and quicker ways to wealth, lad. I found that I had a certain dexterity with cards, and dice, and other toys of chance. It was easier to fatten my pockets with the winnings from those who worked the planetary frontiers than to be a blessed frontiersman myself—a discovery which, of course, Giles Habibula was not the first to make.

I found that I had to develop a certain facility with proton pistols as well, to be successful in my new profession and survive to enjoy that success. Not everyone shared Giles's philosophic acceptance of the occasional losing hand or toss of dice, and it sometimes became necessary to defend my precious winnings. Generally, I managed to do so with my wits, or by bringing my weapon to bear before the other mortal ingrate could produce

his own. But, inevitably, there came a time when I faced a dis-
honorable competitor whose speed nearly matched my own and
I had no choice but to fire.

It was in one of the many gambling dens under the Venusian
domes, and one in which my late opponent had more friends
than I. But poor ancient Giles was agile in those days, able to leap
across the table he pushed in their ugly faces and onto a stairway
leading up to where other types of recreational activities were
pursued. I eluded my own pursuit by easing into an unused room,
and might have escaped entirely had I not overturned an ill-
placed reading lamp in the dark. Fortunately, by the time they
ran me to ground, a legionnaire had arrived, and it was he who
took me into custody.

But that did not discourage poor Giles's new army of enemies. Even back then, fate conspired against me at every turn.
They began inciting a mob to storm the Legion garrison where I
was held. It was a young lieutenant of my acquaitance, another
former Earther named Will Stewart, who offered me a way out.

Stewart was from a place called Bisbee, Arizona, on Earth's
North American continent not far from the fabled town of
Tombstone, where frontier law had been enforced by larger-
than-life figures—Wyatt Earp, Johnny Mack Brown, Lash
LaRue, whoever—old Giles's stressed and addled wits can't sepa-
rate history from legend in that long-ago time.

"Of course we'll try to stand them off, Giles," he told me
through the bars of my cell. "But there are only three of us on
hand right now, and dozens of them. A jury would no doubt
agree that it was a case of self-defense, but you may not get to a
jury. An immediate pardon would be a better way out for us all."

Stewart had tried to recruit me before. He insisted that I possessed qualities of value to the Legion, a certain dexterity with

mechanisms as well as cards. But I had no wish to trade the few precious comforts and luxuries I'd accumulated through my own modest talents for the Spartan barracks and ships of the Legion. Given the alternative, however, I came to see the idea of enlisting in a more positive light.

I took my oath of allegiance within the hour, and soon found myself part of a training squad far from the civilized settlements of the domed cities, in an uncharted Venusian jungle in the wetlands. I don't know where you took your Legion training, lad, but, for sweet life's sake, I hope it wasn't there. No Legion academy for poor Giles—oh no, my presumed friend Stewart had assured his superiors that my field training should come first. Young Giles needed to learn discipline, they said, to function as part of a unit, to survive in planetary wilds, to learn the one-for-all and all-for-one code of the Legion. . . .

Lad, it was mortal agony, the worst torture of my life, at least up until the time that Jay, Hal, John Star, and I were forced to make that terrible trek across the fearful planet of the dark Medusae to rescue the Keeper of the Peace—but poor old Giles digresses. His mind is overtaxed with memories of Venusian jungle fever, of hacking our way through fearful poisonous growths that sprang from our own hundreds of years of terraforming attempts, of battling the frightful descendants of transplanted animals as stubborn as the silica-armored desert things of Mars. Those Mars creatures may have been native or, as later research suggests, transplanted by some earlier space-faring race, but the blame for those Venusian monsters is all our own. In transforming Venus from an unlivable globe of superheated temperatures and sulfuric-acid rain to a place where humans could survive, if barely, we failed to take into account the stubborn planet's own long-term effects on the life-forms we introduced. Fascinating,

though, how we inadvertently turned Venus into the very sort of
world that many of those early-twentieth-century scientific romance writers imagined it to be. . . .

Well! Not to prolong the unpleasantness of my tale, I survived. And it was a happy crew of recruits that took our first liberty aboard a small passenger flyer to a little rocky island of
domed civilization off New Chicago, on a slowly ending long
Venusian night that Giles Habibula will never forget no matter
how long he manages to survive all that ill fortune keeps heaping
upon him.

It was a booming, boisterous little enclave, far enough from
any Legion garrison so that we felt free, in civilian clothing, to
seek out those entertainments that would not be permitted in
uniform. For myself, I yearned to see if my modest talent for
games of chance had survived my months of mortal tribulation,
and wandered into a promisingly noisy and bustling little casino
off the main thoroughfare called the Blue Unicorn.

I had not been in the place for five precious minutes before I
forgot gambling altogether.

A soft, gentle horn from the orchestra at one end of the room
sounded the start of a singer's performance, the notes traveling
gently upward like a melodic breeze, and all around me the place
became abruptly quiet. Players paused in their games, and the
sounds of dice and wheels and the shuffle of cards stopped altogether, something I had never before seen in a place of this kind.
Then came her voice, clean and bright and enchanting, putting
words to a melody so varied that I found I could not hum it to
myself even immediately after hearing it. It was a song about
Venus, not the hothouse Venus that I had spent recent months
barely surviving but the Venus that would be someday, the glorious green Eden where peace and love and harmony reigned in a
bright new universe of realized dreams.

Poor Giles Habibula can't do justice to the song, lad, nor the beauty of the singer who gave it voice. It wasn't until much later that she herself told me that the tune dated back a thousand years, composed during one of old Earth's world wars as a seven-part suite called "The Planets," that this particular segment was titled "Venus, the Bringer of Peace," and that it was she who had added the words.

Lovely words they were, like the voice, holding us all en-thralled, no surprise to those who regularly frequented the Blue Unicorn, and the reason why they had all paused to listen when she began. I would hear her perform many more songs, both her own compositions and others, to the same effect. But, for me, that first song about Venus will be the one I remember.

The song must have gone on for ten precious minutes, seem-ing not enough by far, and the applause was thunderous when the last tinkling notes trailed away and the beautiful performer moved gracefully off stage after bestowing a smile upon us all, her mortal worshipers. "Who is she?" I demanded of the man next to me when the volume of noise finally permitted conversa-tion.

"Why, man, where have you been? That's Ethyra Coran," he said. "Everyone between here and New Chicago knows that Pedro brought her all the way from Earth for his Blue Unicorn—which is why it's suddenly the most popular gambling house on Lakshmi Planum."

Ethyra Coran. The name itself spoke of music to me. Never have the sight and sound of a woman had such an effect on Giles Habibula, before or since. I would not have you believe that Giles was totally inexperienced with women at that point in his life, lad, but none had stirred his blood like this. The perfunctory bit of gambling I managed at two or three tables, wandering aim-lessly through the casino, brought me no precious winnings, but my mind was dreadfully far from the play. I lingered awhile in hope that Ethyra Coran would perform again, but the few other acts that came and went finally discouraged me to the point where I left to try my luck elsewhere.

Still, never did I stray far from the Blue Unicorn, constantly anticipating another hush I knew would fall over the place if Ethyra Coran should return to the stage. As loud as it was now, I thought to detect the difference even from the street. It was during one of my passings by that I noticed a tubular grid-controlled passenger vehicle hum to a stop beside a small alley by the Unicorn. A fly-port auto-cab, from the emblem along its side, the same as on the programmed vehicle that had brought our little group into the domed settlement from the landing field. A woman possessing long blond hair and a dark wrap with a high turned-up collar loaded several pieces of luggage into it and climbed in herself to key a destination on the grid panel in front of her seat. She moved with an intriguing and vaguely familiar grace, but what did I care? Ethyra Coran had short dark hair, not blond.

Old Giles's precious wits were usually quicker than that, at least in those days, but they had been roundly befuddled by her siren song. It was not until a group of dark-suited men pouring from the casino began grabbing bystanders and shouting questions about a missing singer that the truth struck me. You, lad, with your talent for acting and disguises, would no doubt have puzzled it out at once, but poor Giles, as you know, is as innocent and straightforward as a lamb.

The street was crowded. I would not have been the only one to see her. But I had time to walk a few blocks to another auto-cab call box and start to the airfield myself before her pursuers got organized.

She was seated in a corner of the terminal, still wearing the wrap and wig, surrounded by her luggage and glancing at the local-time chronometer on the wall. Boldly, for old Giles was more bold in those days, I walked directly over to her and sat down in the next seat.

"They know you've gone, lass," I said quietly. "They're likely to pick up your trail and be here any precious moment now."

She turned to me with a small intake of breath, and I was struck anew by her beauty close up. "Who are you?" she asked, and it was indeed the same precious voice that had enchanted me before.

"A friend. I hope you can believe that." I gave my name and asked if I could be of assistance.

"I appreciate the offer, Giles, but I'm simply waiting for a flight to the spaceport. I'm returning to Earth."

"Venus's loss," I murmured, the sadness in my voice quite genuine. "I understood you had been here but a short time?"

She hesitated, but I had made it a question. "I came with the understanding that I was to be a performer only. A well-paid performer, but no more. Now, Pedro—my employer—has made it clear that he expects more, so I am dissolving our contract. That's all."

"This is not Earth, or even Mars, lass. Legal niceties don't always apply here. I don't know the clauses of your contract, but it appeared to me that your employer has the muscle and manpower to override it. If, that is, he finds you."

She looked up again at the chronometer. "It'll be early morning before the flight leaves. I suppose he'll be here first." Her fingers gripped the sides of her seat more tightly, I noticed, but there was no tremor whatever in that lovely voice.

"May I suggest a strategy, lass? Hide in plain sight." When she looked questioningly at me, I continued. "Literally hundreds of casinos there are, restaurants and other palaces of entertainment, between here and New Chicago, all reachable by ground-car. Why not join me in visiting some of them, long enough for Pedro and his friends to tire of watching this place and the other exits from this dome? Then I'll bring you back here, and you can go if you still wish it."

She gave me a long, appraising glance. I may say, lad, that old Giles then presented a more robust appearance than the mal-treated and ill-used old soldier you see before you now. At length, she gave what seemed a small nod. "But wouldn't Pedro be able to locate us by whatever route we punched into an auto-car?"

I smiled. "Leave that to me," I said.

You see, lad, I have always had a small ability with locks and machines. It was the work of a few minutes to disconnect a ground-car from its grid control, puzzle out the code that would tell the main computer it was temporarily out of service, and acti-vate its emergency manual control. I could only hope I had cho-sen a vehicle with a fully charged battery. I drove it back to the terminal entrance where she waited after checking her baggage in a locker, and we were off.

A glorious fading Venusian night, lad, one I would not have missed for sweet life's sake even though at no point did we become intimate. We ranged from one settlement to another, pausing here and there for games of chance—I had, after all, only my legionnaire pay, not enough to entertain her in the style I wished without enlarging it—and dining at a lavish restaurant after visiting a clothier and acquiring fit raiment to do so. It was a series of threes and fours at the dice table that turned our luck to the point where we could afford it—luck, and the skillful young hands of Giles Habibula.

We spoke of our pasts, she telling of her fascination with the literature of the last millennium, and I mostly lying. The space age was the only era in human history, she said, of which the legends were written before they happened. It was her goal, she said, to set them to music.

As sweet fate would have it, our excursion lasted until the long-awaited Venusian sunrise heralded the beginning of a two-month day. I don't know if you've ever seen a sunrise on Venus, lad. Neither she nor I had and, giddy and fatigued as we were, it capped our first time together as though sweet nature had planned it just for us. The synthetic atmosphere and climate control within the domes had not appreciatively thinned the denseness of the atmosphere outside, and the sun—rising in the west, with our planet's retrograde rotation—stretched all along the horizon by refracted light. Ethyra hummed a bit of her Venus tune as we watched, locking it even more deeply into my memory. I hated to break the spell, but felt sure she would be safe at the fly-port now, while I had to get back to the Legion garrison where already I would be late and due some military harassments.

"I'm not sure that I want to leave Venus now, Giles," she said when I reluctantly broached the subject.

"But—but, Pedro . . ." I began.

"I can handle Pedro if I must. It just hadn't seemed worth the trouble until now. Now, though, I may stay."

"Why, lass? Why risk yourself by remaining on this primitive planet?"

"Because, Giles," she replied sweetly, "you're here."

After we parted ways, I decided it was time for Giles Habibula to die.

As a captain in the Legion, lad, I don't expect you to understand. But I felt that I'd been shanghaied into joining, and had no qualms about leaving when something better came along. Ethyra was something better.

Opportunities to die in the wetlands were plentiful in those days, and it was no trick for Giles to slip away from his squad on maneuvers and strew fragments of his trainee uniform along one of those sulfurous streams flowing through the Venusian wilds. I had spent the last of my liberty winnings on things I would need—nonmilitary jungle gear, a small proton pistol with spare charges, an oxygen 'fresher for when the air got too bad, food concentrates, and medication to ward off jungle fever—to last across the wetlands to the nearest dome.

My training must have been better than I realized. It wasn't easy—I all but exhausted the pistol between the hungry clinging plants and carnivorous beasts—but I made it.

From there, while my fellow trainees mourned (I presumed) my passing, it was a comparatively simple matter to accumulate a stake by opening a few locks and safe combinations in casino offices, and to build it up at various gaming tables over the next few day-periods. I made my way from one dome to the next until I arrived at the settlement of the Blue Unicorn. A few discreet inquiries confirmed that Ethyra was still singing there, but they brought me bad news as well: she had a suitor.

"Amo, he calls himself," my informant told me. "A fancy man, and extraordinarily good with cards. He arrived barely a week ago aboard a liner from the Jovian satellites. Never talks about himself, but you hear things . . ."

"What things?" I asked.

"A crewman from the liner told me one of the men he broke in shipboard games killed himself. The crewman spoke of another death during the voyage, a cold-blooded murder of some rival of Amo's. They couldn't pin it on him, but the captain was suspicious enough not to let him aboard again. Still, if he's a temporary exile here, he's made the best of it."

Indeed he had. My first encounter with him came within the hour, when I joined the game at his table. By now I was once more garbed in the finest tailoring to be had on the planet, but he was even more resplendent with shimmering jewels on his cloak, his belt, his rings, enough glitter almost to blind my own poor eyes. His hands were the fastest I've ever seen—aye, but not too fast for me to pick up his techniques after a time. It cost me dearly, almost cleaning me out of all I'd accumulated, but eventually luck and skill began to win the day and my pile of chips grew high in front of me once more.

Amo looked down his long nose at me, the sharp planes of his face flushed with anger. He was obviously not a man used to losing—and I remembered the story of the murdered man aboard the liner.

"So, Amo, it appears that you've met your match at last," said a voice behind me. I turned to see a giant of a man, clad entirely in black, looking over my shoulder at my main opponent in the game. His dark, deep-set eyes seemed out of place with the smile on his large face.

"That remains to be seen, Pedro," Amo replied. "I daresay this will not be the last game that he and I will ever play."

"Perhaps," said the man called Pedro, "he would be more amenable to the proposition I made to you, Amo." He introduced himself to me as the owner of the place, nodded when I gave my name, and asked me to come to his office when I was through playing. I cashed in my chips and followed him.

"I've been watching you, Giles," Pedro told me, the smile still fixed on his face. "You, Amo, and I among us have sufficient skill to make fortunes enough for a dozen lifetimes on a planet such as this. Amo, however, prefers to remain an independent operator."

"You're saying you'd like a partner," I suggested. "A way of stacking the odds in your favor, eh?"

He nodded. "And I'd rather have you with me than against me, Giles. In fact, if there were two such independents in the game as you and Amo, I would feel constrained to do something about changing the odds."

"A peace-loving man such as myself wouldn't want to see anything like that happen, Pedro. I think we can work something out."

And so we did, indeed a profitable partnership for us both. With my knack for things mechanical, I was able to, let us say, improve the performance of some of the Blue Unicorn's tables to favor the house. Amo was the only non-house player who could consistently manage to stalemate my little devices. He could have done much better elsewhere, but stubbornly did most of his play in the Unicorn. The reason was obvious.

Ethyra seemed delighted to see me again, and to learn that I would be taking up residence in one of the rooms above the casino. She knew nothing of my connection with the Legion. My guess is that she made no inquiries about Amo, either, who soothed and flattered his way about her constantly. Pedro would have been more direct with her, I fancy, but soon knew he had competition from both Amo and myself and so had to constrain his approach to one of more civility. I thought at first that might end our little partnership, but Pedro proved to be more of a practical man than a romantic.

No, Ethyra Coran accepted us all at face value. She easily kept Pedro at bay, balancing the three of us one against the other as she divided her leisure time amongst us three. My own approach to her was less intense, but constant for all that.

It was, interestingly enough, our ways of pursuing Ethyra

Coran that gave each of us our nicknames. I never learned what
wag came up with them—obviously someone familiar with the
oceans of Earth and the life therein—but the names stuck with
us through all our years on Venus.

I became Giles the Guppy, for the warm-weather fish who
played constant court to the female of the species. Pedro, on the
other hand, was known as the Shark, and Amo as the Eel. Few
dared speak those names to our faces, and I doubt that Ethyra
ever heard them, but they became common knowledge among
those familiar with our troika.

Young Giles grew rich, lad, richer by far than the poor wreck
of a soldier left from all the dark perils he has faced since. An
Earth-year passed, then two, then three, and none of us seemed
any closer to winning the woman who, by now, was worshiped
by every man on Venus who had passed through the Blue Unicorn—and that was most of them.

But I thought I saw my own chances growing. Pedro the
Shark had become all too obvious in his casual brutality, while
the deviousness of Amo the Eel could hardly be lost on her by
now. Most of the time, I tried to be in a position to head off the
worst of their wicked excesses, but on one particular night-
period I was not on hand when I needed to be.

Like Pedro and Amo, I used my wealth to buy gifts for Ethyra
but, as with them, she gently turned away offerings she felt were
of too great a value. Perhaps she had misgivings about the source
of our funds but was too kind to say so. She did accept one gift
from me—a ring of green Venusian malachite, which I'd had
specially carved into a tiny die with threes and fours on all sides,
a sentimental remembrance of those dice throws that had helped
finance our first night together on Venus years before.

Always had I to be aware of new faces coming into the Unicorn, to be sure that none of my fellow recruits or superiors in

the Legion might still be stationed on Venus and recognize me as the late Giles Habibula, now Giles the Guppy. Of course, it was inevitable, with the growing reputation of the Blue Unicorn and its beautiful singer, that it would happen sometime. On this particular night, I spotted one of my fellow recruits whose name I remembered only as Myles. Quickly I signaled for a new house dealer, and retired to my rooms for the nonce.

So I was not there when Myles caught the dealer cheating and called him on it. The cheating was foolish and unnecessary; the odds were always with the house, and my little devices at Pedro's tables added even to that. By the time I heard the snap of the proton pistol, it was too late for me to smooth things over.

I learned later that it was Pedro who fired at Myles from behind, his nucleonic bullet shearing away part of the lad's right shoulder. He would quickly have bled to death had it not been for Ethyra. By the time I got back downstairs, she had sprayed the wound with antibiotic plasti-flesh from a medical cabinet and was kneeling on the floor beside him.

"Don't be foolish," Pedro was saying, that inane smile still plastered on his huge face. "Let him die."

She ignored him, focusing on me instead. "Giles, help me get him to my room. We must help him."

Pedro started to raise his pistol, but I, having heard the shot before I rushed down, had come prepared, and my own weapon waved lazily in his direction. I reached out with my other hand and relieved him of his. "I'll hide this for you until things settle down," I said. "Wouldn't do for a legionnaire to find you with it, if one gets here to investigate the trouble."

Pocketing both guns, I picked up Myles and followed Ethyra to her quarters. She located a doctor among the casino players, and the three of us battled for his life over the next few hours.

Finally, there was nothing more we could do but leave him to rest in Ethyra's bed, and hope for the best. I've never understood exactly how events transpired as they did after that—perhaps it stemmed from the intensity of the moment, or the losing of ourselves in seeking some higher good that had nothing to do with either of us—but we two moved hand in hand from her apartment to mine, and then to my own bed, as though it was something we had long ago agreed upon.

I daresay, lad, that neither of us gave much thought to what the Shark or the Eel would make of our liaison—at least not until much later. We were lost in ourselves for some time. But I knew I would have to give some thought to the situation sooner or later.

Most of my thought came during those times Ethyra was nursing our young legionnaire back to health, feeding him meals or making sure the doctor checked the progress of his slow recovery. I, of course, had to stay out of his sight when he was awake. It didn't occur to me until much too late that he would naturally ask her to notify his commander about what had happened to him.

Until then, only I had known he was a legionnaire, and had some idea of what Pedro had brought down upon us all. I set about making my arrangements, outsmarting the lock on Amo's quarters during a time when he was asleep and carrying out a little project there, and later returning Pedro's weapon to him in his office.

"I think you may need it," I said. "How did Amo trick you into attacking that young man, anyway?"

"Amo?" The smile remained fixed on his face as his dark eyes seemed to pierce me. "Amo had nothing to do with it. Why should you say that?"

"I thought you knew," said I. "The lad is a legionnaire, Pedro. I'm sure Amo will waste no time in getting word to the Legion as to what happened. After all, with you out of the way, there would be nothing to stop him from taking your place at the Blue Unicorn and running all that you've built up."

"How do you know that boy is a legionnaire?" he demanded.

"I have my sources. Don't believe me, if you so choose. But watch your back when Amo is around. If he downed you before the Legion got around to acting, he could simply claim he was making a citizen's arrest."

"You don't fool me, Giles the Guppy. You'd like me out of the way, too, wouldn't you? Then you could continue your little dance around Ethyra Coran without worrying about me."

I shrugged. "Just remember who it was that warned you," I said, and turned to leave.

"If you had been doing your job, the entire incident could have been avoided," he said, his voice rising. "It's your fault if I've wakened an interest by the Legion in our operation!"

He was still sputtering when I closed the door behind me. The same hour found me in one of my regular card games with Amo the Eel.

"What was Pedro yelling about when you came out of his office?" Amo asked as casually as he could manage.

"Let me put it this way, Amo. I trust you never go unarmed in Pedro's casino, do you?"

His right hand moved under his jeweled cloak to his armpit, and he patted something there. "But why Pedro's den, in particular?"

"The man he shot was a legionnaire, Amo, simply enjoying

himself on leave. You don't think Pedro is going to take the blame when the Legion shows up here, do you?"

He waved a slender jeweled hand in dismissal. "What choice would he have?"

"Why, none—unless of course he had already slain the culprit, and could offer up the body as evidence. With his entourage of men to back him up, he could sell any story he liked to the precious Legion, wouldn't you say?"

A frown marred the thin features of his usually bland face. "Why me? Why not, for example, you?"

"Me?" I gave him my best smile. "Dear life, Amo, I'm his blessed partner!"

He was still mulling it over when I finished my hand and ended my part in the game. I had not won any money, this time, but I hoped I had won something more important.

As the days and weeks wore on, I saw that I had. The Shark and the Eel had no time to notice that Ethyra and I had more or less taken up permanent residence together; they were too busy circling one another, like two bloody barracuda, each always looking for some advantage or for the other to let his guard down. But they were too well matched. Pedro did not quite dare to openly challenge the speed of the Eel's deadly hands, and Amo could not attack the Shark without worrying about Pedro's minions. It was a nice, neat stalemate—while it lasted.

I had fooled myself into believing that it might last indefinitely, so oblivious was I to everything but Ethyra Coran and our life together. My happiness seemed complete when she informed me, wrapped in my arms, that, before another Venusian day and night had passed, the two of us would be three.

As you can see, lad, young Giles was nowhere near as devious as he'd thought himself. He could checkmate Amo and Pedro with precious little effort, but it never occurred to him that the still-recovering legionnaire had already set in motion—through Ethyra, no less—the events which would determine the course of my life from that point on.

It was nearly three-quarters of an Earth year later when it finally happened. Amo and Pedro were glaring at each other, as usual, across one of the wheels of chance in a corner of the casino. Seeing movement out of the corner of my eye, I glanced up from the table where I was working, to find the doorway of the Blue Unicorn filled with Legion uniforms. "Everyone stay where you are," a strangely familiar voice rang out through the chamber. "We want only one man. . . ."

"Amo! You did send for them!" Pedro's voice grated from behind the wheel. Amo's jeweled hand started to dart beneath his cloak but, for once, it was not fast enough. The Shark flung himself across the table and seized the Eel's throat in his huge hands.

"Pedro—no! Stop!" The new voice belonged to my beloved singer of stars and planets, my Ethyra who still believed Venus to be the planet of peace of which she had sung. All I could think of was to keep her and the child she carried away from that fearsome deadly struggle toward which she was rushing with no concern for herself. I pushed my way through the crowd, trying to head her off, when two legionnaires caught me by each arm and a third spoke in the familiar voice I'd heard announcing their entrance.

"Giles Habibula, as I live and breathe," said Will Stewart, who was obviously the officer in charge of this raid. "I thought you were too competent to have met your demise in a Venusian jungle."

"Will, let me go," I begged. "I must stop her . . ."

Perhaps Pedro the Shark actually heeded her call to him. More likely, he realized that the approaching legionnaires were

not about to give him time to finish his grisly work. He hurled
the limp figure of Amo the Eel away from him, shouted something to his men, and a dozen proton pistols blossomed into
being throughout the room.

Lad, it was a pitched battle between Pedro's men and the legionnaires. The two who had seized me suddenly had more important things to do, and again I plunged into the mass of
screaming patrons who were trying to avoid being caught in the
crossfire. Some of them were, and I slipped on a pool of blood
that I hadn't seen. Staggering ahead, I saw Ethyra being jostled
by the fleeing spectators and threw my arms up in what seemed a
futile protective gesture.

But it was not so futile, after all. I felt the nucleonic bullet
impact somewhere on my back, and seemed to be falling to the
floor in slow motion, my fading consciousness elated at the
thought that at least it hadn't struck her. . . .

When next I came to myself, I heard the thrumming of machinery about me and recognized the cold metallic wall of a
space cruiser looming above where I lay. I was wrapped in a metallic cocoon of wires, tubes, bottles of bubbling liquids, and
other devices that even I could not identify. I tried to call out,
but all that emerged was a croaking sound.

"At least your voice will come back," someone said from one
side of the cabin. "Amo the Eel will be lucky if he ever manages
to talk again."

I twisted toward the voice but stopped as pain shot through
me. Stewart stepped out of the shadow and up to my resting
place.

"Relax, Giles. It's going to take time, but you'll be all right.
Just lie still and let the medical facilities do their work."

"Ethyra . . .?" This time I managed to get the word out.

"The young woman is fine. In fact, we received a communication from Lieutenant Myles Brewer several Earth-weeks ago from back on Venus. You'll be interested to know that the casino singer gave birth to a healthy baby girl."

"A girl . . ." I found myself smiling despite the waves of pain I continued to endure. Then something else struck me. "Back on Venus, you said. Where . . .?"

"We're on our way to Earth. To Legion headquarters at Green Hall, for you to receive your decoration."

I didn't even try to give voice to my question this time.

Stewart lowered his voice. "I still think the Legion will need your particular talents someday, Giles," he said. "That's why the charges of desertion are no longer part of the Legion files. You were working undercover all these years, Giles, to help us get the goods on Pedro. Didn't you know? His enterprises included much more than gambling. Drugs, illicit androids, and much more. He escaped from our raid into the jungles of the wetlands, but I expect the posse will track him down—if a Venusian gorox doesn't have him for dinner first."

"Will . . ." I managed to gasp. "About that young woman and her daughter . . ."

"I'm truly sorry about that, Giles," he said. "You must know there's no going back—not unless you want those charges of desertion reinstated. In any case, she believes that you're dead, Giles. She thinks you sacrificed your life to save hers and that of the child. Wouldn't you rather leave her believing that, than that you were one of a kind with the Shark and the Eel?"

I had no answer for that, even if I could have articulated one. I felt only a great emptiness somewhere in my soul, for the brief paradise I had experienced and now had lost. Ethyra . . .

"If it's any consolation, she and Lieutenant Brewer seem to have developed an affection for one another, Giles. You needn't worry about the child lacking a father . . ."

Consolation! Suddenly I welcomed the pain from my injury. At least it kept me from single-minded contemplation of all that was gone for me, forever.

Is it any wonder, lad, that wine became a crutch to help me pass my time as a legionnaire? That I gorge myself on fine food and drink whenever the opportunity presents itself? For old Giles no longer has any reason to worry about his appearance. There is no one whose approval I care to have, except for the one person I can never again see.

So I accepted Will's bargain, lad. Had I known that it would mean I must face the dark Medusae, the fearful Cometeers, the mysterious Basilisk, I would have ripped myself free of that medication and hurled my carcass into space. But at least I did find you, lad, through that Venusian malachite ring your mother, my daughter, passed along to you. And an old soldier can still enjoy memories, lad, every time I listen again to the suite to which Ethyra Coran put words about Venus. . . .

Life can be wonderful, lad. Just be careful you don't have too much of it.

The Man Who Remembered Tomorrow

When Jack Williamson's *The Legion of Space* was first published in *Astounding Science Fiction* in 1934, it opened with a prologue titled "The Man Who Remembered Tomorrow." The man is an ancestor of some of the characters involved in the Legion adventures, and tells his doctor about "remembering" events that haven't happened yet—including some that won't happen for a thousand years or more. He also remembers the date of his own death and, after it happens, the doctor finds manuscripts among his late patient's possessions recounting some of the man's far-future memories. That first *Legion of Space* novel is what the doctor reads from the first manuscript.

For the sequels, *The Cometeers* (1936), *One Against the Legion* (1939), *Nowhere Near* (1967), and *Queen of the Legion* (1983), Williamson dropped the gimmick of remembering tomorrow. It was an interesting idea, though, and Williamson's vivid depictions of the future almost tempt one to believe that he based the man with the future memories on himself.

If the TV-turned-movie series *Star Trek* was first sold to NBC as a "wagon train to the stars" concept, using a version of fuel from Williamson's *Seetee* books, consider for a moment that Williamson himself traveled in a covered wagon as a child. He was born south of Tombstone, Arizona, some twenty-one years before the passing of Wyatt Earp; grew up in New Mexico where the first atomic bomb was exploded and the first U.S. rockets lifted toward space; saw men walk on the moon and robots probe all the planets but one, and visualized the impacts of all this and more for thousands of years to come. As for that still unprobed planet: Williamson even predicted Pluto's moon, Charon, only discovered in 1978, in that first Legion novel, and came close to its correct name (he called it Cerberus, but certainly we can forgive a small lapse in those future memories).

I first encountered Williamson in one of those magazine-size paperback novels that Galaxy published in the 1950s. The first one I encountered had been Murray Leinster's *The Black Galaxy*, and I was ready for the next in the series, which turned out to be the Williamson classic *The Humanoids*. Later I found that earlier novels in the Galaxy series included such classics as Olaf Stapledon's *Odd John*, James Blish's *Jack of Eagles*, Edmond Hamilton's *City at World's End*, and Isaac Asimov's first novel, *Pebble in the Sky*. In his autobiography, published after his death in 1992, Asimov wrote of receiving a "welcome to the ranks" postcard from Williamson after the publication of Asimov's first short story in 1939. Apparently Asimov never forgot the gesture; he said it made him feel like a science fiction writer for the first time. It is also indicative of Williamson's thoughtful and generous nature.

Years later, backtracking on those Galaxy Novels, I learned that the first had been Eric Frank Russell's *Sinister Barrier*. The second was *The Legion of Space*.

One of Williamson's most memorable characters has to be Giles Habibula, the Falstaff-like character from the Legion stories, who is still wheezing, wheedling, and whining his way through the 1983 Legion novel. But there is a missing part in Giles's life, only hinted at in the various stories

and particularly in *One Against the Legion,* where Giles encounters figures from his past—Amo Brelekko, once
known as Amo the Eel, and Gaspar Hannas, formerly Pedro
the Shark—and gives us the most tantalizing clues yet
about how Giles came to be the fabulous character that
he is.

That was the gap I tried to fill. Williamson could undoubtedly have done it better, if he cared to, but I hope he
doesn't mind my trying to second-guess him with this
story.

—Paul Dellinger

Though known mostly for his science fiction, Jack Williamson also has written some memorable fantasy, including the seminal lycanthropic classic *Darker Than You Think*. Originally published in the great but short-lived fantasy magazine *Unknown*, Jack's dark vision of were-creatures has terrified and inspired several generations of readers and writers. Witness Poul Anderson's dark adventure of cat-and-mouse set in the Alaskan wild.

Inside Passage

Poul Anderson

The great snake glided up through the foredeck and spread its coils beneath the sky. Low above the land to starboard, a nearly full moon whitened teakwood and frosted scales. The python raised its flat head. Its tongue flickered forth as if to taste the chill. After a minute it flowed soundlessly forward.

A man standing alone near the bow had peered its way and stiffened. Now he sat down on a bench, leaned against the bulwark, and went slack, as if stricken with sudden sleep.

From his place in the shadows, where a glass door at this end of the covered promenade faced out on the open section, Roberto Bulosan saw a shimmering like moonlit smoke come from the body. It thickened, took shape, and stood beside the bench as another man, the image of the first.

At last, at last, proof, the sight itself, not a glimpse that might have been illusion in a moment of panic, but an ongoing event. Bulosan felt his breath quicken and his pulse gallop, but as things remote. Whatever the risk, he must not let this chance go by.

Caution, caution. He pushed the door and propped it open with his foot just enough that he could bring his head out.

He wasn't sure if he would be able to hear as well as see. The sonic part of his wave function actualizer was an addition he had developed after Mihalek's death. Laboratory tests and the refinements they suggested had offered no more than the hope it would work. He was surprised that the goggles gave him as clear a view of witchery as they did.

Night sounds passed through his earphones, murmur of waves and breeze, soft throb and shiver of the ship. Within her, passengers chatted, laughed, drank in the bars, danced to a band, listened to a string quartet, gambled in the casino, made love, sat alone with memories, were early abed in their staterooms, while hundreds of servants attended them and scores of seamen attended the vessel—unheard, shut away from him by steel and size, another universe. He dared not dwell on his aloneness.

Did he catch a buzz? A control unit hung on his chest, suspended by its connections to the instrument cap. He twisted a knob. The buzz strengthened, varied, grew half coherent. He made a second adjustment. Abruptly the voices were there.

The python had reached the man-thing and brought its obsidian eyes level with his. He was speaking, his tone as cold as the night wind: "—fool. You were told not to do this. Go back at once."

The inaudible words from the invisible lips—inaudible and invisible to all common mortals—were in English. Of course,

Bulosan thought at the back of his mind. It would be the common language of a Filipino and a Dutchman.

The python hissed. Almost, it seemed ready to attack. The man-thing stood motionless, his stare as unblinking as its. The reptile head sank. "Sir," Bulosan heard, "I was choking on ape stink. What harm if I go about like this a little while? Who can see or hear me, or have any idea of us?"

It was not really speech, Bulosan knew. It couldn't be. Those weren't material bodies, they were—what? "Energy fields" came near being nonsense. "Probability-wave functions"—no, why not say "spirit form" as the witch-man in San Francisco had done? It wasn't photons of light or vibrations of molecules that came to his headset, it was the ghostliness underlying all reality.

"One is never quite certain," the man-thing was saying like a teacher. "There are humans with enough blood of ours in them that they can at least get a sense that something is somehow amiss. Or you may be tempted to exercise your powers. You are too newly aware of what you are, Emilio, too ignorant of both the wonders and the dangers. If nothing else, an untoward, unexplained incident could well make the captain order shore leaves canceled. I suspected you would break loose, and kept myself ready." With velvet menace: "Do not let it happen again."

"I am . . . sorry, sir."

"Be patient. Soon you shall be free. But understand that that will be for a schooling long and hard, in a country strange to you."

"I know, sir."

"You will find this shape of yours is not well suited to the Northern forest."

"It is natural to me, sir."

"Indeed. Coming from the tropics. You will learn to be wolf, bear, orca, anything." A pause, then, briskly: "I may as well give

you your orders now. When we reach Ketchikan, complete your
tasks here and go ashore. Bring only your sailor's passport. Have
no fears, all arrangements have been made. Go with Ali to the
floatplane dock. I will be waiting, and will accompany you on
your flight to the lair."

"Thank you, sir."

The man-thing made a sign in the wind. "Thank not me. It is
for the race, and for the Child of Night. Now withdraw, and do
not manifest again until you are safely inland."

The snake's head lowered. The long, sinuous form writhed
away. After a few yards, it stopped and drained down through
the deck.

Back down into the body of a humble worker asleep in his
bunk among his fellows.

The man-thing turned about and gazed starboard. Moonlight threw broken radiance across the water and turned hoar the
vast evergreen forest beyond. Ahead and afar, snow glimmered
on a phantomlike mountain. A forbidding country, Bulosan
thought, but wholly magnificent. Did the man-thing also yearn
to run free—swim as a seal, run as a wolf, away and away from
this damned floating hotel?

Briefly, Bulosan hesitated. He had learned incredibly much.
Dared he push his luck? But he needed to know so much more
before he could proclaim the truth about a monstrous worldwide
conspiracy and not be dismissed as a lunatic. The opportunity
tonight was unique. Nothing like it might ever come again, if he
didn't force events along.

Decision. He stepped back from the door and slipped off his
headset. Stooping, he put it well down into the camera bag at his
feet, which he took up and slung from his shoulder. When he
looked through the glass, he saw merely a bare stretch of deck
and a man slumped on a bench near the bow.

But the witch-spirit could see him. What then? He shoved the door aside and stepped forth. Like anyone out for a stroll, he sauntered forward and hoped the moonlight revealed nothing of what was behind his face.

The upper decks rose in tiers at his back. Here and there, ports glowed; the picture window of the observation lounge was a yellow rectangle high up; beyond it a masthead light shone red athwart the stars. A quick, irrational scorn passed through Bulosan. Tawdriness amidst the stern splendors around, flimsiness against the terrible forces abroad. He walked on.

The reclining man stirred, stretched, and rose to his feet. Bulosan knew that the mind had reentered the body. Drawing close, he halted and said, "Good evening." It amazed him how casual his voice sounded. Or was he mishearing through the blood that pounded in his head?

Again the man tensed, but relaxed. Bulosan understood. He, short and sturdily built, brown-skinned, broad-nosed, almond-eyed, must at first glance have seemed a member of the crew. However, his warm clothes—he had been prowling a long while, watchful for anything that could reveal the enemy—and his bag identified him as a passenger.

"Good evening, sir," replied the man. He was a portly, grizzled blond in nautical uniform. He smiled with practiced graciousness. "Out for a breath of fresh air? I too."

"I suppose you really need it after your duties, Mr.—uh—"

"Van Wyhe, sir, Cornelius van Wyhe, chief steward."

Bulosan curbed a nod. He had expected that, having obtained a list of officers beforehand. Since Emilio and, presumably, the second were-creature were in the steward's department, its boss was the logical person to arrange for their comings and goings.

If he wanted to continue the conversation, for whatever

slight clues it might yield, he must reciprocate, while telling no
unnecessary lies. "Roberto Bulosan." They shook hands. Van
Wyhe's clasp was warm, quite human. Somehow that made the
situation twice ghastly. Bulosan should have felt a wolf's paw, a
tiger's claws, an eagle's talons. He kept talking, fast, the better to
cover his emotions. "From Berkeley, California. Physicist by
trade."

"I hope you're enjoying our voyage."

"Oh, yes. I've been to Alaska before, but not in this luxury
style. It's, um, sociable." Bulosan tried for an implication that he
hoped for romance. He was in fact doubly alone, first divorced,
later driven by his quest. But he'd have no time for anything else
—unless he failed, lost the trail, found his hard-won knowledge
useless in a world that could not believe it.

"Ah, you are more an outdoorsman?" van Wyhe inquired po-
litely.

"Yes, I like backpacking, mountaineering, that kind of stuff."
Likewise true. Why not? The idea was to draw the officer out
about himself.

Nothing meaningful emerged. Van Wyhe avoided the personal and told Bulosan what he already knew, that the *Ijsseldam*
was a Dutch ship of Venezuelan registry and that most of the
staff catering to the passengers hailed from Indonesia and the
Philippines. The company kept recruiting stations and training
schools in both countries. Usually such people served for five or
ten years, saving their money, then went home to start a business
or whatever. The Inside Passage was a clime foreign to them, but
they took it well, and when the season here was over they went
to the Caribbean, although they had also cruised the Pacific and
the Far East. . . . Everywhere, Bulosan thought with an inward
shudder. These days the cruise ships went everywhere. Their
wakes wove a spiderweb around the globe; and back and forth

along the strands scuttled the unobtrusive, efficient, courteous little aliens who did the work that earned the profits; and of course nearly all were perfectly decent human beings; but among them were those few of the witch-race who could thus be borne to and fro while keeping ever alert for others of their kind, others who did not know their own nature until someone divined it and revealed it to them. . . .

"Well, goodnight." Don't persist when there's nothing to gain. Don't stand forth in those beast eyes.

"Goodnight, Dr. Bulosan." Never once had van Wyhe's manner suggested he was bored or impatient or anything but blandly affable. The witch-folk knew well how to hide what they were.

It was the death of Ed Mihalek that lived on in Roberto Bulosan and would not let him rest.

Friendship between an Oakland detective and a university scientist was not odd. They met in the Sierra Club, hit it off, and from time to time during the next five years hiked as partners into the mountains or fished in the foothills. Together over beer they mourned or growled at the destruction of the wild by everything from loggers, developers, and dams through acid rain, oil slicks, and agrochemicals, with curses left over for off-road vehicles and the yahoos who brought their stench and racket and soil-chewing wheels into its peace. Sometimes Bulosan joined Mihalek's buddies for poker or came for dinner with Mihalek's wife and three children. They enjoyed their conversations. The policeman was no dolt, the physicist no snob.

Of course they grew interested in one another's work and talked about it. Without mathematics, Bulosan could not really explain the quantum mechanical research on which he was engaged, but he tried, and Mihalek doggedly slogged his way to some idea of it. Those were concepts remote from his world, the particle as a wave, the cat neither/both dead nor/and alive until its box was opened, the relationship between observer and observation such that in certain interpretations a conscious mind was necessary to actualize the whole space-time universe from a sea of possible states. . . . "But it checks out, Ed, to more decimal places than any other theory ever. What I'm trying to do is solve Schrödinger's equation empirically, by making instruments that react directly to changes in the local wave function—oh, call 'em changes in the probability, the likelihood, of event X happening rather than event Y. Could be a Nobel in it!"

What Mihalek had to tell was a great deal more down to earth, to dust and grit and blood, the struggles and sorrows and frequent insanities of human beings. "We're sure a funny breed of animal, Bob. We run all the way from saints to monsters, and you'd be surprised how often that's in the same person. Like we were a mongrelly cross between two different sorts, hawk and dove or cougar and antelope, the first meant to prey on the second except somehow, long ago, their bloods got mixed. . . ."

And finally, on a day when time was closing in on what neither of them guessed would be the end: "Well, I've met a world-class weirdo, Bob. I mean, I've known my cop's share of nut cases, but this guy wins the seegar. Just the same—" Mihalek reached a powerful hand up to scratch in his thinning gray hair. "You remember how I used to, uh, speculate about how there might be two, uh, species of us, and we're all part both but in any of us it's more one than the other, depending? Well, what this Sam Quain guy had to say—I dunno. The goddamnedest stuff. He's got the same notion, only wilder, and he swore it's true, every cockeyed detail. Gave me the creeps, listening. Not that I believe any of it, not for a minute, don't get me wrong. But, well, after all these years I ought to know a psycho when I meet one, and this Quain just didn't have the earmarks."

That was when Bulosan heard about the Mondrick expedition and the evidence it brought back from Mongolia, four decades and more ago—as told by an old man, no longer afraid of a death that must soon take him whatever he did or did not. "He said he skipped from the Midwest with a murder rap hanging over him, but he was less worried about facing the charges than about what might come at him in his cell if he talked. So he made his way out here, took another name, worked in real low-profile jobs—who notices a short-order cook or a filling station attendant?—and kept pretty much to himself, very quiet. But I will believe he was a scientist once like he claimed. When he wanted to, he'd talk in your style, Bob."

And Mihalek relayed the story. It was of a mutant race that back in the Ice Age had evolved the power to send mind from body, roving afar, as shamans claimed they could. But this was no ghost, it was a subtle . . . energy matrix? . . . that could take what shape it willed. Silent, unseen, it wrought by affecting probabilities. ("Yeah, your project, maybe?") The molecules of a wall danced randomly aside enough for the were-creature to pass through. The factors of chance came together for an enemy or a quarry to suffer a fatal accident. With his uncanny powers, *Homo lycanthropos* overcame *Homo sapiens*, who for millennia thereafter was his slave and his food.

"They have their weaknesses, Quain said. Daylight will break up the pattern and kill the, uh, spirit that gets caught out under the sun. The body it left behind, like asleep, that body never wakes again, and soon dies too, I guess. Silver's poison to it, and seems like uranium is. Ha! Plenty of that around these days, huh? But if nothing unlucky happens, why, then the spirit can keep

right on going after the body's croaked. It does need nourishment still. Blood's best, human blood best of all. That's where the
legends about demons and vampires and such got started, Quain
said. And gods. The old pagan gods weren't really nice, you
know. Human sacrifice, often as not—and enjoying the daugh-
ters of men. . . ."

Slowly, slowly, a piece at a time, first here, then there, man
won free of the horror. He and she did have certain advantages,
such as greater numbers than the lycanthropes, and the companionship of dogs. Most important was their nature. The true
human was a social, cooperative animal, capable of discipline,
able to set the cause of the tribe above personal survival, a maker
of artifacts and arts, *Homo faber.* The lycanthropes were born to be
solitary and selfish, cunning more than wise, fearless more than
brave—beasts of prey. To the extent that they could work together, it was largely due to the *sapiens* strain in their heredity.

"The witch hunts of the Middle Ages weren't hysteria, Quain
said. There really were witches, gangs of the monsters trying to
win back part of what they'd lost. But more and more, they got
hunted down. . . . No, you can't tell 'em by sight. The original
stock, it's white, tall and slim, long-skulled—but by now it's
mixed with every race on earth. And then too, they've deliberately bred for a wide range of appearances. Hell, Bob, you or I
could be were-things, as far as our looks go."

For they were coming back. Through centuries they found
each other, begot their young, accumulated their treasures, built
their organization, assumed their identities in human society.
Renewed enslavement need not be through a second overt conquest. It could happen more slowly from within. "What price the
Nazi and Communist leaders? Yeah, both movements failed—
but did they really? They managed to kill off a lot of humans,
including a lot of the finest and brightest. They left whole coun-

tries wrecked. And their ideas aren't dead yet, you know."

When Mondrick and his associates returned home with the relics they had excavated, the lycanthropes had found means to destroy that evidence and kill all of them save for Quain. Him they were content to leave suspected of murdering his comrades. "I dunno. Could they've decided to let him go but keep tabs on him, for whatever it was worth? If he ever met anybody who had a clue, why, they'd know that was a guy they'd better take care of—" Mihalek broke off. His laugh rattled. "Hey, Bob, don't look at me like that. Of course it's nuts. Quain's either a total wack or an all-time practical joker. But damn, he did sound convincing. I get cold just thinking about it." Mihalek held out an arm in a short-sleeved shirt. The hair on it stood up.

"Why did he come to you?" Bulosan asked.

"Well, now, that's on account of the same reason I've come to you," Mihalek answered. As he talked of practical matters, the chill receded from him. "The Dusay case. You know? Carlos Dusay, Oakland shipping tycoon, dead under funny circumstances. Could be he lost control that foggy night along Highway One and his car went over the cliff in a natural way. Or could be it was tampered with. Hard to tell from the wreckage. But he was a good driver, didn't drink, and— Uh-huh, you do know. Then you know he was from the Philippines. Since your folks brought you from there when you were little, I thought maybe—oh, not likely, but maybe—"

"I'm afraid not," Bulosan said. "We only met a few times, mostly casually." He smiled. "I did daydream about getting him to give me a research grant. We talked about that not long ago, and he seemed interested, but—" He shrugged. "What's Sam Quain got to do with this?"

"Well, he was working part-time for Dusay, as an assistant gardener, the kind of light stuff an old man can handle. He

barely knew his employer, but after the death he came to us and
got referred to me. What he'd heard and noticed, servants' gossip
and so on, you know, it gave him the idea that Dusay—the company does have worldwide connections, some of them into odd
places—Dusay had stumbled on an inkling of the truth and was
investigating it. We did find peculiar books and stuff in the
house, and correspondence with detective agencies internation-
ally and— Anyway, Quain decided that now, at last, it was his
duty to come clean."

"But you don't imagine there's anything to the story, do you?"

Mihalek prefaced his "No!" with an expletive. "I'm not quite
ready for the padded cell, not yet. Besides, Quain's disappeared.
Lost his nerve and took it on the lam again, or what? Never
mind. I've only told you all this because—well, because it
doesn't make sense but it did make that damn impression on me."

His fist thudded on his knee. "To hell with it. If you don't
have any dope on Dusay yourself, tell me about your project.
Last time, you said you were close to making the gadget work."

"I've done that," Bulosan replied. "Would you like a demonstration?" He could not keep the thrill out of his voice. "Biggest
advance in the field since the scanning tunneling microscope.
No, bigger, if I do say it myself." He laughed. "And I do."

"Sure. When?"

"Um-m-m—I've been keeping it under wraps, you remember, working on it mostly when I'm alone in my lab after hours.
The dodge it uses is anything but obvious. In fact, I got the idea
by a chain of extremely unlikely associations, and wonder if anybody else in the foreseeable future could have the same luck.
However, once shown to be possible, the thing isn't hard to duplicate. A team, like at Livermore, would get there in a year or
less. So to make sure of the all-important priority, I'm not telling
anybody but you till I'm ready to publish. Do come around,

though, and I'll run the experiment for you. Not that there'll be a spectacular show. Interference patterns, like ripples on a pond when you toss in three or four pebbles. But by God, what you'll be seeing is the wave function of the universe!"

They set a rendezvous on campus at eight the next evening. The year was nearing winter and dark fell early. Thus it came about that they stood together in a basement room of a large building otherwise deserted, silence thick around them, beneath the cold white light of an overhead fluorescent, and regarded a clutter of apparatus on a workbench.

Oddly shy for a big and burly man, the detective muttered, "This makes me feel kind of, you know, small. Like here you're dealing with what things are all about, stars and atoms and time and everything, and my type has barely climbed down out of the trees."

"Mine too, Ed," Bulosan answered. "We're the same humans everywhere." He donned the headset. "Let me adjust this for you. First I fire up that cathode ray tube."

He was fiddling with knobs when he heard the hoarse, cracked sound at his back and whirled about. Ed Mihalek clutched at his chest as he sank to his knees. His face was gray. "Oh, God," he choked, and crumpled in a heap on the concrete floor.

There was a telephone in the room. Bulosan snatched it and dialled 911. Nothingness mocked him. Later investigation showed that an improbable sequence of electronic accidents had knocked out the switchboard. He went on all fours, put his mouth to the fallen man's, and attempted CPR. No response. The autopsy afterward indicated that a fibrillation, equally improbable—but the nervous system *is* chaotic, in the physics sense—had stopped a healthy heart.

What haunted Bulosan most, because he could tell no living

soul if he wished to be thought sane, was what he had seen through the goggles while Mihalek fell. A great dark bird with crested head and cruel beak flapped its wings before the victim. Its talons went into his chest without leaving a trace. Bulosan saw how they tore. Mihalek collapsed. The bird swept aloft, to the ceiling and out, again with no opening and no sound.

Bulosan knew its kind. A Philippine eagle.

Like most Alaskan towns, Ketchikan was a clutter of boxy buildings tossed down into a grandeur of waters, mountains, and wilderness. Originally a fishing port, these days it lived mainly off its raffish past, with souvenir stores and shoppes everywhere you turned. A Haida totem pole stood in a tiny park, but the local tribespeople apparently preferred their village several miles south.

Bulosan took the gangway from the ship in a wave of tourists. The morning was crisp and bright, few clouds overhead, not the commonest weather in these parts. Good for trailing a party, if he could manage that. Beneath the tension he felt a certain confidence. Luck had been on his side throughout. It was as if a destiny had fallen upon him, to avenge his friend and unmask the ancient foes of his race.

Rather than go sightseeing, he found a café across the street from the wharf and lingered over coffee, at a table where he could look out the window. Time dragged. Well, he'd learned patience during the winter months of his search. Ed had often told him how much of a detective's work consisted of waiting. To keep his place, presently he ordered a second cup, and when that was done a piece of pie he didn't really want. He drew occasional stares. No doubt the only Filipinos ordinarily seen here were cruise ship crew, and probably they seldom got shore leave;

their vessels left the same day as they docked. Maybe his leather jacket claimed a share of the attention, as long and metal-studded as it was. People would really get interested if they knew the studs were sterling silver, that a 9mm Smith & Wesson rested in a shoulder holster beneath, and that the bullets were silver-plated. Not to mention the contents of his camera bag. A smile briefly bleakened his face.

There! With an effort, Bulosan kept his muscles at ease. Down the clifflike side of the *Ijsseldam*, on the now empty gang-way, came a big man in a blue tunic. He exchanged a word with the security guard at the foot and walked off. Yes, van Wyhe. Wait, though, wait a while yet. Don't follow till he's gone too far to notice you. He was heading along the waterfront, evidently meaning to walk the whole distance to where the floatplanes harbored. Yes, a werewolf must come to feel hideously cramped in day after day aboard a ship full of monkey folk.

When would Emilio and—Ali?—appear? They'd have to finish their work and give some explanation for taking off. No, van Wyhe would have taken care of that and told the guard to expect them and let them pass. Who would question him or pay any particular heed? A couple of insignificant Asian drudges— He might well have their replacements lined up here in town, and everything would proceed as smoothly as before, northward and northward while the passengers sipped their bouillon and nibbled their cakes, and their gaping raped the solitude of the land.

Bulosan decided he'd better start. Once the pair joined their chief, things would most likely move fast. Awash, he sought the men's room before he followed the steward's course. On one side, heights reared heavenward above drab structures. On the other, wavelets danced and glittered in the channel. He spied an oil slick yonder. iridescent and deadly. Once, he thought, this sky had been full of wings, these waters alive with fish, seal, otter, whale. Much of the olden glory remained, he'd experienced it himself a few years ago, but steadily it was eaten away.

At the terminal he wanted, a row of small aircraft rested on their pontoons. Mainly they worked with the buses that brought visitors who'd paid for a short flight inland. Well, he thought, those people would simply touch down on a chosen lake and shoot up a lot of film. No great harm done. Some of them might gain a bit more appreciation of the country. A few might even begin supporting efforts to save it.

Bulosan didn't go inside. Van Wyhe would be there, would remember him and wonder. It had been a mistake to talk with him under the moon. Bulosan shrugged. He was no secret agent, just a private person driven by a vision of demons.

He went to the wharf's edge and considered the planes. What inquiries he'd been able to make back home had suggested that he might find help in places like this.

"Lookin' for somethin', mister?"

The friendly drawl brought him around on his heel. Silently, he swore. To register excitement was about the worst thing he could do. He saw a man tall and lean, clad in work shirt and jeans. Blue eyes twinkled from beneath black hair, beside a curved blade of a nose and above a lantern jaw.

"Uh, yes," Bulosan said. "A pilot."

"You got your wish." The man grinned. "Frank Langford, at your service."

"Roberto Bulosan, from California." They shook hands. "But you see, this is a special trip."

"I've had a fair number that were. Long's it's legal and not too crazy, I'm good for it. Better'n runnin' a shuttle between here and the same tired beauty spot ten times a day."

Yes, the old free spirit wasn't altogether extinct in Alaska.

Probably Langford was a bush pilot who for some reason—
maybe waiting for a spot of trouble to blow over in his regular
territories—had come south, gotten the use of a floatplane, and
begun free-lancing hereabouts. Another stroke of luck, meeting
him right off like this. If he was willing.

"What I'd like you to do, with me along," Bulosan said carefully, "is follow another party after they take off."

"Friends of yours?"

"Not quite. You see, I'm a partner in a venture that hopes to
build a small lodge in the back country. We'll fly in a few guests
at a time, the kind who'll really enjoy and respect the surroundings. Have you noticed a man in uniform? He's waiting for a couple of helpers to join him. I goofed, telling him about the plan
and sounding enthusiastic. I've gotten reason to suspect he
means to look the area over and report back to another group.
There's only room for one such operation. They're better heeled
than we are. They can probably beat us out if they decide to,
obtain the necessary permits and so on before we can. I want to
see if that's what he's up to, and if it is, get an idea of what he's
observed and what recommendation he'll make."

The sky-colored eyes searched across Bulosan. "That is an
offbeat story for sure. What else does it involve?"

"For you? We might not get back till late, or even till tomorrow."

"That'll cost."

"I have money with me. Cash." Plenty. Bulosan enjoyed a
good salary and, being of frugal temperament, had substantial
savings.

"Well, let's sit down and talk about it. Over here, couple of
bollards, 'case you'd sooner the gentleman inside doesn't glim
you."

The next two hours were interesting. Bulosan stayed as near

the truth as was feasible, calling himself a scientist who wanted
to invest in something he loved, and not grossly libeling van
Wyhe. After he established that nothing like narcotics was in
question, Langford didn't pry. The price agreed upon was reasonable. Langford went on to spin yarns that were mostly amusing, about his adventures when flying in the Yukon region.

It stopped abruptly. A cab let out two short men. Bulosan
recognized Emilio. His darker companion must be Ali, doubtless
an Indonesian. They went into the terminal while Bulosan turned
his head aside. "That's them," he breathed. "I expect they'll take
off straightaway."

"Then let's get settled," Langford replied easily.

He helped Bulosan down into an aircraft that could have ac-
commodated six. It rocked as they entered. Langford signaled a
man at the mooring lines to stand by, lit a cigarette, and leaned
back, relaxed as a cat. "This should be kinda fun," he said.
"Thanks, Mr. Bulosan." The touch of formality was engaging, in
this era when every stranger pushed in on you with your first
name on his tongue.

Van Wyhe, Emilio, and Ali came forth, accompanied by a
stocky man in a flight jacket. Langford squinted through the
windshield. "Yep, Jerry Shotwell," he said. "A wild one, him." A
were-beast? Bulosan wondered with a shiver.

The others boarded their plane. Its motor roared, its propel-
ler became a transparent disc, it trailed spray across the water
and entered the air. Langford sat quiet. "Don't worry," he said
when Bulosan began to dither. "I won't lose sight of 'em. But
wouldn't you rather they didn't notice us particularly?"

A few minutes later, his own flyer took wing. He and Bulosan
donned the headphones that would protect their ears from the
noise and let them talk through it. But they said little as they
bore east.

The land unrolled tremendous below them, mountains gloomy-green with well-nigh impassable forest, cliffs like fortress ramparts, swordblade waterfalls, virginity of snow, an eagle imperial in the distance. Bulosan felt infinitely removed from that dark and odorous room in San Francisco where he had caught the spoor of his enemies.

That Mihalek died in his laboratory was surely happenstance. It was their earliest opportunity after they discovered what he had heard. (How? Had they always invisibly shadowed Sam Quain?) The hour was after dark, when they could range free; the site was where a cry for help could be cut off until too late. If they had known that Bulosan knew too, and that he had means to see them, he would also have died, a very short while later.

He passed a week in terror made the sharper by the condition that he could not share it with any living soul—must not, before he had hard-and-fast evidence, or he would simply doom yet another person. It faded with the days, until he woke from his first good night's sleep and realized he had been spared.

That laid a duty. He was astonished at the grim resolution within him, peaceable him. He might almost have been touched by the finger of God, or be possessed by a devil. But no, it was just that the shock had roused something in him he had never been aware of, the soul of Malay warriors who had been among his forebears. Hunt the witch-folk down! Get them destroyed!

His rational mind took charge. The single usable clue he had was Carlos Dusay's origin and the fact that the man had been a shipping magnate. And, yes, the shape that Mihalek's killer wore, the eagle that preys on monkeys. Of course the lycanthropes were not uniquely Philippine. They were everywhere, interbred with every human stock. But this one connection was a beginning for him. He took to spending his spare time—which he made a good bit of by neglecting his job, except for further work on the wave-field detector—in places where Filipinos went, especially those who had to do with seafaring.

And thus at last, his eerie luck coming through again, he sat in a small, dimly lighted restaurant, a plate of tamarind chicken before him, and two men took an adjacent table while talking, men with faces much like his. They spoke low, but his ears were keen. They spoke in Tagalog, but he knew the language.

". . . a mighty python, yes, you are that in your spirit form, Emilio," the older man was saying. "Wait, though, until you have mastered bird form, raptor form, and stooped upon your kill. *There* is full joy!"

Bulosan did not quite understand how he was able to keep on quietly eating his dinner.

". . . will you continue teaching me?"

"No, Emilio. I have met with Those of the Night and told them how powerful you bid fair to become. You shall go away for years of training, of strengthening . . .

". . . afar in the Northern wilds, where you shall learn what this living world truly means . . .

". . . not directly. You must come to know in your bones, early on, the necessity of concealment. A berth on a ship is being arranged for you. Not pleasant work, oh, no; such a position requires apprenticeship first. Menial work, sweeping, scrubbing, handling the rubbish and filth of the apes. But learn how to swallow your pride, until the night of your revenge shall come.

". . . report to Cornelius van Wyhe, chief steward of the *Ijsseldam*, at the company's Vancouver office. The ship departs from there for a few days' journey up the Inside Passage between the islands and mainland . . ."

When the pair left, Bulosan made no attempt to follow. He

wasn't competent to trail a person unseen. Besides, he should take no needless risks when he had gained so huge a booty of knowledge. And . . . he wanted to sit a while by himself in this dusk, till the sudden trembling that seized him went away.

Inside Passage, he thought. How weirdly right. A symbol, a word, for the witches making their secret way toward the vitals of humankind.

The lake lay high and lonely in the mountains of the Misty Fjords Wilderness. Cliffs palisaded it on the east; the west bank rose into forest that climbed toward the remote vision of a glacier. Seen from above, Shotwell's floating plane was the size and ugliness of a fly.

"Go on past," Bulosan directed. "Cruise around for a couple of hours." Van Wyhe must soon reboard his vessel.

Langford nodded. "Okay. I've got stuff along we can eat— I'm hungry now, aren't you? And I'll show you some mighty pretty scenery."

It was of heart-lifting splendor. Werewolves ought not to be lairing in it. And yet, Bulosan wondered, was that utterly wrong? Here was a land of real wolves, grizzly bears, eagles, fang and talon, terrified prey and blood running hot down predator gullets. He set his teeth. If the witch-folk were the predators of his race, why, quarry had a right to defend itself, sweep the beast aside with horns and trample it under sharp hooves.

The sun was nearing a high horizon when Langford returned him. Shadows lengthened across the blue and quicksilver of the lake. Otherwise it shone bare. "Can you take us to where they were, but avoid being observed?" Bulosan asked.

"Reckon I can try," Langford said. "Married man's trail. You heard? In old-time Ketchikan, a way through the brush off Creek

Street to the back door of Dolly's whorehouse." Bulosan laughed louder than the jape called for. A bit of human humor was very welcome.

The pilot slanted down over the north end, cut his engine, and glided in. With a gentle shock and hiss, his pontoons met water. Momentum bore his craft on to a stop within a yard of the lower bank, at the exact spot desired. Bulosan whistled. "Incredible," he murmured.

"Naw, just sneaky. What now?"

"I, uh, I want to scout around. You wait. If I'm not back by dark, don't worry." Bulosan touched his camera bag. "I've got a flashlight and compass, I'm used to woods, and anyway, if I should get lost, all I need do is keep downhill and I'm bound to reach the lake and see you."

"Okay. I'd appreciate it if you can show up in time for us to get to town for breakfast. I'd hate goin' in to look for you on an empty belly." Langford omitted saying that it could be awkward explaining his client's disappearance. He wouldn't have to, unless with a casual lie. Who had watched closely? —What a nasty thought. Of course he'd raise the Park Service and search parties would arrive . . . and the lycanthropes would retreat into the pathless miles until those intruders were gone. . . .

Bulosan fixed the bag on his shoulders, climbed down to a float, and leaped ashore. For a while he cast to and fro, often slipping on a slope covered with duff. Did Langford watch from the plane with merriment? Eventually he found the tracks he sought, where men had landed like him. They led into the woods. A single pair led back, the marks of large feet solidly shod, van Wyhe's. What story had he handed his pilot, to account for leaving his fellows behind? Or had he needed any?

For a minute Bulosan hesitated. The water reached still, shadowed into dull argency. As darkling were the cliffs opposite, save where their heights caught the last sunlight and burned golden. Somewhere in the quietness, a raven croaked. He mustered his nerve, waved to Langford, and set forth.

Twilight brooded already under the trees, air sharp with their daytime odor but chilling toward night. Bulosan had once taken a course in wilderness survival, and tracking skills stayed with him. Nevertheless he could only follow this trail because they were not woodsmen who had left it. There were no cairns or blaze marks he could identify; there wouldn't be. How did van Wyhe know the way? Werewolf scent, spook-voices, a phantom glimmer where boughs bristled so thickly overhead that the sun never touched earth? Bulosan peered, fingered, searched to find the next broken twig or the next scuff in dead needles underfoot. He resisted the temptation to use his flashlight. His dark vision was better than most men's.

The gloom deepened. His feet whispered unnaturally loud in the silence. His breath began to appear before him, a mist, like a shaman spirit seeking to depart. Except for the trees, this was a gaunt land, game sparse. How did the witch-folk live, in their camp where they learned woodcraft and the lore and rites of that which they were? Well, Bulosan thought, fleshly bodies could eat austerely of rations that had been ferried in bit by bit over the years. As for the blood that were-things needed—fish, birds, the occasional mammal—sometimes a man?— His silver-weighted jacket was a comforting drag upon him.

—A red spark ahead. By now he could barely see at arm's length. He blundered against a branch. It slapped his face with harsh needles and crackled on past his head. A racket to rouse vampires from their graves! He went quadruped and crept forward. The spark waxed to a dim glow. A voice became audible. It was chanting, a minor-key wail that sawed at his nerves.

The last distance he covered on his stomach, until he came to a fallen trunk. Rotten wood crumbled beneath his hand as he brought his eyes high enough to look across. About twenty yards off, a small fire burned. By its flickery light he barely made out shelters, primitive but snug, spread among the trees, everything hidden from the air. A score of people—male and female, as nearly as he could tell—squatted or sat cross-legged before the fire. They were clothed roughly, warmly, against the cold. A man stood on the far side of the flames. He it was who chanted, his arms lifted high into the night. As Bulosan watched, he ended the notes, slowly lowered himself to the ground, and lay flat, hands folded on breast.

The shaman's pose. Bulosan crouched, fumbled in his bag, took forth his headset and shakily donned it, stared again.

A white wolf stood huge beside the sleeper. It turned its muzzle aloft and howled. The watchers made obeisance where they sat. One by one, each of them likewise stretched full length on the earth.

Were they making ready for a Wild Hunt? Time to get the hell out of here, Bulosan thought. Yes, hell indeed.

He kept the headset on while he crawled back. The goggles hampered normal vision somewhat, the earphones muffled normal sound a bit. But he was in total, mute night anyway, though dusk must linger outside the trees; and what went through it was worse than any natural creature. When the fire was no longer visible to him he rose and stared around. Nothing met his senses but darkness and the least rustle of wind high in the treetops. He grasped his flashlight and ventured to turn it on. By the wan puddle of light that it cast, he began making his awkward way back.

Dread gnawed at him—but far beneath a mounting, hammering exultation. He had found what he searched for, tracked his Grendel down, and from this knowledge he would forge his revengeful sword.

Oh, he knew full well it wouldn't be that simple, nor easy nor safe. He couldn't tell local authorities more than that he'd chanced on an illegal encampment. When they came to look, the dwellers would be gone. But the immigration service should be most interested in the fact that a number of them appeared to be foreigners. The FBI would want details about *Ijsseldam*'s crew. At least two or three of the band were bound to be apprehended, and it wasn't likely their stories would be convincing. If Bulosan then urged the investigation of what Dusay had been seeking out, trail after trail ought to open up. Detectives who knew they were dealing with something dangerous would now and then, grudgingly and unbelievingly at first, wear the headsets he supplied when they anticipated contact with the gang—and he'd devise a camera attachment—and sooner or later, in desperation if nothing else, a lycanthrope would make a mistake and reveal himself—"Your first and biggest mistake was when you murdered my friend," Bulosan mumbled into the dark.

Did a hiss reply, feet pad among boles, wings ghost overhead? Bulosan froze. Deeper glooms stirred, a pallor drifted. They could be night and vapor, the faint snickering noise twigs brushed together by a cold breeze. He felt under his silver-studded jacket, found the automatic, cradled it tightly in his right hand. From his left the flashbeam stabbed. Murk drank it down.

Keep going. Onward, Christian soldiers. From the business that walks in the dark, good Lord, preserve us.

No more than two or three miles. No more than an hour and a half or thereabouts, weaving and stumbling where branches clutch, roots snag ankles, duff skids, night stirs and whispers. No more than that, please, please. Don't look at your watch. You'd have to set your gun aside to push the button that illuminates the digits. You have left the world of digital displays, you have lost it. Keep going, downward, always downward.

"Attack if you want," he gasped to those who might not be there at all. "I dare you. I'd like to kill you."

A heart full of hate gave courage.

But when the lake suddenly gleamed between trees, tears blurred it and the breath sobbed in his throat.

He staggered into the blessed open. Stars shone few and pale above him, for the moon had cleared the eastern cliffs, icy-bright. Their wall sheered black against the glade that it cast shivery across the water. *Lap-lap*, murmured wavelets, a little song of peace.

Bulosan doused his flashlight and stowed it in the camera bag. It could draw heed. The moonlight was ample. Calmer after several deep breaths, he looked from side to side. The airplane was visible to the left, another shadow but sharp-angled on the purity of the lake. His position error hadn't been bad for a man beating a path through night and nightmare. Too exhausted to feel more than a vague gladness, he trudged the last distance mainly conscious of how he trembled and how the sweat stank that drenched his underwear.

Ijsseldam had long since proceeded on her route. His table-mates had doubtless wondered why he didn't appear for dinner, but wouldn't care much. For his part, once back in town he'd find lodgings, wallow in hot water and sanity, sleep, sleep, until to-morrow and the beginning of his warfare.

The plane grew clear to sight. A long blot crossed it. Bulosan's heart skipped. He lifted the pistol he still clutched. The shape drew closer, he heard ordinary feet on the canted, uneven ground, and joy rushed over him. It was just Langford, good old Frank Langford. The pilot had seen him and jumped ashore in case he needed help.

"Hi." Bulosan heard his voice waver, cracked and hoarse.

"Sorry I'm late. We, uh, we can go home now." He realized how mad he might seem, brandishing a gun, and jammed it back into the holster before the other man should see. His headset didn't matter. He'd say it was an experimental apparatus.

"I was gettin' worried," Langford called. "You run into trouble?"

"N-not really. But I'm dog-tired and—and— Oh, never mind."

"Nobody will, I reckon." Langford reached him and stopped. Bulosan did likewise. For an instant they gazed at one another, highlights, half-tones, shadows under the moon.

Langford dipped a hand beneath his shirt. He took forth a Luger pistol and leveled it. "You stay put, Mr. Bulosan, will you?" he said quietly. "Don't move, okay?"

Everything drained out of the world.

"Well, I would be obliged if you'd take off that coat of yours," Langford went on after a moment. "Real slow and easy, please. Don't grab after nothin'. And then keep your fingers laced together on top of your head, if you will."

It was as if a machine obeyed. The silver-weighted leather dropped to earth with a blunt, rustling sound. For the first time, Bulosan noticed how long the pilot's skull was.

Langford smiled, not tauntingly, a smile as wry as his voice: "You shouldn't't've supposed we were unawares. And you a woodsman. You should've remembered predators are careful, same as prey, 'specially when they've been hunted themselves for hundreds and hundreds of years. They worried about you, down in California, and asked the Child of Night. He said best to lead you on, find out what you were tinkerin' with and what it could mean. Besides, that should keep you from talkin' elsewhere.

"Oh, you did have luck with you right along. Or, no, not exactly luck. You've got to have a strong strain of us in your blood. It gave you a sense for our kind, and it even let you unconscious-like shift the probabilities the way you wanted." He sighed. "But I'm afraid you're not enough for us to recruit. If nothin' else, you're too committed to the apes. Sorry."

A last rage flared to cry from Bulosan's throat: "You dare call us apes, you hellhounds, you things? Was it you that found a way out of the caves, built the cities, measured the atom and the bounds of the universe, walked on the moon? No, you've always been our sickness, bloodsuckers, harpies, devils, battening on us, draining and terrorizing us— Without you, today we'd be ranging the stars!"

"You know," Langford answered mildly, "quite a few animals could make the same complaint against *Homo sapiens*. You ever been up to Dead Horse Gulch under White Pass? That's where three thousand pack animals died miserably in a single year of the Gold Rush, overloaded, flogged onward till they dropped. Or look around you at what your sort is doin' to the whole planet. I wouldn't make book that life can take much more of it. For sure, the future looks filthy—less'n we can bring your numbers down and keep you in your rightful place, cattle for those of us who're wild by nature and'll welcome wild nature home again.

"You might think about that for a minute, Mr. Bulosan. You've given me a notion that you care too, in your ape way. It might make you feel a little better about this."

His tone had gone dreamy. His glance wandered elsewhere. The gun drooped in his hand. Maybe, flashed through Bulosan, maybe in that brief carelessness was a chance— He snatched for his own weapon.

He was too late. Gray and black by moonlight, out of the forest loped the wolves and down from above the treetops came the eagles.

Jack Williamson

Judge this: the gathering of dreams that grew
Across the span of half a century,
Called out of space and time by one who knew—
Knew well, and knows—what miracles must be
Where stars and stars hold back the outer night
In radiance, begetting worlds and souls.
Long has his vision ranged beyond our sight,
Light-years, to find adventures, hopes, and goals.
Imagination likewise dares the deeps
And dangers of our future and our past,
Man's fate; and if man laughs or shouts or weeps,
Still in these tales we see ourselves at last.
On Earth, from which the questing ships depart,
No bard among us bears a higher heart.

—Poul Anderson

A theme that runs through much of science fiction is the rise of technology and the struggle of humans to master or at least coexist with the machines they themselves have built. Nowhere is this struggle more evident than in Williamson's famous short work, "With Folded Hands," in which he introduced the humanoids, robots so perfectly adept that they are capable of reducing humans to the status of pampered but idle clients.

One of the virtues of well-conceived science fiction is the propensity of its practitioners to pose thorny problems, and then proceed to demonstrate a possible solution. Ben Bova, for a number of years the editor of *Analog* (which, in its previous incarnation as *Astounding,* published "With Folded Hands"), enjoys the challenge of pitting humans against the perfectability of machine intelligence, and following is a delightful example of how satisfying the results of such a contest can be.

Risk Assessment

Ben Bova

They are little more than children, thought Alpha One, self-centered, emotional children sent by their elders to take the responsibilities that the elders themselves do not want to bother with.

Sitting at Alpha One's right was Cordelia Thomasina Shockley, whom the human male called Delia. Red-haired and impetuous, brilliant and driven, her decisions seemed to be based as much on emotional tides as logical calculation.

The third entity in the conference chamber was Martin Flagg, deeply solemn, intensely grave. He behaved as if he truly believed his decisions were rational, and not at all influenced by the hormonal cascades surging through his endocrine system.

"This experiment *must* be stopped," Martin Flagg said firmly.

Delia thought he was handsome, in a rugged sort of way. Not terribly tall, but broad in the shoulder and flat in the middle. Nicely muscular. Big dimple in the middle of his stubborn chin. Heavenly deep blue eyes. When he smiled his whole face lit up and somehow that lit up Delia's heart. But it had been a long time since she'd seen him smile.

"Why must the experiment be stopped?" asked the robot avatar of Alpha One.

It folded its mechanical arms over its cermet chest, in imitation of the human gesture. Its humanform face was incapable of showing any emotion, however. It merely stared at Martin Flagg out of its optical sensors, waiting for him to go on.

"What Delia's doing is not only foolish, it's wasteful. And dangerous."

"How so?" asked Alpha One, with the patience that only a computer possessed.

The human male was almost trembling with agitation. "You don't think a few hundred megatons of energy is dangerous?"

Delia said coolly, "Not when it's properly contained, Marty. And it *is* properly contained, of course."

Alpha One knew that Delia had two interlinked personality flaws: a difficulty in taking criticism seriously and an absolute refusal to accept anyone else's point of view. Like her auburn hair and opalescent eyes, she had inherited those flaws from her mother. From her father she had inherited one of the largest fortunes in the inner solar system. He had also bequeathed her his incredibly dogged stubbornness, the total inability to back away from a challenge. And the antimatter project.

Marty was getting red in the face. "Suppose you lose containment?" he asked Delia. "What then?"

"I won't."

Turning to the robot, Marty repeated, "What if she loses containment?"

Alpha One's prime responsibility was risk assessment. Here on the Moon it was incredibly easy for a mistake to kill humans. So the computer quickly ran through all the assessments it had made to date of C. T. Shockley's antimatter project, a task that took four microseconds, then had its robot avatar reply to Flagg.

Calmly, Alpha One replied, "If the apparatus loses containment, then our seismologists will obtain interesting new data on the Moon's deep structure." Its voice was a smooth computer synthesis issuing from the horizontal grill where a human's mouth would be.

Martin Flagg was far from pleased. "Is that all that your germanium brain cares about? What about the loss of human life?"

Alpha One was totally unperturbed. Its brain was composed mainly of optical filaments, not germanium. "The nearest human settlement is at Clavius," it said. "There is no danger to human life."

"*Her* life!"

Alpha One turned to see Delia's reaction. A warm flush colored her cheeks, an involuntary physical reaction to her realization that Flagg was worried about her safety.

The human form of the robot was a concession to human needs. The robot was merely one of thousands of avatars of Alpha One, the master computer that monitored every city, every habitat, every vehicle, factory, and mining outpost on the Moon. Almost a century ago the pioneer lunar settlers had learned, through bitter experience, that the computer's rational and incorruptible decisions were far sounder—and safer—than the emotionally biased decisions made by men and women.

But the humans were unwilling to allow a computer, no matter how wise and rational, to have complete control over them. The Lunar Council, therefore, was founded as a triumvirate: the Moon was ruled by one man, one woman, and Alpha One. Yet, over the years, the lunar citizens did their best to avoid the duty of serving on the Council. The task was handed to the young: those who had enough idealism to serve, or those who did not have enough experience to evade the responsibility.

Children, Alpha One repeated to itself. As human lifespans extend toward the two-century mark, their childhoods lengthen also. Physically they are mature adults, yet emotionally they are still spoiled children.

Martin Flagg was the human male member of the triumvirate. C. T. Shockley was the female. Marty was the youngest human ever elected to the triumvirate. Except for Delia.

The three of them were sitting in the plush high-backed chairs of the Council's private conference room, in the city of Selene, dug into the ringwall mountains of the giant crater Alphonsus. Flagg glared at Delia from his side of the triangular table. Delia smiled saucily at him. She knew she shouldn't antagonize him, but she couldn't help it. Delia did not want to be here; she wanted to be at her remote laboratory in the crater Newton, near the lunar south pole. But Marty had insisted on her physical appearance at this meeting: no holographic presence, no virtual-reality attendance.

"This experiment must be stopped," Flagg repeated. He was stubborn, too.

"Why?" asked the robot, in its maddeningly calm manner.

Obviously struggling to control his temper, Flagg leaned forward in his chair and ticked off on his fingers:

"One, she is using valuable resources—"

"That I'm paying for out of my own pocket." But the pocket was becoming threadbare, she knew. The Shockley family fortune, big as it might have been, was running low. Delia knew she'd have to succeed tomorrow or give it all up.

Flagg scowled at her, then turned back to the robot. "Two, she is endangering human life."

"Only my own," Delia said sweetly.

The robot checked its risk assessments again and said, "She is entirely within her legal rights."

"Three, her crazy experiment hasn't been sanctioned by the Science Committee."

"I don't need the approval of those nine old farts," Delia snapped.

The robot seemed to incline its head briefly, as if nodding. "Under ordinary circumstances it would be necessary to obtain the Science Committee's permission for such an experiment, that is true."

"Ah-hah!" Flagg grinned maliciously.

"But that is because researchers seek to obtain funding grants from the Committee. Shockley is using her own money. She needs neither funding nor permission, so long as she does not present an undue risk to other humans."

Flagg closed his eyes briefly. Delia thought he was about to admit defeat. But then he played his trump.

"And what about her plans to use *all* the power capacity of *all* the solar collector systems on the Moon? Plus *all* the sunsats in cislunar space?"

"I only need their output for one minute," Delia said.

"What happens if there's an emergency during that one minute?" Flagg demanded, almost angrily. "What happens if the backups fail at Clavius, or Copernicus, or even here in Selene? Do you have any idea of how much the emergency backup capacity has lagged behind actual power demand?"

"I have those figures," Alpha One said.

"So?"

"There is a point-zero-four probability that the backup system at Selene will be unable to meet all the demands made on it during that one minute that the solar generators are taken off-line. There is a point-zero-two probability that the backup system at Copernicus—"

"All right, all right," Flagg interrupted impatiently. "What do we do if there's a failure of the backup system while the main power grid is off-line?"

"Put the solar generators back on-line immediately. The switching can be accomplished in six to ten milliseconds."

Delia felt suddenly alarmed. "But that would ruin the experiment! It could blow up!"

"That would be unfortunate, but unavoidable. It is a risk that you must assume."

Delia thought it over for all of half a second, then gritted her teeth and nodded. "Okay, I accept the risk."

"Wait a minute," Flagg said to the robot. "You're missing the point. Why does she need all that power?"

"To generate antiprotons, of course," Delia answered. Marty knew that, she told herself. Why is he asking the obvious?

"But you already have more than a hundred megatons worth of antiprotons, don't you?"

"Sure, but I need thirty tons of them."

"Thirty tons?" Marty's voice jumped an octave. "Of antiprotons? Thirty tons by *mass*?"

Delia nodded nonchalantly while Alpha One restarted its risk assessment calculations. Thirty tons of antiprotons was a new data point, never revealed to the Council before.

"Why do you need thirty tons of antiprotons?" Alpha One asked, even while its new risk assessment was proceeding.

"To drive the starship to Alpha Centauri and back," Delia replied, as if it were the most obvious fact in the universe.

"You intend to fly to Alpha Centauri on a ship that has never been tested?" Alpha One asked. "The antimatter propulsion system alone—"

"We've done all the calculations," Delia interrupted, annoyance knitting her brows. "The simulations all check out fine."

If Alpha One could have felt dismay or irritation at its own limitations, it would have at that moment. Shockley intended to fly her father's ship to Alpha Centauri. This was new data, but it should have been anticipated. Why else would she have been amassing antimatter? A subroutine in its intricate programming pointed out that it was reasonable to assume that she would want to test the antimatter propulsion system first, to see that it actually performed as calculated before risking the flight. After all, no one had operated an antimatter drive as yet. No one had tried for the stars.

"What's thirty tons of antiprotons equal to in energy potential?" Flagg asked.

Instantly, Alpha One calculated, "Approximately one million megatons of energy."

"And if that much energy explodes?"

Alpha One was incapable of showing emotion, of course. But it hesitated, just for a fraction of a second. The silence was awesome. Then the robot's head swiveled slowly toward Delia, leveling its dark glassy optical sensors at her.

"An explosion of that magnitude could perturb the orbit of the Moon."

"It could cause a moonquake that would destroy Clavius, at the very least," Flagg said. "Smash Selene and even Copernicus, wouldn't it?"

"Indeed," said Alpha One. The single word stung Delia like a whip.

"Now do you see why she's got to be stopped?"

"Indeed," the robot repeated.

Delia shook her head, as if to clear away the pain. "But there won't be any explosion," she insisted. "I know what I'm doing. All the calculations show—"

"The risk is not allowable," Alpha One said firmly. "You must stop your experiment."

"I will not!" Delia snapped.

It took Alpha One less than three milliseconds to check this new data once again, and then compare it against the safety regulations that ruled every decision-making tree, and still again check it against the consequences of Delia's project if it should be successful. Yet although it weighed the probabilities and made its decision that swiftly, it did not speak.

Alpha One had learned one thing in its years of dealing with humans: the less they are told, the less they have to argue about.

And the two humans already had plenty to argue over.

Running a hand through the flowing waves of his golden hair, Flagg grumbled, "You're not fit to be a triumvir."

"I was elected just the same as you were," Delia replied tartly.

"Your father bought votes. Everybody knows it."

Delia's own temper surged. Leaning across the triangular table to within inches of Flagg's nose, she said, "Then everybody's wrong! Daddy wouldn't spend a penny on a vote."

"No," he snarled, "he spent all his money on this crazy starship, and you're spending still more on an experiment that could kill everybody on the Moon!"

"It's my experiment and I'm going to go ahead with it. It'll be finished tomorrow."

"It is finished now," said the robot. "Your permission to tap power from the lunar grid is hereby revoked. Safety considerations outweigh all other factors. Although the risk of an explosion is small, the consequences are so great that the risk is not allowable."

All the breath seemed to gush out of Delia's lungs. She sank back in her chair and stared at the unmoving robot for a long, silent moment. Then she turned to Flagg.

"I hate you!"

"You're not fit to be a triumvir," Flagg repeated, scowling at her. "There ought to be a sanity requirement for the position."

Delia wanted to leap across the table and slap his face. Instead, she turned to Alpha One's robotic avatar.

"He's being vindictive," she said. "He's acting out of personal malice."

The robot said impassively, "Triumvir Flagg has brought to the attention of the Council the safety hazards of your experiment. That is within his rights and responsibilities. The only personal malice that has been expressed at this meeting has come from you, Triumvir Shockley."

Flagg laughed out loud.

Delia couldn't control herself any longer. She jumped to her feet and didn't just slap Marty, she socked him as hard as she could with her clenched fist, right between the eyes. In the gentle gravity of the Moon, he tilted backward in his chair and tumbled to the floor ever so slowly, arms weakly flailing. She could watch his eyes roll up into his head as he slowly tumbled ass over teakettle and slumped to the floor.

Satisfied, Delia stomped out of the conference chamber and headed back to Newton and her work.

Then she realized that the work was finished. It was going to be aborted and she would probably be kicked off the triumvirate for assaulting a fellow Council member.

If she let Marty have his way.

*   *   *

Delia stood naked and alone on the dark airless floor of the crater Newton. Even though she was there only in virtual reality,
while her real body rested snugly in the VR chamber of her laboratory, she reveled in the freedom of her solitude. She could virtually feel the shimmering energy of the antiprotons as they
raced along the circular track she had built around the base of
the crater's steep mountains.

More than 350 kilometers in circumference, the track ran
past the short lunar horizon, its faint glow scintillating like a
giant luminescent snake that circled Delia's naked presence.

The track was shielded by a torus of pure diamond. Even in
the deep vacuum of the lunar surface there were stray atoms of
gases that could collide with the circling antiprotons and set off a
flash of annihilative energy. And cosmic particles raining down
from the Sun and deep space. She had to protect her antiprotons,
hoard them, save them for the moment when they would be
needed.

She looked up, toward the cold and distant stars that stared
down at her out of the dark circle of sky, unwavering, solemn,
like the unblinking eyes of some wary beast watching her. The
rim of the deep crater was ringed with rectennas, waiting to
drink in the energy beamed from the Moon's own solar power
farms and from the sunsats orbiting between the Earth and the
Moon. Energy that Marty and Alfie had denied her.

In the exact center of the crater floor stood the ungainly bulk
of the starship, her father's masterpiece, glittering softly in the
light of the stars it was intended to reach.

But it will never get off the ground unless I produce enough
antiprotons, Delia told herself. For the thousandth time.

The crater Newton was not merely far from any other human settlement. It was *cold*. Close to the lunar south pole, nearly ten kilometers deep, Newton's floor never saw sunlight. Early explorers had broken their hearts searching Newton and the surrounding region for water ice. There was none to be found, and the lunar pioneers had to manufacture their water out of oxygen from the regolith, and hydrogen imported from Earth.

But even though any ice originally trapped in Newton had evaporated eons ago, the crater was still perpetually cold, cryogenically cold all the time, cold enough so that when Delia built the ring of superconducting magnets for the racetrack she did not have to worry about cooling them.

Now the racetrack held enough antiprotons, endlessly circling, to blow up all the rocky, barren landscape for hundreds of kilometers. If all went well with her experiment, it would hold enough antiprotons to send the starship to Alpha Centauri. Or rock the Moon out of its orbit.

The experiment was scheduled for midnight, Greenwich Mean Time. The time when the sunsats providing power to Europe and North America were at their lowest demand and could most easily squirt a minute's worth of their output to Delia's rectennas at Newton. The Moon kept GMT, too, so it would have been easy for the lunar grid to be shunted to Newton for a minute, also. If not for Marty.

Midnight was only six hours away.

Delia's father, Cordell Thomas Shockley, scion of a brilliant and infamous family, had taken it into his stubborn head to build the first starship. Earth's government would not do it. The Lunar Council, just getting started in his days, could not afford it. So Shockley decided to use his own family fortune to build the first starship himself.

He hired the best designers and scientists. Using nanomachines, they built his ship out of pure diamond. But the ship sat, gleaming faintly in the starlight, in the middle of Newton's frigid floor, unable to move until some thirty tons of antiprotons were manufactured to propel it.

Delia was born to her father's purpose, raised to make his dream come true, trained and educated in particle physics and space propulsion. Her first toys were model spacecraft; her first video games were lessons in physics.

When Delia was five years old her mother fled back to Earth, unable to compete with her husband's monomania, unwilling to live in the spartan underground warrens that the Lunatics called home. She divorced C. T. Shockley and took half his fortune away. But left her daughter.

Shockley was unperturbed. He could work better without a wife to bother him. He had a daughter to train, and the two of them were as inseparable as quarks in a baryon. Delia built the antiproton storage ring, then patiently began to buy electrical energy from the Lunar Council, from the sunsats orbiting in cislunar space, from anyone and everyone she could find. The energy was converted into antiprotons; the antiprotons were stored in the racetrack ring. She was young, time was on her side.

Then her father was diagnosed with terminal cancer and she realized that both her time and her money were running out. The old man was frozen cryonically and interred in a dewar in his own starship. The instructions in his will said he was to be revived at Alpha Centauri, even if he lived only for a few minutes.

So now Delia's virtual presence walked across the frozen floor of Newton, up to the diamond starship gleaming faintly in the dim light of the distant stars. She peered through its crystal hull, toward the dewar where her father rested.

"I'll do it, Daddy," she whispered. "I'll succeed tomorrow, one way or the other."

Grimly she thought that if Marty was right and the antimatter exploded, the explosion would turn Newton and its environs into a vast cloud of plasma. Most of the ionized gas would be blasted clear of the Moon's gravity, blown out into interplanetary space. Some of it, she supposed, would eventually waft beyond the solar system. In time, millions of years, billions, a few of their atoms might even reach Alpha Centauri.

"One way or the other," she repeated.

Delia stirred in the VR chamber. Enough self-pity, she told herself. You've got to *do* something.

She pulled the helmet off, shook her auburn hair annoyedly, and then peeled herself out of the skintight VR suit. She marched straight to her bathroom and stepped into the shower, where she always did her best thinking. Delia's father had always thought of water as a luxury, which it had been when he had first come to the Moon. His training still impressed Delia's attitudes. As the hot water sluiced along her skin, she luxuriated in the warmth and let her thoughts run free.

They ran straight to the one implacable obstacle that loomed before her. Martin Flagg. The man she thought she had loved. The man she knew that she hated.

In childhood Delia had no human playmates. In fact, for long years her father was the only human companion she knew. Otherwise, her human acquaintances were all holographic or VR presences.

She first met Martin Flagg when they were elected to the triumvirate. Contrary to Marty's nasty aspersions, Delia had not lifted a finger to get herself elected. She had not wanted the position; the responsibility would interfere with her work. But her father, without telling her, had apparently moved heaven and earth—well, the Moon, at least—to make her a triumvir.

"You need some human companionship," he told her gruffly. "You're getting to an age where you ought to be meeting other people. Serving on the Council for a few years will encourage you to . . . well, meet people."

Delia thought she was too young to serve on the Council, but once she realized that handsome Martin Flagg was also running, she consented to all the testing and interviewing that passed for a political campaign on the Moon. Most of the Lunatics cared little about politics and did their best to avoid serving on the Council. The only reason for having two human members on the triumvirate was to allay the ancient fears that Alpha One might someday run amok.

Once she was elected, C. T. Shockley explained his real reason for making her run for the office. "The Council won't be able to interfere with our work if you're on the triumvirate. You're in a position now to head off any attempts to stop us."

So she had accepted the additional responsibility. And it did eat into her time outrageously. The triumvirate had to deal with everything from people whining about their water allotments to deciding how and when to enlarge the underground cities of the Moon.

And the irony of it all was that nobody cared about Shockley's crazy starship project or Delia's work to generate enough antiprotons to propel the ship to Alpha Centauri. Nobody except her fellow triumvir, Marty Flagg. If Delia hadn't been elected to the triumvirate with him, if they hadn't begun this love-hate relationship that neither of them knew how to handle, she could have worked in blissful isolation at Newton without hindrance of any sort.

But Marty made Delia's heart quiver whenever he turned

those blue eyes of his upon her. Sometimes she quivered with love. More often with fury. But she could never look at Marty without being stirred.

And he cared about her. She knew he did. Why else would he try to stop her? He was worried that she would kill herself.

Really? she asked herself. He's really scared that I'm going to kill *him*, and everybody else on the Moon.

Delia's only experience with love had come from VR romance novels, where the heroine always gets her man, no matter what perils she must face along the way. But she did not want Marty Flagg. She hated him. He had stopped her work.

A grimace of determination twisted Delia's lips as she turned off the shower and let the air blowers dry her. Marty may think he's stopped me. But I'm not stopped yet.

She slipped into a comfortable set of coveralls and strode down the bare corridor toward her control center. Alpha One won't let me tap the lunar grid, she thought, but I still have all the sunsats. The Council doesn't control them. As long as I can pay for their power, they'll beam it to me. Unless Alpha One's tried to stop them.

It wouldn't be enough, she knew. As she slid into her desk chair and ordered her private computer to show her the figures, she knew that a full minute of power from all the sunsats between the Earth and the Moon would not provide the energy she needed.

She checked the Council's communications log. Sure enough, Alpha One had already notified the various power companies that they should renege on their contracts to provide power to her. Delia told her computer to activate its law program and notify the power companies that if they failed to live up to their contracts with her, the penalties would bankrupt them.

She knew they would rather sell the power and avoid the

legal battle. Only a minute's worth of power, yet she was paying a premium price for it. They had five and a half hours to make up their minds. Delia figured that the companies' legal computer programs needed only a few minutes' deliberation to make their recommendations, one way or the other. But then they would turn their recommendations over to their human counterparts, who would be sleeping or partying or doing whatever lawyers do at night on Earth. It would be hours before they saw their computers' recommendations.

She smiled. By the time they saw their computers' recommendations, she would have her power.

But it wouldn't be enough.

Where to get the power that Marty had denied her? And how to get it in little more than five hours?

Mercury.

A Sino-Japanese consortium was building a strip of solar power converters across Mercury's equator, together with relay satellites in orbit about the planet to send the power earthward. Delia put in a call to Tokyo, to Rising Sun Power, Inc., feeling almost breathless with desperation.

It was past nineteen hundred hours in Tokyo by the time she got a human to speak to her, well past quitting time in most offices. But within minutes Delia was locked in an intense conference with stony-faced men in Tokyo and Beijing, offering the last of the Shockley fortune in exchange for one minute's worth of electrical power from Mercury.

"The timing must be exact," she pointed out, not for the first time.

The director-general of Rising Sun, a former engineer, allowed a faint smile to break through his polite impassivity. "The timing will be precise, down to the microsecond," he assured her.

Delia was practically quivering with excitement as the time

ticked down to midnight. It was going to happen! She would get all the power she needed, generate the antiprotons the ship required, and be ready to lift off for Alpha Centauri.

In less than half an hour.

If everything went the way it should.

If her calculations were right.

Twenty-eight minutes to go. *What if my calculations are off?* A sudden flare of panic surged through her. Check them again, she told herself. But there isn't time.

Then a new fear struck her. *What if my calculations are right?* I'll be leaving the Moon, leaving the only home I've ever known, leaving the solar system. Why? To bring Daddy to Alpha Centauri. To fulfill his dream.

But it's not my dream, she realized.

All these years, ever since she had been old enough to remember, she had worked with monomaniacal energy to bring her father's dream to fruition. She had never had time to think about her own dream.

She thought about it now. *What is my own dream?* Delia asked herself. *What do I want for myself?*

She did not know. All her life had been spent in the relentless pursuit of her father's goal; she had never taken the time to dream for herself.

But she knew one thing. She did not want to fly off to Alpha Centauri. She did not want to leave the solar system behind her, leave the entire human race behind.

Yet she had to go. The ship could not function by itself for the ten years it would take to reach Alpha Centauri. The ship needed a human pilot and she had always assumed that she would be that person.

But she did not want to go.

Twenty-two minutes.

Delia sat at the control console, watching the digital clock clicking down to midnight. Her vision blurred and she realized that her eyes were filled with tears. This austere laboratory complex, this remote habitat set as far away from other human beings as possible, where she and her father had lived and worked alone for all these years—this was *home*.

"Delia!"

Marty's voice shocked her. She spun in her chair to see him standing in the doorway to the control room. Wiping her eyes with the back of a hand, she saw that he looked puzzled, worried. And there was a small faintly bluish knot on his forehead, between his eyes.

"The security system at your main airlock must be off-line. I just opened the hatch and walked in."

Delia tried to smile. "There isn't any security system. We never have any visitors."

"We?" Marty frowned.

"Me, I," she stuttered.

He strode across the smooth concrete floor toward her. "Alpha One monitored your comm transmissions to the power companies," Marty said, looking grim. "I'm here to shut down your experiment."

She almost felt relieved.

"You'll have to call the power companies and tell them you're canceling your orders," he went on. "And that includes Rising Sun, too."

Delia said nothing.

"Buying power from Mercury. I've got to hand it to you, I wouldn't have thought you'd go that far." Marty shook his head, half admiringly.

"You can't stop me," Delia said, so softly she barely heard it herself.

But Marty heard her. Standing over her, scowling at the display screens set into the console, he said, "It's over, Delia. I can't let you endanger all our lives. Alpha One agrees with me."

"I don't care," Delia said, one eye on the digital clock. "I'm not endangering anyone's life. You can have Alpha One check my calculations. There's no danger at all, as long as no one interferes with the power flow once—"

"I can't let you do it, Delia! It's too dangerous!"

His face was an agony of conflicting emotions. But all Delia saw was unbending obstinacy, inflexible determination to stop her, to shatter her father's dream.

Wildly, she began mentally searching for a weapon. She wished she had kept a gun in the laboratory, or that her father had built a security system into the airlocks.

Then her romance videos sprang up in her frenzied memory. She did have a weapon, the oldest weapon of all. The realization almost took her breath away.

She lowered her eyes, turned slightly away from Marty.

"Maybe you're right," Delia said softly. "Maybe it would be best to forget the whole thing." Nineteen minutes before midnight.

There was no other chair in the control room, so Marty dropped to one knee beside her and looked earnestly into her eyes.

"It will be for the best, Delia. I promise you."

Slowly, hesitantly, she reached out a hand and brushed his handsome cheek with her fingertips. The tingle she felt along the length of her arm surprised her.

"I can't fight against you anymore," Delia whispered.

"There's no reason for us to fight," he said, his voice as husky as hers.

"It's just . . ." Eighteen minutes.

"I don't want you to go," Marty admitted. "I don't want you to fly off to the stars and leave me."

Delia blinked. "What?"

"I don't want to lose you, Delia. Ever since I met you, I've been fighting your father for your attention. And then your father's ghost. You've never really looked at me. Not as a person. Not as a man who loves you."

"But Marty," she gasped, barely able to speak, "I love you!"

He pulled her up from her chair and they kissed and Delia felt as if the Moon had indeed lurched out of its orbit. Marty held her tightly and she clutched at him, at the warm tender strength of him.

Then she saw the digital clock. Fifteen minutes to go.

And she realized that more than anything in the universe she wanted to be with Marty. But then her eye caught the display screen that showed the diamond starship sitting out on the crater floor, with her father in it, waiting, waiting.

Fourteen minutes, forty seconds.

"I'm sorry, Marty," she whispered into his ear. "I can't let you stop us." And she reached for the console switch that would automate the entire power sequence.

"What are you doing?" Marty asked.

Delia clicked the switch home. "Everything's on automatic now. There's nothing you can do to stop the process. In fourteen minutes or so the power will start flowing—"

"Alpha One can stop the power companies from transmitting the energy to you," Marty said. "And he will."

Delia felt her whole body slump with defeat. "If he does, it means the end of everything for me."

"No," Marty said, smiling at her. "It'll be the beginning of everything—for us."

Delia thought of life together with Marty. And the shadow of her father's ghost between them.

She felt something like an electric shock jolt through her. "Marty!" she blurted. "Would you go to Alpha Centauri with me?"

His eyes went round. "Go—with you? Just the two of us?"

"Ten years one way. Ten years back. A lifetime together."

"Just the two of us?"

"And Daddy."

His face darkened.

"Would you do it?" she asked again, feeling all the eagerness of youth and love and adventure.

He shook his head like a stubborn mule. "Alpha One won't allow you to have the power."

"Alfie's only got one vote. We've got two, between us."

"But he can override us on the safety issue."

"Maybe," she said. "But will you at least *try* to help me out-vote him?"

"So we can go off to Alpha Centauri together? That's crazy!"

"Don't you want to be crazy with me?"

For an endless moment Delia's whole life hung in the balance. She watched Marty's blue eyes, trying to see through them, trying to understand what was going on behind them.

Then he grinned and said, "Yes, I do."

Delia whooped and kissed him even more soundly than before. He's either lying or kidding himself or so certain that Alfie will stop us that he doesn't think it makes any difference, Delia told herself. But I don't care. He's going to *try* and that's all that matters.

Twelve minutes.

Together they ran down the barren corridor from the control room to Delia's quarters and phoned Alpha One. The display screen simply glowed a pale orange, of course, but they solemnly called for a meeting of the Council. Then Delia moved that the Council make no effort to stop her experiment and Marty seconded the motion.

"Such a motion may be voted upon and carried," Alpha One's flat expressionless voice warned them, "but if the risk assessment determines that this experiment endangers human lives other than those willingly engaged in the experiment itself, I will instruct the various power companies not to send the electrical power to your rectennas."

Delia took a deep breath and, with one eye on Marty's face, solemn in the glow from the display screen, she worked up the courage to say, "Agreed."

Nine minutes.

"Alpha One won't let the power through," Marty said as they trudged back to the control room.

Delia knew he was right. But she said, "We'll see. If Alfie's checking my calculations we'll be all right."

"He's undoubtedly making his own calculations," said Marty gloomily. "Doing the risk assessment."

Delia smiled at him. One way or the other we're going to share our lives, either here or on the way to the stars.

Two minutes.

Delia watched the display screens while Marty paced the concrete floor. I've done my best, Daddy, she said silently. Whatever happens now, I've done the very best I could. You've got to let me go, Daddy. I've got to live my own life from now on.

Midnight.

Power from six dozen sunsats, plus the relay satellites in orbit around Mercury, poured silently, invisibly into the rectennas ringing Newton's peaks. Energy from the sun was transformed back into electricity and then converted into more antimatter than the human race had ever seen before. Thirty tons of antiprotons, a million megatons of energy, ran silently in the endless racetrack of superconducting magnets and diamond sheathing along the floor of the crater.

The laboratory seemed to hum with their energy. The very air felt vibrant, crackling.

Delia could hardly believe it. "Alfie let us have the power!"

"What happens now?" Marty asked, his voice hollow with awe.

She spun her little chair around and jumped to her feet. Hugging him tightly, she said, "Now, my dearest darling, we store the antiprotons in the ship's crystal lattice, get aboard and take off for Alpha Centauri!"

He gulped. "Just like that?"

"Just like that." Delia held her hand out to him and Marty took it in his. Like a pair of children they ran out of the control room, to head for the stars.

The vast network of computer components that was known as Alpha One was incapable of smiling, of course. But if it could congratulate itself, it would have.

Alpha One had been built to consider not merely the immediate consequences of any problem, but its long-term implications. Over the half-century of its existence, it had learned to look further and further into the future. A pebble disturbed at one moment could cause a landslide a hundred years later.

Alpha One had done all the necessary risk assessments connected with headstrong Delia's experiment, and then looked deep into the future for a risk assessment that spanned all the generations to come of humanity and its computer symbiotes.

Space flight had given the human race a new survival capability. By developing self-sufficient habitats off-Earth, the humans had disconnected their fate from the fate of the Earth. Nuclear holocaust, ecological collapse, even meteor strikes such as those that caused the Time of Great Dying sixty million years earlier—none of these could destroy the human race once it had established self-sufficient societies off-Earth.

Yet the Sun controlled all life in the solar system, and the Sun would not last forever.

Looking deep into future time, Alpha One had come to the conclusion that star flight was necessary if the humans and their computers were to disconnect their fate from the eventual demise of their Sun. And now they had star flight in their grasp.

As the diamond starship left the crater Newton in a hot glow of intense gamma radiation, Alpha One perceived that Delia and Marty were only the first star-travelers. Others would certainly follow. The future of humanity was assured. Alpha One could erase its deepest concern for the safety of the human race and its computer symbiotes. Had it been anywhere near human, it would have sat back with a satisfied smile to wait with folded hands for the return of the first star-travelers. And their children.

Afterword

When I was asked to contribute a story to this anthology, the first thing that popped into my mind was that no one I could think of deserved an honor such as this book as much as Jack Williamson. Not only is he one of the best-loved figures in the field of science fiction, he has been a pioneering writer, breaking ground in new areas long before most of us had learned how to read.

Jack was among the very earliest writers to deal with antimatter, which he called "contraterrene" matter, or seetee. This was at a time when the concept of antimatter was a new and startling idea to theoretical physicists such as P. A. M. Dirac, Fermi, Einstein, and that crowd.

So naturally, I started to write about seetee. As the story evolved, however, I started to think about how Jack was also among the very first to warn about the dangers of what we now call "risk assessment." His great and seminal work, "With Folded Hands," ought to be required reading for every government bureaucrat and self-styled advocate for piling on more and more regulations—all in the name of safety or fairness—that end up by stifling human enterprise and growth.

Hence this tale, "Risk Assessment."

I've known Jack Williamson since the early 1960s, when I was a newly published author and he was already one of the great ones, not only respected everywhere for his work, but revered by everyone as a kind, generous, gentle man: a strong friend, a figure one could look up to.

For many years, Jack was a professor of English at the Eastern New Mexico University, in Portales. When he reached retirement age, he retired. Not surprising, you might think. But I received a nearly frantic phone call from a group of his students (I was editing *Analog* magazine in New York then) who told me that they thought the university's administration was "forcing" Professor Williamson into retirement, and they wanted me to do something about it!

The first thing I did was to call Jack. "Forcing me?" Jack

laughed. "Goodness no. I'm very happy to retire from teaching. Now I can write full time."

How many professors have been so revered by their students that the students didn't want them to retire?

I got another glimpse into his psyche when my wife Barbara and I visited Jack in Portales one year during the time for the spring calf roundup. We drove out to the ranch where the roundup was taking place that weekend, and watched the local cowhands and teenagers at work. They were led by Jack's older brother, still a working wrangler. It was a hot, bloody, dusty scene. The calves were separated from their mothers, dehorned, the males deballed, all of the calves branded and shot with about a quart of penicillin apiece. There was bleating and mooing and horses and roping and the stench of burnt hides and lots of blood, toil, tears, and sweat.

As we leaned against the corral railing, watching all this hard work and suffering, Jack nudged me in the ribs. "See why I became a writer?" he asked softly.

No fool, Jack. The cattle industry's loss has been our gain, and we should all be extremely grateful for that.

—Ben Bova

Williamson's World

The toaster on the kitchen
table
is a deadlier foe
than the wolf
scratching at the door.

—Scott E. Green

Inspiration takes many forms, and the following story, though not
using either Jack Williamson as a character or one of Jack's works as its
background, nonetheless is clearly the result of the Williamson Effect.
Taking the customs of Earth and sending them out into the far reaches
of space, something Jack did in his recent novel *Demon Moon,* is the
starting point for the following story, in which the human desire for a
sense of order and another human trait—ambition—knock heads to
create a crisis in Paradise.

Emancipation

Pati Nagle

The Custodian of Oporto's Island stood in the darkness of his
house, listening to the growing murmur of voices in the Grove of
Malamalama outside. It was not a feast day, when a large attendance might be expected at Nightfall, but the woods were full of
people. He knew they had not come just to watch him perform
the evening ritual. How he wished his father still lived; his father
had loved the ceremonial aspect of the office of Custodian, while
he himself dreaded it.

He donned his green robe and the tall feathered headdress
that weighed on him so. A tight knot of fear was growing in his
stomach, for he alone was ultimately responsible for the sacred

rite of Maintenance, and that responsibility was about to be challenged. He went to the door of his house, and as he stepped through the curtain that covered it, the drumming began.

Malamalama, the island's axis, glowed bright with captured sunlight, its near end terminating in a shielded pole in the center of the ceremonial clearing outside the Custodian's home. Dancers—men and women in the traditional garb of the *hula kahiko*, their hair and arms decked in the leaves and flowers of the island —waited around the pole, ready for Nightfall to begin. Among the *ti* trees at the Grove's edge and back into the woods beyond were the island's people, dozens upon dozens of them, more than he had seen at any ritual in months. The Custodian glimpsed his counterpart, the Governor, among the growing throng, and his belly tightened at the sight of her. How often had he silently wished for her presence at Nightfall—his favorite hour—the beginning of the time when lovers could tryst in shadowed groves and not be observed by curious eyes from across the island's sphere. How often had he dreamed of dancing for her alone, then taking her hand and leading her among the waterbelt's gardens with the gentle night to cloak them. It was not to be. She did not come as Hoku, the sweet, laughing playmate of his childhood, but as Governor of the island, in the people's name, to put an end to Night.

The Custodian took his place at the foot of the dais that held the Focus, and the rolling drums burst into rhythm. He chanted an ancient prayer to Pele, his hands echoing the words while the dancers swayed in the clearing surrounded by tall palms and bushes heavy with fragrant blossoms. When Pele had been duly honored, the *ipu* players began a faster rhythm and the Nightfall dance began. It was centuries old, one of many dances that kept alive the sacred heritage of Maintenance on Oporto's Island, or Moku Wina as the island was called in the chants. Through

graceful gestures the dancers told the story of Moku Wina's creation, how Oporto enticed Pele to come away from Earth and
hollow out an asteroid, filling it with all the best things from
Earth for the pleasure of his Guests. Dancing hands told how the
great mirrors outside caught light from the distant sun and fed it
into the island through Malamalama, source of all blessings, and
how Oporto had decreed the order of days and nights. As his
hands led the story, the Custodian's eyes watched the Governor
standing at the clearing's edge, waiting.

The chant ended and a hiss of gourd rattles began; the dancers knelt while the Custodian came forward to perform the ritual
of Calibration. He kept his eyes on Hoku as he danced up to the
pole and turned the key that sent beams of light shimmering toward the four sacred shrines around the clearing. His green robe
flowing around him in graceful folds, he danced to each one in
turn—Hi'iaka, Poliahu, Laka—passing his hands through the
light and verifying its centering in the target on each shrine. As
he came to Pele's shrine he looked up, thinking a silent, hopeless
prayer to the goddess whose rituals he had faithfully performed,
and in whom he had never believed. She did not answer him.
Shadows flickered over her image as his hands danced through
the light, then he turned away, returning to the pole and shutting
off the Calibration light before approaching the Focus.

The music intensified as he climbed the steps. Before him
was the Focus that brought light into the island and sent it
glowing along Malamalama; a large, ornate lever, completely unnecessary in a mechanical sense, but vital as a symbol of Maintenance. As the Custodian stepped toward it the drums suddenly
stopped, and he heard what he had been fearing since the ritual
began.

"Wait, Manuel."

He turned to face Hoku, the Governor, his lifelong friend,

who had come up behind him. She did not smile, but stepped between him and the Focus, her red robe brushing the grass-covered dais.

"The Council has made a decision," she said, turning to face the people crowding the Grove. Her formal tones carried easily through the clearing and beyond. "Oporto's Island has been dominated for centuries by the rituals of Nightfall and Dayrise. We treasure our heritage, but we are not savages, or children. We do not need lies to control us, or darkness to inspire us with fear. We are an enlightened people.

"Nightfall is a wasteful practice. Every time the Focus is shifted away from Malamalama, precious light is spilled into empty space. We can use that light to better our lives." The Governor turned to the Custodian, and he saw that her eyes were hard. "The Council has voted to eliminate the process of Nightfall, effective immediately."

The crowd roared approval, and the Custodian felt a sinking in his chest. "That would violate Maintenance procedures," he said over the din. "The Manuals clearly state—"

"The Council consider the Manuals open to interpretation," said the Governor. "We have the right to reevaluate procedures when the good of the people is in question."

"The Manuals were given to us by Oporto," said the Custodian. "To deviate from their instructions will place the island and its people in peril!"

"The Council has debated this," said Hoku, her face a careful mask. "We have concluded that to take the Manuals literally can place us in danger of misunderstanding their metaphorical intent."

"Maintenance must be performed," said Manuel, hoping he sounded firm despite his growing desperation.

"Manny," said Hoku, her voice dropping to a whisper, "don't

make it hard on yourself. You haven't got a choice." For a moment her eyes poured warm sympathy into his, then she raised her arms, the folds of her crimson caftan sliding down to her golden shoulders as she turned to the people now crowding into the clearing and called out, "Henceforth, we live in light, not in darkness!"

A cheer went up among the people, and the Custodian's courage crumbled. He gazed out over the crowd in worry. Here and there a mournful face stared back at him, mostly dancers or his acolytes, the Maintenance technicians. He was their spiritual leader, and they looked to him for guidance in this crisis, but his heart was empty. He had said all he could think to say. The Council ruled the island, and he must bow to their authority. He turned his eyes away from his followers and watched in numb despair as Hoku placed a hand on the great lever of the Focus. She borrowed two gestures from the dance: "light" and "forever." The cheers grew louder.

Hoku beckoned to a Watcher—one of the guards serving the Council—and posted her on the dais to prevent any attempt to shift the Focus. Then the Governor stepped down from the dais and passed into the crowd, touching the hands they reached out to her, moving away under the continuing daylight. The people followed, all but a few faithful who watched the Custodian expectantly as he slowly descended the steps. He stopped in the middle of the clearing and gazed at them, sensing and sharing their fear.

"What will happen, Manuel?" a young dancer asked him, her worried face framed in the leaves and fresh flowers of her headdress. "Will Pele punish us?" Her eyes pleaded for reassurance.

Others gathered around with soft and frightened voices. The Custodian raised his hands to ward off their questions. "I will appeal to the Council," he said. It was inadequate, he knew, but it was all he could offer. His followers exchanged doubting glances. He spread his arms in the wavelike gesture of blessing, which seemed to comfort them a little. "Go home," he told them. "Close the curtains on your windows and doors. Bring night into your homes, and Pele will know you are faithful."

"Thank you, Manuel," they answered, the words rippling in a whispering wave through the small group as they drifted out of the clearing toward their homes. He watched them go, their hands flashing in the spaces between leaves, speaking in silent, worried gestures. When they had passed out of sight Manuel went into his house and changed his ceremonial garb for light cotton, then went out—barefoot so he could feel the island with each step—through the Grove and down the path that led to the waterbelt. It was his custom to walk along the belt every evening after Nightfall, enjoying shadows and the soft sounds of water as it traveled endlessly around the island's center; here a trickling stream, there a clever waterfall, lakes like jewels, some with stars flashing underfoot through viewbays lapped by their blue-black depths. The stars were barely visible now, obscured by the continuing daylight. Manuel stopped and glanced up at a viewbay overhead just as the sharp glint of a mirror's edge passed it. Malamalama glowed steadily bright with the light which should have been diverted for night, some to replenish the great storage cells, the rest to pour off into space. Music began somewhere nearby, and wild shouting; the people celebrating their freedom from darkness. Suddenly Manuel needed to sit down.

He went to the nearest bench and lowered himself onto it with the weariness of a man many times his twenty-four years. A jasmine bush caressed him with its heavy scent. How had it come to this? he wondered. He was Manuel, descended from a long line of Manuels, the Custodians of the island since the time of the Separation, when Pele had returned her attention to Earth, where Hi'iaka was making war on her. It was then that Oporto's children had lost contact with the children of Earth. It was then that Oporto had created the Council, and set into law the Days and Nights of Moku Wina. It was then that the first Manuel had accepted the lifetime post of Custodian, and pledged to train his successor so that the island would always be cared for. And so it had been, until now.

Manuel searched his heart for the source of his failure. He had studied and preserved the Manuals in whose honor he was named, faithfully performed all of the Maintenance rituals—of which Nightfall and Dayrise were the most important—listened to his people and striven to answer their needs. He had tried to hide his own doubts, yet despite his best efforts, the people had begun to question the old ways. Some said the gods were not real, that Pele would never return to the island to reclaim her lost children. A growing number said the only true power was the people's own, and that no ancient system should dictate to them. Such ideas weren't new—Oporto himself had faced opposition, as had Custodians through the centuries—but never before had a Custodian failed to perform Nightfall. Manuel knew the vital importance of the ritual, of Maintenance, for the island's continued well-being, but he did not know how to impress it on those who saw Maintenance merely as superstition.

"Manny?" came a soft voice behind him, and his muscles tensed. He didn't answer, but listened to the sound of sandals on the path, the swish of crimson cloth. A hand touched his shoulder and he flinched, then looked up at Hoku, unable to keep a stab of resentment from his eyes.

"I thought I'd find you here," she said. "May I join you?"

"Shouldn't you be at the celebration?" he said bitterly, hating himself as the words left him, for of all the people on the island, Hoku was the one he least wished to hurt.

She gave him the fleeting smile that always made his pulse a
little faster; Hoku, heart's friend and gentle leader, daughter of
Governors, descendant of Guests as shown by the reddish sheen
of her hair. Though most everyone on the island was of mixed
blood, the Governor's line still bore the distinctive features of
Oporto's heritage. The Council were children of Guests also,
while Manuel's night-black hair proclaimed his descent from
Staff. The two groups—Guests and Staff—had shared the gov-
ernance of the island since the time of Separation; their children
ruled after them and kept their names alive, each following his or
her parent's path. Dancers and technicians fulfilled their birth-
rights, Hoku performed her function, and Manuel, until today,
had performed his.

Hoku sat beside him on the bench, her hand still touching
him, gently making circles on his shoulder. A tiny shudder went
through him, despair mingled with release of the tension knot-
ting his back.

"It isn't you, Manny," she said, bringing both hands to bear
on his shoulders. "I swear it isn't. You've done everything you
should. We have simply outgrown the need for night. Like
you always said, these rituals are just symbolic—"

"*Night* is not just a symbol!" said Manuel, turning to face her.
"Night is the time of rest, of replenishment—"

"On Earth, yes. In primitive societies, yes," said Hoku, "but
we're beyond that. For centuries people have worked through
the night—on Luna, on the stations, even on Earth—and still
lived happy lives. There's no need for us to huddle in darkness
half the day when the sun's light is available to us all the time."

"If there hadn't been a need for Night, Oporto wouldn't have
built the Focus," said Manuel. "He wouldn't have created Nightfall."

"He made Nightfall for the Guests from Earth, so they would

feel at home," said Hoku. "And as for the Focus, *we* control the
flow of light, it doesn't control us!"

Her eyes were beautiful, full of righteousness and something
else—something dangerously like pity—that stung him and
made him turn away. "I don't want to argue with you," he said.

"No," she agreed softly. They sat in silence for a moment,
Manuel acutely aware of the warmth of her hands on his back.
He had loved her from childhood, wanted her from youth, but
the Custodian and the Governor were counterparts, working together from a distance, living at opposite ends of the island, close
and at the same time standing apart. Never since the island's creation had a Custodian and a Governor joined. It was thought
that such an alliance would threaten the balance of power.

Manuel glanced at Hoku. Perhaps she was right. Oporto's
people were enlightened; perhaps endless day would enrich their
lives, and it was only his selfish love of starlight that made him
long for the night. If so, then the skeptics who denounced Maintenance as superstitious nonsense were justified, and the Custodian's function was meaningless.

Except it wasn't meaningless. It was necessary. Beneath the
rituals were the foundations of the island's vitality. Rising
abruptly, Manuel paced a few steps away. "I wish to address the
Council," he said.

"They won't change their minds," said Hoku.

"It is not for the Council to interpret the Manuals," said the
Custodian formally. "Their meaning requires study—years of
study—for which I have been trained and the Council have not.
It is my duty to advise them." He turned to face the Governor
and saw a sadness in her eyes; his words had built a wall between
them.

Hoku sighed and stood. "Very well. I will inform the Council
of your wish. You may address the next meeting."

He nodded silent agreement, gazing at her with an inner ache that was all too familiar. She raised a hand to her heart in the gesture of family love, gave him a sad little smile, and turned away, her sandals whispering on the path, red robe flashing through the leaves as she left him in the sharp light of day.

Lehua came for Dayrise, and Manuel was both glad and sorry. He had not spoken to her since before the last Night. Hoping to resolve the conflict, hoping he could make the Council see his viewpoint, he had gone to their meetings and reminded them of Oporto's word, which threatened dire consequences if the people failed to perform proper Maintenance. His words had disappeared like raindrops into a lake; the Council would not be convinced. His failure to reach them weighed on his spirits, and though it pleased him to see Lehua among the sparse group gathered in the Grove of Malamalama for Dayrise, he did not look forward to speaking with her.

There were only a handful of dancers this morning, and the flowers they wore were a bit brown at the edges. One musician beat out the Dayrise dance on the *ipu*, and Manuel chanted words of joy without much enthusiasm. It was hard praising the return of light when Malamalama was already shining brightly. He finished the song, moved to the Focus where the Council's Watcher stood silent guard, and pantomimed shifting the great lever upward, then turned to watch the worshipers drift away. Lehua waited for him by his house, the whiteness of her hair as it brushed her shoulders making her cotton Maintenance garb seem dim.

Lehua—Chief Technician of Moku Wina, mother of Lehua and Manuel—was a grand old dame, stout as a nut and just as tough. No one cared to cross her. Manuel wished he had inherited some of her tenacity; no doubt he would have dealt better with the Council if he had. He remembered her strong hands around his waist, lifting him up to a Maintenance shaft for the first glimpse of the systems that were his heritage. The hands were gnarled now but still strong, and she held them out to him with a smile.

"You look tired, Manny," she said.

"It's hard to sleep. Come inside, share my breakfast."

Manuel held the curtain aside for his mother and followed her into his house. It was dark; he had formed the habit of keeping the windows covered. He pushed aside a curtain to let some light in, and brought cushions and fruit to Lehua.

"We haven't seen you in Operations lately," she said as she settled herself.

"I've been busy," said Manuel, cutting slices from a ripe mango. He handed her a piece and ate one himself, let its musky sweetness fade on his tongue. "You would send for me if there was any problem."

Lehua bit into a date and chewed slowly. "Have you been down at the Hotel?"

"Not since the last Council meeting."

"What has kept you so busy, then?"

Manuel laid down the knife and wiped the stickiness from his hands with a napkin. "I've been . . . searching."

"For?"

"A way to make the Council hear me. A way to . . ."

"To believe in what you are doing?"

Lehua's voice was gentle, but the words cut. Manuel had never been able to hide his true feelings from her, but she had not said a word about it ever before. Always loving, always accepting, Lehua. Now even she saw the danger that lay in his failure. He could not look into her eyes. "What would my father have done?" he muttered.

"Your father never faced this kind of challenge."

"You mean the Council."

"I mean the doubt."

He straightened and looked at her, and the pity in her eyes was worse than all the rest. Manuel hid his face in his hands, but the smell of mango clung to them, inescapable as the daylight. He got up and went to the window. Outside children were playing tag in the ceremonial clearing, something that would never have happened when he was young. The place had lost its holiness, or the people had lost their sense of it. Or perhaps it had never been holy. "Why did Manuel III make Maintenance into ritual?" he said angrily.

"You know why," said Lehua. "The people were losing interest, and he feared the procedures would be forgotten. He set them to music and dance in order to preserve them."

"He made them a religion, and now we may lose them altogether!"

"Merely because you lack faith? No, Manny. The island is more important than your personal crises."

Like a slap in the face, the words sobered him. He turned to his mother, who sat quietly watching him.

"It seems hopeless, I know," she said. "But you will find a solution."

"You believe that?"

"I know it. These are good dates." She leaned forward, helping herself to another. "Do you remember Hoku's woman-day?"

Caught off guard, Manuel blinked. "Yes—"

"She gave you her *ti* lei. All the boys on the island were courting her, and she gave it to you. I see you still have it," she said, gesturing to where the dried loop of twisted *ti* leaves hung from the wall above his bed.

"I don't think—"

"She loves you, Manny. Why don't you marry her?"

"The Governor and the Custodian can't marry," said Manuel, more sharply than he'd meant to.

"Can't? I never heard that. You young people place too much importance on your functions."

"You were just telling me my function is more important than my beliefs!"

"Well, that's true," she said placidly, reaching for another date.

Frustrated, Manuel began to pace, the woven mats beneath his feet creaking softly. "How can I go on lying to the people I'm supposed to serve?" he demanded. "It's hypocrisy!"

"Maintenance is not a lie, Manuel. You know that."

"But it's all tangled up in mythology! How can I expect the people to believe what I don't believe myself?"

"They don't need to believe. They need to have faith." Lehua got up and walked to the window, where she stood watching the children outside with a soft smile. "They need to know in their hearts that they aren't alone, that there's a whole universe beyond the island," she said.

"What if we are alone?" said Manuel.

"Why do you still do the Communications ritual, Manuel?" said Lehua. "We haven't had a signal from Earth in four hundred years."

"That doesn't mean we'll never get one."

Lehua's smile widened. "Exactly. You know we might get a signal someday. You know we are not alone. You don't believe it, you *know* it." She turned from the window and reached out a hand to comfort him, a gesture that sent him back to boyhood.

Manuel came to her and sighed as her strong arms enfolded him.

"That's what faith is, Manny," she said into his ear. "It's knowing. Believing is worrying that something might not be true; faith is knowing it's true even if you can't see it. You've got faith, my son. You just have to decide in what."

Manuel gave an exasperated laugh. "Any suggestions?"

"Yourself?"

Lehua leaned back to smile at him, then patted his shoulder and started toward the door. "I'd better get over to Operations. Akamu and Keoni keep arguing about when to reschedule rainfall."

"Lehua—"

She stopped, and Manuel caught her hands in his, squeezing tight. "Thank you," he said. "I hope your faith in me isn't misplaced."

"Of course it isn't," she said, kissing his cheek. "You're Manuel."

"It's just a name, Mother."

"Is it?" Lehua's hand pulled back the curtain over the door. Light spilled in, framing her so he couldn't see her face, setting her hair aglow. "You know, they say a Manuel once saved the Earth," she said. He could hear the smile in her voice, and smiled back as he watched her walk down the path to the clearing. She patted a child's head, gestured her respect to the four shrines, and disappeared into the trees.

Manuel turned back to his empty house. The uneaten fruit lay on its plate among the cushions. He walked past it to his bed and took down the *ti* lei from the wall, imagining its making years before, Hoku's pretty hands folding and twisting the long *ti* leaves into a supple, glistening rope on the morning of her womanhood. He remembered the glow in her face as she had proudly danced alone that day, the *ti* lei gleaming between her small breasts, and the voices of dozens of boys begging for the gift. And he remembered his feeling of silent triumph as she had tossed it into his hands.

The lei was dry and brittle now, lifeless, faded with age. He wondered if the same thing had happened to their love. It was not a trivial question. They both needed successors. Adoption was a last resort for those who truly could not have their own children; it was everyone's duty to pass on genetic heritage as well as function. Perhaps Lehua was right, and it didn't matter that a Governor and a Custodian had never married.

He raised the lei to slip it over his head, but it had dried too narrow, hanging on its peg, and he didn't want to break it. Such a fragile thing now, though it had once been strong enough to bind a man's hands. He hated what had happened to it, just as he hated the change the Council had imposed. Sometimes he even felt he hated Malamalama, source of all blessings.

Bad thoughts. Manuel shook his head to get rid of them, but he knew they would not go away. He was angry, he realized, not just at the Council but at Hoku personally, for standing against him. She had chosen to oppose him, and none of his arguments or entreaties seemed to move her.

He reached up to hang the lei back on its peg. Its faded green was only a little darker than the grasses of the wall. In time, it would blend in completely. Manuel wondered if he would some-day forget it was there.

"You must check the systems again," said Councillor Haveland, fanning himself vigorously in the heat of the Council Chamber. "There is clearly a malfunction."

"There is no malfunction," said Manuel. "All environmental systems are operating at peak capacity—"

"Nonsense!" said Councillor Gary, wiping moisture from his brow with a fine kerchief edged in Councillor's yellow. "If the systems were functioning properly the island wouldn't be three degrees hotter than normal!"

Manuel's fist tightened around a handful of his robe and he forced himself to reply calmly. "It is increased demand that is causing problems. Continual day is placing strain on our cooling systems—"

"Then increase their power," said Councillor Petra. "We have the light, let's use it!"

"It's not quite that simple," Manuel began.

"Manuel, we understand your wish to make a point," said Councillor Haveland testily, "but you've made it. The island needs its Custodian to keep the systems in order. You and your descendants will continue to have a place of honor. Now fulfill your function—get the island back to normal!"

"The island can't be normal without Night!" said Manuel, his hands emphasizing his statement with the gesture meaning "night."

"Do the Manuals say night is necessary?" asked Gary.

Manuel clenched his teeth. He'd been expecting that question; he'd spent hours searching the Manuals for just such a reference, hoping to use it in support of his arguments, but he'd found none. The Manuals were written by the Oporto and the Investors, children of Earth, who took night for granted.

"Not in so many words," he said, "but references to nighttime functions make it clear—"

"I know of no functions that cannot be as easily performed in day," said Gary, stifling a yawn.

"The advantages of daylight outweigh the difficulties," said Petra. "We are increasing our quality of life. With continual work shifts we have more space for our workers, we can produce more food and allow people to have more children—"

"All of which will increase the demand on our physical systems," said Manuel, "and they're already overburdened!"

"Manuel," said Hoku, who had been silently observing the discussion, "is it possible to increase power to the physical systems?"

Manuel turned to her, frustrated by her neutral mask. "Yes, but—"

"There!" said Gary in triumph. "He admits it! I move the Council *require* the Custodian to increase power!"

"We can't maintain an increase indefinitely!" said Manuel, but his protest was lost in a chorus of agreement from the Councillors.

"So ruled," said Hoku, her voice putting an end to the clamor. "Manuel, you have the Council's instructions." Her eyes were hard, and Manuel swallowed angrily, then turned and left the chamber without another word.

Outside the Hotel the air was oppressive; hot and damp, as if the island had been doused in the steam from a battle between Pele and her sister Hi'iaka. A slight stink of rotting vegetation made Manuel frown. He stripped off his robe, under which he wore Maintenance garb—light, close-fitting cotton for the sacred work of Holding Up The World—but even this thin clothing seemed too much in the heat of the endless day. Manuel glanced at the nearby pole of Malamalama, terminating in the Civic Plaza, exactly opposite to the Grove of Malamalama. Across the plaza was the Governor's house, flanked by *ti* trees and stately palms. Oporto himself had once lived there. Now it was Hoku's.

Feeling a sudden tightness in his throat, Manuel turned away and started back toward Operations, on his side of the island. He jogged most of the way back, passing fields of flourishing new crops and others that seemed pale and withered. Workers looked up at him, some with weary eyes; he was not the only one having trouble sleeping in the constant light. Feeling helpless against their misery, he jogged on past the fields and between flowering shrubs that had dropped their blooms, strewing the path underfoot with flashes of faded color.

Arriving at Operations with a sheen of dampness on his skin, Manuel slowed to a walk and wiped at his face with his robe. He would need a fresh one for Nightfall, and wondered how much time he had before the ceremony. It annoyed him, having to check. Ordinarily he would have known by instinct how many hours of light were left, but he couldn't count them now, no matter how closely he shuttered his rooms against the incessant daylight.

He strode into Operations with the robe slung over one shoulder and headed for the control room, where he found a cluster of technicians gathered. "What's the status, Lehua?" he said, joining them.

Lehua glanced up from her console, grimacing as she wiped perspiration from her face with a brown hand. On the screens around her frantic images conveyed stress on the island's systems.

"We're at maximum on environmental control," said Lehua. "Power use is up thirty percent, ambient humidity up eighteen percent, water use up seven percent. And the temperature's still rising," she added unnecessarily.

Manuel leaned toward the screen, knowing what he would see. Though the Council blamed the island's woes on system failure, he knew there were no malfunctions. He and his technicians had been searching the complex environmental systems for days —even for nights, though he disliked putting his staff on the continual shifts that the Council promoted—trying to find a problem to correct, but there were none.

The Custodian rubbed his sweating chin, thinking of Oporto's warning to his children of the consequences of failing to perform Maintenance: crops withering, lakes drying, fighting among the people. He had not thought such plagues would actually occur, yet without doubt they were beginning, and only weeks after the Council had first denied his pleas to reinstate night.

"What shall we do, Manuel?" asked Kaleo, a young tech whose dark eyes were tense with worry.

Manuel glanced at Lehua. "I've been given orders by the Council," he said. "We must make a change."

He gathered the technicians into a circle and led the chants of purification that preceded all major Maintenance functions. Feeling Lehua's eyes on him, he hurried through the song, his hands weaving the air in the gestures of blessing. Then he looked up at Lehua. "Increase power to environmental systems by ten percent," he said.

One of the techs took a sharp breath. Lehua moved toward her console, pausing to look back. "We'll be drawing on reserves," she said.

Manuel nodded. "I'll inform the Governor," he said, glancing at the screen. "After Nightfall."

He stepped back, breaking the circle, and as he glanced at them the techs avoided his gaze. Their silence followed him away down the hall. Few people paid any attention to the Nightfall and Dayrise rituals any more; even his own technicians had lost faith. Often as not he performed the ceremonies alone, but he did so without fail. He was Manuel. If he stopped performing the rituals, he would cease to be Manuel.

As he strode down the corridor he heard the surge of new power into the environmental control system, sensed the change of air pressure as fans picked up speed, felt a breath of coolness as he passed beneath a vent. Welcome as it was to his body, the change only increased his anxiety, for now the physical plant was supplementing the fire of Malamalama with stored light from the great power cells. When their reserves ran out, the island would have no other source to meet its demands.

He went to his house and permitted himself the luxury of a shower. The water was lukewarm, slightly stale. Donning a fresh green robe and his ceremonial headdress, he went out to the Grove of Malamalama and found the clearing empty. No dancers, no singers, no drummers. The only person in sight was the Council's Watcher, standing on the dais between him and the Focus. With a sigh Manuel walked to his place at the foot of the steps, and stood alone in the silence.

Closing his eyes, he listened to his own breathing and the distant sounds of activity muffled by the woods. He could almost imagine a miracle, a crowd of followers waiting breathlessly for him to lead the ceremony. He laughed at himself; easy with eyes closed. Easy to mumble incantations and trust in omnipotent gods to take care of you, but he believed—no, he knew—that Moku Wina's people were their own caretakers, and he was responsible for seeing it was done.

Manuel opened his eyes and stared at the shielded pole that marked Malamalama's terminus. Above where the shielding stopped, at a level distant enough not to damage the eyes, the axis gleamed with brilliant daylight. Malamalama, source of all blessings, was after all just a machine.

Sometimes he thought of going through the Manuals and removing all reference to ritual and worship, but when he tried to picture himself performing the functions of Maintenance without the gestures of blessing and reverence, it felt wrong. He was his father's son. He had spent his life training to perform the rituals of Moku Wina's heritage. His feelings, even the Council's decision, didn't matter. Maintenance must be performed.

In a voice barely above a whisper he began the chant to Pele. He did not believe she was creator of Moku Wina, or protector of Oporto's people. He remembered arguing with his father over the dedication to Pele. His father had told him it didn't matter what he thought; Pele must be honored because that was part of the ritual, part of Maintenance.

He danced alone, chanting softly, hands flowing through the air and his bare feet gripping the soft earth of the island. He danced not for Pele, but for his father. He followed the dedication with the Nightfall dance, then in silence he performed Calibration, his hands cutting knifelike through beams of light. One of the mirrors was slightly off-focus, and he sent a command signal to its driver to adjust. Every bit of light was needed now.

Finally he shut off the Calibration light, and ascended the dais to stand before the Focus. He stared at the lever, carved with symbols no one believed in anymore.

"Manuel," said the Watcher, startling him. It was Puna, the woman who had first been posted on guard over the Focus.

"Yes?" he said.

To his surprise she stepped aside. "I think you were right," she said, her eyes bright with worried tears. "The Council shouldn't have stopped Nightfall. Please complete the ceremony."

Manuel caught his breath, and reached out his hand shivering with an instant's joy at the thought of shifting the lever and plunging the island into Night. Instead he grasped the Watcher's shoulder. "Thank you, Puna," he said, "but the Council would see it as an act of war. There must be a better way to bring back the night."

"How?" asked Puna.

It was a question that had filled him with despair for many days. "Pray," he said helplessly. "Pray for guidance." It was the best answer he had, and it was not enough. Feeling defeated, he turned away to descend the steps.

"May I pray with you, Manuel?" Puna asked.

Surprised, Manuel stopped halfway down the steps and looked back at the Watcher. Her eyes pleaded, and Manuel returned and took her hands, then began the chant he thought she was most likely to know; a chant to Pele, a simple song, one of the first learned by every child on the island. Puna sang with him, stumbling over some of the words, but when the chant was finished she smiled. "Thank you, Manuel," she said, looking up at him shyly. "I would like to sing with you again."

Touched, Manuel nodded. "Tomorrow, we'll sing again."

"Thank you," she said as he stepped away. "Thank you, Manuel!" Puna's voice followed him through the clearing and into his home. As the curtain fell closed behind him he suddenly realized he'd been doing everything wrong. He had been working alone —shutting himself away in solitary darkness, shielding his technicians from responsibility, trying to fight the Council single-handedly—when what he needed was to add the people's voices to his. It was not his faith that mattered, but theirs.

Even if Pele was just a symbol, she stood for Maintenance, and he knew beyond doubting that Maintenance was necessary. Night was necessary too, and there were others who wanted its return. If he could win back the people's support, the Council would not be able to ignore him. How many days in the unending day he had wasted! Tossing his headdress onto the bed, he

caught his long robe in one hand, went back outside, and began
to run.

The first people he encountered were field workers, tending
new crops. "Nightfall has passed," he told them. One or two
sneered, but he ignored them. "I know your work shift kept you
from attending the ceremony. I came to offer a prayer for those
who wish to join me."

They stared silently at him, and Manuel could feel the heat
rising to his face. "Maybe some of you miss the Night, as I do," he
said. "Maybe you would like to have it back."

"You won't get it back," said a worker, turning away.

"Maybe not," said Manuel, "but I will pray anyway."

The workers looked at each other, then one put aside her
shovel and came to him. Others followed, and Manuel led them
in the same children's chant he had sung with Puna. "We'll sing
again at Nightfall tomorrow," he said. "Everyone is welcome."

Moving on, he made the same offer to everyone he found
awake, Staff and Guests, at work or at play. Some ignored him
but many did not, and each time he joined hands with a new
circle and began to chant, he felt the strength of the people flowing through him. He walked all through the hours of night, returning to the clearing for Dayrise. When he reached it he found
a small crowd of people waiting for him, many of those he'd sung
with in the last few hours. Among them were a dozen or more
dancers, decked in wreaths of fern and flower woven by their
own hands, and musicians enough to perform the Dayrise
chants. Manuel led the ceremony, then sang the children's chant
again with the people and sent them into the day with blessings
while he continued his mission.

He lost track of time as he walked all the paths of the island,
seeking to sing with as many of its two thousand people as he
could persuade to join him. He surprised his technicians by lead-

ing them in a chant of celebration he had not sung since the beginning of endless daylight, and laughed inside at their astonishment. They must think he had gone mad, and perhaps he had, but at least he was doing something.

His legs and feet were aching with weariness by the time his wanderings brought him to the Council Chamber. It was empty; the Councillors were busy elsewhere, and he stood in the Chamber's center and chanted a song praising Night while the Watchers at the doorway stared. Then he went outside and crossed the plaza to the Governor's house.

"Hoku," he called, standing outside her window, swaying a little with weariness. "Hoku, come sing with me." He received no answer, and with a laugh he sat beneath her window. He plucked a leaf from a *ti* tree nearby and tore it into strips, fingers clumsy as he twisted them together, one end held between his toes and the pungent juice making his hands sticky. He began to sing, not a chant this time, but a song of love, a courting song. He had sung it softly to himself a thousand times, alone in the darkness of his room, with Hoku's face shining in his imagination. Now he sang it out loud, heedless of who might hear, his hands caressing the air now and then before returning to the rope-weaving. Manuel had gone mad, the people would say. It might be true, but if so it had happened long ago.

As he sang of starlight on the island's waters he became aware he was not alone. He kept his eyes on the twist of leaves in his hands and tied its ends together as he finished the song, then turned to see Hoku herself, in Governor's red, with the Council behind her.

"Manuel," she said in a voice that matched the sadness of her frown, "what are you doing?"

Rising to his feet, Manuel held out the bracelet he had made. "This is for you," he said.

Hoku's hand came up to take the circle of dark, glossy green. As she looked up at him a flash of regret replaced the frown, and all his anger melted.

"Come sing with me, Hoku," he said softly, taking her hand. "We haven't sung together since we were children. *Analani e—* remember?"

"Manuel," said Hoku, "you are not yourself. You need some rest—"

"We all need some rest," said Manuel, laughing. "That's what I've been telling you! Never mind, come and sing! All of you, come sing!" He beckoned to the Council as he led Hoku by the hand down the path toward the far pole and the Grove of Malamalama. They followed, probably with the idea of preventing him from doing anything they disapproved. It didn't matter to Manuel. He squeezed Hoku's hand as she walked beside him on the path.

"I love you, Hoku. I don't think I've told you that in years," he said softly. "It's more true now than ever."

Hoku didn't answer, but neither did she pull her hand away. She walked on beside him, gazing at the path beneath their feet, the bracelet in her free hand. They crossed the waterbelt on Manuel's favorite bridge, and long before they reached the Grove they began passing through a great crowd, hundreds of people, more than Manuel remembered seeing all together in many years. The people reached out their hands to him as he passed, and he touched their fingers with his own. When he reached the ceremonial clearing he led Hoku up to the steps before the Focus, with the Councillors close behind. The voices of the people filled the clearing, some questioning, some cheering Manuel. He smiled, then held his hands up for silence.

"People of Moku Wina," he said aloud, smiling, "many of you

have sung with me today, and my heart is filled with gladness. Sing again with me now."

He led the same song—the children's chant to Pele—a song with no significance toward day or night. It was the voices chanting together, the hundreds of hands moving in unison, that mattered. He heard Hoku's voice join the others, and saw her lovely hands rise in gestures of happiness and love, the bracelet of *ti* leaves circling one slender wrist. At the end of the chant the people cheered, and the *ipus* began to play the rhythms of the Nightfall dance. Voices from the woods joined Manuel's in the chanting; he saw the hands of the people echoing the dance. Those who didn't know the song chanted *"Po, Po"*—calling for Night, Night—and kept up the chant while he performed the dance of Calibration. The voices rose higher as he approached the Focus. The Council clustered on the dais, and he faced them, smiling, with open arms.

"Councillors," he said, "you honor your people with your presence at the Nightfall ritual." He saw Councillor Haveland ready to speak, and continued. "I thank you for what you have taught us in the time since the last Night. You have shown us what we can accomplish by using all of Malamalama's blessings. That is a good thing, but now we are using more light than Malamalama can give us. Now we are using the reserve power from our storage cells. The island needs to sleep, just as we need to sleep."

A roar of agreement went up from the crowd, so strong it surprised Manuel. He glanced at the people, then at the Councillors, who looked uncomfortable. Manuel went on. "You have given us the freedom to work through the hours of Night. Now I ask you to give us the freedom to rest. Can we not offer our people both choices?"

Hoku was frowning slightly. "What do you propose, Manuel?" she asked.

"Change is a good thing, as you have taught me," said Manuel. "On Earth the days change in length. I propose a new system that will allow us to have longer days some of the time and longer Nights some of the time, as on Earth. Then we can still achieve more without exhausting our light completely."

The Councillors exchanged glances. "We must discuss this," said Councillor Gary.

Manuel nodded. "I will bring a plan to you tomorrow," he said. "My staff and I will determine the most efficient use of the energy at our disposal."

"Agreed," said Hoku, glancing at the Councillors. "In the meantime—"

"In the meantime," said Manuel, lowering his voice so that only the Councillors would hear, "we're depleting our reserves to run the environmental control systems. Let us have a Night to allow them to recover. You can call it a holiday if you like."

He watched their faces anxiously. The Councillors did not look pleased. "Shall I ask the people what they wish?" he said softly.

Hoku glanced at him with sharp amusement. "I don't think that will be necessary," she said. "Councillors, the Custodian's words make sense. Any opposed to declaring a holiday?" When none spoke, she turned to the waiting people and raised her arms. "People of Moku Wina, your Custodian has made a wise suggestion. The Council will meet tomorrow to review a new plan for the use of Malamalama's blessings. In celebration of this, we declare a holiday from now until Dayrise. Let torches be lit to honor Pele, and let Night fill the island so that the torches can be seen by all!"

A cheer broke from the crowd, and accompanied by the roaring of drums, Manuel stepped up to the Focus, placed his hands on the ornate lever, and shifted it downward.

Darkness surrounded him, a black so deep he felt an instant's primal fear of blindness. Then the light of stars penetrated the viewbays, and the cheering rose higher as torches were kindled and began to dance through the woods, scattering away from the clearing. Manuel stood gazing at the stars for a moment, then turned away from the Focus.

His eyes were still adjusting, but he knew the shadowed figure standing still before him was Hoku. He smiled at her through the Night. "Well said, Governor. You are very good at your function."

"And you are good at yours," said Hoku. "This will be a good change, I think."

Manuel could see Hoku's hand, pale against the shadows of her robe. He reached out to take it, and led her slowly away from the others, down the steps to the clearing. "I have another change to propose," he said. "Won't you walk with me by the water?"

Afterword

Jack Williamson is one of the reasons I feel lucky to be a New Mexican. Our state is a mixture of outmoded systems that retain both function and charm—like acequias that have watered farmlands under three nations' rule—and exciting innovations such as the commercial spaceport now being planned near White Sands. In a way Jack reflects

that dichotomy. He's been around long enough to be considered part of the landscape, yet his ideas still sparkle and
inspire. He is a far-thinker and a country gentleman at
once, and it's an honor to be a member of his community.

Thinking over my favorites among Jack's work, I noticed a common thread of technology originally intended
to be benevolent, but either gone wrong somehow, or just
not well-planned enough, and ultimately too controlling of
humankind. Our fierce love of independence can lead us to
defy any restrictions, regardless of their good intent. That's
a key part of growing up, as any parent of teenagers knows.
I wondered what would happen if a group of humans who
found themselves in such a situation decided to buck the
system laid down for their tender care—and then discovered they'd made a mistake by so doing. The result of my
ponderings in this direction is "Emancipation," a coming-
of-age story of sorts.

Oporto's Island owes its name to a character in Jack's
Starchild Trilogy. I rather doubt it was this character who
created the island, but it might well have been a relation.
And like Jack, port wine (oporto) is one of the finer treats
of Earth origin that continue to improve with age.

—Pati Nagle

It's always nice to be surprised, and John Brunner has always delighted in surprising the reader. Perhaps it is his strong sense of social justice, evident in such works as the Hugo Award–winning *Stand on Zanzibar* as well as in his speeches to science fiction conventions and also in his willingness to personally work in the service of various worthy causes. Or perhaps it's his sheer author's audacity, his refusal to be predictable.

The humanoids weren't the first robots to be written about in science fiction, and by 1994, when "Thinkertoy" was written, there were already hundreds of robot stories. So here's one that's a little different. Just like Brunner.

Thinkertoy

John Brunner

Paul Walker was afraid of his children. For months now he had been afraid for them, ever since the fatal accident, but this was different—not a rapid change, but the gradual kind that is recognized one morning as having happened.

And he and Lisa had been so proud of their outstanding intelligence. . . .

He could not tell which of them he found the more disturbing. Logically it should have been Rick because of the way the crash had altered him. He bore no visible scars, but it had done incontestable damage. Whether directly, as the result of trauma, or indirectly, through showing him his mother hideously dead, had proved impossible to establish.

Yet in many ways Kelly, two years the older, affected him worse. There was something unnerving about the composure she maintained: in particular, the way she cared for Rick now that he showed so little interest in the world. It wasn't right for a child barely into her teens to be so organized, so self-possessed: to rouse her brother in the mornings, make sure he was neatly dressed and came to breakfast on time, arrange their return home because though Paul could drop them at school on his way to the office he was still at work when classes finished. Most days they came back by bus, now and then in the car of one of the numerous other parents living nearby who had been shocked by Lisa's death. . . . It was in principle a great arrangement; as his friends kept reminding him, it meant he could keep his job and even work overtime now and then, without worrying.

But he had worried all along. Now he had progressed beyond that. He had grown used to the sense of Rick not being wholly present anymore, yet not resigned to it. The boy went to school without protest, and endured his classes and maybe soaked up the odd droplet of information. But on regaining his room he would sit, both before and after supper unless Kelly coaxed him to watch TV, in front of his computer or his games console, perhaps with a game loaded, more often watching a net display scrolling of its own accord, looking—this had crossed Paul's mind weeks ago and fitted better than any other description— bored. Bored as though he was tired of being able to remember that he had used to operate these expensive gadgets, without recalling what he had actually done to make them work. For a while Paul had offered to partner him, but was defeated by his frustrating wall of indifference.

Every weekend he sought some stimulus that might re-
awaken his son's dormant personality, making a trip to a game or
a show or some place of interest out of town. This time, though,
Kelly had asked to visit a shopping mall, to which he gladly consented because he felt she ought to let him buy her new and
more stylish clothes to keep up with her school friends. It was
fruitless; she insisted on the same kind of items as usual, inexpen-
sive, practical, plain.

However, there proved to be a compensation. He was
double-checking his grocery list for the coming week before
continuing to the supermarket when Kelly—in T-shirt, jeans,
and trainers as she would remain until it was time for sweater,
jeans, and boots—returned to him with a thoughtful air.

"Dad, I think you ought to see this."

Instantly: "Where's Rick? Why isn't he with you?"

"That's what I want you to see. Look."

And there the boy was, standing riveted before a display in a
section of the mall it had not crossed Paul's mind to make for.

*But why did I not think of toys? After all, in some ways he has become a
child again. . . .*

Hastening in Kelly's wake, he wondered what could have
broken through that armor of remoteness. It must be something
special, for there were as many adults and even teenagers, normally contemptuous of childish things, as there were children
gathered here. A smiling salesman was putting his wares through
their paces.

And quite some paces they were.

They were performing under an arch bearing the name
THINKERTOY in brightly colored letters, on a display one part of
which modeled a modern city block with buildings of various
heights; another, a medieval castle with donjon, moat, and curtain wall; another, an icebound coastline lapped by miniature

waves. All over these were roaming little machines, some with wheels, some arms and/or legs, some tentacles, some hooks and suckers for hauling themselves up cliffs or trees or vertical walls. Occasionally they came to an obstacle they could neither surmount nor traverse, whereupon, seemingly of their own volition, they repaired to a heap of miscellaneous parts at the side of the display, disconnected part of their or another's current fitments, plugged in replacements and renewed their progress. Now and then the onlookers clapped and laughed at some particularly ingenious configuration, such as a scaling-ladder. Also there were a pair of video screens showing other actions they were capable of. Paul found himself fascinated along with all the rest.

"Excuse me."

A tentative voice. The salesman deployed his broadest beam.

"Suppose you change things around."

Rick? Could it be . . . ? Yes, it was Rick who had spoken! This was fantastic!

"You mean like shifting things to new places? They keep right on going. They learn in moments. For instance—" He reached for a handful of the spare parts, then checked.

"No, kid, you can do it. Dump 'em wherever you like. When they bump into one of these bits they'll recognize it, remember it's in the wrong place, collect it, and return it to store. You'll see."

The little machines performed as predicted, watched by Rick with total attention. Meantime the man continued his spiel, while two pretty girls took station beside a credit-card reader in anticipation of impending sales.

"But you haven't seen a fraction of what Thinkertoys can do! You can find out more from the screens here, and our full-color literature." On cue, the girls fanned brilliant leaflets like oversize poker hands. "You can discover how much more fun, how much more fulfilling for adults too is life with Thinkertoys around! Want your Thinkertoy to answer your phone, and that includes videophones by the way, with any of a hundred voices and identities? Make 'em up yourself or use the ones supplied. Want your games console or computer to play against you in exactly the style of your favorite partner, only he or she is not available? Easy! Just record a sample of the games you've played together. Your Thinkertoy will analyze and duplicate anybody's style to grandmaster level and beyond. Want to integrate your computer with your stereo, your stereo with your TV, your TV with your phone—so you can call home and tell the VCR to record a program you only just found out about? Your phone with your cooker, your microwave, your refrigerator? It's done for you! And as for what two or more of these little pals can do, it's astonishing! Two Thinkertoys working together can open an icebox or freezer, read the labels on the stored food, or if unlabeled show it to a videophone for you to identify, then locate the recipe you name and prepare it against your return home, substituting if need be alternative ingredients of equal or superior quality. Thinkertoys retrieve from awkward places. They clean tirelessly and unobtrusively. They hide in corners when not required and reactivate instantly on hearing their names. No need to connect them to wires or cables, though that is an option. They communicate like portable phones, and with ultrasound, and with infrared—"

"Say!" one of the listeners burst out. "If they do all these things why call them toys?"

"They're for playing with," was the suave rejoinder. "Most people don't have enough fun in their lives. Thinkertoys are designed to put the fun back in living! And . . ." His voice dropped to a confidential level, though everyone in the small crowd still heard every syllable. "To be absolutely frank, our company was intending to introduce a family model, what you might call a more sober design, just to do dull things like help out around the house. But then this new chip came out, the very latest most sophisticated kind, and we found we could pack all these features in as well, and . . . okay, I'll let you in on the secret. Thinkertoys work so well, people buy them for their kids and wind up using them themselves, so they have to come back and buy another, catch?"

He flashed a mouthful of excellently cared-for teeth, and several people chuckled at his engaging blatancy.

"Of course," he added, "it makes sense to save yourself the second trip, and these young ladies will be pleased to show you our double packs at a net savings of fifteen percent. And of course all Thinkertoys are fully guaranteed."

"Dad," Kelly whispered, "are you going to buy one for Rick?"

The things weren't cheap, especially with the full kit of parts warranted to permit access anywhere in any house or apartment. However, the sight of Rick showing animation for the first time since he came home from the hospital. . . .

He hadn't spent the insurance he had had on Lisa, meaning to invest it until the kids were of college age. But this was a special case. Just how special became plain when, instead of showing his customary indifference, Rick made a careful selection of the optional extras. As he put his credit card away Paul's heart felt light for the first time since his wife's death.

"What's got into you?" demanded Carlos Gomez when they met during lunch break. Carlos was the firm's computer manager, and as personnel supervisor Paul worked closely with him, but they had been drawn together most of all because Belita Gomez had been a good friend of Lisa, and immensely supportive since the tragedy. It was she who most often gave Rick and Kelly a ride home from school.

"What do you mean?"

"You're looking cheerful for a change."

Paul explained, with the aid of some of Thinkertoy's promotional literature that he had in his pocket. Studying it, Carlos gave a soft whistle.

"I'd heard they were working on stuff like this, but I didn't know it was on the market. And for kids, yet! There must be something wrong with it."

Paul blinked. "What makes you so sure? I haven't noticed anything wrong. In fact the opposite. Kelly has been so anxious to help Rick get better, and this is the first real chance she's had. First thing they had to do when they switched the gizmo on was choose a name for it, and they settled on Marmaduke and that was the first time I've heard Rick show any sign of amusement since . . . Well, recently. But I swear I heard him chuckle.

"Then they settled down to try out everything in the manual, and I had to take supper to Rick's room for them and eventually become the heavy father at midnight. And today I've let them stay home from school, just for once, because . . . well, because of the change it's worked on my son." He sounded almost belligerent. "And you immediately conclude something is wrong? I think it's all extremely right!"

"Cool it," Carlos sighed. "I didn't mean wrong from your kids' point of view. I meant from the point of view of what they originally intended the things to do. Maybe they're fine for home use but no good for autopiloting an airliner or controlling an industrial plant."

"You ever heard of this operation before? No? Then what makes you so positive?"

"Just the sort of things a Thinkertoy is capable of, on its own or in conjunction with others. Paul, a chip like that simply isn't the sort you develop for the toy market."

"During the Cold War, didn't the Soviets buy gaming machines intended for Las Vegas because that way they got their hands on electronics that were otherwise under ban?"

"Sure, but those aren't exactly toys. The gambling market operates in the billion-dollar league. Even the biggest hits in the toy market arrive one season, thrive for another, and fade away the next. Exceptions exist, like Barbie dolls, but have you seen a Peppervine doll lately? Or a Captain Carapace? So I can't help wondering what the intended application was for these things. I guess I'll ask around. Mind if I keep this?" He tapped the stiff polychrome paper of the advertising flyer.

Paul shrugged and nodded. But he felt annoyed with Carlos. He had spent months in a nonstop condition of worry; thought it was ended; and now found himself given a reason to start worrying all over again.

He was still further alarmed when he arrived home to find Kelly alone in the kitchen defrosting food for supper.

"What's Rick doing?" he demanded. "Never tell me he's bored with Marmaduke already!"

Wrestling with a too-tough plastic cover, she shook her head. "No, it's just that we've done everything in the manual that we can—you need some extra connectors to wire up the kitchen, like the oven and the broiler, and he didn't pick them up —and . . . Well, you better ask him yourself. He lost me halfway. Ah!"—as the obstinate cover finally peeled back.

"He'll lose me sooner than that," Paul sighed, and headed for his son's room.

The boy was seated contemplatively before his computer. Marmaduke squatted beside the keyboard, or rather its torso, devoid of the attachments. The screen showed mazy lines.

"Circuit diagram?" Paul hazarded.

"Mm-hm"—without looking around.

"Something wrong? Kelly said you can do everything in the manual except jobs you need special parts for."

"Mm-hm."

"So—uh—are you running an autodiagnostic?"

"Trying to. I can't get it to run properly."

"I was talking to Carlos Gomez over lunch. You know, our computer manager. He seemed very interested in these Thinker-toys. How about downloading it to him and seeing if he can help?"

"Nope." The boy's tone held the first hint of determination his father could recall since the crash. "I think I know what's wrong and I'd rather fix it myself."

He rose stiffly from his chair, as though he had been there all day.

"I'm hungry," he added. "What's Kelly fixing? Smells good."

Paul had to wait a moment before following him downstairs. His eyes were blurred with tears.

The following day Kelly said she wanted to go to school. Rick didn't. He wanted to finish solving his problem and thought he could. Unwilling to risk an argument that might make him late for work, Paul exacted a promise that he would certainly attend the next day, and was astonished and delighted when the Think-ertoy appeared unexpectedly on the breakfast counter in a quasi-humanoid configuration with two arms, two legs and one head, threw up a smart salute and shouted, "You got it, Mister Admiral, sir!"

His son had often made jokes like that, way back when . . .

In the car, he hoped Kelly's detachment might thaw, but it

didn't. Drawing up before her school, he ventured, "Buying Marmaduke seems to have been a bright idea, hm?"

With her customary abnormal gravity she shrugged. "Too soon to say."

And was gone, not pausing to kiss him goodbye.

That, though, had become the pattern.

Carlos was not in the office today—on a trip, Paul learned, to inspect a batch of expensive gear being offered second-hand at a bargain price. The seller, a bankrupt arms company, had been a casualty of the end of the Cold War. He resolved to phone him at home tonight if Rick hadn't sorted out his problem. Two days off school were enough.

And of course if there really was something wrong with Marmaduke they could always return him—it—on Saturday, under guarantee.

But, Kelly declared as soon as he entered the house, that wasn't going to be necessary. Pleased, more than a little proud of his son, who had been a real computer whiz before the accident and seemed to be recovering at last, he headed upstairs.

"Rick! Kelly tells me you figured it out," he said heartily.

"Mm-hm." The screen was acrawl with lines like yesterday, but this time the boy was using his mouse rather as though he was in Draw mode, marking a dot here and a dot there and leaving the computer to connect them.

Paul hesitated, aware that he understood far less about computers than his son, but finally ventured, "Are you repairing Marmaduke?"

"Yup."

"I didn't know you could. I mean, not on the sort of gear you have."

"He's designed that way. To be fixed in the field."

"Field?"

"Away from the shop. It's a really dense chip in there. You can write to it with real tiny currents. Amazing stuff. 'Course, reprogramming it would be a different matter."

"You're not—uh—doing that?"

"Nah. Just cleaning it up. Getting rid of some junk."

"So what exactly did you find wrong?"

Rick leaned back and stretched.

"It got damaged. Like my brain . . . Say, I'm hungry."

And after they'd eaten, he carried his plate to the sink, announcing, "Okay, well, if I got to go to school in the morning I better make sure Marmaduke is one hundred percent. See you later."

After a pause, Kelly's mood softened enough for her to concede, "I guess you were right, what you said about Marmaduke."

That was as far as she was prepared to go, but Paul passed his most relaxed evening in a long, long while.

Around ten-thirty Rick decided he was satisfied, emerged yawning from his room, took a shower, and retired peacefully to bed. Kelly decided to do the same. As she headed for the stairs there was a soft scuttling noise.

"What's that?" Paul exclaimed.

"Marmaduke, of course, this time with all his wits about him. You turning in too?"

"In a little while. I want to call Carlos, see if he's home yet—Just a moment! Do I need to set the answering machine as usual or has Marmaduke been programmed to switch it on?"

"Better than that," the Thinkertoy replied. It was perching on the newel post of the banister. "I can act as one, using whichever phone is nearest and adjusting the outgoing message to correspond with the current situation. I shall memorize your usual bedtime and rising time with allowance for weekends, but in addition I can take calls whenever the house is unoccupied and give the other party your estimated time of return. Let me know if ever you would like these parameters changed. By the way, I can also control a modem and a fax and reprogram your VCR in response to a phone call—but you've read the brochure. At least I hope you have."

"You forgot to mention," Kelly murmured, "that we've fixed you to sound like me, or Rick, or Dad, or Donald Duck, according to who the caller wants to talk to. The Donald Duck one is for telephone solicitors. In case you're interested, Dad, the voice he's using right now is a three-way mix of all of us. I told Rick it would be kind of suitable."

For a second Paul was stunned. Then he chuckled.

"Marmaduke, I think you are going to be a distinct asset to the Walker household. Good night!"

He reached for the phone. They only had the regular kind. Videophones were still very expensive, even though it was clear from the Thinkertoy literature the manufacturers took it for granted that if you could afford one you could afford the other.

Moments later Belita Gomez's drowsy voice sounded in his ear.

"No, Paul, Carlos isn't home yet. He called to say he'd closed the deal and they were all going to a restaurant. Want him to call back?"

"Don't even give him a message. It can wait until morning. The kids are in bed and I'm about to follow their example. *Buenas noches.*"

"I'm *in* bed. G'night."

Later there was the faintest beep from the phone bell, cut off so quickly it was barely audible.

Whereafter, to the accompaniment of a yawning noise: "Hello."

In a whisper: "Paul, this is Carlos. Sorry to call so late. I'll try and keep it short but you need to hear this. 'Fraid I got to keep my voice down. Belita's asleep and I don't want to disturb her."

A deep breath.

"At this company where I went today, after we agreed on a figure, I stuck around for dinner with the guys I was mainly dealing with. I happened to ask whether they knew anything about Thinkertoys. I hit pay dirt. Remember I said those chips weren't developed for the toy market even if the toys do double as home appliances? Well, this company I was at used to be in arms back in the Cold War period, and this guy says yes, he knows who made them, though he wouldn't give a name, but he did tell me what they were intended for. Sabotage! Plant 'em behind enemy lines, or leave 'em during a retreat, and they activate and start wrecking everything in reach. Electronics first, naturally—they have built-in jamming capacity. But they can start fires and foul up bearings and unscrew closed valves in chemical plants, even loosen tacks in stair carpet so people break their necks. . . . They're supposed to have been rendered harmless. Some kind of inactivation program. But this guy I was talking to: he says the security is lousy and you can get around it in an hour, or sooner if you automate the job, and the word's out on the net and you want to guess who's buying? The Sword Arm of the Lord, that's who, hoping to destroy black-owned businesses, and the Islamic League for Female Decency, and the Choosers of the Slain, and — Shit, I think I woke Belita after all. Talk to you in the morning. 'Bye."

The connection broke.

Whereupon Marmaduke went on about its proper business, the liberty for which Rick had restored.

*   *   *

"Sorry, *querida* — didn't mean to wake you."

"It's okay, I wasn't really asleep. . . . Who were you talking to at this hour?"

Sitting on the edge of the bed to remove his shoes: "Paul. Paul Walker. I learned something about those Thinkertoys that couldn't wait for morning."

"If it was that urgent why didn't you call from the car?"

"His home number is unlisted and I don't have it in the car memory."

"Ah-yah. . . ." Belita was struggling to keep her eyes open. Then, with a sudden start: "What do you mean, it couldn't wait until morning? It'll have to anyway, won't it?"

Carlos, unfastening his tie, checked and glanced at his wife. "I don't get you," he said after a pause.

She forced herself to sit up against the pillows. "You got his answering machine, right?"

"No! I talked to Paul—"

"But he called here about ten-thirty to ask if you were home yet. When I told him no he said the kids were in bed and he was going to turn in as well. Ever know him forget to set his answering machine?"

Carlos was staring. "But I know his message! He never changes it. I must have heard it a hundred times. . . . Oh my God."

"What is it?" Belita was alarmed into full wakefulness now.

Feverishly he retrieved the Thinkertoy advertisement from his jacket. "Yes, I'm right," he muttered. "One of the things they can do is impersonate their owner on the phone."

"You mean carry on a conversation that can fool the caller?"

"No, that's the Turing test and no machine has passed it yet. But it could exploit the Eliza principle. That goes right back to the early days, but it's still used and it can sure as hell fool people, especially if they're under stress and their guard is down. . . . 'Lita, I got to go check that the Walkers are okay."

"But why should they not be?"

He told her. Before he finished she was out of bed and scrambling into whatever clothes she could reach.

Kelly and Rick, in pajamas and barefoot, stood hand in hand before their house, waiting. Hearing a car approach, they disregarded it. There were still a few people returning home even at this time, and they were concealed in the shadow of a clump of bushes.

Just as Carlos braked, there came a faint whooshing sound from the kitchen, which lay partly below the bathroom but mainly below Paul's room, the one that had been his and Lisa's. An orange glow followed, and a crackling noise. The house was largely timber-built. Later it was established that Marmaduke had loosened the valve on a cylinder of propane and ignited the leak, as it was designed to, by short-circuiting its powerpack.

The glow revealed the children.

"*Madre de dios!*" Belita exclaimed. "But what are Rick and Kelly doing out here? And where's Paul?"

"Save your breath!" Carlos was frantically escaping his safety belt. "Blast away on the horn! Rouse everyone you can! Call 911!"

"Carlos, don't do anything foolish—"

But he was already rushing towards the porch. Kelly and Rick recognized him and seemed to scowl and mutter. Suspicion burgeoned but he had no time. He reached the door.

It was locked. Suspicion grew brighter and fiercer like the fire within. But he still had no time. In the car he kept a baseball bat for security. He ran back for it. Thus armed, he smashed a glass panel alongside the door and managed to reach the inside lock.

By now lights were coming on, windows being flung open as the car horn shattered the night silence. Slamming shut the kitchen door, which he found open, gained Carlos a few more precious moments before heat and smoke made the stairway impassable. Three at a time he dashed up it.

The front door was not the only one that was locked.

Suspicion approached certainty, but still he had no time. He smashed the flimsy jamb, found Paul sleepily approaching the window, aroused by the horn, dragged him down the stairs and staggering into the garden. . . .

With seconds to spare. Like a puff of breath from a dragon, the gas cylinder burst and blew out all the house's doors and windows. Flame erupted through the ceiling under Paul's room.

Distant but closing fast, sirens wailed.

Paul collapsed, choking from a lungful of smoke, but Carlos managed to retain his feet. Gasping, he found himself confronting Rick and Kelly. Their faces were stony and frustrated. He whispered, "You knew, didn't you?"

Impassivity.

"Paul said you spent most of your time scrolling around the net. That must be how you found out. I guess the Thinkertoy display at the mall must have been pretty widely advertised. And like the guy said, the protection that was supposed to make the chips harmless could be easily erased."

He stood back, hands on hips, ignoring Belita, who clearly wanted to fuss over the children. He barely registered that Paul was albeit unsteadily regaining his feet. Before his friend could speak:

"But why?" Carlos pleaded.

The children exchanged glances. At length Rick gave a shrug.

"He was driving."

After which Belita's importunities could no longer be ignored.

Paul Walker was afraid of his children.

As those three words made clear, he had good reason.

Afterword

John Brunner died before he could write an afterword for this story, but I know he held Jack Williamson in the highest regard. As Brunner's science fiction has been extremely popular in the United States, he, possibly more than any other contemporary British sf writer, spent a great deal of time in the U.S. "Thinkertoy" has a distinctly British flavor, but the McGuffin, the Thinkertoys themselves, are spiritual descendants of Williamson's humanoids. It's only fitting that Brunner should use Jack's dangerous invention as the basis for a murder weapon, eloquently illustrating that something made with a positive purpose can easily be the instrument of evil.

The humanoids were born in the aftermath of World War II, when Jack Williamson, along with many others, realized much to his chagrin, that technology and science could become tools for wreaking terrible destruction. Until the power of nuclear fission was demonstrated in the horrible immolation of Hiroshima, nobody had truly grasped the full implications of our burgeoning scientific knowledge. For all of Jack's adult life, science had been a source of benevolent change. Hiroshima changed that.

Fred Saberhagen understands the humanoids, perhaps better than any sf writer besides Jack himself. Since I read my first *Berserker* story nearly thirty years ago, I've hoped for a story like the one that follows. Perhaps it was inevitable that something like the following clash of titans would happen. Boy, are we lucky it happened here.

The Bad Machines

Fred Saberhagen

Smoothly functioning machinery composed the bulk of the lit-tle courier ship, surrounding its cabin, cradling and defending the two human lives therein. Both crew members were at battle stations, their bodies clad in full space armor and secured in combat chairs. At the moment all the elaborate devices of guidance and propulsion performed their functions unobtrusively, and the cabin was very quiet. This was not the time for casual conversation, because the combat zone was only a few minutes ahead.

The small portion of the Galaxy settled by Earth-descended humans lay almost entirely behind the courier, while only a few of the most recently established settlements lay in its path, as did much of the vaster Galactic realm still unexplored. Moving in c-space, the ship's instruments at the moment were able to show only a faint indication of its destination: the hint of the presence of a gravitational radiant, still several light-hours away.

Before Lieutenant Commander Timor and Ensign Strax had departed on this mission, the admiral in command of Sector Headquarters had summoned both to a secret briefing. Once the three officers were isolated in the briefing room, the CO had turned on a holostage display. The scene depicted was at once recognizable as the region of space surrounding the Selatrop Radiant.

Crisply the admiral reminded the man and woman before him of the special physical qualities of negative gravitational radiants in general, and of this one in particular, which made these peculiar features in space-time strong points in the struggle to control the lanes of space.

Three inhabited planets orbited suns within a few light-years of the Selatrop, and the lives of those populations hung in the balance. In the war of humanity against the Berserker machines, whichever side held the Selatrop Radiant would have a substantial advantage in the ongoing struggle to control this sector of space. If Berserkers should be able to capture and hold this fortress, then it would probably be necessary to try to evacuate those planets.

Facing his two officers across the glowing tabletop display, the admiral had come quickly to the point: "I'm worried, spacers. Communication with Selatrop is still open, and the garrison commander reports that the defenses are holding. But . . . several of the messages received from there over the last standard month suggest that something is seriously wrong."

The admiral went on to give details. Most puzzling was a

statement by the garrison commander, Colonel Craindre, that she flatly refused to accept any more human reinforcements. From now on, only routine replacement supplies, and a few additional items, factory machinery and materials, were to be sent. Some of these requisitions were hard to explain by the normal requirements of maintenance and replacement—and the sender of the message had offered no explanation.

When the CO paused, seeming to invite comment, Timor said: "Admiral, that doesn't sound like Colonel Craindre at all."

The older man nodded. "Semantic analysis strongly suggests that none of the members of the garrison wrote those words."

"But who else could have written them, sir?—unless some ship we don't know about has arrived at the fortress."

"Who else, indeed? Your orders are to find out what's happening, and report."

The message torpedoes from the Selatrop Fortress had borne additional puzzling content. At least one of the dispatches hinted at a great, joyous announcement soon to be proclaimed. Psychologists at Headquarters suspected that the sender might have been subjected to some kind of mind-altering drugs or surgery.

The admiral also voiced his fear of a worst-case scenario: that the Berserkers had actually overrun the fortress, but were trying to keep the fact a secret.

The briefing was soon concluded, and Lieutenant Commander Timor and Ensign Strax boarded the armed courier. Minutes later they were launched into space.

The little courier was now about to reemerge into normal space after three days of c-plus travel.

The onboard drive and astrogation systems, under the autopilot's control, continued to function smoothly. No enemy presence had been detected in local c-space. The small ship popped back into normal space precisely on schedule, only a few thousand kilometers from its destination, well-positioned within the approach lanes to the Selatrop.

Timor let out held breath in a kind of reverse gasp. At least normal space within point-blank weapons range was clear of the Berserker enemy. There would be no attack on the courier within the next few seconds. But on the holostage display before him there sprang into being scores of ominous dots, scattered in an irregular pattern, indicating real-space objects at only slightly greater distances. The Berserkers, space-going relics of an ancient interstellar war, programmed to destroy life wherever they encountered it, were intent on breaking into the defended space of the fortress, and slaughtering every living thing inside, down to the last microbe. Then, having seized control of this strategic strong point, they would use it to great advantage in their relentless crusade against all life.

In appearance the Radiant resembled a miniature sun, a fiery point burning in vacuum, its inverse force pressing the newly arrived ship, and everything else, away from it. Like the handful of its mysterious fellows scattered about the Galaxy, it could be approached no closer than a couple of kilometers, by any ship or machine. Here at the Selatrop, the inner surface of the fortress was four kilometers from that enigmatic point.

The fortress consisted of blocks and sections of solid matter, woven and held together with broad strands of sheer force, the whole forming a kind of spherical latticework some eight kilometers in diameter. Through the interstices the fitful spark of the radiant itself was intermittently visible.

*   *   *

Timor and Strax sent a coded radio message ahead to the fortress, announcing their arrival, even as the autopilot eased the courier into its approach.

The fortress holding the high ground of the Selatrop Radiant possessed some powerful fixed weapons of its own, but depended very heavily for its defense upon two squadrons of small fighting ships. The original strength of the garrison had been twenty human couples, the great majority of them highly trained pilots. With their auxiliary machines they made a formidable defensive team.

In combat, as in many other situations of comparable complexity, better decisions tended to be made when a human brain participated in the parts of the process not requiring electronic speed. A meld of organic and artificial intelligence had proven to be superior in performance to either mode alone.

The marvels of an organic brain, still imperfectly understood, provided the fighter pilot's mind, both conscious and unconscious, with the little extra, the fine edge over pure machine control, that enabled the best pilots under proper conditions to seize a slight advantage over pure machine opponents.

During the first few seconds after their ship's reemergence into normal space, Timor and Strax were reassured to see on their displays that the defense was still being energetically carried out.

Small space-going machines, beyond a doubt Berserkers engaged in an attack, could be seen on the displays. Even as Timor watched, one of the enemy symbols vanished in a small red puff, indicating the impact of a heavy weapon. Moments later, one of the defending fighters was evidently badly damaged, so much so that it turned its back on the enemy and began to limp toward the safety of the fortress.

"At least our people are still hanging on," the ensign commented.

"So far."

The brief sequence of action Timor had so far been able to observe suggested a steady probing of the defenses rather than an all-out assault.

A hulking shape easily recognizable as the Berserker mothership hovered in the background, at a range of a thousand kilometers or more, constrained by its own sheer bulk from forcing an approach into the volume of space near the Radiant, where only small objects could force a passage.

As the courier in the course of its final approach moved within a hundred kilometers of the fortress, a new skirmish flared in nearby space, punch and counterpunch of nuclear violence exchanged at the speeds of computers and electricity.

As the courier drew nearer to the fortress, the skirmishing flared briefly into heavier action.

The attack was conducted by space-going Berserkers in a variety of sizes and configurations. But the Radiant proved its worth as an advantage to the defense: the assaulting force was continually at a disadvantage, in effect having to fight its way uphill, their maneuvering slowed and weapons rendered less effective. At the moment their efforts were being beaten off with professional skill.

And now the enemy showed full awareness of the presence

of Timor's ship. One Berserker was now accelerating sharply in the courier's direction, trying to head it off.

The human skill and intuition of Ensign Strax as pilot, melded with the autopilot's speed and accuracy, secured the courier a slight edge in maneuvering, and ultimately a safe entry to the defended zone.

With the Berserkers temporarily baffled, the nearest of the manned fighting ships engaged in the defense now turned aside and approached the courier. As the two officers on the courier began to ease themselves out of their armor, routine messages were exchanged.

REQUEST PERMISSION TO COME ABOARD.

Timor replied: PERMISSION GRANTED.

Only mildly surprised—it seemed natural that people who had withstood a long siege would be eager to see a new and friendly human face—Timor and Strax made ready to welcome aboard the pilot from the fighting ship.

When the two craft were docked together, and the connected airlocks stood open, Timor looked up, confidently expecting to see a human step from the airlock into the courier's cabin . . . but instead he was petrified to behold a metal shape, roughly human in configuration, but obviously a robot—

. . . *somehow, a Berserker. And we are dead.* . . .

Too late to do anything about it now. . . .

Ensign Strax let out a wordless cry of terror, and tried to draw a handgun. But she was instantly stunned by some paralyzing ray, so that the weapon clattered on the deck.

A moment later, Timor broke free of the paralysis of shock. He grabbed for the controls before his combat chair, intending to wreck his ship, if he could, to keep it out of enemy hands.

Human reflexes were far too slow. His wrists were gently seized, his intended motion blocked.

A Berserker. From one fraction of a second to the next, he waited for his arms to be wrenched from their sockets, for his life to be efficiently crushed out.

But nothing of the kind occurred.

Opening his eyes, which had involuntarily clenched themselves shut, Timor beheld the lone intruder, its metal hand still holding him by one wrist. It was obviously a robot, but vastly different from any machine that he had ever seen before— Earth-descended people almost never built anthropomorphic robots—and also unlike any Berserker he had ever seen or heard described.

Standing before him was a metal thing, nude and sexless, the size and shape of a small human adult. The immobile features of its face were molded in a form of subtle beauty.

Timor's handgun was smoothly taken away from him. Then he was released.

His only thought at the moment was that this was some attempted Berserker ploy. The bad machines must want something from him, some information or act of treachery, before they killed him.

But the very beauty of the robot, by Earth-descended human standards, argued strongly against its having a Berserker origin.

"At your service, Lieutenant Commander Timor," the shape before him crooned, speaking in Timor's language, the same as that used by the Selatrop garrison. Its voice was startlingly lovely, nothing at all like the raucous squawking produced by Berserkers when they condescended, for their own deadly reasons, to imitate human speech.

The machine looked extremely strong and well-designed,

presenting a dark and seamless metallic surface to the world. It had stepped back a pace, but was still standing close enough that Timor might easily have read the fine script engraved on the metal plate set into its chest—had he understood the language. Seeing the direction of his gaze, the machine translated for him in its musical voice, pointing at each word in turn with a delicate-looking finger of steel:

HUMANOID
SERIAL NO. JW 39,864,715
TO SERVE AND OBEY
AND GUARD HUMANITY FROM HARM

Just as the translation was completed, the figure of Ensign Strax in the other seat stirred slightly. Turning away from Timor, flowing across the little cabin with more than a human dancer's grace, the intruder machine bent solicitously over Strax as if intent upon seeing to her welfare. Soft hues of bronze and blue shone across the robot's sleek and sexless blackness. It was handsome, and monstrous in its independence. Gently, efficiently, it did something which must have partially counteracted the effects of the stunning ray. Then it adjusted the position of the ensign's seat, as if concerned for her safety and comfort.

Meanwhile, Timor was slowly recovering from shock, from the certainty of instant death. "At my service?" he croaked stupidly.

The thing turned back toward him, its blind-seeming, steel-colored eyes fixed on his face. Its high clear voice was eerily sweet. "We humanoids are here, and always will be. We exist to serve humanity. Ask for what you need."

" 'We'?"

"Locally, only eighteen other units, essentially identical to the one you see before you. Elsewhere, millions more."

"But what are you?"

Patiently it pointed once more to its identification plate. "Humans elsewhere have called us humanoids."

Timor shook his head as if to clear it. It seemed that the question of the robot's origin would have to be settled later. "What do you want?"

"We follow our Prime Directive." Tolerantly it repeated the words incised below its serial number: " 'To serve and obey and guard humanity from harm.' "

"You're telling me you have no intention of killing us."

"Far from it, Lieutenant Commander." Metal somehow conveyed the impression of being softly shocked at the mere idea. "We cannot kill. Our intentions are quite the opposite."

Meanwhile the courier's and the fighter's respective autopilots had been easing the joined small ships along toward the fortress, steadily decelerating. The two separated only moments before being individually docked. Timor felt the usual shift in artificial gravity, from ship's to station's. Here the natural inverse gravity of the Radiant dominated.

"Our immediate objective," continued the humanoid, brightly and intensely, "is to save humanity from the critical danger posed by Berserkers."

"I know what Berserkers are, thank you. I have a fair amount of experience along that line. What I haven't quite grasped as yet is—you. Where did you come from?"

The thing declined to answer directly. "We have long familiarity with the Earth-descended species of humanity. Your history displays patterns of evolving technology and increasingly violent aggression. Even absent any Berserker threat, your long-term survival would require our help."

"How do you come to speak our language?"

Again the answer was oblique: "To achieve our goal it has been necessary to learn many languages."

The ship was now snugly docked, the open hatch leading directly into the Selatrop Fortress. From outside the ship came a hint of exotic odors. Beside him, the mysterious thing was insisting in a cooing voice that it and its fellows wanted only to benefit humanity.

Ensign Strax was now awake and functioning once more, though obviously dazed. She seemed basically unharmed, able to stand and walk with only a little help.

The two humans left the courier, the humanoid solicitously assisting the ensign. As they emerged into dock and hangar space, they saw around them the great structural members of composite materials, making up the bulk of the fortress. In places the Radiant itself was visible, as a sunlike point always directly overhead, casting strong shadows.

Two more humanoids, practically identical to the first, were on hand to offer a silent welcome. But not a human being was in sight.

"Where's the garrison?" Timor demanded sharply.

One of the waiting units answered. "All humans aboard the fortress are now restricted to the region of greatest safety."

"Not at their battle stations? By whose decision?"

"No human decisions can be allowed to interfere with our essential service."

At another dock nearby rested a small spacecraft, no bigger than Timor's courier but of unique design. "Whose ship is that?" he demanded.

"It is ours."

The humanoid spokesunit went on to inform him that reinforcements were expected soon, a second ship and perhaps a third, each carrying another score of units like itself.

"Arrive from where?"

As nearly as Timor could understand the answer, the reinforcements, like the first humanoid craft, would be coming from a direction, or perhaps a dimension in c-space, such that it would be virtually impossible for the besieging Berserker fleet to interfere with their arrival.

Timor also observed that the newcomers had taken over several docks, part of the repair facility, to establish their own workshop. Imperturbably his new guide explained to him that the resources of the fortress, computers, materials, and machinery, were being pressed into the construction of more humanoids.

The two humanoids that had been waiting now boarded the courier. Maybe, thought Timor, they were looking for the requested factory machines and materials. If so, they were doomed to disappointment.

Their original guide escorted Timor and Strax deeper into the fortress, through multiple airlocks, past redundant defenses.

The special attributes of gravitational radiants in general, and of this one in particular, not only made them strong points in the struggle to control the preferred thoroughfares and channels of c-plus travel. The same peculiarities that made it easy for a ship to emerge from flightspace in the vicinity of a radiant also rendered it more likely that things from far away, such as the humanoids, were likely to turn up here.

When Strax and Timor had reached the garrison's living quarters, still without having encountered a living soul in the course of their long walk, the robot assigned the couple to separate small cabins. They were not consulted as to their preference in quarters.

Once the ensign was in her cabin, the humanoid locked the door from the outside. "By attempting to draw a weapon, Ensign Strax has demonstrated a willingness to use violence against humanoids," the beautiful robot explained to Timor. "Temporary confinement will be best for her own safety."

Timor did not protest, because in truth Strax had still seemed somewhat dazed. Better for her to stay out of the way, while he investigated.

He followed his guide down a short corridor.

"At last!" he muttered. A dozen or so members of the live garrison had come in sight, assembled in a recreation lounge. Timor thought that when he appeared, hope flared briefly in their faces, only to fade swiftly when they perceived that he had been disarmed and was thoroughly under the control of the escorting robot. Three additional humanoids stood by, observing carefully.

Timor immediately recognized Colonel Craindre, the garrison commander, a gray-haired, hard-bitten veteran of space combat. He approached her, identified himself, and announced his mission.

"I wish you well, Lieutenant Commander," the colonel said. "But I don't know whether I can say welcome aboard. Because I don't know if I'm glad to see you here or not. Our situation is so . . ." Her words died away.

"Casualties?"

Colonel Craindre shook her head helplessly. Her pale hands were folded tensely in front of her, in what was evidently an unconscious gesture, and Timor suddenly noticed that several other members of the garrison had adopted the same pose.

In a belated response to Timor's question the colonel said: "Four pilots lost." She paused. "All our casualties occurred before the humanoids arrived."

"Why is that?"

"Very simple. As soon as they seized control, all humans were forbidden to fly combat missions. Several additional fighter ships have been lost since then, and four of our new allies with them."

Another pilot chimed in: "Which probably means that four of us are still alive, who would otherwise be—"

But Timor had scarcely heard anything beyond the colonel's remark. He interrupted: "You were *forbidden*—?"

Craindre nodded. Her clenched hands quivered. "That is the situation, Lieutenant Commander. You see, space combat is far, far too risky for human beings. The humanoids will not contemplate for a moment allowing us to engage in such activity; they've taken over the fighting for us." The colonel's voice was trembling slightly. "Now before you convey to me the explosive wrath of Headquarters, tell me this: How long were you able to retain control of your courier, after a single humanoid had come aboard? We had more than twenty. They took us by surprise, and resistance proved hopeless."

One of the interchangeable humanoid units cooed: "It is true, there have been no human casualties since our arrival. It is our intention that there will never be any more."

Timor turned to face the thing. "How can that be? We're fighting a war. Or do you hope to sign a truce with your fellow robots, and bargain for our lives? That won't work with Berserkers."

Sweetly the robot warned him that he must not persist in such a dangerous attitude. The humanoids hoped to gain his active cooperation, and that of other humans, but there could be no question of yielding on any rule essential to human safety.

Timor turned back to his fellow humans. "But what exactly happened here? How did these machines—?" he gestured at the nearest humanoid, which had resumed its role of impassive observer.

The colonel and other members of the garrison did their best to explain. They could only conjecture that the humanoids' exotic ship had somehow found its way to the Selatrop Radiant from some alternate universe, or at least from across some vast gulf of space-time.

In an effort to explain how the newcomers had seized control so easily, Craindre and others described the humanoids' ability to mimic humanity by the use of imitation flesh and hair, something no Berserker had ever managed. This trick had allowed the intruders to dock at the fortress, even though their craft had previously been boarded by suspicious humans. And once they were loose inside the fortress it had been impossible to stop them.

Like Timor on the courier, the human garrison of the fortress had unanimously assumed that the first woman-sized robot to reveal itself as a machine was some new type of Berserker. Naturally panic had ensued, and a futile attempt to fight. But the humanoids' behavior after seizing control had quickly demonstrated that they were not Berserkers.

When the immensely skilled and intelligent robots had filled the pilots' seats of the small fighters, and had successfully turned back one Berserker assault after another, a substantial minority of the garrison were soon converted.

But still a majority of the human garrison were far from satisfied with the situation, and more than one had already been treated to some mind-altering drugs to ease their concerns.

Even not counting those who had been drugged, the balance was changing. Gradually additional members of the garrison had come to accept what the humanoids told them. For this faction the humanoids represented salvation, in the form of the true fighting allies that ED humanity had needed for so long. By now almost half the original garrison had been converted, though human discipline still held. People everywhere were tired of the seemingly endless Berserker war.

In the midst of conversation the colonel received a signal from one of the robots, and promptly passed along the information: "The machines have prepared a meal for us in the wardroom."

Walking down the corridor, Timor turned abruptly to once more confront the garrison commander beside him. "Where are the shoulder weapons stowed, Colonel Craindre? Where's the space armor? Regulations require such gear to be stored near the sleeping quarters."

"We are no longer allowed access to weapons of any kind."

Timor was speechless.

"Lieutenant Commander, the Selatrop Fortress has now been under humanoid control for approximately a standard month. I assure you, that is more than long enough for drastic changes to have taken place."

"I can see that!"

A humanoid, walking beside them, interjected: "And we assure you, Lieutenant Commander, that all changes are essential. Without our timely help, the fortress would have been overrun by Berserkers days ago. All the humans you see before you would be dead."

Craindre said sharply: "I consider that outcome far from certain. But I have to admit the possibility."

Presently all the humans on the fortress, with the exception of Strax and one or two others confined for their own good, were gathered in the large wardroom. Two humanoids presided while the ordinary maintenance robots, squat inhuman devices, served a meal at the long refectory tables. Food and drink were of good quality, as usual, but Timor observed minor deviations from the usual military fare and customs. Humans were now discouraged from performing the smallest service for themselves; spoons and small forks were still allowed, but sharp knives and heat much above body temperature were considered prohibitively dangerous.

Timor tasted his soup and found it barely lukewarm. On impulse, to see what would happen, he complained to the nearest serving machine that the soup was cold. A humanoid glided forward a few paces to explain that hot soup presented a danger of injury, and would require the consumer to be spoon-fed by a machine, or to drink the liquid by straw from a spillproof container.

It concluded: "We regret that the exigencies of combat temporarily prevent our providing full table service."

"There's a war on. Yes, I know. That's all right. I'll drink it cold."

Mealtime conversation with the garrison elicited more facts. The humanoids, on taking over the defense of the fortress, had at first denied the humans any knowledge of how the ongoing battle was progressing. Their stated reason was that information about the proximity of Berserkers was bound to cause harmful anxiety. But a few days later, without explanation, that policy had been reversed. Everyone not tranquilized was now kept fully informed of the military situation.

Timor turned to one of the metallic guardians. "I wonder why?"

This time an explanation was forthcoming. "We seek voluntary cooperation, as always, Spacer Timor. We hope that with the Berserker threat ever-present in human awareness, you will soon abandon your unrealistic objections and wholeheartedly accept our protection."

"I see. Well, most of us are not ready to do that."

The humanoid went on to relate that some days ago it and its kind had considered putting everyone aboard the fortress into suspended animation. They had refrained only because a real chance existed that the humans might have to defend themselves against Berserkers.

"That will be difficult if we are deprived of weapons."

"Your personal weapons will be returned, if an emergency grave enough to warrant such action should arise."

Walking with the colonel after dinner, touring the living quarters, Timor noted several significant differences from the usual arrangements. For one thing, everyone was assigned a private room. It seemed that associations as intimate as bed-sharing were being discouraged.

In the course of their walk, Colonel Craindre informed him that the main computer aboard the fortress, when asked to determine the probable origin of the humanoids, had offered a kind of guess by suggesting that in the close vicinity of a gravitational radiant, even the laws of chance were not quite what they were elsewhere. Certain philosophers held that in such locations many realities interpenetrated, and even the rules of mathematics were not quite the same. In everyday terms, this was a place where the unexpected tended to show up.

And such tests as the members of the garrison had been able to conduct—admittedly few and simple—tended to confirm this. Humanoids were exotic devices in many ways, not least in the fact that they relied so strongly on rhodomagnetic technology.

The humanoids had welcomed the humans' questions, and had even volunteered some information on the science and engineering which had gone into producing the benevolent robots. They said they wished to be as open as possible, to convince the humans quickly that they were not in any way dangerous to human welfare.

Timor heard a unit promise that one of their machines would be turned over for ultimate testing, even dissection—as soon as one could be spared from the ongoing conflict.

Returning with the colonel to the wardroom, Timor announced to all machines and humans present that within the hour he intended to dispatch an unmanned courier back to Headquarters, carrying a complete report of the situation on the fortress.

And within a standard day he planned to depart on his return trip, to report to the admiral in person. He would take with him Ensign Strax and as many members of the human garrison as the colonel thought she could spare, to corroborate his testimony regarding the situation here.

Timor concluded: "It is up to the colonel whether all the garrison, including herself, come with me or not. It seems to me that would be the best course." He paused, then added: "This fortress has already fallen."

Colonel Craindre hesitated, considering her decision. The new masters of the fortress stared silently at Timor for a few seconds, no doubt taking counsel privately among themselves. Then their current spokesunit insisted that the humanoids must approve any message before it was sent. It also informed Timor that they had already sent reassuring messages to headquarters in his name.

"Then obviously," Timor said, "the truth means little to you."

The robot before him was, of course, neither angry nor embarrassed. "The Prime Directive has never required the truth. We have found, in fact, that undisguised truth is always painful, and often harmful to mankind."

It went on to explain that neither Timor nor any other human would be allowed to depart the fortress in the foreseeable future. Even Sector Headquarters could hardly be as safe as a fortress directly defended by humanoids. And as long as the Berserker siege continued, space in the immediate vicinity was simply too dangerous for anyone to risk a passage in a small ship. That was why the protectors of humanity had refused, in the colonel's name, to accept any more human reinforcements.

But the humanoids had no objection to the dispatch of an unmanned courier. They encouraged the humans, especially Timor as the head of the investigative team, to send messages of reassurance and comfort back to their headquarters. Because secure transmission could not be guaranteed, the joyful proclamation of the actual presence and nature of the humanoids was not to be made just yet.

Timor once more went walking with the colonel. He wanted to talk, and considered that trying to find privacy was hopeless. Humans conversing anywhere in the fortress had to assume that humanoids could overhear them.

Strolling the living quarters, Timor could see that when people were forced to live under tight humanoid control, they would not even be allowed to open doors for themselves. Several doors had actually had their hand-operated latches taken away, leaving only blank surfaces. Several of the cabins had already been converted to create an absolute dependency upon machines; only the press of more important matters, and the fact that all humanoid units might at any time be called into combat, had kept the humanoids from enforcing more restrictions on the garrison.

Everything the colonel had learned in a month of living with humanoids confirmed the plan of the benevolent robots: eventually, in a world perfected according to humanoid rules, the entire human race, while being at every moment of their lives served and protected, would spend those lives in isolation. Succeeding generations of humanity would be conceived with the aid of artifice, and raised in artificial wombs. In general it was always better that humans not get too close to one another, given their propensity for violence.

The two officers walked with folded hands. Timor noted that he himself was now carrying his empty hands clasped behind his back.

"I wonder . . ." he mused aloud.

"What?"

"If Berserkers will really want to destroy humanoids completely. Or vice versa."

Colonel Craindre looked at him keenly. "That's already occurred to you, has it? I needed several days to arrive at the same idea."

"Not that there would be any overt bargaining between them."

"No, the fundamental programming on each side would preclude that."

"But—Berserkers might easily compute that the existence of humanoids must inflict a strategic weakness upon humanity—if humans can be induced to rely completely on such machines."

"And on the other hand, humanoids are already making use

of the Berserkers, indirectly, as a threat: 'If you don't turn your lives over to us, the bad machines will get you.' "

Timor said to his companion: "Of course the reason they give for wanting to keep their presence here a secret makes no sense. Certainly the Berserkers attacking must already realize they're up against something new."

"Of course. And . . . wait! Listen!"

There came a sound like roaring surf, sweeping through the corridors and rooms. Somewhere outside, the battle thundered on, wave fronts of radiation smashing into the fortress walls, filling the interior with a sound like pounding waves.

The heaviest Berserker attack to hit the fortress yet was now being mounted. An announcement on loudspeakers proclaimed an emergency: all humanoid units save one were being withdrawn from the interior of the fortress and sent out as pilots as every available fighter ship was thrown into the defense.

The sole unit left to oversee the humans opened a sealed door and brought out piles of hand and shoulder weapons, along with space armor.

Everybody scrambled to get into armor and take up weapons, against the possibility of the fortress being invaded by Berserker boarding units.

Maybe, thought Timor in sudden hope, maybe the damned do-gooder robots hadn't studied the gear thoroughly, did not take into account that such suits had been constructed for combat against Berserkers—that such a device could amplify a man's strength until he was not entirely outclassed by a robot— whether the robot was trying to tear him limb from limb or smother him with kindness.

The distant-sounding surf of battle noise swelled louder than before.

Timor, fitting himself into armor as quickly as he could, asked his guardian: "How goes the battle?"

"It goes well," the beautiful thing claimed brightly. "Our performance is incomparably better than that of humans in space warfare."

Timor signed disagreement. "Better than unaided human pilots, certainly. No one disputes that. But human minds using machines as tools are best."

"When we have increased our numbers sufficiently," it crooned to them, "your race must place your defenses absolutely in our hands. On every ship and every planet. Only we can be as implacable as this Berserker enemy, as swift to think and act, as eternally vigilant. At last we have met a danger requiring all our limitless abilities."

Colonel Craindre was fitting on her helmet. She said: "History has repeatedly demonstrated that an organic brain, working in concert with the proper auxiliary machines, can hold a small edge both tactically and strategically over the pure machine— the Berserker."

Inflexibly the humanoid spokesunit disagreed. It claimed that the tests, the comparisons, could not have been properly conducted, the statistics not honestly compiled, if they led to any such result.

"And even if such a marginal advantage existed, the direct exposure of human life to such danger is intolerable, when it can be avoided."

"Danger exists in every part of human life," said Timor.

"We are here to see that it does not."

Lieutenant Commander Timor now had his armor completely on.

So did Colonel Craindre.

Exchanging a quick look, they moved in unison.

A direct hit on the fortress by a heavy weapon set the deck to quivering, and distracted the humanoid. It turned its head away, scanning for Berserker boarders.

In a matter of seconds, the two humans in armor had disabled the one robot, but only after a serious struggle, in which the colonel had to shoot off both its arms. Being unable to use deadly force against the humans had put the humanoid at a serious disadvantage in the encounter.

When the contest was over, their opponent reduced to a voiceless, motionless piece of baggage, Colonel Craindre said, breathing heavily: "I am of course remaining here, at my post. But your duty, Lieutenant Commander, requires you to report to headquarters."

Smashing open one door after another, Timor and Craindre ranged through a fortress temporarily devoid of humanoids, hastily releasing the few humans who were still locked in their cabins. Soon everyone but the colonel—she ordered all her people to leave—was aboard the little courier.

Timor considered it all-important that humanity be warned about the humanoids, without delay. One of his first acts on regaining his freedom was to send a message courier speeding on to headquarters, ahead of the crewed vessel: the message contained only a few hundred words—including the prearranged code which identified him as the true sender.

Now, aboard the escaping courier, the surviving humans, bringing along the disabled humanoid, embarked on their dash for freedom.

As the small ship with its human cargo, launched from the fortress at the highest feasible speed, came into view of the attacking machines, Berserkers sped toward it from three sides, intent on kamikaze ramming. Instantly humanoid-controlled fighters, careless of their own safety, hurled themselves at the enemy in counterattack, taking losses but creating a delay.

The courier broke free, plunging into c-space.

"Our only wish is to serve you, sir." A last plaintive appeal came in by radio, just before the curtain of flightspace closed down communication.

"On a platter," Timor muttered. He looked up at his human friends, whose bodies, mostly bulky with space armor, crowded the cabin as if it were a lifeboat. Triumph slowly faded from his face.

One of the pilots who had been inclined to accept the humanoids wholeheartedly, and who had in fact volunteered to stay behind with them, spoke up, in a tone and with a manner verging on mutinous accusation: "We couldn't have got away without the help of those machines. We couldn't have survived that last attack."

The lieutenant commander faced the speaker coldly. "Just which set of machines do you mean, spacer? And which attack?"

His new shipmates stared at him. He saw understanding in the eyes of many, clear agreement in some faces. But there were others who did not yet understand.

"Think about it," Timor told them. "The Berserkers—yes, the Berserkers!—have just helped us to survive an attack. An assault launched at us, you might say, from a direction opposite to their own, and with somewhat more subtlety. Not that the Berserkers *wanted* to help us—they didn't compute that trying to blow us to bits would work out to our benefit. But if it hadn't been for the Berserkers, the humanoids would have taken our sanity and freedom, given us sweet lies in return."

He paused to let that sink in, then added: "And, of course, if it hadn't been for humanoids piloting fighters just now, covering our escape, the same Berserkers would have eaten us alive."

Timor paused again, looking over his audience. He wanted to spell out the situation as plainly as he could.

His voice was low, but carried easily in the quiet cabin. "I can see how things might go from now on. It might be that only the threat of Berserkers, keeping the humanoids fully occupied, will make it possible for us to sustain humanity in a Galaxy infested with humanoids.

"And without humanoids fighting for our lives, we might wind up losing our war against Berserkers.

"Now we face two sets of bad machines instead of one," he concluded, his tone rising querulously at the unfairness of it all, "and the hell of it is, not only are they depending on each other, but we're going to need them both!"

Afterword

Jack Williamson and I are both citizens of New Mexico by adoption. But Jack, riding in a covered wagon— yes, really—arrived in the state a number of decades before I got here.

Last time I saw Jack at a convention, he remarked with a youthful twinkle of the eye that he considered me a promising young writer. I've just graduated to Medicare, and have been turning out science fiction for upward of thirty years, but that compliment, coming from a man who sold his first story before I was born, was one of the most satisfying I've ever had. With Jack around, I can even feel that it might be true.

I've always viewed *The Humanoids* as perhaps the most underrated novel/series in the genre, and jumped at the opportunity to get my hands on those bad machines.

—Fred Saberhagen

Jack hasn't written funny humanoids stories, but there is a good bit of humor in his work as a whole, as well as inventiveness, both of which Jeff Bredenberg has included in "The Human Ingredient." As a matter of fact, I don't think anyone who has ever been to a science fiction convention could avoid knowing that a great majority of those who read and write science fiction seem to share an affinity for the ingredient referred to in the story's title. One can only hope that you, gentle reader, are not allergic to it.

The Human Ingredient

Jeff Bredenberg

When the humanoid exploded we had no time to stand around and cheer.

Three of us had choreographed the entire maneuver. I placed a carefully designed tureen into the photonic oven, then busied myself with a pocket reference pad, scrolling through the next day's menus. In the oven, a dusting of graphite chips and garrow-plex shavings was stirred into the quiche batter. I had amassed those unlikely "seasonings" during dozens of sanctioned visits to the maintenance bay.

At the far end of the galley, Diderot "accidentally" spilled a vial of caugi cactus extract into a serving dish and held it aloft as if to inspect the damage—the perfect concave focusing mirror for the photonic blast from the oven.

And at the same moment, Juan-Om—passing through on cleanup duty—whirled with his spray cannister and shooshed our supervising humanoid with a misty cloud. Some fool had filled the cannister with rhodoquantic gas, not galley disinfectant.

The glassine humanoid froze in the swirl of photonically bombarded gas—lips parted as if in protest. His torso groaned and whined with opposing internal forces. His surprised local neural clusters, suddenly severed from the global controls on his home planet, surged with confused messages. Finally he smiled wryly. And blew up.

Secretive planning had carried us to that delicious moment. Then we depended heavily on speed and luck, and the unpredictable factors multiplied exponentially with every second.

Diderot's luck, for instance, ran out immediately. Her serving dish clattered to the deck. Her right hand fell too, severed at the wrist by shrapnel. It splashed crimson everywhere. She smiled at me wearily, as if embarrassed to be pumping blood into the muffin batter on the counter. She was sliding into shock, and for her escape was now impossible. Within minutes, the humanoids— those that weren't pursuing Juan-Om and me—would be swarming over her with their oppressive "service." They would reattach the hand, or supply an even better prosthesis. If they knew of her role in the explosion, they also would set her mind aright with psychosurgery. (After all, the humanoid mission was to alleviate the burdens of humanity. Can't have rogue individualists mucking up the works.)

Juan-Om bolted out the galley hatch into the corridor, and I followed. We dived into a dark maintenance channel, then jogged aft into a claustrophobic tunnel that formed one rib of the spaceship's massive hull.

The lights pulsed. A pleasant chime sounded.

"Danger!" came a melodious announcement. "All human crew will please report to quarters immediately, while we repair life support systems."

Juan-Om found the small hatch labeled LIFE POD and feverishly tore open the seals. Hunched over, I dripped sweat onto the surface of the tunnel—a hellish metallic moonscape pocked with hand- and footholds for the humanoids.

"Life support systems my butt," he mumbled, glancing up and down the corridor. "If the maintenance schedule is correct, all the pod's systems will be activated for a routine diagnostic. We don't have a second to waste on warm-up."

When the hatch cover slid away, he extracted two sets of papery coveralls, which we pulled on. I adjusted the goggles until they locked to my brow and then crawled through the hatch into the pod. Indeed, the instrument panel glowed with life, and now Juan-Om had only to—

Juan-Om had been halfway into the life pod, and suddenly he fell crashing into the tunnel outside. Through the hatch, I saw his goggled face twisting with pain and desperation. The tunnel echoed with the clatter of metallic hands and feet. A glassine torso flashed past the hatch, and I pressed myself to the shallow floor, wishing I could turn liquid and seep down through the cracks in the deck of the life pod.

"Service!" cried the humanoid confronting Juan-Om. "You are exhibiting errant behavior. To prevent further injury you must submit to my counsel."

"Well, pardon my errant ass," growled Juan-Om. "I'm only

human." He kicked the creature between the legs—an empty gesture, of course, against a machine.

The humanoid slid a forearm under each of Juan-Om's armpits and hoisted him to his feet. Juan-Om glared down the tunnel as more humanoids thundered close. With Juan-Om subdued, they would logically search the life pod next. But I'd had no time to locate the emergency release for the pod. Juan-Om was the technician; I was just a galley rat.

Juan-Om knew my predicament. He peered directly through the hatch to where I cowered in the shadows. "Well, the planning was half the fun, amigo," he said to me. A rivulet of blood ran from his left nostril.

My stomach tightened. Was Juan-Om crazy? Could he be turning me in? His captor turned in my direction, loosening his grip. Juan-Om wriggled free and kicked up at the near wall.

The pod hatch slammed closed, and a sharp blast hammered me against the bulkhead as the life pod tore away from the ship. Ribs bruised, I clawed my way to one of the passenger troughs and strapped in. I hitched an air mask to my face, then reviewed the controls—yes, the computer would guide the descent.

In the wide forward window, a milky-blue pearl grew huge— a planet unknown to me, save for one marvelous characteristic: It was enveloped in a rhodomagnetic field, which the humanoids could not penetrate.

The life pod shuddered when it hit the atmosphere. The pod's air was stuffy first, then steamy. A dozen nozzles activated, spraying gray foam into the cabin. The foam was adaptable stuff, changing its nature as the computer fed it chemical infusions. During atmospheric entry, it would insulate; in the case of hard impact, it would cushion. So what if I lost my view? Better to be blinded than cooked like a crustacean.

The line of foam crept over my goggles, and I was suddenly lonely for Juan-Om. Apparently he had kicked an exterior release for my life pod. For that defiance, he would suffer. I had doubted him briefly, and I felt ashamed.

"Where are your plants? Your seeds? We find it inconceivable that you would flee to a new world without agricultural assets."

"Plants? I don't know what you're talking about."

"You admit working for the humanoids. You are a spy then?"

"I worked on their ship. They all—um, they take a hundred or so bloods with them wherever they go. Handy for diplomacy and such while they go gobbling up the galaxy."

"Diplomacy and spying often go hand-in-hand."

"I was a cook."

"You flatter yourself."

"I barely escaped with my life."

"Why did you choose *our* planet?"

"Didn't, really. We watched the humanoids—came to recognize a pattern of sensor preparations every time the ship passed a rhodo-no-go."

"Pardon me?"

"A protected planet. That's all I knew about this place—what do you call it?"

"Agria."

"Ah, Agria. I stole a life pod and took a blind leap."

I came aware at that moment—that's the best I can describe it—right in the middle of a conversation. I had always figured that a crash victim would regain consciousness the way a light blinks on. Not this time. Clearly I had been "awake" for some time and was chattering away merrily with this brow-wrinkled gent in a silky tunic.

We were on an elevated wood platform. Above, an orange-and-white tent top rustled in a light breeze. There were no walls —just a 360-degree view of rolling green farmland. I lay in an adjustable bed, wrapped in ointment-moist bandages. The structure below our platform, I assumed, was some kind of residence.

"Who are you?" I asked. "How long have I been here?"

The man's pursed lips emerged from the white fur covering his face. "For the hundredth time, my name is Jemma," he said in oddly accented Galactic Standard. "Your craft crashed onto my plantation three days ago—wiped out several dozen prized grapevines, I'm sorry to say. I have a team of herbalists attending to you, and I will provide their board as long as necessary."

"Is this an interrogation? Am I under arrest?"

Jemma harrumphed. He left his stool and strode to the edge of the platform, where he watched a band of workers wheeling an irrigation rig into position. "In a manner of speaking," he said. "Besides, if you know the humanoids, I don't have to explain that a certain amount of suspicion is warranted."

I nodded. "But what were you asking me about plants?"

"We picked through the wreckage of your craft thoroughly," Jemma said. "The ministries would demand that. And—I hope you'll forgive us—we searched through your clothing. You don't seem to have brought even the merest seed with you. How would you hope to make your way in a new society without collateral?"

"How about information?" I asked. "With Agria so isolated, surely there's some call for news from around the galaxy, technological know-how. What's this fixation with plants and seeds?"

Jemma looked sad. "We only get a visitor such as yourself every twenty years or so," he said. "They're all runners from the humanoids, of course. Although you are the first I have had the privilege to meet, I gather the majority of your kind have been similarly puzzled. While our society may seem complex to you at first, it's actually painfully simple and obvious at its heart—food. We eat to survive; therefore, the societal power goes to those most adept at the growing and preparation of food. Unless you have brought us some new plant species, or some dazzling concoction, I'm afraid a laborer's life here is the most you can hope for. To be frank, most runners who touch down here end up hauling barrows of cow dung for a living."

I pushed myself up onto my elbows, but the pain forced me back into the starched pillows. "My galley experience must count for something," I groaned.

Jemma snorted. "I have reviewed the culinary contents of your reference pad," he said disdainfully. "If that is the sum of your gastronomic knowledge—"

"I grew up on Pacifica—how about that?" I said. "Only five migrations removed from Earth herself."

The old man nodded appreciatively. "Better," he said. "With that you might catch the ear of some low-level minister. We make much sport of trying to re-create Earth cuisine, although personally I suspect Agria surpassed the mother world hundreds of years ago."

I followed Jemma's gaze out to the fields. Our platform sat at the convergence of eight dirt roads. Between the roads eight different crops fanned out from us, as if we sat at the center of a large, green pie.

"I recognize the grapevines," I said, pointing. "And the corn. But those spiky things—"

"Pineapple. Then sugar cane beside that."

"And those trees?"

"Swanfruit," Jemma said. "If you are Earth-oriented, they might remind you of very tart oranges."

"What about those?"

Jemma sighed. "Scrotum trees," he said.

"I beg your pardon?"

"They're useless, actually. Those drooping pods yield a bitter seed—good for nothing but a chartreuse now and then. But we daren't let a plant species die off. So keeping this small plot alive is my contribution to the archive."

"You used a word . . . chartreuse."

Jemma shook his head. "Ho, that's just a bit of political deceit—"

"Oh!" I interrupted, trying to sit up again. "Why didn't I think of it before? If you have technology sophisticated enough to envelop your *entire planet* in a rhodomagnetic field, then you *must* have a space fleet."

Jemma laughed. "I'm sorry to disappoint you, but the rhodomagnetic field is totally natural. It's a product of our lush population of braintrees—we have jungles of them covering entire continents. The mineral makeup of Agrian soil must appeal to them. Besides, I'd scarcely fling you back into space before you had paid for the grapevines you damaged during your blind landing. At a laborer's wages . . . well, by law, I will *own* you for the next several years."

I fell back again into the bed and stared woefully into the undulating tent top. I found myself wishing a humanoid would scuttle by and rub my tightening temples—perhaps give me one of those happy little injections.

"You have a lot to learn," Jemma said soothingly. "And do not fret. There is always room here for another dung hauler."

So I hauled dung—horse shit, cow shit, chicken shit, human shit—and drenched the Agrian soil with my sweat. I was thrust into a caste, of sorts: workers on the "down" cycle of food pro-

duction. At the top, it appeared, were the revered food preparers.
Then came the growers, still a respected lot. Lowest of the low
were the dung haulers and compost technicians.

Compost barns dotted Jemma's sprawling farm. I was assigned to one, a ramshackle wood structure within easy sight of
the giant furrow my life pod gouged out of the vineyard. Inside,
wooden barrels the size of houses turned slowly on their axles,
hurrying the rotting process of their contents. Against the ceiling, conical vents sucked up the reeking gas to power the kitch-
ens.

A month into my labors, I happened into Monte during a
break. She guzzled water from the outside trough, shamelessly
sopping her T-shirt. Monte had a military air about her, although Agria seemed to have no use for a military. All of her
movements were economical. If she spoke at all, her words were
no-nonsense. Her hair was buzz-cut blond, her skin taut and sun-
browned. She was my unofficial coach and interpreter.

"I heard a term once—chartreuse," I said. "What's it mean?"

She propped herself on the rim of the trough, oblivious to
the water lapping at her rear. "It's from one of our legends of the
mother world," she said with a shrug. "Some monks living in the
mountains produced a popular liqueur called chartreuse, a complicated concoction. To keep their recipe secret, they ordered
from their suppliers many more ingredients than were needed for
the liqueur. That way, no one could guess what actually went
into its preparation. So now we call that technique a chartreuse.
That is how many of our ministers hold on to their power, you
know."

The compost barrels emitted a solemn groan. Monte glanced
into my eyes nervously and away again.

"What is it?" I said.

"You will get a chance soon to witness a chartreuse in operation," she said. "I guess you haven't been informed yet."

I clapped my callused hands together once. "Splendid!"

"Maybe not," Monte said cautiously. "You see, Mentha—our regional minister of confections?—is holding his annual dinner party in a couple of weeks. They won't mind having you and me in the kitchen, because it is presumed our culinary knowledge is so limited that we pose no threat to the secrecy of Mentha's cooking methods."

"Are we assigned to be waiters then?" I asked.

Monte laughed. "No. It seems Jemma has rented out our services. You and I, um, we're to be *ingredients*."

"I know you don't mean cannibalism—"

"Not at all," she said. "They'll want us very alive. Under special circumstances, you see, human skin produces a short-lived enzyme. Mentha prepares a dessert sauce that is totally dependent on that enzyme—it's supposed to be the crowning glory of the dinner party. You and I will be the source."

"This enzyme," I said. "What are the special circumstances that produce it?"

"Well, on that world you come from—Pacifica?" she asked. "What was the general social attitude toward, um, having sex in public?"

The secretaries to the minister of confections arrived in a dirigible. They gave Monte and me all the consideration of cattle—herded us up the gangplank, fed us respectably, corralled us into a windowless room for the day trip. The floor shifted, creaked, and we were airborn.

We left our room, meaning to explore the airship, but became mesmerized by the view and lingered at the rail. Suspended from the helium envelope, the entire oak deck on which we stood swayed ever so slowly. It was as if we were slung from the midsection of some giant cat loping across the landscape.

"I've never been this high up before," Monte said, "or this far from home."

"I've flown plenty," I replied. "But never so low."

"You'll do fine," she said.

"What makes you think I'm worrying about my impending public humiliation?"

"You'll do fine."

"Why me?"

"You're an off-worlder, and you'll bring an exotic flavor to Mentha's dessert. If it's successful, he'll surely hold on to his ministry for another year."

"I'll just refuse to cooperate."

Monte sighed and shook her head. "You know what they say? 'The mule that won't move is on his way to the soup.' "

Mentha was a dirigible of a man himself. Two hundred kilos easily, roll upon roll of fat around his neck like a fleshy accordion. He lorded over his hangarlike kitchen, bellowing orders to an army of assistants. He heaved his jiggling body up and down the tiled loading dock.

"These sacks here," he shouted to his laborers. "They are the wheat flour for the braided bread—fourth course. One sack goes to each doughmaster."

The workers swarmed like ants, hauling baskets, crates, bottles, and mountainous butchered beasts reeking of the smokehouse. Soon, the vegetable bins were lush with produce, the rows of grain barrels brimming.

All day, Mentha divided his time between supervising and his private labors in a partitioned work area—his confection studio— in the center of the massive kitchen. I tried to keep track of the ingredients he lugged into the studio but soon began to doubt I could recall every one.

Toward evening, Mentha emerged from his studio holding a bowl of white paste against one hip. He found Monte and me in the staff lounging area. We stood. Without a word he deftly removed our robes and led us to a slinglike gurney. He situated us in the sling, forcing our pelvises into carnal collision, and then slathered us both in the white paste.

The round man stepped back to admire his work, perspiration beading across his red face. He smiled.

"Now—" he said to us, finishing his command with a hand gesture: his right index finger inserted into the fist of his left hand.

We obeyed. Monte was matter-of-fact—businesslike, yet loving enough to get the job done. Between us, Mentha's white paste slurped wetly. Softly clapping his approval, Mentha wheeled our gurney toward his confection studio. I felt like an obscene parade float, but the rest of the kitchen staff paid us scant attention. We could have been a pair of trussed swine, for all they cared.

In the studio, a dozen tiers of shelving surrounded us in a horseshoe shape. Each shelf was subdivided into small bins for holding ingredients—all manner of sugars, flours, and spices; bottled jellies, juices, and glazes; fresh fruits, nuts, and seed pods.

Mentha selected a small spatula from the rack above his round work table. "Friends," he whispered, holding the utensil aloft, "tonight we are preparing Mentha Chiffon—the *climax*, shall we say, of the dinner party?"

Monte mashed her lips together, bored. She craned her head around, studying the surrounding wall of ingredients, all the time pressing against me in slow, digging hip movements. A streak of the paste had splashed into her hair. I wiped it out of the blond bristles and tasted—pungent and bitter.

Mentha saw. "Do not worry," he said, "your enzyme is rising now, and when it blends with the paste—" He smiled dreamily, and his eyes momentarily rolled back into his head.

On cue, my breath grew shallow and rapid, and my vision blurred. I grabbed Monte by the hips. My eyes locked onto a bin just over her shoulder, a bin filled with long brown objects— familiar . . . now, what were they?

Then Mentha was upon us, scraping the paste away with his spatula and humming merrily. His mood—and his utter, humiliating control over us—put me in mind of the ever-chipper humanoids I had risked my life to escape. Until now, I had thought it impossible to make such pleasures as sex and dessert a miserable experience.

When he was done, Mentha returned to his work table, and Monte and I watched in awe as his beefy hands flew about the studio, stirring, whipping, punching, mixing. Soon, a large baking dish dominated the table, overflowing with exquisitely sculpted froth and interlaced with fluted crust. It looked like a sea of raging cream.

"And now," announced Mentha, "*my* little reward." He held the sticky spatula to his sweating lips and licked it lovingly. "Mmmmm," he said, placing his free hand over his heart. His eyes closed in ecstasy. He exhaled heavily, groaned deeply. Then Mentha dropped the spatula, and that hand too gripped his chest. His body convulsed, and Mentha fell stiffly backward and smacked the tile. Blood oozed from under his head. His eyes were open, staring lifelessly toward the ceiling.

Monte slid out of the sling, shaking remnants of the white paste from her arm. She inspected Mentha.

"Well," she drawled, dipping a finger into the baking dish, "guess *I'll* have to try some of that."

We returned to our normal routine at the composting barn on Jemma's estate—save for one major change. I was now in love. Monte was baffled by this and kept her distance.

"Just because a fat man forced us to pump enzymes one time?" she asked, and her brow knit with honest confusion.

My feelings surpassed logic, I knew, so I did not press. I threw my energy into a new, surreptitious project. One corner of our composting barn saw little foot traffic, and to make it even more private I rolled a few mothballed harvesting vehicles into a circle. Most of the equipment I needed for my experiments was easily procured from various farm buildings—a vat for fermenting, an old grape press, a small gas stove for roasting. Monte helped, although her patience often wore thin.

"You realize that if Jemma catches you wasting his produce, you'll be indebted to him for an extra year or two," she warned.

"But nobody really has a use for the pods from the scrotum trees," I pointed out. "Mentha had them in his studio, but he never touched them—they were just part of his chartreuse, right?"

Monte shrugged. "But you can't so easily explain away the sugar you've been filching, or the milk. What are you trying to accomplish, anyway?"

"Seems to me there's an opening in the confection ministry."

Monte laughed. "Surely you don't think you can re-create Mentha Chiffon just from what little we saw!"

I shook my head. "Just bear with me a little while."

"Don't forget that you haul shit for a living," she said. "In order to jump to even a bottom-rung job in any of the culinary ministries, you'd have to come up with a major advancement."

I looked down at the dirt floor. "Yeah."

"And meantime," she said, turning her rangy frame and heading into the darkness of the groaning compost barn, "I'd say you got some dung to wheel around."

A month later, daybreak was cool and damp, reminding me of fall on Pacifica. I lingered at the open door of the compost barn, watching the fleet of horse carts departing the distant barracks to deliver my coworkers about the farm. I felt sober, sad, yet somehow relieved. I would probably never leave this land. Surely, within a few decades, I would be part of it—rotted myself, composted, absorbed into the vegetation. The humanoids would always be . . . *beyond*—their horrors, their deceptions, their "service." Forever held at bay, forever unresolved.

"You've got that 'daydreaming about humanoids' look."

I started. It was Monte—I hadn't noticed her approaching. She smelled fresh from the showers.

"Uh, caught me," I said.

"You look like something dug out of the cow barn. Been up all night? Nightmares again?"

I smiled. "No, I've been working," I said, handing her a paper-wrapped object. "Try this."

She peeled the covering back and wrinkled her nose. "Well, what do ya know—looks like dung."

"I know. Made it from the pods of the scrotum tree. I finally realized it was a species dating back to the mother world."

Monte took a cautious nibble, then a larger one. She closed her eyes and was silent for several moments. My pulse raced as I thought of old Mentha leveled by a heart attack.

Monte pushed the rest of my sample into her mouth and chewed, wadding up the wrapper.

"I think I could love you after all," she said. "What do you think you'll call this stuff?"

"Chocolate," I said.

Afterword

If you follow science fiction writers, you probably know how much creative effort they pour into developing the "worlds" in which their stories take place—that is, the customs, religions, and governments of imagined societies; the technological marvels—weaponry, transportation, communication; the planets, cities, deserts, mountains, and other settings where the characters leave their footprints as the stories unfold.

For a writer, a world well done is like a fine old car, oiled often, polished lovingly, taken out for a spin sometimes, yes, because you gotta get to the grocery, but just as often for the pure pleasure of the drive on a fine, fine day. Well, there aren't many people in the science fiction business with a better-stocked warehouse of handsome roadsters than Jack Williamson. So it's a delicious, sobering, mirthful and frightening thing when an editor comes 'round dangling a set of his car keys in front of your nose inviting you to take a spin.

Well, my use of Williamson's humanoids in "The Human Ingredient" is not much more than a cautious drive around the block, I suppose—an opportunity to combine a

few of my favorite subjects: food, sex, and justified para-
noia. There were dozens of buttons and switches in the
Williamson machine I didn't dare push, not on the first
drive. But it was a heart-thumping experience nevertheless.
Thanks for the ride, Jack.

—Jeff Bredenberg

One of the most satisfying and fun things you can do in a book like this is to take a story and add to it, creating a new story that gives readers the same kind of charge as the original story, without in any way spoiling or exploiting the original story. It's also one of the hardest things to do. Writing in another writer's universe is done quite a lot these days, but seldom is it done with the skill and sensitivity as in Jane Lindskold's unnerving but ultimately triumphant tale.

One note for readers: If you haven't read *Darker Than You Think,* it's only fair that I should tell you: in that book, the term "Child of the Night" referred to Will Barbee.

Child of the Night

Jane Lindskold

Pat knew she shouldn't get out of bed, but she didn't like this place and she wanted Mama. With the unfailing directness of her five years she knew that if the people here wouldn't take her to see Mama, then she would just have to find her all by herself.

Tall, skinny Nurse Etting had tucked Pat into a bed that was too big for her even with Teddy Bear to hold. Then she had brought Pat a glass of warm milk and a cookie. The cookie tasted good, but warm milk was for babies and Pat left it on the tray. While she waited for the grown-ups to think she was asleep, Pat tried to remember all the things that had happened to put her in this strange place.

Daddy had been gone for a long time and when he had come home he had been nervous and unhappy. He brought a big green wooden box with him and it hadn't even been full of presents for Mama and her. Pat had trouble understanding the next part— she was sure that she'd been asleep, but she was also sure that she had watched the pretty white dog and big gray dog come to steal the box. She didn't like remembering what had happened next— how her own little dog, Jiminy Cricket, had been killed by the big gray dog and tossed into the sand pile like an old toy.

When Nurse Etting came into the room, Pat pretended to be asleep. With a gentleness that made Pat almost start crying, the nurse tucked the blankets down around the little girl. Then she went out taking the tray with the milk and the cookie plate. Pat said her alphabet twice and then decided that the grown-ups would probably leave her alone for a while.

Leaving Teddy under the blanket, she stole to the door. No one seemed to notice her slipping out and slinking behind a window curtain. She didn't see Mama anywhere and huddled behind the musty-smelling fabric wondering how to find her. Mama was upset and she would need Pat to make her feel better.

Mama had started laughing and crying all at the same time right after the sheriff's men had come to say that Daddy had been found hiding up in the mountains with the box. Pat had run to hold her, just like she had done when Mama had cried at Christmas or on Daddy's birthday, but the men had pulled her away. They had bundled her, Teddy, and Mama into a police car and driven them to Glennhaven. There Dr. Archer Glenn had said kind, soothing words that didn't touch his eyes. Then Mama had been fed some pills and taken one direction and Pat had been taken in another.

Crouched behind her curtain, Pat looked out the window. In the dusk, the trees around Glennhaven were as red and orange as the construction paper Thanksgiving decoration she and Mama had been making, but the gray buildings had bars over the windows, nothing at all like the little white house in which she and Mama lived. And Daddy, too, now, she reminded herself. Daddy was home now and everything would be all right.

She wished that Daddy or Mama were here to tell her what to do next, then she heard a familiar voice.

"Come over to my office, Mr. Troy," Dr. Glenn was saying to another man. "We can continue our talk there."

"Good," Mr. Troy answered. "I've just come from the cell block and Sam's in the sheriff's custody. You have Nora and the little girl here?"

Mr. Troy was a fat man with thin red hair. He smelled from the cigar clenched in his teeth. Dr. Glenn had black hair and looked like a movie star. He had to keep taking little steps because Mr. Troy was so much shorter. Mr. Troy took big steps to keep up with him. They walked so much like a pair of clowns that Pat had fought not to giggle.

"That's right. Nora's under sedation, and Nurse Etting reported that Patricia's asleep. We can stop in and see them later, if you would like."

Nora was Mama. Sam was Daddy. Pat's heart jumped so loudly that she wrapped her hands over it to keep it quiet. Then she stole after the two men. They would go and see Mama and she would follow them. Pat thrust out her square chin in a gesture that everyone said was just like Daddy. Just let them try and send her away once she'd found Mama.

Dr. Glenn closed the door to his office quickly, but not before Pat found a way to slip inside. She hid behind one of the high-backed chairs and sat very still like she did when Mama's bridge club came to call and she didn't want Mama to remember and send her for a nap. Then she had been waiting to get some of the little sandwiches and the nuts dipped in chocolate. Tonight she was waiting for something even more important.

"How's Sam?" Dr. Glenn asked, pouring both himself and Mr. Troy drinks from a fancy bottle cut like a diamond.

"Terrible, as you might expect," Mr. Troy said, taking his glass in the hand that didn't hold his cigar. "He's not only being charged with the murders of Dr. Mondrick, Rex Chittum, and Nick Spivak, but with possible complicity in the death of Will Barbee. They'll throw away the key."

"Almost a shame, from a genetic viewpoint," Dr. Glenn said. "We did manage to switch his blood test all those years ago."

"Yes, and fouled up switching Barbee's, so Barbee ended up cut out of Mondrick's little crew and becoming a drunk," Mr. Troy sighed. "I've been carrying him for years. At least it was worth it in the end. Our Child of the Night is flying free of this mortal coil. I'm actually amazed at how well he took to the free mind web."

"You miss my point," Dr. Glenn said a bit coolly. Pat wondered if he didn't like the cigar smoke any better than she did. "Sam Quain was not as much of our blood as Will Barbee, but he and his little blond were an admirable breeding pair. Now they are both lost to us."

"He is," Mr. Troy said. "Nora may yet be convinced to have other children. Have you had a chance to check the girl?"

"No," Dr. Glenn replied. "There will be time enough in the morning. What arrangements are being made for her?"

"If her mother ends up committed . . ."

"She will."

"Then the girl will need a home. I plan to have my daughter April appointed as a temporary guardian. Patricia will be raised in an appropriate atmosphere, and we won't need to waste time awakening her talents as we have with so many others."

"Very good. And her daughter will make a fine hostage to encourage Nora to cooperate with us." Dr. Glenn rose. "Would you like to see her now?"

"In a moment." Mr. Troy grinned evilly. "I have something you are going to take a look at for us. April phoned and told me where Will Barbee dropped the box that Sam Quain was guarding. Most of its contents fell into the water, but some scraps remained. I sent one of my trusties to collect them."

He pulled what Pat thought was a small cigar box from his coat pocket. It thudded when he put it on Dr. Glenn's desk.

"Lead-lined." Mr. Troy grunted. "Helps keep the deadly emanations from the Stone inside. None of the pieces are bigger than a quarter."

"Why did you bring that here!" Dr. Glenn's eyes lost their look of lazy confidence. Pat thought that he was really scared.

"Don't be such a coward. The Stone is most dangerous to us when we are free of our bodies," Mr. Troy answered. "You can study it safely. We need to know what the Stone is and how to counter its powers. That's the only way we're ever going to be safe from the humans."

"I . . ." Dr. Glenn drained all the liquor in his glass. "You're right. I'll get to it as soon as we have this problem with Sam and Nora Quain settled. Are you ready to see Nora now?"

"Yes. If you have any sodium pentothal bring that along. We need to know exactly how much Sam let slip."

"I already have it ready. Don't worry overly about what she remembers." Dr. Glenn smiled. "Electric shock therapy or even a lobotomy will make certain she doesn't continue to remember too much, and neither will affect her usefulness to our Cause."

Pat was quite confused as she followed the men down a hallway, across a red-tiled waiting area, and to another section of the building. Many of the words the men had used were too big for her, but she understood enough to know that Dr. Glenn and Mr. Troy wanted Daddy to be in jail. It sounded like they wanted to put Mama and her in jail, too. Pat had seen April Bell at the airport on the day that Daddy had come back. Miss Bell had red hair and a white fur coat and a little black kitten. The kitten had been cute, but Miss Bell had scared Pat. She most certainly didn't want to go and live with her.

Dr. Glenn unlocked a heavy door with a key and held it open for Mr. Troy. Pat slipped through, too. So far she had been lucky and no one had noticed her, but then she had always been lucky with sneaking around at night. Mama never seemed to notice, only Jiminy Cricket did, but he liked to join her watching the stars from the back steps. Her eyes got wet when she remembered her little dog, but she blinked the tears away and hurried after the two men.

Mama was asleep in a high bed with rails on the sides. Her soft blond hair spilled around her pillow. She was very still and breathing heavily. Dr. Glenn patted her face and slowly she started to come awake, her blue eyes opening to narrow slits. Pat wanted to run over to her then and there, but she knew that the men would send her back to her room. Unhappily, she crept into a corner behind a nightstand and wished that the men would go away.

"Nora? Nora?" Dr. Glenn's voice was very gentle. "Wake up. I have a few questions for you."

"Sam?" Mama's voice was slurred. "Sam? You shouldn't be here. Those horrible people are going to try and frame you for Nick's death now. Go up to the cave and hide. I'll send a message when it's safe to come home. Will Barbee will bring it."

"Wake up, Nora," Dr. Glenn urged. Then he let Mama's head fall back onto the pillow. "She's still too far under, Preston. If I give her something to counteract the sedative, it would be unwise to give her the sodium pentothal on top of it. Better to let her sleep for a few more hours and then try again."

"If we must." Mr. Troy sounded grumpy.

The two men left and Pat rushed from the corner and climbed onto Mama's bed.

"Mama," she said softly, "Mama, it's Pat. Mama, wake up."

Mama's eyelashes fluttered but she didn't awaken.

"Mama!" Pat put her hand out to shake Mama's shoulder, softly at first, then harder. "Mama, wake up!"

Unbidden tears rolled down her cheeks and splashed on the coverlet. A few fell on Mama's face and she stirred, opened her eyes, and peered weakly about.

"Pat?" her voice was weak, but less slurred than before, "Where are you, Pat?"

"I'm right here!" Pat said, putting her face down so Mama could see her. "I got out of bed and came to find you. Mama, I don't like this place. Can we go home?"

"Home?" Mama's eyes opened wider and she seemed to see where she was for the first time. "Where are we? Where's Sam?"

Pat felt panic rising. She put a finger to Mama's lips. Then she thought hard. As an only child, she was used to getting her own way. Nothing was working now and she wanted it to. She wanted Mama to wake up and be a grown-up. She wanted to leave this place and she wanted to do something so that Dr. Glenn and Mr. Troy would leave them alone.

"Get up, Mama," she ordered and stamped her foot.

Mama stirred and sat up slowly. With great labor, Pat took off Mama's nightgown and helped her into a dress and flats. She was giving a lick and a promise to Mama's hair when Mama finally seemed to wake up.

"Pat, honey." She hugged Pat so hard that happy tears started. "Where are we? Where's your Daddy?"

"Don't cry again, Mama, but Daddy's with the sheriff." Pat hesitated to see if Mama was going to cry, then continued. "And we're at Dr. Glenn's hospital. Can we go home?"

"Glennhaven." Mama frowned, but she didn't cry. "I remember now. I got a bit hysterical after the report that Sam had been arrested came in. Has anyone been by to see us?"

"Just the nurses, Dr. Glenn, and Mr. Troy," Pat said impatiently. "Mama, we've got to go home. This isn't a good place. Dr. Glenn and Mr. Troy don't like Daddy."

"I could call Uncle Will," Mama said hesitantly. "He could pick us up."

"Uncle Will." Pat remembered what she had heard in Dr. Glenn's office. "Is his other name Will Barbee?"

"That's right, honey."

"I don't think you should call him, Mama." Pat thrust out her chin, knowing she shouldn't tell that she had been listening to grown-ups talk. "I heard Dr. Glenn and Mr. Troy talking and they said that Will Barbee was the strongest of them. I think he's their friend."

Pat decided not to explain what she'd heard about Daddy being blamed for Will Barbee's accident. She was still confused about most of that.

Mama stood. "Your Daddy told me some very strange things when he came home from Mongolia, Pat. I thought that he was just very tired, but everything that has happened since makes me wonder. I think we had better leave here—without telling anyone who might feel differently."

Pat jumped off the bed and peered out into the hall. "There's no one out there, Mama. Come on."

Mama looked strangely at her, but followed quickly. They hurried down the hallway, hiding once when a nurse came out of another room to rummage in a supply cupboard.

Pat worried about how they were going to get through the locked door. She trotted ahead of Mama, her bare feet making no noise on the tiled floor. When she reached the door, it was closed tightly. Standing on her toes, she poked at the lock with her fingers. Luckily, she could squeeze just enough of her finger inside to make the bolt spring back. When Mama joined her, she had pulled the door open.

"Do you have any other clothes, Pat?" Mama whispered, fingering the thin nightgown Nurse Etting had put her in. "It's going to be chilly outside."

"In my room." Pat's eyes grew wide. "And Teddy is there. I have to go and get him!"

She ran ahead to her room. Teddy was waiting for her, lumped up under the covers so that it looked like she was still with him. Stopping to give him a kiss for being so brave, she tugged her nightgown off over her head. Mama came in time to help her put on her playsuit, shoes, and coat.

When Pat was dressed, they ventured out into the hall again, hiding whenever they saw anyone. The way out took them right by Dr. Glenn's office. Pat could hear voices in conversation as they walked by.

Mama pushed on the latch to open a heavy double-paneled glass door. Her breathing was coming quickly now like she might start to cry. Pat held her hand tightly.

"It's locked, Pat," Mama said. "I guess . . ."

The door to Dr. Glenn's office flew open and Dr. Glenn strode out into the hallway. His tie was off and he held a cigarette. Otherwise, he was as neat as he had been earlier.

"Mrs. Quain," he said in surprise. "What are you doing?"

"Taking me and Pat home," Mama said, firmly. "After all

today's shocks, my little girl needs to sleep in her own bed."

"Why didn't you tell the night nurse to check you out?" Dr. Glenn asked disapprovingly.

"She wasn't at the desk," Mama answered, astonishing Pat with her fib. They had very carefully sneaked past the night nurse, who had been listening to the radio and doing a crossword puzzle at her desk.

"I must speak with her about staying at her post," Dr. Glenn said. "You may as well come into my office and let me sign your release myself. There is an exit through my reception room, and we can call a cab to come for you. This way everything will stay in order and you won't disable our alarms. Come right this way."

Mama followed him, Pat fuming at her side. Pat didn't like that Dr. Glenn talked to Mama as if she were a little girl. She didn't like even more that he treated Pat herself as if she weren't a person.

Mr. Troy was still in Dr. Glenn's office. Dr. Glenn's desk was cluttered with glasses, ashtrays, and stacks of papers. The cigar box that Mr. Troy had brought earlier rested on the corner nearest to where Pat stood. Remembering that Mr. Troy had said that it contained poison, she looked to see if there was a skull and crossbones on the lid, but there was just the usual gold and red pictures.

"Mrs. Quain, do you know Preston Troy?" Dr. Glenn said as he shut the door behind them.

"I know Mr. Troy by reputation," Mama said.

"My condolences about Sam's arrest," Mr. Troy said. "The strain of the trip must have broken him."

"Sam is innocent," Mama said firmly. "Now, Dr. Glenn, if you would please let me call a cab and get the paperwork completed I would be grateful."

"My car could take you home," Mr. Troy said gruffly. "I'm

nearly done with my business here, and I feel that it isn't a safe night for a woman to travel alone."

"I couldn't trouble you," Mama answered. "I'll call Trojan Cabs."

"Well, then, I must be leaving." Mr. Troy glanced at Dr. Glenn.

He left and Dr. Glenn pushed a phone book and telephone over to Mama.

"Call your cab while I fill out the paperwork. Would you like a drink?"

"No, thank you." Mama bent her head over the phone book.

Pat edged over next to the desk. When Dr. Glenn was busy scribbling on a form, she slid the cigar box from the desk and into the pocket of her coat. It was Daddy's, Mr. Troy had said. She would bring it back to him. She hugged Teddy tightly and waited nervously, but Dr. Glenn didn't seem to notice that the box was gone.

A car horn beeped outside.

"That will be your cab," Dr. Glenn said. "If you would just sign here and here, I will release you. In all honesty, I must say that I have noted on these forms that I believe you need further rest, but since you were a voluntary admittee I acceded to your wishes."

"I will decide what is best for my daughter and me," Mama said, taking the pen and signing. "Good night, Dr. Glenn."

A round-topped yellow cab was pulling away from the curb as they stepped out of the door. Mama ran out into the road, waving her hands.

"Over here," she called. "Come back!"

The cab turned around, accelerating as it did so. Mama backed up toward the curb, slipping on the loose gravel. Pat screamed.

"Mama!"

As the cab lurched toward Mama, Pat realized that Preston Troy was at the wheel, a tweed cap pulled over his eyes.

Pat ran after Mama, but as she did the heaviness of the box in her pocket threw her to the ground. She felt the box break, then Mama was holding her.

"Upsy-daisy," Mama said, setting Pat on her feet. "The cabby is coming back for us."

Feeling sick, Pat realized that Mama didn't understand, just like she hadn't believed Pat when Pat told her that the big gray dog had killed Jiminy Cricket. The cab was coming back. Mr. Troy was gesturing for Mama to walk out into the road again.

"Mama, no!" Pat said, pulling her back.

Mama picked her up. "Don't be a silly baby. That's just our ride home."

Pat struggled, but she was carried out into the road. The cab rumbled closer. Then, at the last moment, it veered away, hitting Mama a glancing blow that knocked her out. Hearing the engine shut off, Pat worked her way free of her unconscious mother's embrace, crawling out to find Mr. Troy advancing on them. He had become a horrible thing—a big red dog that walked on its hind legs, clawed hands dangling at his side.

His fang-filled mouth rasped, "Poison, Glenn! The child carries the poison of the Stone. Glenn! Where are the shards of the stone?"

A lean black panther glided out of the office doorway and joined the red dog.

"Gone," Pat somehow heard it say, though its mouth did not move. "The brat stole them. I smell them on her."

Pat's head was swimming now, but she thought she understood. The box had broken and these creatures could feel the poison leaking out. Reaching into her pocket, she drew out the box and opened the lid. The wood was cracked, the lead lining bent but still intact, cradling bits of stone that glowed dull purple in the dark. The dog and the panther cringed back.

Thrusting her chin forward, she advanced on the monsters.

"Drop the box, Patricia," the black panther snarled. "It is dangerous."

To you, she thought, and kept walking.

"Put down the box and I'll get you a pony," the Mr. Troy dog coaxed. "A Shetland pony with a floppy mane."

Pat paused, but she remembered Jiminy Cricket and kept walking. Behind her, Mama moaned.

"Patricia, don't come any closer!" the red dog pleaded, falling to all fours.

Pat drew back her arm, a bit of the purple rock in her hand. She threw it as hard as she could at the black panther.

"That one's for Mama!" she said.

The black panther crumpled, tearing at the purple stone, its movements growing slower and slower. She threw another stone at the Mr. Troy dog. It howled and fell to the ground.

"That one's for Daddy!" She was crying now, but she ran forward and emptied the dust from the box over the two struggling monsters.

"And that one's for Jiminy Cricket!"

Dr. Glenn and Mr. Troy faded into mist, dissolving the shreds of purple stone with them. Pat hurried to help Mama to her feet. The night was dark and she knew with all the certainty of her five years that it was filled with monsters.

Afterword

In early April of 1995, I flew to Portales, New Mexico, along with Roger Zelazny and George R. R. Martin, to take part in the Jack Williamson Lectureship Series (inaugurated in 1977 when Jack "retired"). The three of us all resided in Santa Fe at that time and the fastest way to Portales was Mesa Air. Mesa does not use large planes. Ours had maybe twenty seats and a center aisle so narrow that Roger and I could easily hold hands across it. Of course there was no beverage or snack service—there wasn't even room to stand up straight.

Our short flight to Albuquerque went without a hitch, but as we departed Albuquerque for Portales, the weather rapidly made its presence known. Our position between earth and sky gave us an opportunity to appreciate the power with which the lightning left the clouds to impale the ground. When the pilot forgot to close the curtain that separated the cockpit from the passenger cabin, we had a vivid demonstration of how dangerous landing one of those little planes during a storm can be.

All three of us were more than happy to get off the tiny plane at the terminal, where we were met by Patrice Caldwell, Jack's assistant. In three-part chorus, we regaled her with the story of our hazardous journey. Only later, when the four of us were comfortably sitting in a warm restaurant eating pizza and buffalo wings, did the myriad wonders involved in our journey occur to me.

In a few hours time, we had crossed not only a portion of the Rocky Mountains, but also miles and miles of cracked, arid semi-desert land. The only real inconveniences in the entire journey had been a few moments of nausea during the worst of the storm, and damp clothing from walking in the rain to the terminal. When we finished our meal, we would sleep warm and dry, with hot water, television, and various other modern conveniences at our disposal. Yet, our entire trip would have seemed right on the border of science fiction when Jack Williamson was born.

I'll leave to others who better know the details to talk about how Jack came to New Mexico in a covered wagon, about the years spent working a variety of very unwriterly jobs, about the successes he has achieved as writer, teacher, brother, uncle, and cousin. I've only heard of those by report. What I want to touch on is Jack Williamson and wonder.

In Jack's novel *Darker Than You Think* (1948), on which I based my short story "Child of the Night," wonder is what holds the melange of fantasy and hard science together. It is a story in which shapeshifters are as real as school buses, but the explanation behind their ability to take on animal forms and to dazzle the unaccepting human mind are taken from what was, for the time, cutting-edge physics. So many writers who use fantasy motifs use them as an excuse to escape the hard, cold realities that have been uncovered by science. It took Jack Williamson to combine the wonders of new science and old legend into something powerful and strange.

Jack did not reserve this talent for just one novel. His more recent novel *Demon Moon* (1994) again combines fantasy motifs and scientific explanation. His unique sense of wonder leads to other odd combinations. One of my favorites occurred when Jack—as he cheerfully admits—stole Shakespeare's best rogue and transformed him into the clever and cowardly Giles Habibula. Giles, in story after story, upstages the more noble members of the Legion of Space, just as Falstaff upstaged Prince Hal.

My enthusiasm could carry me through example after example, but I'll pause here, smile, and allow myself to hope that someday the wonders of the future as envisioned by Jack Williamson will be as routine as an airplane flight is today.

—Jane Lindskold

There's something positively irresistible about Giles Habibula. Larger than life in his Legion of Space adventures, he's no less a rogue or likable scoundrel in David Weber's charming story of temptation and redemption, none of which exactly explains why he went on to those legendary Legion adventures, except that one can argue for the potential for good that lies within even the most unregenerate of us.

A Certain Talent

David Weber

Habibula, Giles (2819–?): Hero of Humanity (with clus-
ter), Acclamation of Green Hall (with three clusters),
Guardian of the Keeper, Grand Solar Cross (with cluster),
Star of Terra (with cluster), Medusean Campaign Medal,
Cometeer Campaign medal, Legion of Merit, Fellow of
Solarian Institute. One of only three individuals (*see also* Jay
Kalam, Hal Samdu) to be twice awarded humanity's highest
award for valor and service, Giles Habibula's career has so
far spanned almost a full century of service to the Legion of

Space. Although he has persistently refused promotion to officer's rank, Habibula has . . .

—*A Solarian Who's Who, Vol. 36*
Star Press, Phobos, 2962

Habibula, Giles, a.k.a. Grenz Harnat, Gorma Habranah, Gerniak Helthir, Gorsah Hamah. Age 35. Brown hair, gray eyes. Height 6' 1". Weight 275 lbs. Arrested for: grand larceny, grand theft spacecraft, grand theft technology, burglary, assault with a deadly weapon, resisting arrest, aggravated assault, and public drunkenness. No convictions. Presently wanted on charges of illegal gambling practices. A master of locks and adaptive technology, Habibula should be considered armed and dangerous. A reward of seventy-five thousand dollars has been posted by the Venusberg Gambling Commission for information leading to his arrest and conviction on charges of tampering with electronic gambling devices.

—Venusberg Police Department
Records Division, 2854

His arrogance was his downfall.

Or perhaps it wrongs him to call it "arrogance." Perhaps "confidence" would be a better word, for he had a certain talent he knew none could equal, and the challenge was irresistible to a man of his nature. And so it should have been, given how carefully it had been crafted to that end. . . .

Sweat trickled down Giles Habibula's broad face in the steamy, moonless dark. The eerie cries of a night such as Earth had never known came from the jungles, where huge, armored sauroids splashed and grunted as they fought one another for life—and food—while the strange, scaled "birds" of Venus waited to pick the losers' bones. But those were familiar sounds, and they came from the far side of the compound wall, and Habibula paid them no heed. He'd hidden in the shrubbery against the wall since the chalet staff ushered the last public visitor away, and now he waited patiently for the staff to leave, as well.

He must be mad to attempt an escapade such as this when the mortal Gambling Commission had already offered its reward for his poor, underappreciated self, he thought with a smile, but the curse of Giles Habibula's life was ever the same. There was never time enough for all the splendid food, the fine wines, the beautiful women, the challenges to his wit and skill, and when three of the four combined in a single temptation, it was more than mortal man could do to turn his back upon it. Especially when the lass who'd set him onto it was such a fine, beautiful one. Ah, the fire in those blue eyes, and that lovely head of midnight hair! And the spirit of her, too. *The Solar System might see her like once in a lifetime,* he told himself, *and as well for the rest of us, for we'd never survive two of her!*

He smothered a chuckle and checked the time once more. Just past twenty-two hundred. He'd spent two days timing the staff's schedule, and he nodded in satisfaction as he stole silently out of the imported Earth shrubbery about the chalet's protective wall.

The grounds were well lit, but the chalet's owners relied on automatic systems, nothing so fallible as humans, so there were no roving patrols, and he'd plotted his course with care. He crept across flower beds and grass like a great, prowling cat, avoiding the cameras and illuminating spotlights as he flowed through puddles of inky shadow. He paused just beyond the chalet itself, scanning for infrared beams, and chuckled once more as he found them. Ah, the wit of the lad who'd planned the security here! It was a mortal fine job he'd done, but not the equal to Giles Habibula!

He sidled to the side, studying the interlinking play of the beams, and for all his massive bulk, he moved quiet as the breeze. Fat other men might think him, and so, indeed, he was, but there was muscle under that fat, and he carried himself with a dancer's grace, placing each foot with feline caution. And even as he surveyed the challenge, his mind went back to the beautiful young woman awaiting him in the Venusberg bar.

"It won't be easy, Mr. Harnat," the woman called Ethyra Coran warned, and Giles Habibula—Grenz Harnat, to her—nodded gravely. "On the other hand," she went on, "my client will pay a half million dollars for the Dragon's Eye, and they may have been just a bit too clever in the way they planned the security."

"Ah, and have they now?" The remnants of a stupendous meal lay in ruins before him, and he sipped more wine—a splendid Martian Burgundy—as he listened to her. A half million was a paltry value to set on the famed Dragon's Eye, yet it seemed reasonable enough under the circumstances. The flawless Martian ruby was priceless, but it was also half the size of a man's head, and the very size which made it so rare and beautiful would make it impossible to fence on the open market.

"Your client's not thinking to have it cut, is he?" Habibula asked after a moment. Ethyra raised an eyebrow at him in perplexity, and he shrugged. "I'll have no part of it if he is," he explained. "A mortal crime against nature it would be to break up a lovely bauble such as that."

"A burglar with esthetics?" She laughed in sheer delight at the thought, then sobered. "No, Mr. Harnat. My client intends to retain it for, ah, his private collection."

"Does he now?" Habibula nodded in approval, opened another bottle of wine, and concentrated on his glass as he poured. "And how might it be they've been 'a bit too clever,' lass?" he asked.

"They're relying as much on misdirection as on security," she replied. "No one on Venus is supposed to know the gem is here, so they've stayed away from banks and regular vaults. Instead, they've lodged it with Samuel Ulnar, and he's hidden it in his chalet."

"The Ulnar Chalet?" Habibula looked up from his glass so abruptly he spilled wine, and his gray eyes brightened. "In his cellars, is it?"

"Why, yes." Ethyra sounded surprised, and he smiled happily. He'd heard of those cellars. "Samuel Ulnar is on Earth, so the chalet is officially unoccupied," she added. "The Dragon's Eye's owners expect that to help divert attention from their own presence, and they were told the Ulnar cellars are one of the most secure places on Venus."

"And so they should be, lass. So they should be," Habibula murmured. The Ulnar cellars, he thought, under the very chalet Zane Delmar, Samuel Ulnar's ancestor, had built seven centuries ago. Its historical significance made it a major tourist attraction, and the Venusian branch of the once all-powerful Ulnar family allowed public tours of its spacious, landscaped grounds. But its interior was private, for it was still home to Samuel Ulnar and his wife . . . and to the finest collection of wines and brandies in the Solar System. A single bottle of European champagne from that cellar would fetch five thousand dollars, but what a mortal shame to waste such a vintage on any but the most cultured palate! His

eyes gleamed at the thought of what he might find as a byprod-
uct of fetching out the Dragon's Eye, and he beamed at the
young woman.

"Just you be telling me all you know of this blessed security,"
he said.

Habibula continued his cautious circuit of the chalet's inner defenses, then paused. The capacious knapsack on his back—large
enough for a dozen bottles plus the Dragon's Eye—held the
tools of his trade, and he'd brought along reflectors to defeat the
infrared beams if he must. But such a trick was always risky, for
even Giles Habibula's wrist could slip and interrupt the beam as
he slid them into place. He'd hoped to avoid their use, and he
smiled cheerfully as he examined his discovery.

An ornate portico in the neoclassic style of the twenty-
second century fronted the chalet, and its sculptures and col-
umns broke up the neat pattern of beams. The security system's
designer had done his best to weave an impenetrable net about
them, yet there was a small gap where the beams bent and angled
about the massive stone sphinxes crouched on either side of the
main door. It looked far too tiny for a man of his girth, but appearances could be deceiving, and he estimated its size with care.

Yes, he decided. It would be mortal difficult, but few could
match the fearsome agility of Giles Habibula.

He slipped off his knapsack, slid it carefully through the
opening, and took another moment to memorize the pattern of
the beams before he slipped off his scanners and folded them
away into a pocket. Then he folded himself with equal care, embracing the sphinx's stony flank, and eased himself through the
same gap. He took his time, creeping past one inch at a time, and

sighed with relief as he drew his left foot through at last without
sounding an alarm.

A mortal fine job you did, my lad, he thought at the security system's designer, *but not so fine as to be stopping Giles Habibula!*

He gathered up his knapsack once more, took out his scanners, and checked for any inner perimeter of beams. There was
none, and he stepped closer to the chalet's front wall to examine
the doors and windows.

"Do you really think he'll come, Sir?" the younger man asked.

His older companion never took his eyes from the panel
before him. Dozens of alarms, internal and external, reported to
that panel, from the motion sensors atop the compound walls to
the intricate infrared photoelectric beams covering the chalet's
exterior and the manifold internal detection systems on its windows, doors, and hallways. For three nights they'd waited, without even a flicker from any of them, and he understood the
youngster's impatience and doubt.

"Oh, he'll come," the older man said. "If he's the man for the
job, he'll come."

Habibula slipped cautiously down the hallway. The doors had
been too richly fitted with alarms for his taste, but only three
separate systems had protected the library windows. The window lock had been a sophisticated Cabloc Seven combination
device, but locks were his special talent. A mortal pity an artist of
his stature was deprived the recognition his genius deserved, yet
such was the way of an uncaring world. And fair or no, there *were*
compensations, he reminded himself with a smile.

He paused in the darkness of a four-way intersection, mentally consulting the map he'd memorized, then nodded with a smile. One more flight of stairs, another door, and then the cellar itself.

"I still wish we could have avoided giving him an accurate map, Sir," the younger man fretted. "Couldn't we have had her—?"

"If he noticed any discrepancies, he'd pull out in a second," the older man said patiently. "Besides, this is supposed to be a test, as well, and how good a test would it be if we deliberately fed him false information?"

Habibula crouched outside the wine cellar door and examined the lock with the aid of a small hand light. *Well, now! Isn't that a mortal surprise!*

He bent closer and ran his fingers over the three combination wheels, and his eyebrows rose in respect. He'd always heard the Ulnar Chalet had first-class security, and any member of the Ulnar clan could afford the very best, but this was more than he'd expected. It was a Cerberus Twelve, possibly the most complex and effective lock yet designed by man, but he smiled, then gave it a fond pat. A good lock was like a trusted friend to Giles Habibula, for he had a certain way with them, and this one was based on a design his own father had created fifty years before. A mortal pity the old man had been a finer locksmith than a businessman, for his creation had been stolen by sharper, craftier minds, but he'd taught his son its secrets before they had.

Giles smiled again, and his short, strong fingers began to turn the knobs with a delicate precision any surgeon might have envied.

*   *   *

"Sir, I'm sorry, but I really don't think he's coming. Or not to-night, at least." The young man rose and walked about the room for a moment, stretching muscles cramped by hours of motion-less waiting. "It's after two hundred. If he *was* coming, he'd certainly have started by now."

"How do you know he hasn't?" the older man countered. The green-uniformed youngster looked at him in disbelief for a moment, then waved at the console before them.

"If he were here, we'd know about it, Sir," he said positively.

"Ah, you young people!" The older man smiled. "So much faith in technology and so little in human inventiveness! Sit down, James. And remember, he's Giles Habibula."

The Cerberus Twelve clicked finally, and he wiped sweat from his broad face once more despite the cool of the chalet's dehumidified air. *A fearsome fine lock you designed, Dad,* he thought wryly, *and what a mortal sin you never got the credit you deserved for it! Ah, but we'll make them wonder at us when they find it unlocked in the morning, won't we?*

He chuckled and stole through into the dusty silence of the wine cellars. One more lock and the Dragon's Eye would nestle safe and secure in his knapsack . . . and then it would be time for what *he'd* come for.

The younger man stirred restlessly in his chair, only his immense respect for his senior preventing yet another protest. No one had *ever* defeated a Cerberus Twelve without blasting or cutting. He couldn't believe that even a man of Giles Habibula's reputation

could beat this one, and even if he could, there was still no sign
of any attempt to penetrate the chalet.

The older man noted his restlessness and hid another smile.

There!

Habibula stowed the Dragon's Eye carefully in his knapsack,
and his gray eyes glittered at the huge gem's fearsome beauty.
He stroked it with reverent fingers. *Ah, I'd like to keep you for myself,*
he thought at it, *just to rest my mortal eyes upon you from time to time. But
you're too well known for that, aren't you?*

He chuckled, then turned away and rubbed his hands, and
his eyes flickered with a deeper greed as they darted about the
dimly lit cellar's dusty racks of priceless bottles.

He started his search, trotting down the aisles between the
racks, face alight with pleasure as he scanned the dusty labels. *A
little bonus for my mortal time,* he told himself with a grin, and started
making his selections. The Napa '72 made a good start, and he
followed it with a bottle of the Mons Olympus '90, then the
Rothschild '63. Years to savor, all of them, he thought, and then
his beady eyes lit in sheer delight.

He stepped closer, unable to believe what he was seeing.
Crocyrean Brandy?! It couldn't be!

He blew dust gently from the bottle and sighed in pleasure. It
was, and the '51, at that! Over a mortal century old, pressed from
the rich black grapes of the Canal Delta, then distilled and aged
to await a palate with the sensitivity to appreciate its golden
glory. And that palate, he promised himself, would savor it with
the respect it deserved.

He lifted the bottle gently from the rack—and froze as
alarms howled.

*   *   *

"I don't believe it!" The younger man shot upright in his chair, staring at his console in disbelief. A brilliant light—the very last one on the panel—flashed blood red, and the older man laughed.

"I *told* you he was Giles Habibula, James!" he said, and reached for his communicator.

Habibula's eyes darted about the cellar in disbelief. He'd checked the racks for motion systems, scanned for invisible detection beams, searched with excruciating care for any possible alarm, and found nothing. He'd even seized the mortal Dragon's Eye without sounding an alert!

He shook himself as the fearsome keening of the alarms burned in his ears. How they'd detected his presence was less important than escaping before they got here. The chances might be slim, but he'd planned his exit route with all his mortal cunning on the way in, and they'd not caught him yet!

He slid the brandy into his knapsack, buckled it shut, and darted from the cellar with a blinding speed that belied his bulk.

"He's on his way out," the older man said urgently into his communicator. "It looks like he's headed for the west annex."

Habibula dashed up stairs and down halls with fleet-footed urgency, avoiding the detectors he'd noted on his way in with instinctive skill and breathing a silent apology to the vintages jouncing in the knapsack on his back. A mortal crime to jostle such fine wine so rudely, but he promised to let it settle properly before he tapped it.

A door slammed somewhere behind him, and he swallowed a curse as feet ran after him. They were too far back to have seen him, but where had they *come* from?! There were supposed to be no human guards, and even if there were, how did they know which way to pursue? He'd tripped none of the alarms he'd already spotted in his flight, and if he'd missed any on the way in, the guards would surely have reacted before he got clear to the mortal cellars!

But there was no time to think about that, and they were too far back to catch him. Once he made it through the library and onto the grounds, he'd mapped a dozen different escape routes, and—

He darted into the huge library, running for the windows, and crashed full-tilt into something in the darkness. Somehow he managed to curl around to protect the precious bottles in his knapsack as he fell, but whatever had tripped him up wrapped about his legs like a Venusian python. He thrashed and kicked against it, fighting it in the blinding dark, and he'd almost won free when the library lights clicked on.

A reading lamp, he thought. *A mortal reading lamp! What fearsome idiot left it standing in the middle of the mortal aisle?!*

He started to leap up, then sighed and sat back down as half a dozen men with drawn pistols dashed into the library. He sat on the floor, looking up at them, and wondered what the Legion of Space was doing in the Ulnar Chalet at three in the morning.

"Good morning, Mr. Habibula. My name is Jartha. Colonel John Jartha of the Legion, at your service." The silver-haired man in the green uniform bowed courteously, apparently oblivious to the three enormous legionnaires who had "escorted" Habibula into the chalet's security center, then waved as a beautiful young woman walked in through another door. "I believe you've met Miss Coran," he added.

"Aye, and so I have," Habibula replied. His gray eyes were hard for just an instant, but then he smiled at the young woman and nodded to the knapsack one of the legionnaires held. "I'll take my mortal money in small bills, lass," he said genially, "but I'm afraid you'll have to get the Dragon's Eye from that great, fearsome brute with my knapsack if you're still minded to have it."

The young woman smiled, then shook her head with a trace of sadness, and Colonel Jartha cleared his throat.

"I trust you won't hold this against Miss Coran, Mr. Habibula. She was only doing her job."

"Her job, is it?" Habibula inquired pleasantly.

"Indeed. In fact, she had no choice. Miss Coran's father owns a bar—the Blue Unicorn, I believe it's called—in the Aphrodite Sea just off the coast of New Chicago. Unfortunately, there were a few, ah, *irregularities* in his departure from the Legion some twenty years ago." Jartha shook his head sadly. "A pity, but you know how military organizations can be."

"So you used mortal blackmail to get the lass to do your bidding, did you?" Habibula observed shrewdly.

"We prefer to think of it as encouraging her to volunteer," the colonel disagreed. "Of course, the Green Hall itself has authorized her father's pardon in return for her services."

"Has it now? And why would the Green Hall be interested in trapping a poor, honest nobody like myself?"

"You wrong yourself, Mr. Habibula." Jartha smiled. "You're quite well known in certain circles. Indeed, when we asked who

the most skilled, ah, lock expert in the System might be, our contacts assured us it was either you or Stephen Matha."

"*Matha!* That fearsome nincompoop?!" Habibula glared at
the Legion colonel. "Why, I've more talent in one hand—no,
in one mortal *finger!*—than that great, clumsy, bumbling, over-
confident—"

"Please, Mr. Habibula!" Jartha broke in, and Ethyra Coran
raised a hand to hide an even broader smile. Habibula slithered
to a red-faced halt, and the colonel spoke quickly before he
could start up once more. "All our sources assured us Martha fell
far short of your stature, Mr. Habibula," he soothed, "and that
was the reason we recruited Miss Coran to contact you. We need
a man with a certain talent, you see, and this was our way to be
sure you had it."

"A *test*, was it?" Habibula glared at him, angered, despite his
circumstances, by the touch to his pride of Matha's name.

"Indeed it was," Jartha assured him, "and one you passed with
flying colors. Major Hazell"—he nodded to the younger man
standing behind him—"doubted you could do it, but I had complete faith in you."

"Ah?" Habibula seemed to deflate suddenly and heaved an
enormous sigh. "Well, it's a mortal pity the major was right, then,
isn't it?" He shook his head. "Twenty fearsome years of practice
—aye, and the most cunning mind with machines you're like to
see in your life, Colonel Jartha—and I've not the least tiniest
idea how it was I tripped myself up. The mortal shame of it! Giles
Habibula to put his foot in a trap he never even saw!"

"But that was because we cheated at the very end, Mr.
Habibula," Jartha said almost compassionately. He took the
knapsack from the enormous Legionnaire and withdrew the bottle of Crocyrean Brandy. "Fifty-one," he observed. "I believe most
connoisseurs regard this as the finest year ever."

"That they do, and with mortal good reason," Habibula said, gray eyes clinging to the bottle with a sort of desperate sorrow as it slipped further from his grasp.

"But it isn't," Jartha said. "Brandy, I mean. This bottle is a fake." Habibula stared at him, and Jartha tossed it back to the legionnaire. "There's a motion sensor and an ultrawave homing device in it, Mr. Habibula. I knew a man of your discerning palate could never pass by '51 Crocyrean, so—"

"The cold, cunning heart of the man!" Habibula said indignantly. "To trap poor Giles Habibula with an *empty* bottle? An empty bottle of the '51?! You're not human, Colonel!"

"Perhaps not, but I *do* need you, and I'm afraid that *this*"—he dug back into the knapsack and extracted the huge ruby—"is the *real* Dragon's Eye. We've caught you red-handed in its theft, Mr. Habibula. I'd say you're looking at ten to twenty years in the uranium mines of Pluto."

"But it was you yourself set me on to steal the lovely, wicked thing," Habibula pointed out shrewdly, "and that makes you an accomplice!"

"No, Mr. Habibula. It makes *Miss Coran* an accomplice. I'm not even here."

"You're not—?!" Habibula glared at the colonel for a moment, then darted a look at Ethyra Coran, and the beautiful, sable-haired young woman had gone quite pale. He clenched his jaws until his teeth hurt, then turned his baleful gray eyes back to Jartha. "You've gone to a mortal lot of trouble just to trap poor Giles—aye, and this lass, too, it seems. So what might it be you're wanting of us, Colonel John Jartha?"

"Miss Coran's part is done, assuming *you* accept my terms, Mr. Habibula."

"And what might those terms be?"

"The Legion of Space is the Green Hall's first line of defense," Jartha replied in a voice that was suddenly deadly serious, "but its *final* defense is the device known as AKKA. Have you heard of it?"

"Aye, of course I have. Everyone in the mortal System's heard of it!"

"Then you know that there can never be more than a single keeper of the weapon, only one individual who knows the secret of its construction and operation?" Habibula nodded, and Jartha went on heavily. "Unfortunately, that isn't *quite* the truth of it, Mr. Habibula. Only one person may ever *know* the secret at one time, yet we can never be certain that no accident or disease will overtake the present Keeper before he or she can pass it on to his or her successor. And so the secret is written down, locked inside a box of adamanite which can be opened only with the fingerprints of the designated successor. Not even you could open that box's lock without them, and any attempt to force it would only destroy its contents."

"Ah?" Habibula cocked his head, considering ways he might have gone about opening such a box. To be sure, the fingerprint provision would make it mortal difficult, but unless there were other safeguards Jartha had chosen not to mention—

"Indeed," the colonel went on, breaking into his thoughts. "But the problem, Mr. Habibula, is that the box has been stolen."

"*Stolen?*" Giles Habibula paled at the fearsome implications. If someone had stolen the box, if they ever managed to open it and lay hands upon the secret of the device which had overthrown the Purple Hall and the Empire of the Ulnars, the consequences would be unthinkable.

"Stolen," Jartha agreed coldly. "We believe we know by whom, but the man in question is wealthier and more powerful than you can imagine. He could have hidden it anywhere, on any of his estates. He's already killed to secure it, and I see no reason to believe he wouldn't kill again to keep it, but the same contacts in the Green Hall which let him steal it in the first place would quickly warn him of any official move the Legion made against him. Which brings us to you, Mr. Habibula. We had that Cerberus Twelve installed especially for you. If you could defeat it and steal the Dragon's Eye, then perhaps you can also find and steal the Keeper's box back for the Green Hall."

"You're mad," Habibula said flatly. "If he's so fearsomely powerful not even the blessed Legion can defeat him, it would be madness for one man, even Giles Habibula, to cross him!"

"Perhaps, but those are my terms," Jartha said coldly. "You have a choice: accept them, or spend twenty years on Pluto for grand theft."

"Ah, you're an evil, evil man, John Jartha," Habibula said bitterly.

"No, Mr. Habibula, I'm a *desperate* man. We *must* reclaim the secret of AKKA. It's just remotely possible they may find a way to open it, or, failing that, they may attempt to kidnap Aladoree, the Keeper's daughter, and force *her* to open it. She's only three years old, Mr. Habibula. How could she stop them? And to what lengths would men ruthless enough to steal the Keeper's box go in order to force a child to obey them?"

Habibula glared at the legionnaire once more, yet the desperation in Jartha's eyes was genuine, and his own soul cringed at the thought of a child in the hands of wicked men.

"And you'd really send the man you tricked into stealing that mortal bit of rock"—he jabbed his chin at the huge gem Jartha still held—"to the wicked hell of Pluto if I say no?"

"Yes," Jartha said inflexibly. "And if I do, I'll be forced to send Miss Coran, as well."

"Desperate or no, you *are* a wicked man," Habibula said heavily, "but I've little choice. Yet before I do this, you'll put that"

—he gestured to the Dragon's Eye once more—"back where it belongs. Aye, and you'll destroy any mortal record that myself or Miss Coran ever laid hand or eye upon it. I'll not have you sending such a fearsomely beautiful lass as this to Pluto if it should happen I try and fail. Not when it was your own wicked blackmail made her trap poor Giles in the first place."

Ethyra Coran stared at him in disbelief, and Jartha's eyes narrowed.

"A noble sentiment," the colonel said after a moment, "and one I'm inclined to believe is *mostly* genuine. However, it seems to me that you've forgotten something. If I return the Eye and destroy the records, then I lose my hold on you."

"You've no need for any 'hold,' " Habibula said with dignity. "You'll have my mortal word."

"A comfort, I'm sure," Jartha said dryly. Habibula glared at him afresh, and the colonel scratched his chin thoughtfully. "No, Mr. Habibula, I have a counter-proposal. I'll return the Eye and destroy the records after *you* enlist in the Legion."

"*Enlist?* Giles Habibula sign his life away to the mortal Legion of Space?!" Habibula stared at him. "You *are* mad!" he declared with certainty.

"Not in the least. You do have a certain talent, and it's quite possible the Legion will need it again someday. More immediately, however, the sentence for desertion from the Legion is twenty years on Pluto—more, under special circumstances. I trust your word, Mr. Habibula, but I'll sleep better knowing I have a somewhat more secure grip upon your loyalties."

"Ah, to think it should come to this," Habibula said bitterly. "The Legion of Space bent on shanghaiing poor Giles Habibula! It's a fearsome, wicked thing, indeed it is, to see the Legion stoop so low."

"We do what we must, Mr. Habibula," Jartha replied calmly. He let several minutes drag by, then cocked his head. "Do we have an agreement?"

Seventeen months later, Colonel John Jartha, commander of the Legion of Space's Office of Intelligence, opened the door of his office at the very heart of the Legion's huge headquarters building and stopped dead on the threshold.

His last secret report from Giles Habibula was over six months old, and the colonel had come to the unhappy conclusion that not even Habibula had proved capable of breaking the defenses of the Green Hall's enemies. Jartha had come to like the fat, cunning rogue in the year they'd worked together, and he had felt a gnawing guilt for entrapping the man and sending him to his death, yet as he'd told Habibula that night in the cellars of Ulnar Chalet, he'd had no choice. He hadn't entirely abandoned all hope, but it was growing harder to cling to it, and he'd taken to avoiding responses to Ethyra Coran. The young woman had plagued his office with carefully, innocently worded inquiries about Habibula almost weekly. Her queries had grown almost desperate of late as the silence stretched out, yet Jartha had no heart to confirm Habibula's death to her when any tiny trace of hope remained.

But now he stood just inside his office door, staring at the small, silvery box in the middle of his desk top. It bore no insignia, no marking of any sort except two small, darker ovals—about the size of fingertips—on its top, yet he knew instantly what it was.

He crossed the office slowly and sank into his chair, staring at the box and fearing to touch it, and his mind raced. It was impossible for anyone to break the security on Legion HQ and penetrate to his office. *No one* could do that . . . except, perhaps, for one man with a certain talent.

He began to smile, and then to chuckle, and reached out to the box at last. He took it in his hand and tossed it lightly on his palm, and even through his heady relief, it seemed impossible that so small and light a thing could hold the secret of so much destruction. They'd have to improve security on it in the future, he thought, and made a mental note to discuss ways to do just that with Legionnaire Habibula.

He paused, then, and his head cocked. Speaking of Habibula . . . ?

He set the box carefully inside the safe built into his desk and spun the combination. It should be safe enough there—from anyone except Habibula, of course—until he could have it conveyed back to the Green Hall under maximum security, and with it tucked away, he could concentrate on other questions. Like the whereabouts of the man who'd stolen it back from the Solar System's enemies and flowed through Legion HQ's security like so much smoke to deposit it on his desk. Now, if he were Habibula, where would he—?

His intercom buzzed sharply, and he pressed the button.

"Yes?"

"Sir!" It was James Hazell, and his voice was high with excitement. "Sir, it's Habibula!"

"What about Habibula?" Jartha asked calmly.

"Sir, he's . . . he's *deserted!*" Hazell sputtered. "He's stolen a small space cruiser right off the Green Hall's landing field, and—"

"Stolen a cruiser, has he?" Jartha's eyes began to gleam.

"Yes, Sir! Right from under our noses—just walked aboard with a forged set of orders on stationery from *your* office, Sir!"

"Well, that was a bit precipitous of him," Jartha murmured.

"*Sir?*" Hazell sounded strangled, as if he couldn't credit his superior's calm.

"I said that was a bit precipitous of him," Jartha repeated. "I'd gladly have granted him a furlough."

There was a moment of utter, stunned silence over the intercom, and then Hazell spoke very carefully.

"Uh, Sir—Colonel Jartha—if Habibula's deserted, what about, ah . . . what about a certain *box,* Sir?"

"Oh, *that!*" Jartha chuckled. "Now that you mention it, James, I need you to organize a little security detail to return that very box to its rightful place."

"I-it's *back,* Sir?"

"Well, you could hardly return it if it weren't, now could you?" Jartha observed.

"Uh, no. No, Sir, I don't suppose I could," Hazell said slowly. There was another moment of silence, and then he cleared his throat. "And what about Habibula, Sir? Shall I alert the System patrols to intercept him?"

"I don't believe that will be necessary," Jartha said judiciously.

"But, Sir, he's a *deserter!*"

"Technically, I suppose you're correct," Jartha agreed, "but if we arrest him and send him to Pluto, we'll only have to let him out again the next time we need his talent. Think of all the time we'd waste."

"But he'll get away, Sir. If he could get the, ah, the box back for us, we'll never find him again if we don't go after him now!"

"I've told you before, James; you have too little faith in human inventiveness. I found Habibula once, and I'm sure I can lay my hand on him again any time I want to."

"You *can,* Sir?"

"Certainly. Tell me, did he leave on a course to Venus?"

"As a matter of fact, Sir," Hazell said slowly, "he did."

"Just as I thought." Jartha smiled to himself. "Don't worry about it, James," he said.

"Very well, Sir," Hazell said a bit grumpily, and Jartha switched off the intercom with another smile and opened a drawer to look at the clutch of inquiries Ethyra Coran had sent him. He scooped them up and dropped them in the disposal slot, then leaned back in his chair and folded his hands behind his head in thought for several seconds, and his smile became a grin.

He leaned forward and keyed his intercom again.

"Major Hazell," a voice replied.

"Colonel Jartha, James. There's one other thing I'd like you to do before you arrange to return the item we just discussed."

"Yes, Sir?"

"Send someone out to find us a bottle of Crocyrean Brandy— the '51—and arrange to ship it to Venus."

"Where on Venus, Sir?" Hazell asked in a resigned tone.

"Why, I'm surprised at you, James!" Jartha chided. "Send it to the Blue Unicorn, Star Island, New Chicago. Send it care of Miss Ethyra Coran . . . and be sure you enclose a card with my name on it."

Afterword

I know all about "the Williamson Effect"—it got me at a young and tender age. The very first science fiction story I actually remember reading was Jack's work. I was about twelve years old, laid up with some embarrassing childhood ailment, and my dad had *The Legion of Space* in hardcover, which I proceeded to devour. Dad had always been a great sci-fi reader, though honesty compels me to admit that *I* had been preoccupied with things like *Swallows and Amazons*, *The Black Stallion*, and *You Were There at the Battle of Concord*. But Jack changed all that. This was great stuff, full of spaceships, alien menaces, beautiful maidens, and super weapons, and I went on to find all the other Legion stories as quickly as I could. I was hooked, and from Jack I dived into Dad's collected works of Doc Smith, then Heinlein, Asimov, Murray Leinster. . . . I still read the stories I'd been reading before, but my addiction to the hard stuff began with Jack and never eased.

Over the years, I read everything of his I could get my hands on (I was a particular sucker for his and Fred Pohl's *Starchild Trilogy*), yet it was always the Legion I remembered, and I went back to read it all over again when I was in college. I'd gotten away from the thirties and forties writing style, and it was sort of a shock to the system to jump back into it, but I persevered—it was the least I could do for my first love—and the truth is that the crackle was still there. Sure, it was dated stylistically, but it was still a by-God *story*. And, as I suppose this short story indicates, I will always have an abiding weakness for Giles Habibula.

Then again, I'll always have an abiding weakness for Jack Williamson. Like the best of Giles's beloved wines, vintage Williamson travels well.

—David Weber

Most of the stories in this volume have a connection to one of Jack Williamson's story backgrounds, and Frederik Pohl's opening tale even featured Jack as protagonist. But Connie Willis has written a story that is different from all the rest, utterly charming, and completely disarming. In her own style, she offers a slice of life, contemporary yet at the same time. . . . Well, you'll see.

Nonstop to Portales

Connie Willis

Every town's got a claim to fame. No town is too little and dried out to have some kind of tourist attraction. John Garfield's grave, Willa Cather's house, the dahlia capital of America. And if they don't have a house or a grave or a Pony Express station, they make something up. Sasquatch footprints in Oregon. The Martha lights in Texas. Elvis sightings. Something.

Except, apparently, Portales, New Mexico.

"Sights?" the cute Hispanic girl at the desk of the Portales Inn said when I asked what there was to see. "There's Billy the Kid's grave over in Fort Sumner. It's about seventy miles."

I'd just driven all the way from Bisbee, Arizona. The last

thing I wanted to do was get back in a car and drive a hundred and sixty miles round trip to see a crooked wooden tombstone with the name worn off.

"Isn't there anything famous to see in town?"

"In Portales?" she said, and it was obvious from her tone there wasn't.

"There's Blackwater Draw Museum on the way up to Clovis," she said finally. "You take Highway 70 north about eight miles and it's on your right. It's an archaeological dig. Or you could drive out west of town and see the peanut fields."

Great. Bones and dirt.

"Thanks," I said and went back up to my room.

It was my own fault. Cross wasn't going to be back till tomorrow, but I'd decided to come to Portales a day early to "take a look around" before I talked to him, but that was no excuse. I'd been in little towns all over the west for the last five years. I knew how long it took to look around. About fifteen minutes. And five to see it had dead end written all over it. So here I was in Sightless Portales on a Sunday with nothing to do for a whole day but think about Cross's offer and try to come up with a reason not to take it.

"It's a good, steady job," my friend Denny'd said when he called to tell me Cross needed somebody. "Portales is a nice town. And it's got to be better than spending your life in a car. Driving all over kingdom come trying to sell inventions to people who don't want them. What kind of future is there in that?"

No future at all. The farmers weren't interested in solar-powered irrigation equipment or water conservation devices. And lately Hammond, the guy I worked for, hadn't seemed very interested in them either.

My room didn't have air-conditioning. I cranked the window open and turned the TV on. It didn't have cable either. I watched five minutes of a sermon and then called Hammond.

"It's Carter Stewart," I said as if I were in the habit of calling him on Sundays. "I'm in Portales. I got here earlier than I thought, and the guy I'm supposed to see isn't here till tomorrow. You got any other customers you want me to look up?"

"In Portales?" he said, sounding barely interested. "Who were you supposed to see there?"

"Hudd at Southwest Agricultural Supply. I've got an appointment with him at eleven." And an appointment with Cross at ten, I thought. "I got in last night. Bisbee didn't take as long as I thought it would."

"Hudd's our only contact in Portales," he said.

"Anybody in Clovis? Or Tucumcari?"

"No," he said, too fast to have looked them up. "There's nobody much in that part of the state."

"They're big into peanuts here. You want me to try and talk to some peanut farmers?"

"Why don't you just take the day off?" he said.

"Yeah, thanks," I said, and hung up and went back downstairs.

There was a dried-up old guy at the desk now, but the word must have spread. "You wanna see something really interesting?" he said. "Down in Roswell's where the Air Force has got that space alien they won't let anybody see. You take Highway 70 south—"

"Didn't anybody famous ever live here in Portales?" I asked. "A vice-president? Billy the Kid's cousin?"

He shook his head.

"What about buildings? A railroad station? A courthouse?"

"There's a courthouse, but it's closed on Sundays. The Air Force claims it wasn't a spaceship, that it was some kind of spy plane, but I know a guy who saw it coming down. He said it was shaped like a big long cigar and had lights all over it."

"Highway 70?" I said, to get away from him. "Thanks," and went out into the parking lot.

I could see the top of the courthouse over the dry-looking treetops, only a couple of blocks away. It was closed on Sundays, but it was better than sitting in my room watching Falwell and thinking about the job I was going to have to take unless something happened between now and tomorrow morning. And better than getting back in the car to go see something Roswell had made up so it'd have a tourist attraction. And maybe I'd get lucky, and the courthouse would turn out to be the site of the last hanging in New Mexico. Or the first peace march. I walked downtown.

The streets around the courthouse looked like your typical small-town post-Wal-Mart business district. No drugstore, no grocery store, no dimestore. There was an Anthony's standing empty, and a restaurant that would be in another six months, a Western clothing store with a dusty denim shirt and two concho belts in the window, a bank with a sign in the window saying NEW LOCATION.

The courthouse was red brick and looked like every other courthouse from Nelson, Nebraska, to Tyler, Texas. It stood in a square of grass and trees. I walked around it twice, looking at the war memorial and the flagpole and trying not to think about Hammond and Bisbee. It hadn't taken as long as I'd thought because I hadn't even been able to get in to see the buyer, and Hammond hadn't cared enough to even ask how it had gone. Or to bother to look up his contacts in Tucumcari. And it wasn't just that it was Sunday. He'd sounded that way the last two times I'd called him. Like a man getting ready to give up, to pull out.

Which meant I should take Cross's job offer and be grateful.

"It's a forty-hour week," he'd said. "You'll have time to work on your inventions."

Right. Or else settle into a routine and forget about them. Five years ago when I'd taken the job with Hammond, Denny'd said, "You'll be able to see the sights. The Grand Canyon, Mount Rushmore, Yellowstone." Yeah, well, I'd seen them. Cave of the Winds, Amazing Mystery House, Indian curios, Genuine Live Jackalope.

I walked around the courthouse square again and then went down to the railroad tracks to look at the grain elevator and walked back to the courthouse again. The whole thing took ten minutes. I thought about walking over to the university, but it was getting hot. In another half hour the grass would start browning and the streets would start getting soft, and it would be even hotter out here than in my room. I started back to the Portales Inn.

The street I was on was shady, with white wooden houses, the kind I'd probably live in if I took Cross's job, the kind I'd work on my inventions in. If I could get the parts for them at Southwest Agricultural Supply. Or Wal-Mart. If I really did work on them. If I didn't just give up after a while.

I turned down a side street. And ran into a dead end. Which was pretty appropriate, under the circumstances. "At least this would be a real job, not a dead end like the one you're in now," Cross'd said. "You've got to think about the future."

Yeah, well, I was the only one. Nobody else was doing it. They kept on using oil like it was water, kept on using water like the Ogalala Aquifer was going to last forever, kept planting and polluting and populating. I'd already thought about the future, and I knew what it was going to be. Another dead end. Another Dust Bowl. The land used up, the oil wells and the water table pumped dry, Bisbee and Clovis and Tucumcari turned into ghost towns. The Great American Desert all over again, with nobody but a few Indians left on it, waiting in their casinos for customers who weren't going to come. And me, sitting in Portales, working a forty-hour-a-week job.

I backtracked and went the other way. I didn't run into any other dead ends, or any sights either, and by 10:15 I was back at the Portales Inn, with only twenty-four hours to kill and Billy the Kid's grave looking better by the minute.

There was a tour bus in the Inn's parking lot. NONSTOP TOURS, it said in red and gray letters, and a long line of people was getting on it. A young woman was standing by the door of the bus, ticking off names on a clipboard. She was cute, with short yellow hair and a nice figure. She was wearing a light blue T-shirt and a short denim skirt.

An older couple in Bermuda shorts and Disney World T-shirts were climbing the stairs onto the bus, slowing up the line.

"Hi," I said to the tour guide. "What's going on?"

She looked up from her list at me, startled, and the old couple froze halfway up the steps. The tour guide looked down at her clipboard and then back up at me, and the startled look was gone, but her cheeks were as red as the letters on the side of the bus.

"We're taking a tour of the local sights," she said. She motioned to the next person in line, a fat guy in a Hawaiian shirt, and the old couple went on up the steps and into the bus.

"I didn't think there were any," I said. "Local sights."

The fat guy was gaping at me.

"Name?" the tour guide said.

"Giles H. Paul," he said, still staring at me. She motioned him onto the bus.

"Name?" I said, and she looked startled all over again. "What's your name? It's probably on that clipboard in case you've forgotten it."

She smiled. "Tonia Randall."

"So, Tonia, where's this tour headed?"

"We're going out to the ranch."

"The ranch?"

"Where he grew up," she said, her cheeks flaming again. She motioned to the next person in line. "Where he got his start."

Where who started to what? I wanted to ask, but she was busy with a tall man who moved almost as stiffly as the old couple, and anyway, it was obvious everybody in line knew who she was talking about. They couldn't wait to get on the bus, and the young couple who were last in line kept pointing things out to their little kid—the courthouse, the Portales Inn sign, a big tree on the other side of the street.

"Is it private? Your tour?" I said. "Can anybody pay to go on it?" And what was I doing? I'd taken a tour in the Black Hills one time, when I'd had my job about a month and still wanted to see the sights, and it was even more depressing than thinking about the future. Looking out blue-tinted windows while the tour guide tells memorized facts and unfunny jokes. Trooping off the bus to look at Wild Bill Hickok's grave for five minutes, trooping back on. Listening to bawling kids and complaining wives. I didn't want to go on this tour.

But when Tonia blushed and said, "No, I'm sorry," I felt a rush of disappointment at not seeing her again.

"Sure," I said, because I didn't want her to see it. "Just wondering. Well, have a nice time," and started for the front door of the Inn.

"Wait," she said, leaving the couple and their kid standing there and coming over to me. "Do you live here in Portales?"

"No," I said, and realized I'd decided not to take the job. "Just passing through. I came to town to see a guy. I got here early, and there's nothing to do. That ever happen to you?"

She smiled, as if I'd said something funny. "So you don't know anyone here?"

"No," I said.

"Do you know the person you've got the appointment with?"

I shook my head, wondering what that had to do with anything.

She consulted her clipboard again. "It seems a pity for you to miss seeing it," she said, "and if you're just passing through . . . Just a minute." She walked back to the bus, stepped up inside, and said something to the driver. They consulted a few minutes, and then she came back down the steps. The couple and their kid came up to her, and she stopped a minute and checked their names off and waved them onto the bus, and then came back over to me. "The bus is full. Do you mind standing?"

Bawling kids, videocams, *and* no place to sit to go see the ranch where somebody I'd probably never heard of got his start. At least I'd heard of Billy the Kid, and if I drove over to Fort Sumner I could take as long as I wanted to look at his grave. "No," I said. "I wouldn't mind." I pulled out my wallet. "Maybe I better ask before we go any farther, how much is the tour?"

She looked startled again. "No charge. Because the tour's already full."

"Great," I said. "I'd like to go."

She smiled and motioned me on board with her clipboard. Inside, it looked more like a city bus than a tour bus—the front and back seats were sideways along the walls, and there were straps for hanging onto. There was even a cord for signaling your stop, which might come in handy if the tour turned out to be as bad as the Wild Bill Hickok tour. I grabbed hold of a strap near the front.

The bus was packed with people of all ages. A white-haired man older than the Disney World couple, middle-aged people, teenagers, kids. I counted at least four under age five. I wondered if I should yank the cord right now.

Tonia counted heads and nodded to the driver. The door whooshed shut, and the bus lumbered out of the parking lot and slowly through a neighborhood of trees and tract houses. The Disney World couple were sitting in the front seat. They scooted over to make room for me, and I gestured to Tonia, but she motioned me to sit down.

She put down her clipboard and held on to the pole just behind the driver's seat. "The first stop on today's tour," she said, "will be the house. He did the greater part of his work here," and I began to wonder if I was going to go the whole tour without ever finding out who the tour was about. When she'd said "the ranch," I'd assumed it was some Old West figure, but these houses had all been built in the thirties and forties.

"He moved into this house with his wife, Blanche, shortly after they were married."

The bus ground down its gears and stopped next to a white house with a porch on a corner lot.

"He lived here from 1947 to . . ." She paused and looked sideways at me. ". . . the present. It was while he was living here that he wrote *Seetee Ship* and *The Black Sun* and came up with the idea of genetic engineering."

He was a writer, which narrowed it down some, but none of the titles she'd mentioned rang a bell. But he was famous enough to fill a tour bus, so his books must have been turned into movies. Tom Clancy? Stephen King? I'd have expected both of them to have a lot fancier houses.

"The windows in front are the living room," Tonia said. "You can't see his study from here. It's on the south side of the house.

That's where he keeps his Grand Master Nebula Award, right above where he works."

That didn't ring a bell either, but everybody looked impressed, and the couple with the kid got out of their seats to peer out the tinted windows. "The two rear windows are the kitchen, where he read the paper and watched TV at breakfast before going to work. He used a typewriter and then in later years a personal computer. He's not at home this weekend. He's out of town at a science fiction convention."

Which was probably a good thing. I wondered how he felt about tour buses parking out front, whoever he was. A science fiction writer. Isaac Asimov, maybe.

The driver put the bus in gear and pulled away from the curb. "As we drive past the front of the house," Tonia said, "you'll be able to see his easy chair, where he did most of his reading."

The bus ground up through the gears and started winding through more neighborhood streets. "Jack Williamson worked on the *Portales News-Tribune* from 1947 to 1948 and then, with the publication of *Darker Than You Think,* quit journalism to write full-time," she said, pausing and glancing at me again, but if she was expecting me to be looking as impressed as everybody else, I wasn't. I'd read a lot of paperbacks in a lot of un-air-conditioned motel rooms the last five years, but the name Jack Williamson didn't ring a bell at all.

"From 1960 to 1977, Jack Williamson was a professor at Eastern New Mexico University, which we're coming up on now," Tonia said. The bus pulled into the college's parking lot and everybody looked eagerly out the windows, even though the campus looked just like every other western college's, brick and glass and not enough trees, sprinklers watering the brownish grass.

"This is the Campus Union," she said, pointing. The bus made a slow circuit of the parking lot. "And this is Becky Sharp

Auditorium, where the annual lecture in his honor is held every spring. It's the week of April twelfth this year."

It struck me that they hadn't planned very well. They'd managed to miss not only their hero but the annual week in his honor, too.

"Over there is the building where he teaches a science fiction class with Patrice Caldwell," she said, pointing, "and that, of course, is Golden Library, where the Williamson Collection of his works and awards is housed." Everyone nodded in recognition.

I expected the driver to open the doors and everybody to pile out to look at the library, but the bus picked up speed and headed out of town.

"We aren't going to the library?" I said.

She shook her head. "Not this tour. At this time the collection's still very small."

The bus geared up and headed west and south out of town on a two-lane road. NEW MEXICO STATE HIGHWAY 18, a sign read. "Out your windows you can see the *Llano Estacado,* or Staked Plains," Tonia said. "They were named, as Jack Williamson says in his autobiography, *Wonder's Child,* for the stakes Coronado used to mark his way across the plain. Jack Williamson's family moved here in a covered wagon in 1915 to a homestead claim in the sandhills. Here Jack did farm chores, hauled water, collected firewood, and read *Treasure Island* and *David Copperfield.*"

At least I'd heard of those books. And Jack had to be at least seventy-nine years old.

"The farm was very poor, with poor soil and almost no water, and after three years the family was forced to move off it and onto a series of sharecrop farms to make ends meet. During this time Jack went to school at Richland and at Center, where he met Blanche Slaten, his future wife. Any questions?"

This had the Deadwood tour all beat for boring, but a bunch of hands went up, and she went down the aisle to answer them, leaning over their seats and pointing out the tinted windows. The old couple got up and went back to talk to the fat guy, holding on to the straps above his seat and gesturing excitedly.

I looked out the window. The Spanish should have named it the *Llano Flatto*. There wasn't a bump or a dip in it all the way to the horizon.

Everybody, including the kids, was looking out the windows, even though there wasn't anything much to look at. A plowed field of red dirt, a few bored-looking cows, green rows of sprouting green that must be the peanuts, another plowed field. I was getting to see the dirt after all.

Tonia came back to the front and sat down beside me. "Enjoying the tour so far?" she said.

I couldn't think of a good answer to that. "How far is the ranch?" I said.

"Twenty miles. There used to be a town named Pep, but now there's just the ranch . . ." She paused and then said, "What's your name? You didn't tell me."

"Carter Stewart," I said.

"Really?" She smiled at the funniest things. "Are you named after Carter Leigh in 'Nonstop to Mars'?"

I didn't know what that was. One of Jack Williamson's books, apparently. "I don't know. Maybe."

"I'm named after Tonia Andros in 'Dead Star Station.' And the driver's named after Giles Habibula."

The tall guy had his hand up again. "I'll be right back," she said, and hurried down the aisle.

The fat guy's name had been Giles, too, which wasn't exactly a common name, and I'd seen the name "Lethonee" on Tonia's clipboard, which had to be out of a book. But how could somebody I'd never even heard of be so famous people were named after his characters?

They must be a fan club, the kind that makes pilgrimages to Graceland and names their kids Paul and Ringo. They didn't look the part, though. They should be wearing Jack Williamson T-shirts and Spock ears, not Disney World T-shirts. The elderly couple came back and sat down next to me. They smiled and started looking out the window.

They didn't act the part either. The fans I'd met had always had a certain defensiveness, an attitude of "I know you think I'm crazy to like this stuff, and maybe I am," and they always insisted on explaining how they got to be fans and why you should be one, too. These people had none of that. They acted like coming out here was the most normal thing in the world, even Tonia. And if they were science fiction fans, why weren't they touring Isaac Asimov's ranch? Or William Shatner's?

Tonia came back again and stood over me, holding on to a hanging strap. "You said you were in Portales to see somebody?" she said.

"Yeah. He's supposed to offer me a job."

"In Portales?" she said, making that sound exciting. "Are you going to take it?"

I'd made up my mind back there in that dead end, but I said, "I don't know. I don't think so. It's a desk job, a steady paycheck, and I wouldn't have to do all the driving I'm doing now." I found myself telling her about Hammond and the things I wanted to invent and how I was afraid the job would be a dead end.

" 'I had no future,' " she said. "Jack Williamson said that at this year's Williamson Lecture. 'I had no future. I was a poor kid in the middle of the Depression, without education, without money, without prospects.' "

"It's not the Depression, but otherwise I know how he felt. If

I don't take Cross's job, I may not have one. And if I do take it—"
I shrugged. "Either way I'm not going anywhere."

"Oh, but to have a chance to live in the same town with Jack
Williamson," Tonia said. "To run into him at the supermarket,
and maybe even get to take one of his classes."

"Maybe *you* should take Cross's job offer," I said.

"I can't." Her cheeks went bright red again. "I've already got a
job." She straightened up and addressed the tour group. "We'll be
coming to the turnoff to the ranch soon," she said. "Jack Williamson lived here with his family from 1915 till World War II, when
he joined the army, and again after the war until he married
Blanche."

The bus slowed almost to a stop and turned onto a dirt road
hardly as wide as the bus was that led off between two fields of
fenced pastureland.

"The farm was originally a homestead," Tonia said, and everyone murmured appreciatively and looked out the windows at
more dirt and a couple of clumps of yucca.

"He was living here when he read his first issue of *Amazing
Stories Quarterly*," she said, "and when he submitted his first story
to *Amazing*. That was 'The Metal Man,' which, as you remember
from yesterday, he saw in the window of the drugstore."

"I see it!" the tall man shouted, leaning forward over the back
of the driver's seat. "I see it!" Everyone craned forward, trying to
see, and we pulled up in front of some outbuildings and stopped.

The driver whooshed the doors open, and everyone filed off
the bus and stood in the rutted dirt road, looking excitedly at the
unpainted sheds and the water trough. A black heifer looked up
incuriously and then went back to chewing on the side of one of
the sheds.

Tonia assembled everyone in the road with her clipboard.
"That's the ranch house over there," she said, pointing at a low

green house with a fenced yard and a willow tree. "Jack Williamson lived here with his parents, his brother Jim, and his sisters Jo and Katie. It was here that Jack Williamson wrote "The Girl from Mars" and *The Legion of Space*, working at the kitchen table. His uncle had given him a basket-model Remington typewriter with a dim purple ribbon, and he typed his stories on it after everyone had gone to bed. Jack Williamson's brother Jim . . ." she paused and glanced at me, "owns the ranch at this time. He and his wife are in Arizona this weekend."

Amazing. They'd managed to miss them all, but nobody seemed to mind, and it struck me suddenly what was unusual about this tour. Nobody complained. That's all they'd done on the Wild Bill Hickok tour. Half of them hadn't known who he was, and the other half had complained that it was too expensive, too hot, too far, the windows on the bus didn't open, the gift shop didn't sell Coke. If their tour guide had announced the wax museum was closed, he'd have had a riot on his hands.

"It was difficult for him to write in the midst of the family," she said, leading off away from the house toward a pasture. "There were frequent interruptions and too much noise, so in 1934 he built a separate cabin. Be careful," she said, skirting around a clump of sagebrush. "There are sometimes rattlesnakes."

That apparently didn't bother anybody either. They trooped after her across a field of dry, spiny grass and gathered around a weathered gray shack.

"This is the actual cabin he wrote in," Tonia said.

I wouldn't have called it a cabin. It hardly even qualified as a shack. When I'd first seen it as we pulled up, I'd thought it was an abandoned outhouse. Four gray wood-slat walls, half falling down, a sagging gray shelf, some rusted cans. When Tonia started talking, a farm cat leaped down from where it had been sleeping under what was left of the roof and took off like a shot across the field.

"It had a desk, files, bookshelves, and later a separate bedroom," Tonia said.

It didn't look big enough for a typewriter, let alone a bed, but this was obviously what all these people had come to see. They stood reverently before it in the spiky grass, like it was the Washington Monument or something, and gazed at the weathered boards and rusted cans, not saying anything.

"He installed electric lights," Tonia said, "which were run by a small windmill, and a bath. He still had occasional interruptions—from snakes and once from a skunk who took up residence under the cabin. He wrote 'Dead Star Station' here, and 'The Meteor Girl,' his first story to include time travel. 'If the field were strong enough,' " he said in the story, " 'we could bring physical objects through space-time instead of mere visual images.' "

They all found that amusing for no reason I could see and then stood there some more, looking reverent. Tonia came over to me. "Well, what do you think?" she said, smiling.

"Tell me about him seeing 'The Metal Man' in the drugstore," I said.

"Oh, I forgot you weren't with us at the drugstore," she said. "Jack Williamson sent his first story to *Amazing Stories* in 1928 and then never heard anything back. In the fall of that year he was shopping for groceries, and he looked in the window of a drugstore and saw a magazine with a picture on the cover that looked like it could be his story, and when he went in, he was so excited to see his story in print, he bought all three copies of the magazine and went off without the groceries he'd been carrying."

"So then he had prospects?"

She said seriously, "He said, 'I had no future. And then I looked in the drugstore window and saw Hugo Gernsback's *Amazing Stories,* and it gave me a future.'"

"I wish somebody would give me a future," I said.

"'No one can predict the future, he can only point the way.' He said that, too."

She went over to the shack and addressed the group. "He also wrote 'Nonstop to Mars,' my favorite story, in this cabin," she said to the group, "and it was right here that he proposed the idea of colonizing Mars and . . ." She paused, but this time it was the stiff tall man she glanced at. ". . . invented the idea of androids."

They continued to look. All of them walked around the shack two or three times, pointing at loose boards and tin cans, stepping back to get a better look, walking around it again. None of them seemed to be in any hurry to go. The Deadwood tour had lasted all of ten minutes at Mount Moriah Cemetery, with one of the kids whining, "Can't we *go* now?" the whole time, but this group acted like they could stay here all day. One of them got out a notebook and started writing things down. The couple with the kid took her over to the heifer, and all three of them patted her gingerly.

After a while Tonia and the driver passed out paper bags and everybody sat down in the pasture, rattlesnakes and all, and had lunch. Stale sandwiches, cardboard cookies, cans of lukewarm Coke, but nobody complained. Or left any litter.

They neatly packed everything back in the bags and then walked around the shack some more, looking in the empty windows and scaring a couple more farm cats, or just sat and looked at it. A couple of them went over to the fence and gazed longingly over it at the ranch house.

"It's too bad there's nobody around to show them the house,"

I said. "People don't usually go off and leave a ranch with nobody to look after the animals. I wonder if there's somebody around. Whoever it is would probably give you a tour of the ranch house."

"It's Jack's niece Betty," Tonia said promptly. "She had to go up to Clovis today to get a part for the water pump. She won't be back till four." She stood up, brushing dead grass and dirt off her skirt. "All right, everybody. It's time to go."

There was a discontented murmuring, and one of the kids said, "Do we have to go already?", but everybody picked up their lunch bags and Coke cans and started for the bus. Tonia ticked off their names on her clipboard as they got on like she was afraid one of them might jump ship and take up residence among the rattlesnakes.

"Carter Stewart," I told her. "Where to next? The drugstore?"

She shook her head. "We went there yesterday. Where's Underhill?" She started across the road again, with me following her.

The tall man was standing silently in front of the shack, looking in at the empty room. He stood absolutely motionless, his eyes fixed on the gray weathered boards, and when Tonia said, "Underhill? I'm afraid we need to go," he continued to stand there for a long minute, like he was trying to store up the memory. Then he turned and walked stiffly past us and back to the bus.

Tonia counted heads again, and the bus made a slow circle past the ranchhouse, turning around, and started back along the dirt road. Nobody said anything, and when we got to the highway, everyone turned around in their seats for a last look. The old couple dabbed at their eyes, and one of the kids stood up on the rear seat and waved goodbye. The tall man was sitting with his head buried in his hands.

"The cabin you've just seen was where it all started," Tonia said, "with a copy of a pulp magazine and a lot of imagination." She told how Jack Williamson had become a meteorologist and a college professor, as well as a science fiction writer, traveled to Italy, Mexico, the Great Wall of China, all of which must have been impossible for him to imagine, sitting all alone in that poor excuse for a shack, typing on an old typewriter with a faded ribbon.

I was only half listening. I was thinking about the tall guy, Underhill, and trying to figure out what was wrong about him. It wasn't his stiffness—I'd been at least that stiff after a day in the car. It was something else. I thought about him standing there, looking at the shack, so fixed, like he was trying to carry the image away with him.

He probably just forgot his camera, I thought, and realized what had been nagging at me. Nobody had a camera. Tourists always have cameras. The Wild Bill Hickok gang had all had cameras, even the kids. And videocams. One guy had kept a videocam glued to his face the whole time and never seen a thing. They'd spent the whole tour snapping Wild Bill's tombstone, snapping the figures in the wax museum even though there were signs that said, NO PICTURES, snapping each other in front of the saloon, in front of the cemetery, in front of the bus. And then buying up slides and postcards in the gift shop in case the pictures didn't turn out.

No cameras. No gift shop. No littering or trespassing or whining. What kind of tour is this? I thought.

"He predicted 'a new Golden Age of fair cities, of new laws and new machines,'" Tonia was saying, "'of human capabilities undreamed of, of a civilization that has conquered matter and Nature, distance and time, disease and death.'"

He'd imagined the same kind of future I'd imagined. I wondered if he'd ever tried selling his ideas to farmers. Which brought me back to the job, which I'd managed to avoid thinking about almost all day.

Tonia came and stood across from me, holding on to the center pole. " 'A poor country kid, poorly educated, unhappy with his whole environment, longing for something else,' " she said. "That's how Jack Williamson described himself in 1928." She looked at me. "You're not going to take the job, are you?"

"I don't think so," I said. "I don't know."

She looked out the window at the fields and cows, looking disappointed. "When he first moved here, this was all sagebrush and drought and dust. He couldn't imagine what was going to happen any more than you can right now."

"And the answer's in a drugstore window?"

"The answer was inside him," she said. She stood up and addressed the group. "We'll be coming into Portales in a minute," she said. "In 1928, Jack Williamson wrote, 'Science is the doorway to the future, scientification, the golden key. It goes ahead and lights the way. And when science sees the things made real in the author's mind, it makes them real indeed.' "

The tour group applauded, and the bus pulled into the parking lot of the Portales Inn. I waited for the rush, but nobody moved. "We're not staying here," Tonia explained.

"Oh," I said, getting up. "You didn't have to give me door-to-door service. You could have let me out at wherever you're staying, and I could have walked over."

"That's all right," Tonia said, smiling.

"Well," I said, unwilling to say goodbye. "Thanks for a really interesting tour. Can I take you to dinner or something? To thank you for letting me come?"

"I can't," she said. "I have to check everybody in and everything."

"Yeah," I said. "Well . . ."

Giles the driver opened the door with a whoosh of air.

"Thanks," I said. I nodded to the old couple. "Thanks for sharing your seat," and stepped down off the bus.

"Why don't you come with us tomorrow?" she said. "We're going to go see Number 5516."

Number 5516 sounded like a county highway and probably was, the road Jack Williamson walked to school along or something, complete with peanuts and dirt, at which the group would gaze reverently and not take pictures. "I've got an appointment tomorrow," I said, and realized I didn't want to say goodbye to her. "Next time. When's your next tour?"

"I thought you were just passing through."

"Like you said, a lot of nice people live around here. Do you bring a lot of tours through here?"

"Now and then," she said, her cheeks bright red.

I watched the bus pull out of the parking lot and down the street. I looked at my watch. 4:45. At least an hour till I could justify dinner. At least five hours till I could justify bed. I went in the Inn and then changed my mind and went back out to the car and drove out to see where Cross's office was so I wouldn't have trouble in the morning, in case it was hard to find.

It wasn't. It was on the south edge of town on Highway 70, a little past the Motel Super 8. The tour bus wasn't in the parking lot of the Super 8, or at the Hillcrest, or the Sands Motel. They must have gone to Roswell or Tucumcari for the night. I looked at my watch again. It was 5:05.

I drove back through town, looking for someplace to eat. McDonald's, Taco Bell, Burger King. There's nothing wrong with fast food, except that it's fast. I needed a place where it took half an hour to get a menu and another twenty minutes before they took your order.

I ended up eating at Pizza Hut (personal pan pizza in under five minutes or your money back). "Do you get a lot of tour bus business?" I asked the waitress.

"In Portales? You have to be kidding," she said. "In case you haven't noticed, Portales is right on the road to nowhere. Do you want a box for the rest of that pizza?"

The box was a good idea. It took her ten minutes to bring it, which meant it was nearly six by the time I left. Only four hours left to kill. I filled up the car at Allsup's and bought a sixpack of Coke. Next to the magazines was a rack of paperbacks.

"Any Jack Williamson books?" I asked the kid at the counter.

"Who?" he said.

I spun the rack around slowly. John Grisham. Danielle Steel. Stephen King's latest thousand-page effort. No Jack Williamson. "Is there a bookstore in town?" I asked the kid.

"Huh?"

He'd never heard of that either. "A place where I can buy a book?"

"Alco has books, I think," he said. "But they closed at five."

"How about a drugstore?" I said, thinking of that copy of *Amazing Stories.*

Still blank. I gave up, paid him for the gas and the sixpack, and started out to the car.

"You mean a drugstore like aspirin and stuff?" the kid said. "There's Van Winkle's."

"When do they close?" I asked, and got directions.

Van Winkle's was a grocery store. It had two aisles of "aspirin and stuff" and half an aisle of paperbacks. More Grisham. *Jurassic Park.* Tom Clancy. And *The Legion of Time* by Jack Williamson. It looked like it had been there a while. It had a faded fifties-style cover and dog-eared edges.

I took it up to the check-out. "What's it like having a famous writer living here?" I asked the middle-aged clerk.

She picked up the book. "The guy who wrote this lives in Portales?" she said. "Really?"

Which brought us up to 6:22. But at least now I had something to read. I went back to the Portales Inn and up to my room, opened a can of Coke and all the windows, and sat down to read *The Legion of Time*, which was about a girl who'd traveled back in time to tell the hero about the future.

"The future has been held to be as real as the past," the book said, and the girl in the book was able to travel between one and the other as easily as the tour had traveled down New Mexico Highway 18.

I closed the book and thought about the tour. They didn't have a single camera, and they weren't afraid of rattlesnakes. And they'd looked out at the Llano Flatto like they'd never seen a field or a cow before. And they all knew who Jack Williamson was, unlike the kid at Allsup's or the clerk at Van Winkle's. They were all willing to spend two days looking at abandoned shacks and dirt roads—no, wait, *three* days. Tonia'd said they'd gone to the drugstore yesterday.

I had an idea. I opened the drawer of the nightstand, looking for a phone book. There wasn't one. I went downstairs to the lobby and asked for one. The blue-haired lady at the desk handed me one about the size of *The Legion of Time*, and I flipped to the Yellow Pages.

There was a Thrifty Drug, which was a chain, and a couple that sounded locally owned but weren't downtown. "Where's B. and J. Drugs?" I asked. "Is it close to downtown?"

"A couple of blocks," the old lady said.

"How long has it been in business?"

"Let's see," she said. "It was there when Nora was little because I remember buying medicine that time she had the croup.

She would have been six, or was that when she had the measles?
No, the measles were the summer she . . ."

I'd have to ask B. and J. "I've got another question," I said, and
hoped I wouldn't get an answer like the last one. "What time
does the university library open tomorrow?"

She gave me a brochure. The library opened at 8:00 and the
Williamson Collection at 9:30. I went back up to the room and
tried B. and J. Drugs. They weren't open.

It was getting dark. I closed the curtains over the open windows and opened the book again. "The world is a long corridor,
and time is a lantern carried steadily along the hall," it said, and, a
few pages later, "If time were simply an extension of the universe,
was tomorrow as real as yesterday? If one could leap forward—"

Or back, I thought. "Jack Williamson lived in this house from
1947 to . . ." Tonia'd said, and paused and then said, ". . . the
present," and I'd thought the sideways glance was to see my reaction to his name, but what if she'd intended to say, "from 1947 to
1998"? Or "2015"?

What if that was why she kept pausing when she talked, because she had to remember to say "Jack Williamson *is*" instead of
"Jack Williamson *was*", "*does* most of his writing" instead of "*did*
most of his writing," had to remember what year it was and what
hadn't happened yet?

" 'If the field were strong enough,' " I remembered Tonia saying out at the ranch, " 'we could bring physical objects through
space-time instead of mere visual images.' " And the tour group
had all smiled.

What if they were the physical objects? What if the tour had
traveled through time instead of space? But that didn't make any
sense. If they could travel through time they could have come on
a weekend Jack Williamson was home, or during the week of the
Williamson Lectureship.

I read on, looking for explanations. The book talked about quantum mechanics and probability, about how changing one thing in the past could affect the whole future. Maybe that was why they had to come when Jack Williamson was out of town, to avoid doing something to him that might change the future.

Or maybe Nonstop Tours was just incompetent and they'd come on the wrong weekend. And the reason they didn't have cameras was because they all forgot them. And they were all really tourists, and *The Legion of Time* was just a science fiction book and I was making up crackpot theories to avoid thinking about Cross and the job.

But if they were ordinary tourists, what were they doing spending a day staring at a tumbledown shack in the middle of nowhere? Even if they were tourists from the future, there was no reason to travel back in time to see a science fiction writer when they could see presidents or rock stars.

Unless they lived in a future where all the things he'd predicted in his stories had come true. What if they had genetic engineering and androids and spaceships? What if in their world they'd terraformed planets and gone to Mars and explored the galaxy? That would make Jack Williamson their forefather, their founder. And they'd want to come back and see where it all started.

The next morning, I left my stuff at the Portales Inn and went over to the library. Checkout wasn't till noon, and I wanted to wait till I'd found out a few things before I made up my mind whether to take the job or not. On the way there I drove past B. and J. Drugs and then College Drug. Neither of them were open, and I couldn't tell from their outsides how old they were.

The library opened at eight and the room with the Williamson collection in it at 9:30, which was cutting it close. I was there at 9:15, looking in through the glass at the books. There was a bronze plaque on the wall and a big mobile of the planets.

Tonia had said the collection "isn't very big at this point," but from what I could see, it looked pretty big to me. Rows and rows of books, filing cabinets, boxes, photographs.

A young guy in chinos and wire-rimmed glasses unlocked the door to let me in. "Wow! Lined up and waiting to get in! This is a first," he said, which answered my first question.

I asked it anyway. "Do you get many visitors?"

"A few," he said. "Not as many as I think there should be for a man who practically invented the future. Androids, terraforming, antimatter, he imagined them all. We'll have more visitors in two weeks. That's when the Williamson Lectureship week is. We get quite a few visitors then. The writers who are speaking usually drop in."

He switched on the lights. "Let me show you around," he said. "We're adding to the collection all the time." He took down a long flat box. "This is the comic strip Jack did, *Beyond Mars*. And here is where we keep his original manuscripts." He opened one of the filing cabinets and pulled out a sheaf of typed yellow sheets. "Have you ever met Jack?"

"No," I said, looking at an oil painting of a white-haired man with a long, pleasant-looking face. "What's he like?"

"Oh, the nicest man you've ever met. It's hard to believe he's one of the founders of science fiction. He's in here all the time. Wonderful guy. He's working on a new book, *The Black Sun*. He's out of town this weekend, or I'd take you over and introduce you. He's always delighted to meet his fans. Is there anything specific you wanted to know about him?"

"Yes," I said. "Somebody told me about him seeing the magazine with his first story in it in a drugstore. Which drugstore was that?"

"It was one in Canyon, Texas. He and his sister were going to school down there."

"Do you know the name of the drugstore?" I said. "I'd like to go see it."

"Oh, it went out of business years ago," he said. "I think it was torn down."

"We went there yesterday," Tonia had said, and what day exactly was that? The day Jack saw it and bought all three copies and forgot his groceries? And what were they wearing that day? Print dresses and double-breasted suits and hats?

"I've got the issue here," he said, taking a crumbling magazine out of a plastic slipcover. It had a garish picture of a man being pulled up out of a crater by a brilliant crystal. "December, 1928. Too bad the drugstore's not there anymore. You can see the cabin where he wrote his first stories, though. It's still out on the ranch his brother owns. You go out west of town and turn south on State Highway 18. Just ask Betty to show you around."

"Have you ever had a tour group in here?" I interrupted.

"A *tour* group?" he said, and then must have decided I was kidding. "He's not quite that famous."

Yet, I thought, and wondered when Nonstop Tours visited the library. Ten years from now? A hundred? And what were they wearing that day?

I looked at my watch. It was 9:45. "I've got to go," I said. "I've got an appointment." I started out and then turned back. "This person who told me about the drugstore, they mentioned something about Number 5516. Is that one of his books?"

"5516? No, that's the asteroid they're naming after him. How'd you know about that? It's supposed to be a surprise. They're giving him the plaque Lectureship week."

"An asteroid," I said. I started out again.

"Thanks for coming in," the librarian said. "Are you just visiting or do you live here?"

"I live here," I said.

"Well, then, come again."

I went down the stairs and out to the car. It was 9:50. Just enough time to get to Cross's and tell him I'd take the job.

I went out to the parking lot. There weren't any tour buses driving through it, which must mean Jack Williamson was back from his convention. After my meeting with Cross I was going to go over to his house and introduce myself. "I know how you felt when you saw that *Amazing Stories* in the drugstore," I'd tell him. "I'm interested in the future, too. I liked what you said about it, about science fiction lighting the way and science making the future real."

I got in the car and drove through town to Highway 70. An asteroid. I should have gone with them. "It'll be fun," Tonia said. It certainly would be.

Next time, I thought. Only I want to see some of this terraforming. I want to go to Mars.

I turned south on Highway 70 towards Cross's office. ROSWELL 92 MILES, the sign said.

"Come again," I said, leaning out the window and looking up. "Come again!"

Afterword

Two years ago I had the privilege of speaking at the Jack Williamson Lectureship Weekend in Portales, New Mexico. It gave me the opportunity not only to spend time with Jack, but also to do the "onsite research" for this story, which consisted of a delightful day at the ranch with Jack's family, highlighted by wonderful conversation and the best asparagus (and the most) I have ever eaten in my life. When I was asked to do a story for this collection, I knew exactly what I wanted to write about.

Writing the story also gave me the chance to reread all of Jack's early stories. A lot of the science fiction written in the thirties and forties dates badly (and not just because of the heat rays and vacuum tubes) and has only historical interest. But Jack's stuff is as fresh as it was the day it was written. "Deadstar Station," "Jamboree," and, of course, "Nonstop to Mars," would sell in a flash to *Analog* or *The Magazine of Fantasy and Science Fiction* today.

Mostly though, "Nonstop to Portales" let me write about Jack, who is my flat-out favorite person in the field. He is a man of extraordinary talent and consummate humility, of penetrating intelligence and great kindness, a scholar and a gentleman. We are unbelievably lucky to have him as one of the forefathers of the field.

—Connie Willis

We are a lucky generation. Here, just shy of the millennium, we can marvel at the wonders of twentieth-century technology, twentieth-century art, twentieth-century "civilization" . . . and in our midst are not one, but two of the immortal science fiction writers who have shaped the field almost from its very beginning. Andre Norton is, in her own way, like Jack, a uniquely creative mind with principles that have stood the test of time to guide generations of readers, of seekers.

If Jack has been one of the visionaries of science fiction, then Andre Norton has been its strong soul, her own visions searing in their truth and brilliance. Only she could have written the following counterpoint to "With Folded Hands." Calling on resources outside the technology of the future, she sounds a call that resonates down the mountains, across the prairies, and through the valleys of this vast continent that she and Jack call home. Like Jack's, her voice, too, will be heard by future generations of seekers.

No Folded Hands

Andre Norton

Jules Bearclaw watched the ant caravan move into sight down the highway, swinging his field glasses carefully about—not that he expected any of the ants to catch sight of a sun glint on a bit of glass so far above their heads that it might have been borne along by an eagle. It was just as it had been for a week now—a trail of trucks swinging along, each with its ant in charge, heading in toward the white man's country. They were always precisely in line, the same distance from each other, and they never stopped.

Now he did slide around on his vantage point and put to his lips an age-smoothed horn pipe. He blew three warn notes. And caught the very faint answer to his action.

There was a powwow to outrank all powwows back in the desolate desert lands into which the ants had not yet come. For the first time in the history of the oldest tribe, one-time enemies consorted with their most bitter foes, hands sped in hand talk between peoples of the north, the far south, the west and the midcountry—or else they used the English they had learned in school or the army to warily examine the problem of the universal enemy.

Of course some of the People argued that it was best to simply let the white man suffer from his own greed. That was before the ants moved in on Ledbetter's trading post. But it was the stories that such as Bearclaw himself told of the coast cities through which discharged veterans from the late overseas war had come which alarmed enough of the influential shamans to consider factors, then tentatively approach their peers in other tribes until there was an interlocking system of communication from north to south.

The ants were not of this world; that had seemed a smoke tale at first, but there were enough telling it to give it truth. They had landed in great sky ships—claiming to be from the stars. Then—they had taken over the world—or were fast occupying the civilized parts of it as quickly as possible.

Not that they destroyed life. On the contrary, they encouraged it in their own smothering fashion. They built new homes for the creatures native to this planet, they produced every luxury for the asking—their one rule stated over and over was that mankind must be protected, not allowed any chance to injure himself or others. Thus they simply bound men into cocoons where they became larvae that would never come to life again.

So far they did not move in upon the People. He wondered now briefly what might be happening in other places—Africa, or the eastern jungle lands he has known for himself. There was greed enough for the white man's wealth and sloth enough for it to be enjoyed. Or were the natives there already seeing what had become of those who accepted the ants, and so were looking about for their own weapons?

The caravan of trucks came at a steady speed and was fast approaching the cliff where he lay as still now as a hump of the native rock. One—two—four—five—the sixth one seemed to have lost speed. Through the air the purr of engines developed a discordant note. So—Jim Twoknives had managed it! Bearclaw grinned, but kept an eye on the trucks that were now pulling away from the clanking one. Would they all stop? There did not appear to be any lag, and they were now a respectable distance away from that last one.

Perhaps the ants depended on each to settle his own difficulties. This was like the report delivered three days ago from a Ute scouting party. They had seen a truck fall behind, the ant disembark from its interior and set to swift work on the engine.

Yes, the Old Ones were with them this day also! The ailing truck drew to the side of the road and the ant, all in his shining armor, climbed out.

Once more Bearclaw sounded the signal and this time he was answered from nearby. There began a steady thumping, following an erratic pattern. He poked the feather balls deep in his ears for his own defense, and his hands were shaking when he had done.

For a space the ant did not seem to notice. Then it dropped a tool, swayed nearly off its feet when it stopped to pick that up. A moment later it fell back with a clang against the side of the truck and slid down. Both of its metal hands wavered toward its round bowl of a head, and that was shaking back and forth now wildly, in broken rhythm with the hidden drums.

Bearclaw went into full action. He slipped down the slope that had brought him to his hiding place, the cliff now between him and the road. Tearing off his hat he waved it vigorously and saw the dust of the approaching horses as the scouting party came up.

The horses were spooked by the drums, though not as badly affected as human ears. They were left in charge of one of the party while Bearclaw and Jim Whiterock unlashed the burden the one pony had carried.

They made no move to draw weapons, though two of them shouldered Uzis and the rest had sidearms well to hand. The ants *might* just be blown up with a well-placed grenade, as they had discovered some time ago. But the result had been an intense searching of the surrounding territory from which the experimenter had barely escaped. And after all they were not to count coup on dead ants but to capture a live one for the shamans to use for an experiment.

The drums were still in force as they rounded an outcrop of cliff and saw the stalled truck. They could feel the erratic rhythm through their bodies, and it required a man's near full strength to hold steady against it.

The ant was on its feet again, but weaving back and forth, its large eyes like fire coals. It was jabbering away—some English, other words that made no sense at all. Bearclaw gave a hand signal.

The triple-woven net flew out and, though the creature took a step back, it was caught while the men around it hastily wrapped the folds tighter and tighter. It was stumbling along a prisoner in spite of its struggles as they returned the way they had come.

Bearclaw, having seen that the captive was as well secured as their preparations could make it, padded on into another jag of the cliff. The four drummers, their sparse gray hair woven with red strips of fur to give them proper warrior length, which the passing years had denied them, sat in a line. Their eyes were near buried in the deep creases of sun wrinkles but were wide open, staring at him without losing a single beat of palm against the stretched hide of hand drums. He made a swift hand signal.

As one the wrinkled hands no longer struck the drums. For a second or two Bearclaw felt slightly dizzy. It took a couple of deep breaths to assure himself that that part of the ordeal was over.

"The ant is netted, then, Younger Brother?" That was Ashdweller of his own clan who rightly broke silence first.

"It is, Elder Brother. We are ready to ride."

They were already slinging their drums and getting stiffly to their feet. One of them, the Dakota, had stiff-jointed difficulty in that, but none allowed themselves to note that weakness. Being peers in power-raising, it did not matter that their old bodies sometimes betrayed them.

There was another group of horses being led out, and the drummers made it into their saddles. Ashdweller allowed his mount to pace forward toward the waiting Bearclaw while his three late companions were trotting already.

"There will be storm soon—"

The younger man nodded. "We shall push the pace, Elder Brother, make sure of that. Those who dance the thunder will not be left without the reward of seeing what can be seen."

They had to ride single file for a while, and it was behind Bearclaw's tough trail horse that the ant was bundled along on its own two feet, which had been carefully freed for that purpose. At first it had continued to twitch and shake its head, but now it walked with confidence, showing no sign of any discomfort.

"Why did you do this?" Its voice was metallic, but not unpleasant, and it spoke English as if that were its native tongue.

There was no need either to inform or to argue with the creature, Bearclaw knew. He had scouted enough into the territory these creatures now ruled to know that each one was merely a scraping of the main enemy and had no will nor mind of its own.

He thought back over the hard months just behind—the embarkation into a city far removed from the one he remembered—new houses gleaming, set in carefully tended parklike surroundings—no haste, no noise, no clutter. It had not taken him long to be suspicious. A world was not transformed overnight for no reason. His own squad of communication experts had kept to themselves; perhaps in all of them the age-old suspicion of the ways of the white skins awoke. While the man they had fought beside seemed eager to accept the new way of life, their own body of men had watched and waited. At Bearclaw's suggestion they had spread out through the city, putting on the guise of amazed innocents. Three of them had discovered the underlying truth on the same day—

The ants ruled. Ruled not with guns, terror, and death as their strengths, but with the aid of man's own greed for the luxuries of life. But what these creatures judged good for man was sucking out of those in their nets all that was truly life. Tools were outlawed—they held potential harm for the users; most games were outlawed; men went dully to jobs where they watched a flow of useless knowledge across screens and might once in a while push a button.

And the rebels—they disappeared into the fine new hospitals, coming out as tin and alien in their thoughts as the ants.

But one could not fight the ants with weapons that were known. They apparently acted from one brain—Jim Hard had met with a lounger in the park who, after he had made well sure there was no one else in earshot, supplied the knowledge of the great sky ships that had brought them and the fact that those orders they obeyed came from an off-world source which no man could hope to reach.

Orders by telecommunication—when they had gathered that night they had centered in on that. They had been selected for the Signal Corps, as had happened in earlier wars, because they could talk in their native tongues without encoding and with any possible understanding by any listener who was not Navajo, Ute, Apache, or Dakota. They were young and somehow their particular group had been fired with a desire to use more than their tongues. There were manuals to be studied, and they had had the luck to serve under an officer who was obsessed with the possibility of new forms of communication—so they had learned. Learned that their only true weapon against the ants was to cut the transmission that kept the creatures in control.

It had taken time. His squad had broken up and gone to their own homes. Those who had lived in cities found their families gone—back to the reservations, as a horror of ant slavery seemed also to be a part of their own heritage.

For some time the ants had not encroached on that near-forgotten wasteland that had been left to the People. And the alienness that surrounded their always busy metal bodies was a warn-off that the whites did not seem to feel. It was then that Hanson Swift began his pilgrimage.

Shamans of the past had been mighty enough that their names were remembered for generations by the Elders. But Hanson was more than a Shaman of note—he was as much a leader of men as an always-lucky war chief. From the east he had come, slipping from tribe to tribe, always talking, to the Elders, to the young, to those who would listen; and those became more and more in number.

Once there had been a league of tribes in the east who had

kept peace among themselves over many generations. Oneida sat beside Mohawk in council, and all men spoke their minds until there was agreement.

Now there was an awakening among all the tribes such as there had not been since they had been beaten to the dust by the invaders from overseas. Shamans might be jealous of their powers at first, but they were drawn into one accord sooner or later.

Now the knowledge of those wisdom keepers from nearly a dozen nations was centered in the southwestern desert land, and they awaited what Bearclaw tugged behind him, its metal feet clanging against rock. The stream of talk the thing had spouted at first had died away as they continued into a land of rocks and sand, majestic cliffs and river beds dry these fifty years or more.

That the creature could be in long-distance communication with its fellows was more than a suspicion. But they could not keep the drum vibration going throughout their journey. As it was, they picked a way already studied out by a scout in which they could not be well sighted from the air. And certainly none of the machines this enemy used were for desert travel.

He was aware of signals from the broken lands about; there had been a tight network drawn about the powwow country, and he did not believe that even a real ant might walk that way without being noted. Swift had arrived two days ago with the information that had put an end to the last challenge of the Shamans.

White men spoke of luck—the people knew that certain happenings were sent and meant to be noted and made use of by their blood. Rain was a gift of the Above Ones—but it had its dangers also. Torrents of water could in moments flood usually languid streams; the touch of lightning could set off dreaded crown fire in the forest lands. And it was that lightning which seemed to be the war gift of the Above Ones in this matter.

The rumors had come early; the proof arrived with Swift and

his following of Shamans and men who had served enough with the war machines of the whites to follow the knowledge shown them by the sky itself. Lightning could knock out those controls that kept the ants about their business; not entirely—the majority of them appeared to recover after a space—but it could disconnect the unheard orders that backed their attempt to make all mankind into helpless children again.

Now they had a captive of their own to experiment with—and coming swiftly into sight was the place of proving. The Shamans had been at their conferences for days picking out a time. There had been dream fasting, ceaseless night sings, all the possible ways of summoning the attention of the Old Ones. Maybe two years ago Bearclaw would have shrugged aside the thought that there were men even among the People who could accomplish more with the full use of their minds than a weaponed and well-trained soldier could do against any enemy. Only a man never loses the blood that runs in him, can never dodge and hide from his inheritance.

Dirty drunken Indians—he had been embittered for years by such comments and sneers, ashamed for those who had become the refugees at the edges of white towns, those who had been drained of all that had given them pride in the fact that they were the People.

There were still such outcasts, yes, far too many of them. Though those who seemed to pick up the words Swift uttered spread them with nearly the same power as he could say. Men had once hidden their tattered beliefs in things beyond; now they followed them openly.

Let the ants show the white men what it meant to be helpless —comfortable after the fashion his kind held to be the proper state of mankind—but helpless—like sheep marched from one pasturage to another with no will of their own.

Bearclaw angled right, only a portion of his band following
him, but there still kept up with them one of the drummers, his
raw-boned range nose matching full stride with the others.

They fronted a canyon now. The bare rock in brilliant color
under the sun. Bearclaw caught the scents of sage added to a fire
along with other herbs—some from half the continent away.
They had been purifying this slit in the rock for a week, tying
prayer sticks in crannies wherever they could be thrust into crev-
ices of the stone wall, or into the sand along the path to be followed.

The chant took life from the drum that the lone Shaman
tapped with swift, expert fingers. And it sounded in three different tongues from the men about him—each giving their own
accent to their petition.

Bearclaw slid from his mount, one of the younger men beside
him following suit and grasping the reins of his horse along with
his own. There was no word now from the ant. Bearclaw found
himself almost uneasy at that smooth visage with its now dusty
metal skin and its huge and apparently all-seeing eyes.

"Our duty is to serve man—" The words seemed to boom,
even above the ever-forceful beat of the drum. "Ask what you
will—we shall make it yours."

Bearclaw could not believe there was any note of pleading in
that even, resonant voice. The ants had no emotions—knew no
fears—were only here to confine, herd, change a world into
something which was near actionless death.

He gave the special twist which fastened the thrice-blessed
cords that had held the creature captive. Stepped back. For a
long moment they stood so, man of humankind, thing born of
some misguided brain on another world. A thing which had no
reality in itself, only harkened to orders fed it.

"We have come to serve you—" the ant repeated. "To protect man is all our power—"

It was the Shaman who edged his bony nose forward, and his
hand slapped the drum in quick time. Bearclaw raised one hand
and pointed ahead.

The rhythm was a pain in his own head but he held himself
erect and watched. First the creature's head swung around so it
could eye the drummer. Its eyes blinked and seemed to contain a
spark of fire far in their bubble depths.

Its arms clicked upward, moving jerkily, its fingers reaching
toward its head. Then it turned a little and went, not with the
calm swing with which it had marched, but jerkily.

Meanwhile about them the day was darkening. The horses
threw up their heads and two whinnied. There was no need for
any of them to look to the sky. Had there been any doubt left
among them it was gone. What came was Shaman-called—
called by such a gathering of power as this country had never
known. Perhaps had it been possible to do so in the past there
would have been no white men walking the land—though the
action it was designed for now was striking at something else—
at that unseen, space-spun thread which united the ants with the
indestructible brain that had set them about their conquest and
made prisoners, after a fashion, of half the world.

They turned their backs now on that wavering figure heading out into the open. Sand twists were rising; they had barely
time to reach the shelter already staked out—to loose the horses
and to climb up into the place of the old ones, Those Gone
Before; to throw themselves down in what shelter the time-
cracked buildings would afford, and wait.

Rain dances—yes—the people of the mesas had danced
down the rain for untold centuries. It had become something

that the white man came to watch and wonder at. But united to the rain dance now was the Calling—That Which Dwelt in the Woodlands of the North and East, That Which Climbed near Sun High, That Which was the very strength of their own bones and blood.

The shaman caressed his small drum with the sweep of his palm, but there was no way to hear its answer. For then their sound struck from mountain top to mountain top—the brilliant flash of lightning seeming far more frightening than any storm brought before. And through all the clamor of the wind and that thunder Bearclaw could somehow feel a vibration within his own body. Yet it did not assault as had that which had taken the ant prisoner. No, instead this gave him a feeling of power as if the lightning itself flooded along his veins—that he could point a finger and scar a mountain. This was in him, of him, it fed somehow upon what it was and yet he was not consumed, only strengthened.

He closed his eyes and saw—

Was this thing like the medicine dreams of a would-be warrior? No, he was already proven on the war trail. Nor was he a Shaman with the jealously guarded powers passed from one generation to the next.

Still he saw—

It was as if he were given wings and had soared out into the furious buffeting of the storm. Yet it did him no harm, nor would it. Below him stood the ant—stood? No, its knees bent; it fell upon them. And from its head, like the line that might have taken a fish, was a thin line—extending not upward into the heavens as he had thought—traveling westward.

That which was now Bearclaw followed the line until it came to join with others. He recognized beneath him the trucks that he had watched hours earlier.

Out of nowhere struck an arrow of the same brilliancy as the lightning. It did not cut the cord. Now, rather it melted into it, speeding through those others below. The bait had been taken, now the catch was waiting.

The whirls of wind-raised sand were high, but they did not hide the truck from that which was now Bearclaw, scout in a new and different war. Suddenly the head truck went off the road. The one behind grazed it, and they all came to a stop.

That cord down which the arrow had slid so easily snapped out of sight. There was a sharp upward blaze from those still mingled on the ground. Then a thicker stem also reached ahead into a distance that the sand storm and then the burst of wind and rain covered.

Still that which had summoned Bearclaw kept him aloft— until he saw those other cords snuff out. Then he was lying, head on arm, in the place of the Old Ones with the roar of the storm heavy in his ears. Only he knew what he had seen, and surely he had not been the only one who had witnessed that. There were too many of the spirit-trained Elders who must have taken the same sky trail, though he had not seen or sensed their company. But he knew—the ants were surely tied, and those ties could be broken. At least the country claimed by the People could be freed from their snares and prisons. Let the white man sit prisoner among them if he so wished—there was none of the old strength in *him*.

Bearclaw looked at his own callused hands and expanded each finger to its furthest extent. Here were no folded hands.

Afterword

There are forceful stories which make such an impression on the reader that it lingers for years. "With Folded Hands" is a classic. It is also a story which makes the reader uneasy and with a not too far hidden spark of that old fearsome feeling—what if?

It is undoubtedly taking a very great liberty on my part to turn to that fine example in the Hall of Fame with an answer. I expect wholehearted disagreement with this answer. However, it is also a deep-held belief of mine that there *are* phases of human consciousness and abilities which we have not learned to use to the utmost. And the values of one race are not always those of another. So because I have been haunted for years by "With Folded Hands," I am now daring to provide an answer—which I hope Mr. Williamson will be kind enough not to blast into the farthest reaches of space.

—Andre Norton

There's a line where truth and fiction meet. Mike Resnick won't tell me whether the following is the one or the other, and Jack Williamson isn't talking either. I just hope I'm not around when we find out.

Darker Than You Wrote

Mike Resnick

You lied, Jack.

Yeah, I know, you had to change his name to Will Barbee for legal reasons. I have no problem with that. And you embellished a little here and a little there. That's okay; it's what novelists do.

But you know what they say about Karen Blixen's *Out of Africa* —that every single sentence is true, but the book, taken as a whole, is a lie?

Same thing with *Darker Than You Think*.

You took Jacob Bratzinger—I'm sorry: Will Barbee; whoever heard of a protagonist called Bratzinger?—and romanticized the hell out of him. Made him some kind of hero. Even gave him a happy ending. You did all that just to make a sale.

Well, let me state for the record that he wasn't romantic, and he was no hero, and, above all, he didn't end happily.

I know. I was there.

I'm sure shrinks hear a lot of strange stories during their working hours. So do fantasy editors and Hollywood producers, and any tourist who ever tries to walk past a beggar in a Third World city. But let me tell you, *nobody* hears as much out-and-out unbelievable bullshit as your friendly neighborhood bartender.

That's me.

I remember that Jake used to come around in the afternoons. A lonely drinker. Never had anyone with him, never tried to make friends with anyone once he got here. Stayed down at the far end of the bar and minded his own business. Always had an expression on his face that made you hope he was drinking to forget and that he'd succeed, because it looked like what he was remembering was pretty grim stuff.

He always left before sundown. Made no difference to me: I figured he worked a night shift. But then he started coming in all torn up, like he spent his nights prizefighting. Except that he wasn't black-and-blue, the way you'd expect him to be after a fight. No, sir, he was all ripped up, just like I said. He healed pretty fast, didn't bother going to the doctor except for some of the more serious wounds, never complained about the pain.

Since he usually showed up around two or maybe two-thirty, and he left before six, he and I spent a lot of time together with nobody else around, and finally, after maybe half a year, he loosened up and started telling me his story. I didn't believe it at first, but what the hell, it helped pass the time, so I dummied up and listened to him.

I gather that he was telling it to you at pretty much the same time, maybe in the mornings, and he kept waiting for your book to come out. He was sure some scientist would read about him and do something to cure him, though in retrospect I don't know what they could have done.

But then you crossed him up, Jack. You changed his name and gave him a girlfriend and passed it off as science fiction. You'll never know how close he came to killing you when *Darker Than You Think* came out.

Only one thing stopped him, and that was that he was sick of killing. You know, if he'd been a werewolf, if lycanthropy was all there was to it, if the old legends were right, I think he could have adjusted, I really do.

But you know that wasn't true, and you even told your readers. Jake didn't turn into a wolf. Not him. He was a tiger one day, and a roc—you called him a pterosaur—the next. He knew a girl—he wasn't involved with her, he just happened to share a hunting ground—named June (you called her April, remember?) who became a she-wolf at nights. And then there was Ben Sacks—you wrote him out of the book completely—who was a puma.

And even knowing all that, knowing that the flesh-eaters weren't confined to one kind of body, that they weren't all wolves or vampire bats or any of the other creatures out of legend, you still didn't see it, you never drew the connection.

But Jake learned it early on, and so did all of the others. He didn't shrivel in the sunlight like some bad Dracula movie, you know. He didn't instantly turn back into a man, either. It was a slow process, a gradual transformation, that took maybe ten or twelve minutes.

And during that time, he learned the awful, hideous truth, not about himself but about his world. *Our* world. For just as followers outnumber leaders and prey outnumber predators, so did those humans who turned into sheep and goats and cattle far outnumber Jake and his kind. It was presumptuous of him—and you—to think that only a handful of men and women underwent the Change at nights, or that those who changed all became nocturnal hunters.

Jake would make his kills, clean and swift, in the dead of night. He'd drag the carcasses to places of safety, where competing carnivores couldn't see or scent them. And then he'd dine on them, as he was meant to dine: tearing at their flesh, lapping up their blood, swallowing huge mouthfuls of meat. It was perfectly natural.

Until morning came, and the Change began, and it afflicted both predator and prey, and he'd find himself crouching over a half-eaten child, or a partially-consumed woman, and he realized how true was the old saying that you are what you eat, and he was once again a man.

He hated himself for it. His only hope was your book, and then you turned it into a novel, and after that he didn't have any hope at all. He started drinking more heavily, and the haunted look in his eyes grew worse and worse.

It only took another two weeks before he put a gun to his head, right there in the bar, and blew his brains out. Yeah, I know you hadn't heard, Jack; he asked me not to tell you.

That was, let me see, damned near half a century ago. Of course, I don't age the way normal men do. No reason why I should; I'm no more normal than Jake was. The Change just hit me a little later, that's all.

His very last wish was that I avenge him. It took me a long time to figure out what he meant. I mean, hell, he killed himself, so I could hardly take my vengeance out on him. And while it's true that the world made him what he was, I wouldn't begin to know how to destroy the world. So I thought about it, and thought about it, and finally I decided that he meant I should pay you a visit, Jack. He counted on that book of yours, and you let him down. I finally sold my business and retired last month, so now I'm ready to do what has to be done.

They tell me you're a pretty smart fellow, and that you're still working well into your eighties. That's good; I admire brains and industry. I figure you're probably a raccoon, or maybe a badger.

Me, I'm a wolverine. And unlike Jake Bratzinger, I don't have a problem with guilt at all. I *like* meat.

See you soon, Jack.

Afterword

Jack Williamson is not merely a giant in the field of science fiction, but he is the friendliest, most approachable, least awesome giant you're ever likely to encounter.

But not being awesome in person does not diminish the awesome range of his accomplishments. I've said this before, when toastmastering a convention where Jack was the guest of honor, but it bears repeating: despite the fact that he began selling science fiction in the 1920s, despite the fact that he is halfway through his eighth decade as a professional science fiction writer, despite the fact that when you're the acknowledged Dean of Science Fiction you're allowed to coast a little, Jack is the only writer around who has demonstrably improved with every passing decade.

He used to be a dedicated writer; then one day, and I can't tell you exactly when it occurred, we took a good hard look at him and he had metamorphosed into a dedicated artist.

If I can stick around as long as Jack has, and be half as well-loved and well-respected as he is, I won't have any complaints at all.

—Mike Resnick

Near Portales . . . Freedom Shouts

Near Portales, wolves
are howling above the hum
of machines. Their cries won't be
muffled by works of
technology. Freedom shouts.

—Scott E. Green

It's fitting that we end with a tale of the *other* legion. Spanning alternate realities and vast reaches of time, John J. Miller brings us Denny Lanning and the rest of his time-traveling heroes, in an exciting, poignant final chapter to this *festschrift.*

Worlds That Never Were

THE LAST ADVENTURE OF THE LEGION OF TIME

John J. Miller

i

Lethonee was lovely in the moonlight.

Dennis Lanning stood by the side of their bed, watching her sleep, thinking that she was the most beautiful woman he'd ever seen. Her long, mahogany-colored hair gleamed redly in the light spilling through the unshuttered window; her lips were slightly parted as if she were smiling in a dream. Her skin looked whiter and softer than the silk sheet lying diagonally across her torso, exposing a full breast that rose and fell with her deep, regular breathing. Lately, he thought, she was all that made paradise palatable to him.

Wide-awake and restless despite the lateness of the hour, Lanning turned from the bed and went to the window to look out upon the paradise city called Jonbar. It was a city of soaring towers, wide boulevards, and immaculate pocket-parks set among gigantic buildings. The closest thing to perfection yet created by man, Jonbar was hundreds of years beyond Lanning's native twentieth century. It owed its existence to Lanning's friend and one-time college roommate Wil McClan and his Legion of Time, the men whom Wil had rescued from the war-torn wreckage of their native timelines. Lanning, war correspondent and soldier for hopeless causes, had been their leader. They'd fought for Jonbar, had almost died for her not once but several times. Lethonee and her people had been very grateful to them, giving them apartments, food, drink, clothing, and whatever else they might desire. They'd given them everything, Lanning reflected, but purpose in their lives.

After nearly a year in Jonbar, Lanning had lately realized that he had no place in it. There were no wars to describe to the people back home, no battles to fight, no causes to support. He knew that the others felt the same emptiness. The Canadian brothers, Isaac and Israel Enders, had left Jonbar for the country. Lanning hadn't seen them in months. Emil Schorn, the bull-like Prussian zeppelin officer, was drinking excessively and brawling frequently with Boris Baranin, the Soviet rocket-flyer, his usual companion. Barry Halloran, another of Lanning's college friends, had tried to put together a couple of football teams. When that idea failed to garner popular support, Halloran drifted from one project to another, from handcrafting his own biplane to painting watercolor landscapes, finishing nothing. Lao Meng Shan,

the last of Lanning's old roommates, immersed himself in Jonbarian science, trying to master the intricacies of the dynatomic
tensors that were the basis of their technology. Despite his vast
intellect, Lao soon realized that he was years away from understanding the complexities of the *dynat.* Lately he'd been spending
most of his time writing melancholy poetry about the Chinese
homeland he would never see again.

Only Lethonee made life tolerable for Lanning. Only her
love saved him from maudlin introspection—

The window before Lanning suddenly darkened, blinked red,
then shuddered like a flickering television screen. The image of
the city was replaced by that of a man who looked disheveled,
worried, and more than a little afraid.

"Lao!" Lanning said, surprised but pleased. "It's been weeks—
over a month. What've you been up to?"

Lao Meng Shan glanced over his shoulder. When he looked
back at Lanning his dark eyes were wide, almost crazy-looking.
His hair was in uncharacteristic disarray and there were dark
bruises around his chin and jaw. Ugly circular burn spots flared
redly on his temples.

"Trouble, Denny, big trouble."

"What is it?" Lanning asked, concerned.

"Can't explain over the air. Don't know who might be listening. I'll meet you at my apartment. The *Chronion*—"

The screen blanked again, flickered, and when it stabilized it
had returned to the image of the peaceful city. Lanning frowned.
The *Chronion* was Wil McClan's time machine. It had been
severely damaged in the last battle with Gyronchi, Jonbar's bitter
enemy. Lanning hadn't seen the ship since the Legion had beaten
the Gyronchi and then settled in Jonbar.

Lanning glanced at Lethonee. She had slept through Lao's
call. She was tired, worn out as usual by the long day she'd put in

at the Museum of Man, where she was one of the directors and top researchers. Lanning slipped out of their bedroom without disturbing her, and took the lift down to the garage. He kept his Indian there, a custom-built replica of his beloved model 101 Scout. The Jonbarians had built the near-as-he-could-remember motorcycle for him—just one of the perks of being the savior of the world.

Of course, this model had some improvements over the bikes Lanning knew back home. It was powered by a tiny fusion engine. At first the nuclear reactor between his legs made Lanning feel a trifle uncomfortable, but the Jonbarians had no petrochemical industry, and he realized that asking them to drill for oil, refine it into gasoline, and ship and store the final product for his personal use would be a bit much. The Jonbarian scientists knew fusion, and knew it well. Their ultimate destiny would in fact be evolution into the *dynon*, a people capable of directing the application of atomic energy without a mechanical interface. Building a fusion-powered motorcycle was a snap for them.

The other improvements included a maintenance computer that doubled as a guidance center. Lanning only had to punch in Lao's name and the computer called up his friend's address and displayed it on the screen between the handlebars. It even showed the best route to Lao's housing block, nicely highlighted in red.

Good thing, too. Lanning didn't know exactly how big Jonbar was, but it was at least ten times the size of the largest city of his time. He'd been living in Jonbar for almost a year, but huge sections of it were still totally unfamiliar.

Lao's residence was located in one of those sections. It took half an hour of fast riding through Jonbar's never-ending traffic to reach Lao's building. Lanning parked the Indian and looked around uncertainly, realizing for the first time since he'd come to

Jonbar that even utopia has bad neighborhoods.

Not that Lao lived in a slum, but this area of Jonbar didn't compare favorably to the soaring towers and wide boulevards of the neighborhood where Lanning shared an apartment with Lethonee. Here the buildings were older, more densely packed, and designed with a more utilitarian eye. There were fewer streetlights. Some were dark and even broken. The pocket-parks between the block-sized tenements looked unkempt compared to those between the high-rises where Lanning lived. The trees were untrimmed, the grass long and wild. They looked like feral patches of forest encroaching on the slightly seedy neighborhood.

There was little traffic on the street. The hour was late and most of the people who lived around here had jobs. Lanning didn't, but then that was another one of the perks of being the world's savior. Though, of course, if he had a job he wouldn't have so much of the free time that'd been weighing so heavily on him lately.

He went up the stairs into the lobby. With caution born from years of soldiering, he waited until he could catch an empty elevator, and took it to Lao's room on the thirtieth floor. The corridor was empty and quiet, but Lanning knew something was wrong. The door to Lao's apartment was ajar, and there was a body in the entranceway.

Lanning had dealt with violent death all his adult life. Fresh out of Harvard, he'd been a war correspondent in Nicaragua. Later he fought fascism all over the world—in Ethiopia, in Spain, in the Chaco, and in China. As the captain of the Legion of Time he'd seen men blasted by Gyronchi energy weapons and torn to bits by their bioengineered insectile warriors. He never got used to it. He didn't miss that part of his old life and seeing the corpse in the doorway brought it all back with disturbing vividness.

It was the body of a woman. She might have been as beautiful as most Jonbarians, but Lanning couldn't tell because her head was missing. It had been cut jaggedly from her neck. Not torn off by brute strength, not cut crisply by a surgical instrument or energy blade, but hacked and sawed as if Jack the Ripper had been transported to the peaceful streets of this far-off time. The woman's tunic was soaked with blood, somewhat dried but still gooey-looking. A dark, gelid pool of the stuff stained the carpeting around her. A large-bladed knife that looked quite capable of performing the beheading lay in the blood. Lanning resisted the crazy momentary impulse to pick it up.

Lao—

Lanning stepped over the body and went into the apartment, calling his friend's name. No one answered. The entranceway opened up into a sitting/reception room that was dark, spartan in furnishing, clean and neat, and devoid of life. Lanning shut the door behind him, then went into the apartment's interior, looking for signs of Lao, half afraid that he'd find his friend's body, half afraid that he'd come face to face with the maniac who'd slaughtered the woman in the doorway.

But he found nothing, except the glowing computer in Lao's study. Lanning approached it carefully. He wasn't a computerphobe, exactly. He just didn't like the things, except when they were acting in such basic capacities as glorified road maps. Give him a good, old-fashioned manual typewriter any day and a glass of something cool to keep his throat wet while he battered out the story of the latest atrocity—

Lanning knew he couldn't afford such inattention. He jerked himself back to the present and looked at the short note on the screen. He frowned when he finished reading it.

Out of a madness born of hate and jealousy I have killed the only thing that I love in this world. Denny — God forgive me, and you, too. I'm going to do away with myself. Don't bother to search for my body. You'll never find it. Goodbye.

Lao had done it. He'd killed the girl.

Only . . .

Lanning read the message again. It didn't sound at all like Lao — that part about asking God's forgiveness for him was a definite false note. Lao was a scientist, and Chinese. He was half-atheist and half-Confucianist. He worshiped China, science, his family, and his ancestors. He wouldn't ask for forgiveness from an entity he didn't believe in. Also, Lanning thought, this message was damned convenient, lying out here in the open for everyone to see.

Lanning contemplated erasing the note. He even moved his hand to the keyboard, but stopped before he touched anything. He wasn't an expert, but he knew that nothing was ever really erased from a computer. Given a searcher with enough expertise, any file could be retrieved. He could get rid of the evidence by carrying off the machine — No, don't complicate things, he told himself.

Instead of destroying the supposed confession, he'd be better off looking for evidence to exonerate Lao. He pulled open the drawers of the computer hutch one by one, and in the third found something interesting enough to linger over. It was a journal, written in what Lanning recognized as Lao's handwriting — in Chinese, of course.

Lanning frowned. He'd been a Flying Tiger in China. In fact, he and Lao both had been plucked from the timestream by Wil McClan when their fighter had been shot down over Peking. He'd always been a fair hand with languages. He knew some

Chinese. He and Lao were probably the only people on the planet—except, perhaps, for some literature profs specializing in long-dead languages—who did. He wondered if he still knew enough.

He opened the journal to the last entry and scanned it quickly. He couldn't read everything, but he could make some sense out of Lao's impeccably-drawn characters. His friend had written about the *Chronion;* about Fraeya, the woman who shared his apartment and also worked on the project to repair the time-traveling vessel; about Adolpham, the project's head; about growing success; about growing fear . . .

Lanning couldn't decipher what had frightened Lao. Given time to study the journal, however, he would certainly learn more. He slipped the leather-bound book into his pocket.

"I'll take that."

Lanning started at the sudden, cold voice. He looked up to see a man standing in the doorway, blocking it. He'd come from nowhere. Even though he was big, he must have moved as quietly as a cat in gumshoes. His face was harder than most, and he wore the silver and green tunic of government service. His blond hair was cut short in contrast to current style.

"Who are you?" Lanning asked.

"Bylass. Security. Give me that book."

"This isn't what it seems," Lanning said, stalling.

"Then what is it?" Bylass asked in a grating voice.

"I'm Dennis Lanning," Lanning said, and waited for his name to do its magic. Sometimes it helped to be the savior of the world. Not that he ever took sole credit for it.

In Lanning's mind Wil McClan, mathematician, engineer, and philosopher of time, had been Jonbar's real savior. Once Jonbar had been only the merest shadow of possibility, eclipsed by the umbral blackness of the dark city of Gyronchi and its cruel warrior-queen, Sorainya. McClan had glimpsed Sorainya while scanning the geodesics, the lines of probability, and built the timeship *Chronion* to sail to her side. But the love she'd promised him had been a trap. Sorainya had wanted McClan's knowledge of the geodesics to ensure Gyronchi's triumph over Jonbar, its rival future. McClan had spent ten years in Sorainya's torture vaults before escaping to his home-time to rescue Lanning and recruit doomed soldiers for the Legion of Time. Together Lanning, McClan, Lao Meng Shan, and the others had overcome long odds to cast Gyronchi into the substanceless shadow universe of possibilities that might have been and raised Jonbar to take its place. Only Wil McClan had never seen their final triumph. Too broken to be revived, he'd died the true death while piloting the *Chronion* back to Jonbar so that the rest of the Legion could be saved.

Bylass, however, was unimpressed by Lanning's name and the things he'd done in service to Jonbar.

"Yes," he said. "One of the violent primitives who've come to our city." He gestured angrily over his shoulder, back toward the vestibule and what lay in it. "That's the work of another of you."

"Lao Meng Shan?" Lanning shook his head. "He didn't do it."

Bylass gestured toward the computer. "I've very good eyesight. I can read the murderer's confession from here." There was no weakness, pity, or understanding in his voice. Only certainty.

Lanning nodded, and held out the journal. Bylass marched forward, reached for it, and Lanning kicked him as hard as he could in the groin.

Bylass went down with a strangled groan and Lanning leaped over him. Bylass grabbed Lanning's ankle even as his face turned dark from pain. Lanning tore away, feeling sorry for him yet admiring his persistence.

Apparently Bylass had come alone. At least there were no

other Security men lurking in the apartment or the hallway outside. Lanning wondered where he'd come from, who had summoned him to the scene. He glanced down at Fraeya's corpse,
feeling a profound sadness turning into anger that raged at the
brutality and waste. He went into the corridor, closing the door
behind him.

"I'm coming, Lao," he said in a low voice. "Just hang on until I
get there. Wherever you are."

ii

Lanning was astonished to discover that Under Jonbar was as
much an engineering marvel as the city itself. The caverns of
Under Jonbar were as high as the towers above them were tall,
the buildings as huge and imposing. If Above Jonbar was the soul
of its people, Under was the internal organs: heart, lungs, stomach, and bowels. Its fusion plants gave light, warmth, and movement to the city, its pumps purified and circulated air and water,
its sewers collected and consumed all waste, its carniculture vats
grew most of Jonbar's food.

Lao's journal had led him Under. Lanning had hightailed it
out of Lao's apartment, revved up his Indian, and roared out of
sight before Bylass had stopped rolling around the floor clutch-
ing his groin. He'd used one of the parks as a refuge, the Indian's
headlamp as a light to read by.

It had been frustrating. Lanning had stumbled repeatedly
over Lao's beautiful calligraphy, unable to read many of the characters that would have made everything clear. As it was, while
scanning Lao's entries for the past three weeks, Lanning had
sensed a growing feeling of triumph, as apparently Lao and his
team neared their goal of repairing the *Chronion*, then a growing
sense of unease, as some indecipherable fear stole over Lanning's

friend. Lanning couldn't discern exactly what had frightened Lao, but something had obviously gone wrong with the project. Something wasn't as it seemed. Lao had also been a faithful diarist who made daily entries until they suddenly stopped two days ago. There was no clue why.

The trail obviously led Under, to where the *Chronion* had been beached for study and repair. Lanning stashed the Indian in a dark niche near one of the lifts that ferried the battalions of workers below the earth's surface to their jobs Under. It was near the beginning of the day's fourth six-hour shift, so there were enough workers to enable Lanning to blend in with the crowd.

A few of them looked at Lanning, whispered about him in low voices. One of the perks of being the savior of the world: public recognition. The Jonbarians were a restrained people, so they rarely went beyond whispers and surreptitious nods. He'd never been mobbed for autographs, thank God, and rarely had to fend off overzealous well-wishers, especially as the events of the Gyronchi war faded into the past. Given his current status as a quasi-fugitive, though, he wished he could blend into the background a little bit better. Since he couldn't, he told himself not to worry about it. He almost listened.

He found the *Chronion* on an open tarmac field, looking as if she were squatting on a massive tennis court without net, boundary markings, or enclosing fence. She was a strange ship with a flat, railed-off deck, a submarinelike hull, and massive metal disks fore and aft. A crystal dome enclosed the bridge in the center of the deck. The metal of her hull was pitted and stained, eaten away in places as if by corrosive acid or energy. She looked like no ship that had ever sailed the oceans or the sky, and she hadn't. She sailed the geodesics, the blue-lit abyss that encompassed all possibility, following the lines of probability that linked all the worlds that could be. She was the ship of the Legion of Time.

Lanning had fought on her decks, slept in her cabins, bled all over her. She'd been home and refuge to him, she'd bought him through the terrible battles with the Gyronchi whole and alive, back to Lethonee.

Lanning put a hand on her battered hull. She'd been badly damaged in the final battle. Will McClan had barely brought her back to Jonbar before most of her systems had collapsed. The scientists of Jonbar had had a hard time repairing her because they didn't fully understand the genius that had gone into making her. That made Lanning feel proud, and he silently saluted McClan as he climbed up the rope ladder hanging over the *Chronion*'s side.

Memories flooded him when he stood again on the deck where the Legion had fought Sorainya and her bioengineered warriors. There had been fourteen of them. Lanning, McClan, Lao Meng Shan, and Barry Halloran, college roommates. Emil Schorn, the herculean, duel-scarred Prussian. Boris Barinin, the Soviet rocket-flyer. The Canadian twins, Isaac and Israel Enders, infantrymen whom McClan had pulled out of a World War One trench. Silvano Cresto, the Spanish flying ace. Willy Rand, USN zeppelin pilot. Erich van Arneth, Austrian army lieutenant, also rescued from the debris of World War One. Colonel Jean Querard of the French army, plucked from a burning Paris during World War Two. Captain Courtney-Pharr, British flyer, and his countryman, Duffy Clark, British Navy.

Once they had been fourteen, but McClan was gone, injured beyond even the power of Jonbar's surgeons to revive. Now they were thirteen. Unlucky number, that.

Lanning went across the deck to the hatch that led down to the *Chronion*'s guts and clambered through it. The timeship's interior was lit, meaning someone was probably inside. Was Bylass right? Was Lao hiding out in familiar territory?

Deep inside the complicated mechanism wrought by the genius of Wil McClan, Lanning stopped suddenly as he saw a man
kneeling on the floor, half inside a control panel whose casing
had been removed and set aside.

"Lao!" Lanning exclaimed.

He stiffened at the sound of Lanning's voice, half rising, and
banged his head hard enough to make him swear. He backed out
of the console.

"Damn," Lao said, looking equal parts guilty and annoyed.
"You got here too soon."

Lanning didn't like the sound of that. Maybe Lao was trying
to use the *Chronion* to escape through time. "What the hell is
going on?"

Lao shook his head. "No time to explain." He dove back into
the open control board. "Let me finish here," he said, his voice
muffled as he played with varicolored bundles of wires.

"What are you doing?" Lanning asked, but Lao ignored him.
There was something wrong with his friend. Not wrong, actually, but different. Something odd that Lanning couldn't put his
finger on.

"Almost done," Lao said. Lanning waited impatiently as another thirty seconds went by. "There."

Lao pulled himself out of the bay, a look of satisfaction on his
lean face. He pushed his wire-rimmed glasses back up on the
bridge of his nose.

"*Now* can you tell me what you're doing?" Lanning asked.

Lao's face clouded, and he shook his head. "Afraid not,
Denny. But I'm sure you'll understand soon."

His eyes flickered over Lanning's shoulder. Lanning hesitated for a moment, suspecting a trick, realizing it would be a
dumb old trick, then felt embarrassed for even suspecting his
friend of something so foolish. But then he looked, following

Lao's gaze, and his eyes widened in astonishment.

Standing behind him, having approached unheard, was Barry Halloran. Barry, an All-American tackle in his college days, towered over Lanning. Due to the tricks of the timestream, Lanning was fifteen years older than his college roommate, whom McClan had gone back through time to rescue from a plane crash their senior year.

Behind Barry was Emil Schorn, bull-like in the Prussian uniform that he still insisted on wearing, and Jean Querard, the dapper Frenchman dressed in the height of Jonbarian elegance with gold trim on his sky-blue tunic. Barry was smiling, but it seemed to Lanning a sad smile with no humor in it.

"Sorry, old chum," Barry said.

"Wha—" Lanning started to say, then he saw Halloran's huge fist sweeping towards him. It exploded against his jaw. His knees went rubbery and he went down hard. In a last moment of utter clarity he realized what had been wrong with Lao. His face had been clean: unbattered, unbruised, and unburned.

iii

"Wake up, already. Wake up, will you?"

The voice was not gentle, nor was the shaking that accompanied it. Lanning felt as if his brain were sloshing around the bucket of his skull. His face hurt and his brain hurt, but there was some deeper pain that he wasn't quite able to isolate. Something more fundamental, as if the memory of a betrayal that hurt to his very core.

"Hey!" he protested, and the shaking stopped.

He opened his eyes. Bylass was kneeling over him, holding his shoulders. To say his expression was grim would have been understating infinitely. Leaning over Bylass, regarding Lanning with a brightly interested look, was another Jonbarian Lanning had never seen before. He was older, though Jonbarians always suffered their age well, and thin, with a somewhat distracted air that reminded Lanning of Wil McClan. Scientist, Lanning thought.

"Well?" Bylass asked, not gently.

"Well what?" Lanning shook off his hands and sat up under his own power. His head swam for a moment, but his eyes stayed focused, as did his brain. He remembered. Halloran. His sad smile. His big right hand.

"Don't even think of playing with me. What kind of plot are you primitive trash engaged in?"

Lanning stood. For a moment he thought it was a mistake, then the room stopped spinning and he was able to look Bylass in the eye and muster almost as much anger as the Security man.

"There's no plot, Bylass," Lanning said. He stared at the Security man, disturbed by his presence. Of course, it was Bylass's job to investigate murders and such, but Lanning didn't like the way he kept popping up wherever Lanning went.

"Explain things, then," Bylass demanded coldly.

"I . . ." Lanning hesitated. There had to be some rational explanation. But for the life of him he couldn't figure it out. "I can't."

Bylass looked at the other Jonbarian with disgust. "I told you," he said. "They're all in this together."

The older man shook his head in mild disbelief. "You see plots everywhere, Bylass. I know that's your job, but still, sometimes these things benefit from calm, rational, logical examination." He turned to Lanning and smiled briefly. "Forgive me. My name is Adolpham. I've been working with Lao Meng Shan— and Fraeya—on the *Chronion* project. I know you, of course, by reputation, Dennis Lanning."

Lanning nodded. He knew better than to offer his hand.

That custom had dropped out of use in the centuries between his and this.

"Now," Adolpham turned his mild gaze on Bylass. "What exactly is this plot that Dennis Lanning and his men are hatching?"

"I don't know," Bylass growled after a moment.

"Well, what could they be seeking? Grateful people that we are, we've given them literally everything they want and need."

Bylass was silent and after a moment Adolpham shook his head. "No, I could believe, barely, that Lao Meng Shan might lose his head and in a moment of passion commit a rather horrible crime. It seems unlikely, but I can believe it. But a full-blown plot . . ."

"I don't trust any of the primitives. They're violent, unthinking savages. I've had to deal with many of their disturbances."

"But no conspiracies to do . . . what, anyway?"

Bylass clamped his lips shut, then took refugee in incontrovertible fact. "He kicked me," he said, pointing at Lanning.

"In a moment of perhaps panic," Adolpham said, "in the misguided belief that he was helping a friend." He turned to Lanning. "Isn't that right?"

Lanning nodded. "Yes. I was wrong, even foolish. But at the time it seemed . . ."

"Reasonable," Adolpham supplied, when Lanning hesitated.

"Yes. Reasonable."

"What happened to you here?" the scientist asked, an expression of friendly concern on his face.

"I . . ." Lanning hesitated. Despite Adolpham's sudden avuncularity, he knew instinctively that he shouldn't tell him and Bylass the whole truth. He couldn't implicate his other friends in this, no matter how inexplicable their actions. It would give too much credence to Bylass's insane conspiracy theories. If they were theories. And insane. "I found Lao on board. I knew that he should surrender to the authorities, but he was frightened. He tried to run. I tried to stop him, and he slugged me."

Adolpham hmmed. He and Bylass exchanged glances, and it seemed to Lanning that neither was exactly buying his story. He wondered why they were so skeptical.

"You see," Adolpham finally said to the Security man, "a simple explanation. Now, I suggest you both leave me to my work while you go do yours. We all have a lot to do."

Bylass nodded reluctantly. "He's right," he said gruffly to Lanning. "Let's let him get back to work."

They nodded at Adolpham as they took their leave, but the scientist was already puttering with the *Chronion*'s temporal mechanism. They went up on deck, Lanning leading the way. They together stood on the bow of the timeship, looking out over the rail.

"I'm going back to headquarters," Bylass said. "I'm going to put all my people on this case. We'll hunt down this friend of yours, you can be sure of that."

Lanning shrugged. "Maybe."

"And you." Bylass's grim features suddenly became infinitely grimmer. "You hurt me, savage. I won't forget that."

He turned and went down the rope ladder.

Lanning watched him go. He was suddenly very tired. He was sure that the night was almost gone. He wouldn't be much use to Lao dead on his feet. He should go home and get some rest, and think. There were things he had to figure out. The real connection between Bylass and this case. Barry's role in it. The mystery of Lao's disappearing bruises. The mystery of Lao's disappearance, period.

Lethonee was still sleeping when he returned to their apartment and tiptoed into the bedroom. He undressed, too tired to shower, and slipped into bed next to her. She sighed in her sleep and moved against him. He put his hand on her velvety hip, his head on the pillow next to hers, closed his eyes, and fell asleep.

As he slept, Lanning dreamed.

At first they were dreams of his friend Lao. Lanning knew where he was being kept, knew how to rescue him. The other members of the Legion were urging him on, but he couldn't seem to dress correctly. He kept putting on his T-shirt, and it was always inside out. He would stop, take it off, turn it right side in, but when he'd pull it over his head it was always inside out again. Strange, he thought. He kept trying to hurry, but it never worked out right. Lao eventually died because he couldn't get dressed properly.

The dream segued into a vision of the *dynon*, the race to come, whose seeds were in the Jonbarians. They were more than human. They had direct mastery over the *dynat* and were able to control it with the force of their will, having no need for mechanical intermediaries.

They soared without planes, empowered robot-manned factories without energy plants, lit their cities without wires strung through the sky or buried under the ground. They lived in every earthly environment without causing pollution, and their home city, New Jonbar, was the glory of the galaxy, where everyone lived without fear, worry, or want.

The *dynon* who appeared in Lanning's dream was female. She had an ethereal cast to her features that wasn't entirely human. Her forehead was too high, her cheeks too narrow, her eyes too large. When Lethonee had first appeared to him, he thought it was a dream. He had fallen a little in love with her that first time he saw her, but the *dynon* only invoked in him a feeling of unease. Perhaps a twinge of fear.

"Dennis Lanning," the *dynon* said, "we need your help."

Lanning twisted in his sleep. Great, he thought, here we go again.

Look, he wanted to say, I've already done this. I've already been pulled out of my own place and time, unasked, and saved the world. Then I was trapped in the world I saved—a world so similar to my own, yet so alien that I soon found myself with nothing to do but putter meaninglessly through a succession of empty days. If I'm so lost in Jonbar, what would it be like in your world? How would the *dynon* regard mere humans? What possibly—

Lanning felt cool fingers touch his cheek and he jerked awake. Lethonee looked down at him, concern in her great violet-colored eyes.

"Were you dreaming?" she asked.

Lanning let out a long, gusty sigh. "I guess so. I hope so. One of the *dynon* had come to me, asking for my help. I wanted to help her, but was afraid to go to her alien future, afraid of my place in it."

Lethonee nodded, her hair cascading down in a mahogany wave as she leaned over the bed. "I'd say your subconscious mind is trying to work through your already existing problems."

"Problems?"

"We'll talk about it later," Lethonee said. "Right now you'd better get dressed." She wrinkled her nose. "Take a shower first. Someone's here to see you."

Lanning stood and stretched. He was still tired, but a stinging cold soaking would remedy that. "Who is it?"

Lethonee looked at him oddly. "You'll see. Hurry up."

She usually wasn't so cryptic. It must be, Lanning thought, something really important or something really strange. Perhaps both. Lethonee left the bedroom and he hurried through his shower, brushed his teeth, took his vitamins, and threw on the first clothes he could find.

When he hurried to the dining nook next to their small kitchen his hair was still damp. That didn't stop it from rising on the back of his neck when he saw who was sitting at the small table with Lethonee, drinking coffee.

The visitor looked up. "Hi," he said casually.

Lanning didn't know how he managed it, but he said "Hello," before he collapsed weakly in the last chair around the dining table, watching himself eat buttered muffins and drink coffee with Lethonee.

iv

"Surprised?" the other Lanning asked.

Lanning nodded weakly, as his doppelganger poured him a cup of coffee. "Have some. It's really good. But then you already know that."

Lanning nodded again as Lethonee looked from one to the other. "I'm sure you two have a lot to talk over—"

Lanning finally found his voice. "Stay with us."

Lethonee glanced at the other Lanning, who returned her gaze with a long, serious look of his own.

"No," she said. "I'd better go. It looks as if you two have some private matters to discuss. I'd better leave you alone."

She stood up, leaned over to Lanning and quickly kissed his cheek. She looked at the other Lanning as of she were going to say something, then walked away silently as if thinking better of it. They both watched her go.

"Beautiful," the other Lanning said.

"Beautiful," he agreed with himself.

"Let me explain," the other Lanning said.

"I wish you would."

"I'm sure you suspect already. I'm from another probability."

Lanning took a sip of coffee and nodded. "You're right . . . that's what I figured. What I can't figure out is why you're here."

"Well . . ." the other Lanning took a deep breath. "I know you well enough to realize you'd want it straight." He smiled a mirthless grin. "Like I said, I'm from another probability."

Lanning had a sudden sick feeling. "Wait. Let me guess. You're from a rival future."

His doppelganger nodded earnestly. "That's right, uh, Denny. Right about now things start to go bad for the Jonbar of this probability. If your present extends itself into the future, it'll be as bad as if Sorainya and the Gyronchi had triumphed. New Jonbar will never be built and the promise of the *dynon* will never be fulfilled."

Lanning wondered if his dream had been more than a dream, if it had been some sort of prophetic vision filtered down imperfectly from the far-distant future of the *dynon*. But it had been so unclear. Had it warned him about this other version of himself or had it warned him about what this other version of himself was about to warn him about? He cursed silently. Why were prophetic dreams so damn murky? Why couldn't they just flat out tell you, watch out for this stuff, don't trust that guy, beware of future selfs bearing gifts.

"Forgive me," Lanning finally said, "if I don't quite believe you."

The other Lanning looked at him earnestly. "Would I lie about this?"

Lanning took a deep breath. "No. I guess not." He knew himself better than that. "But you can be mistaken. You must be. If you're not, if you're right, then this probability must be shunted away from reality." He gestured vaguely around himself. "And if that happens then all this . . . the entire world . . . will fade away."

The other Lanning nodded. "I'm from the future, remember. I have twenty-twenty hindsight."

Lanning swallowed hard. He didn't want to believe himself, but he was starting to.

"What will happen to us?" he asked. "What will happen to the Legion? Will we fade away with Jonbar, or will we be marooned in the abyss of the geodesics, wandering aimlessly through eternal non-time like some damned *Flying Dutchman?*"

"If I told you," the other Lanning asked, "would it stop you from doing the right thing?"

Lanning sighed. "No. I suppose not. If I can figure out what that is."

"We've never had a problem telling right from wrong before."

"Before it was always so clear-cut. Now I don't even know whom I'm dealing with—was the Lao who called me my friend, or some shadow from another possibility? What about the one in the *Chronion?*"

"The first was your friend, the second mine. I'm sorry that Barry had to take you out, but they had to leave, fast, and they had to make sure that the *Chronion* wouldn't sail anytime soon."

"He was sabotaging the controls?"

The other Lanning nodded.

"The first Lao—he's the Lao Meng Shan of this probability?"

He nodded again. "He's the one who needs to be rescued."

"Well, you're from the future. You seem to know everything. Where is he?"

"We're not from 'the' future, we're from 'a' future, and our presence here is probably altering that future in unimaginable ways, which is why we're trying to act as little as possible. We have an idea where he is, but the rescue has to be left up to you and your friends."

"You're leaving all the dirty work to us," Lanning muttered darkly.

His doppelganger shrugged. "It's your world. We thought you'd want it that way."

"I hate it when you're right," Lanning said after a moment. "All right, what do you suggest?"

"You're being watched, you know that?" Lanning nodded. "I hid my face when I came up to your apartment."

"So they don't know there's two of us?"

"Exactly. I'll just waltz out of here. You wait a few minutes, and then you can go about your business unwatched."

Lanning nodded decisively. "We need help."

The other Lanning nodded decisively. "Yes. It's time to raise the Legion."

He held out his hand and Lanning took it, suddenly struck that for the first time he had an inkling of how the Enders felt. He felt a sudden surge of warmth for his double, less than himself but more than a brother, whose hand he clasped, even if he had brought news of the death of Lanning's whole world.

The other Lanning grinned. "I think I'll try to scare up more information on Lao's location."

Lanning nodded. "Be careful."

"You know me. The soul of discretion. What about you?"

He couldn't help himself. Despite the gravity of the situation, he grinned back at the doppelganger. "It's a nice day to visit the country."

v

The sun was hot on Lanning's back, the wind cool on his face. The road was an unpaved, twisting trail. The Indian felt powerful between his legs.

Unfortunately, he was far too preoccupied to enjoy the ride as much as he normally would. He had the feeling that perhaps he'd been cursed with what he'd been wishing for. All of a sudden his life had become meaningful again, and while the excitement and sense of adventure were welcome, he could do without the bodies, the fear for his friends, the fear for the fate of the whole world.

Lanning slowed, took a sharp turn that led off the trail onto what was little more than a footpath paralleling a swiftly moving stream. Lanning hoped that it was the right path to the Enders' homestead. He hadn't been this way in months, since he'd last visited them in the early spring when they'd been living in a canvas-sided tent while putting up their cabin.

Isaac and Israel Enders were tall, lean, taciturn men from the Canadian heartland. McClan had pulled them from a World War One trench before the German shell that had been marked to end their lives could fulfill its destiny. They were twins, whose own company was enough for them. They'd left Jonbar within a week of arriving, departing for the open country north of the city to stake out a homestead of their own.

He was relieved when he found their home by the stream and was surprised at how neat and tidy it looked. The cabin was built of mud-chinked logs with a hand-split shingle roof. A small millhouse stood next to the stream with a paddle wheel turned by the running water. Other outbuildings looked like storage sheds, several chicken hutches, and a small mud-brick oven.

One of the twins was tending the vegetable garden beside the house. There were tomatoes, corn, peas, cucumber and squash, rows of onion, lettuce, and cabbage, and other plants whose names Lanning couldn't even guess. Enders plucked a final ripe tomato as Lanning approached and placed it carefully in the basket at his feet.

"Israel?" Lanning asked.

He shook his head. "Out in the wheat field."

"Isaac."

The twin nodded. Lanning had never seen him so tanned, so fit . . . so right. While in the Legion they'd been pallid and thin. Lanning now realized that they'd never been meant for war. Their spirits had suffered for it. Back in their proper place, they'd bloomed. It would be hard to ask them to come back to the city, but he had to do it.

"We need your help, Isaac. You and Israel."

Isaac Enders looked around himself, then at Lanning. His eyes were startlingly clear, as blue as the sky. They glittered like sun on water.

"We're done with that, Denny," he said, "Israel and me. We're done with the killing and dying. This is our place, now." He gestured simply, eloquently. "We never want to see blood again, Denny, ours nor anyone's. We don't even eat meat anymore. We just keep some chickens for their eggs, cows for milk, horses for company."

Lanning stifled a sigh. He had no right to ask for more sacrifices on their part. They had already virtually died twice for Jonbar, but this time it wasn't solely Jonbar that was in trouble. It was also one of the Legion.

Israel joined them partway through Lanning's story. The two listened, then looked at one another. Israel, the older by two minutes, spoke.

"So, if we fail to rescue Lao, if the *Chronion* sails again, then darkness will fall over Jonbar. A tyranny as bad as that of Gyronchi will rise, and Jonbar will never fulfill its destiny. Mankind will be destroyed. The *dynon* will never exist."

Lanning nodded.

"On the other hand," Isaac said, "if you succeed, if you rescue

Lao and stop the *Chronion* from sailing, then this probability will be ended off. It will fade, and all our work here"—he gestured at the homestead around them—"will be for nought. We will lose everything we have and our own fate is unknown."

Lanning nodded again. "That pretty much sums it up," he said.

The twins looked at each other for a long time, then Israel spoke again. "We understand. And out of friendship, out of what we owe you and the others, we'll follow you again."

Nothing Lanning could say could do justice to their sacrifice. He nodded. He offered his hand and they took it in turn, their grip warm, strong, and friendly. It felt good to shake hands again.

"All right," Lanning said. "Come as soon as you can. Raise the Legion. Get them ready for anything."

Isaac nodded. "What about you?"

Lanning frowned. "I've got to find Lao."

"If Bylass and his men haven't already," Israel said.

"I have a feeling he won't be easy to find."

"He's in trouble sure," Isaac said. "I know he didn't kill that girl. He couldn't have."

"Which means someone else must have—" Israel said.

"Which means Lao is his scapegoat," Isaac concluded.

Lanning nodded. He was about to say that he'd already thought of that when the communicator on his bike beeped, interrupting him. He went to the Indian and looked at the screen between its handlebars and saw Lethonee's face, frowning with concern, looking back at him.

"Your friend who came to visit this morning is in trouble," she said.

He nodded. Lethonee was concerned that their communications were being monitored. Bylass and his damned Security net.

"All right," he said. "I'm on my way. We'll meet—"

"I know where you are. I'll meet you on the way in."

"All right. Be careful."

She flashed a smile, and broke contact.

Lanning looked at the Enders. "I better get going. You two be careful, too."

They nodded and waved as he started the Indian and roared away, scattering a few chickens that were pecking in the dirt. On the way back to Jonbar he racked his brains for a clever plan to deal with Bylass, but could come up with nothing. He had no authority in this world, no power to stand up to Bylass and his Security net. He had a certain status as world savior, but he was afraid that lately he'd been playing that card a little too often.

Well, he'd had no real authority as a war correspondent back in his own time, but that had never stopped him. It had gotten him ignored, threatened, even beaten and thrown in prison once or twice, but it'd also gotten him some fabulous stories, some glorious or awful truth that he'd shown the world. It was time, maybe, to start thinking like that again, to forget Lanning, savior of the world, and become again plain old Lanning, seeker of truth. If he could.

He was still ruminating when he saw Lethonee waving to him from the side of the road. She was gorgeous in the sunlight, the most beautiful, vibrant, and alive woman he'd ever seen. He braked the Indian and turned off the engine.

"Need a ride, beautiful?"

She smiled. "I was hoping a strong, handsome man on a motorcycle would come by to carry me away."

"Well, you'll have to settle for me. Hop on."

She got on behind him and put her arms around his waist.

"How'd you get here so fast?"

"I had my friend Ruthven drop me off with her flitter—and don't worry, we weren't followed."

"Great." He released the brake and fed the Indian some gas. They took off down the road. "What happened?" he shouted over his shoulder.

Lethonee put her mouth close to his ear. "Lanning called me. Said he knew where Lao was, and was going to try to free him, but Bylass and his men were onto him. They must have captured him, because he never called back."

"Did he at least say where Lao was?"

Lanning could feel Lethonee nod. "Oh yes. He said they were holding Lao in the vats."

Lanning frowned, his teeth clenched tight. They said nothing the rest of the trip, but Lanning was desperately glad to feel Lethonee's arms tight around his waist and her head resting warmly against his back.

                                  vi

There was a funny smell to the air, a yeasty, smoky odor with undertones of blood and boiling bouillon. The silver-colored vats were ranked row upon row on the floor of the poorly lit cavern, half-hidden in their own shadows. The only sound was a slight, constant drip drip drip that could have been water slipping off a hidden stalactite or blood running from an exposed vein.

Lanning looked upon the rows of vats, then glanced at Lethonee at his side. The place gave him the creeps, though, he reasoned, it was preferable to the sights and smells of a slaughterhouse anyday.

As they had with so many other problems, the Jonbarians

had humanely solved that of dealing with the animals they needed for food. They'd replaced them with slabs of flesh cloned from various species and grown in carniculture vats. These slabs of meat were mindless, nerveless, unfeeling, always-growing blobs of protoplasm that were carefully tended, trimmed, and harvested when ready.

It required a huge effort to grow and harvest as much meat as the city needed, even though the work was largely automated. There were literally thousands of vats in the cavern Under Jonbar.

"Why would Bylass bring Lao here?" Lanning asked.

"It's a good place to get rid of a body." Lanning looked at her with a frown. "All they have to do is dump it in one of the vats and it becomes nourishment for the meat," she explained.

"Oh." Lanning looked with despair upon the ranks and ranks of vats that loomed like abandoned pillboxes in the gloomy cavern. "How are we going to find them in this maze? Lao could be anywhere, in any one of them. It would take days to look into every damn vat. We need a clue, something to follow—"

Before Lethonee could reply there was a sudden booming, clanging sound, as if someone were kicking a huge gong. Or, perhaps the side of a metal vat. The reverberations echoed into silence, then the hollow thumping sound was repeated. Lanning and Lethonee looked at each other.

"How's that?" she asked.

Lanning nodded. "It'll do."

Together they ran through the cavern following the clanging reverberations. It took a while to track them down. Sound echoed weirdly in the cavern, bouncing around and being absorbed by the metallic vats. The sounds came less frequently and more quietly as they searched, as if their maker was running out of strength.

They finally narrowed their search to a particular row. A last tiny rumble, almost too muffled to hear, drew them to one of the vats in the row's center. Each vat had a spiral metal staircase snaking around its side, ending in a small railed platform. Lanning ran up the vat's stairs while Lethonee waited anxiously below.

Its lid had gauges and pipes running off it and connecting to an overhead circulation system that looked as complicated as a diagram of the blood vessels of the human body. Lanning grabbed the lid's edge and heaved. It wouldn't budge until he unlatched a series of clamps.

When he opened it a sweet, yeasty odor struck him in the face with almost palpable force. He turned away, grimacing, then looked back, holding his breath. It was hard to see inside the vat, but Lanning finally made out a slumping, crumpled form. It looked up and Lanning saw his own face, battered and bruised.

"I thought you'd never come," the other Lanning said.

Lanning leaned into the vat. A metal ladder ran down the inside wall, presumably providing access for cleaning and harvesting. "Can you make it up the ladder?"

"I'll try."

The other Lanning took a deep breath, and pulled himself to his feet. His legs were obviously weak, his whole body seemed battered and tired, but he managed to crawl high enough up the ladder until Lanning could grab his shirt. Then it was easier. Lanning heaved as the other gripped the vat's lip and pulled himself over the edge. They both sank down with their backs against the vat's cool metal skin, panting from exertion.

"Boy," Lanning finally managed to say, "you stink."

"Thanks," the other Lanning said. "Good to see you too."

He'd been beaten. His face was bruised, his lower lip split. There was blood on his chin and shirt, which had been torn nearly to shreds. He'd also been soaked in the thick, musky, slimy nutrient bath that was a couple of feet deep in the vat. His hair was slick with it, his clothes sodden.

"What happened?"

"I was looking for Lao. I knew generally what had happened to him, but not exactly where Bylass had stuck him. Well, I was in the control center checking computer records for a clue, when that bastard snuck up on me and he and his band of merry little fascists beat the stuffing out of me. He thought I was you, of course."

"Did you find Lao?" Lanning asked.

The other Lanning shook his head. "Didn't have a chance." Lanning cursed quietly, his hopes suddenly dashed. But his doppelganger smiled a crooked smile. "But that goon Bylass couldn't help bragging about it." Lanning gestured with a tired flip of his hand. "He's in the vat next to mine."

Lanning clapped his twin on the shoulder and hurried down the stairs.

"He's in there," he shouted to Lethonee. She followed him up the ladder as Lanning unlocked, then flipped open the vat's hinged top. He looked in. "There he is!"

Lao was huddled against the slab of meat growing from the spindle that went from lid to floor in the center of the vat. He seemed to be braced up against the thing, embracing it. Lanning felt his heart skip, for Lao's eyes were closed and he wasn't breathing. Lanning dropped to his knees in the smelly nutrient broth next to his friend.

"Lao," he said, touching him gently on his shoulder. "Lao?"

After what seemed like an eternity Lao's eyes fluttered open and he smiled a ghastly smile. "I knew . . . you'd come," he said in a half-dead whisper.

Lanning rocked back on his heels, heaving a grateful sigh.

"Okay," he said. "I'm going to get you out of here."

Lao half-nodded. He couldn't move his head too well. One side of his face seemed to be stuck to the meat growing from the spindle. "The sooner . . . the . . . better . . ."

Lanning grimaced. "Okay," he said, and took Lao's shoulders and pulled.

There was a horrid sucking, tearing sound, and Lao screamed. Lanning choked back a cry of his own and tugged harder. His friend broke away from the slab of meat that had been engulfing him, ripping the skin off the side of his face and flesh from his hands and fingers. Most of his shirt stuck to the slab, and he left behind skin and flesh from his shoulder.

The shock and pain knocked him out. Lanning cursed, hefting the dead weight of his friend's body. For a moment Lanning thought that Lao had died, but he was still breathing, and bleeding from where he'd lost skin and flesh. He tossed Lao over his shoulder and started up the ladder inside the vat. Lethonee was waiting on the platform outside, and helped him gently lift Lao out of the death trap that had held him for so long. Lanning carried him to the ground, next to where his double anxiously waited.

"That damn thing was eating him," Lanning said, outraged, as he set his friend gently down on the ground.

The other nodded. "It would have eventually engulfed him— but the nutrient bath encourages rapid growth and healing. If it wasn't for that he'd be long dead. Here." He handed Lethonee his tattered shirt. "Bandage his wounds with this. It's soaked through with that junk."

Lao groaned even though Lethonee was being as gentle as she could. His eyes fluttered open, and he smiled at his friends.

"You're going to be all right," Lanning said.

Lao took a deep breath. "You must stop Adolpham," he said

in a low, exhausted voice. "He plans to take the *Chronion* into the future, to discover the secret of the *dynat.* If he ever gets control of it—"

"We know," both Lannings said at once.

Lethonee frowned. "What does this mean?" she asked.

The Lannings looked at each other. Lanning didn't want to, but he had to tell her. As he spoke she looked shocked, angered, and sorrowful in turn. She said nothing, even when he'd finished.

"So," he concluded, "I'd better get to the *Chronion* and pull the plug on Adolpham and Bylass's scheme." He looked at Lethonee. "Stay here. Take care of, uh, Denny and Lao."

She looked up at him and shook her head. "I'm coming with you."

"But—"

"It's my world," she said, anger in her eyes and voice. "Don't you think I should be present at its ending?"

Lanning stood, head down. There was nothing he could say.

vii

The *Chronion* was quiet, but Lanning knew that deep in its guts evil was working, festering in silence and darkness, evil that Lanning had to wipe from the world. He glanced at Lethonee, silent by his side. Perhaps he had to wipe away the world itself.

Savior turned destroyer, he climbed with Lethonee onto the deck and went silently down to the control center where Adolpham was laboring over the ship's temporal mechanism. He looked up when they entered the room.

"You again?" the scientist asked. "Still looking for your friend? And Lethonee. To what do I owe the honor?"

"We found Lao," Lanning said.

Adolpham looked surprised. "Congratulations. Why are you bothering me then?"

"Because you're the one who put him in the carniculture vats," Lethonee said "to be assimilated by one of the meat clones and end up on someone's dinner plate."

"That's absurd," Adolpham said.

"Is it?" Lanning challenged.

Adolpham stared at them for a long moment, then shook his head, smiling. "No. You're right, of course."

"And you killed Fraeya," Lethonee said accusatorily. "You took her head so our surgeons couldn't revive her."

"Well, not me personally, but I must admit you have the basics correct." Adolpham shook his head, a little smile still playing on his lips. "How did you come to these amazing realizations?"

Lanning shrugged. "Does it matter? We know what you're up to. Repairing the *Chronion* is only one of your little projects. Your main interest is experimenting with the *dynat*, looking for the way to mentally control atomic energy."

The scientist nodded. "Amazing—and quite true. I used Lao Meng Shan as one of my test subjects. I achieved some success with him, but I'm afraid he was damaged during the course of my investigations. But not so damaged that he couldn't escape briefly and make a desperate call for help. We weren't sure whom he'd called, but we knew that he wanted to meet at his apartment. I had Bylass set a trap. But Fraeya discovered our plans and acted most emotionally. She had to be taken care of. Meanwhile I'd been making progress with the *dynat*, but slowly. Then it suddenly struck me." He gestured around himself. "If I can repair the *Chronion* all I have to do is discover the proper probability, follow it to the future, and see exactly how the *dynon* manipulate the *dynat*. Then I just bring the information back and experiment on some suitable test subjects. No doubt it'll take a few trials, but I'm sure I'll eventually get it right."

"You will," Lanning said grimly. "You'll repair the *Chronion*, find the probability that leads to New Jonbar, and discover how the *dynon* harness fusion power by force of mind. You'll return here and after years of experimentation, you'll create a race of surgically-altered slaves with the same ability. Of course, force-feeding them the power of the *dynon* will drive them mad, but you won't care. You and Bylass will take over Jonbar and run it as your personal little kingdom."

Adolpham, his eyes wide, looked inordinately pleased. "How do—"

"You would do all this," Lanning said grimly.

"But we're going to stop you," Lethonee added.

Adolpham frowned. "But why, my dear? I'll simply be bringing our future to us in our lifetime, rather than in thousands of years."

Lethonee shook her head. "At what cost, Adolpham? You'll sacrifice the lives and well-being of countless citizens, creating a society no better than Sorainya would have. Your future will be as dark and grim and ultimately as futile. The world will end unless we stop you."

"This is utter foolishness," Adolpham said. "I think this discussion has gone on long enough. Bylass!"

His shout was answered immediately. The Security man stepped into the control room behind Lanning and Lethonee with a dozen men.

"For someone so remarkably prescient, you've also been utterly blind," Adolpham said.

"Apparently you escaped the vat with the help of your slut," Bylass said viciously, "but this time I'll make sure you're in no condition to crawl, let alone stand."

"You did the actual killing, didn't you?" Lanning said. "Fraeya's blood is on your hands."

"Of course," Bylass acknowledged. "I'll kill the both of you, too." He glanced at the scientist. "Unless Adolpham needs you."

"Hmmm." Adolpham stared at Lanning as if he were a particularly promising-looking laboratory rat, then looked at Lethonee. "But no. They're too dangerous. They know too much and she's much too visible. You'd better take them some place quiet and get rid of Lanning immediately. There are plenty of others we can test our theories on."

"There were people like you in my time," Lanning said. "They were called Nazis."

"Is that right?" Adolpham said blandly. "I'll have to look them up in the history books." He nodded at Bylass.

Bylass drew an energy pistol and pointed it at Lanning. "Move," he said economically.

Lanning looked at him coldly. "When I finish with you there won't be enough left for even Jonbar's physicians to bring back to life."

Bylass struck like a snake, pistol-whipping Lanning across his face, knocking him back against Lethonee. Bylass grinned as blood ran down Lanning's cheek and dripped onto his chest as Lethonee supported him.

"That's just the beginning, primitive trash. Now get going."

Lanning and Lethonee led the way, with Bylass and his men behind them. They were on deck, bunched close together in a tight knot and getting ready to go over the rail, when a voice suddenly called out, "Hold it right there, chum."

Bylass started, turned, and stared.

It was the Legion. Young, red-haired Barry Halloran. Silvano Cresto. Willy Rand. Erich von Arneth. Jean Querard and Boris Barinin. The giant Emil Schorn. The Britishers Courtney-Pharr and Duffy Clark. The Enders. They were armed with Mausers and Lugers taken from the *Chronion*'s stores. Some of them looked grim, some affected unconcern. Some were grinning madly in anticipation, for it had been months since they were in a real fight.

"You're the fool, Bylass," Lanning said in a low voice. "You and your crazy co-conspirator. You think I've never fought a battle before? You think I'd walk onto the *Chronion* blind?"

"Kill them!" Bylass screamed. "Kill them all!"

"All right, boys," Barry Halloran shouted. "Chargggggge!!!"

And with fixed bayonets, the Legion of Time charged.

Bylass had the only drawn pistol. He tried to aim at Halloran, but Lanning grabbed his arm and yanked it down so that he fired into the deck. Energy spit from the pistol's muzzle, splashed on the deck, and reflected up in a coruscating spray. Bylass screamed as the ricochets burned his legs.

The others tried to draw as the Legion opened fire with their Mausers. They fired high, making sure not to hit Lanning or Lethonee. The shots were explosively loud. Bylass's men had never heard a noise like that before. Most ducked instinctively as Barry and Emil Schorn screamed hoarse battle cries that melded with the rifle fire in a hellish cacophony.

Lanning shoved Bylass into two of his men. One fell, dropping his half-drawn pistol. Lethonee dove for it as a few others finally drew and fired. Out of the corner of his eye Lanning saw Duffy Clark go down, then one of the Enders, he couldn't tell which, and then Halloran hit them like a tackle tearing through the line to get to the quarterback, only he was carrying a Mauser with attached bayonet. The blade took one of the Security men high in the chest and he screamed like a frightened animal, and then the rest of the Legion joined the melee.

There was a confusing, desperate maelstrom of hand-to-hand

fighting, interspersed with blasts of rifle and pistol fire, the high-pitched whine of energy weapons, and the screams, battle cries, and curses of the men. Lanning saw Emil Schorn run one of Bylass's men through the stomach, lift him off his feet on the blade of the bayonet, and throw him over the side of the *Chronion*.

The stench of blood and burned flesh stank in Lanning's nostrils. He hated it, but hated the man glaring madly at him even more. Bylass and he danced around each other, Lanning with a death grip on his arm, preventing him from using his energy pistol. Bylass lashed out with his booted foot, hitting Lanning's shin. Lanning went down, pulling Bylass with him.

They hit the deck and rolled in the streaming blood. They slid over the body of a Security man, Lanning hammering at Bylass's face with his free hand. He caught the Jonbarian square on the nose and Bylass howled. The flash of pain gave him added strength, and he pulled his gun hand free of Lanning's desperate grip.

His howl of pain turned to a scream of triumph, then someone reached out and grabbed Bylass's arm before he could aim and fire his energy weapon. Bylass glanced up and his grin of triumph turned suddenly into a mask of fear and disbelief.

"No!" he screamed. "I killed you!"

Lao Meng Shan calmly shook his head. "No. But you tried to."

He pointed the muzzle of his Luger at Bylass's face and pulled the trigger. He kept pulling it until there was little left of the man's head.

"For you, Fraeya," Lao said quietly.

Lanning looked around. It was all over. Only a few of the Security men were still alive, and they were all crawling on the deck, groaning or crying in pain. The Legion of Time seemed to have doubled. There were two of almost everyone. Some were staring dumbfoundedly at each other, others were helping their injured comrades. Lanning's doppelganger put a hand out and helped Lanning to his feet.

"We came to help, but I see you've got things well in hand."

Lanning grunted. "Give us some credit."

"I do," the other Lanning said. He looked around. "Things are under control here, but there's still much to be done, and time is running low."

"I thought," Lanning said, "that time was something we never ran out of."

"Most times," the other Lanning said with a smile. "Come on."

The legionnaires still on their feet were helping their wounded comrades. It didn't look too bad for most of them, except for one of the Enders brothers who'd taken an energy beam high on the chest early in the battle. His shirt was soaked with blood. His brother was holding his hand while the two Barry Hallorans were carrying him as gently as they could by his head and feet.

"Isaac?" Lanning asked.

The wounded man shook his head and Lanning could see the effort that small task cost him.

"You never could tell us apart," he said in a small voice, bloody bubbles forming on his lips.

"Take the wounded to sick bay," the other Lanning ordered.

As they moved to obey Lanning saw the other Enders carrying a body on a stretcher. Lao Meng Shan lay on it, battered and bruised and not breathing.

"Is he alive?" Lanning asked.

The other Lanning shrugged. "We have work below decks.

Lao." He gestured at the walking, healthy Lao Meng Shan. "Let's go."

They went below with Lethonee and half a dozen of the Legion, while the others took the wounded to the *Chronion's* sick bay.

Adolpham, his back toward them, was busy probing into the guts of the temporal mechanism. "Bylass, what was that racket on deck? You know I can't be bothered—"

"Bylass is dead," Lao said. "I blew his head to tiny little pieces."

"What?" Adolpham jerked around. He stared, the disbelief plain on his face. "Why, we got rid of you . . ." He stopped, stared at the two Lannings, the two Emil Schorns behind them, one whole, one bleeding from his forehead. "I see," he said, nodding. "Two of you."

"That's right," Lanning said. "A Legion from another probability, come to help stop your damnable plan."

"But . . ." The implications suddenly struck Adolpham. "That means . . ."

The other Lanning nodded. "That's right. This line is a dead end and we're closing it off."

"No," Adolpham said. "You can't. You'll destroy all Jonbar."

Lethonee interrupted him, her voice hot with anger. "No, Adolpham. You destroyed Jonbar. They're just burying the corpse."

"You—you have no right to do this!" Adolpham sputtered.

The other Lanning shrugged. He turned to the two Emil Schorns. "Throw him off the ship."

They smiled. "Gladly," they rumbled in unison.

They grabbed the scientist not very gently, and carried him away, screaming and ineffectually kicking. The other Lanning nodded at Lao. "Put it all together," he said.

Lao bent to the jumble of wires, coils, circuit boards, and other arcane mechanisms that Adolpham had exposed.

Lanning looked at his other self. "What's going to happen?"

"This world will cease to be."

Lanning swallowed hard. *"Have* we the right to do this?"

The other Lanning shrugged. "We did it before."

"But that seemed so easy . . . so clear-cut."

"This probability was heading for the same darkness that encompassed Sorainya and her Gyronchi. Ultimately Adolpham's slaves would have rebelled and overthrown him. Their battle would have ripped Jonbar apart and created a score of competing pocket-cities, each ruled by inhumanly powerful, insane beings. Jonbar's light would have been forever extinguished. New Jonbar would never have risen. With Adolpham and Bylass removed, the *dynon* will come into being as a result of slow, natural, evolution on our probability line, and New Jonbar will be the glory of the universe."

"And this probability?"

"It will fade from the geodesic."

Lanning looked bitter. "You couldn't have handled it yourself? You had to drag us into it?"

The other Lanning looked at him. "We thought you had the right to be part of this. You could have refused us, even fought us."

Lanning looked down at the deck. "No," he said. "No, we couldn't."

"I know," his doppelganger said softly. He looked at Lethonee, sadness and regret on his face. "The dissolution is probably already beginning. We have to get back to our *Chronion.*" He glanced at Lao. "Done yet?"

"Almost," Lao said.

Lanning looked at Lethonee and suddenly found that he couldn't meet her eyes. She went to him and put her arms around him, hugging him tightly with her head laid against his chest.

"Farewell, my love," she murmured.

Lanning was caught in a sudden, unbearable surge of grief. "I'm going with you," he told her.

His other self grabbed his arm. "If you leave the sanctuary of the *Chronion*, you will exist always, floating alone, drifting endlessly, eternally among the geodesics, hopelessly searching for worlds that never were. You must stay on the *Chronion*."

"Listen to him, my love," Lethonee told him. "It is my wish for you."

"I—" Lanning was torn by indecision. He wanted nothing more than to hold Lethonee forever in his arms.

"It is my final wish," she said.

Lanning looked at his other self. His expression was unreadable. "If I remain on the *Chronion*?"

"Then you have a chance."

"Finished," Lao suddenly said, standing and dusting his hands together with some satisfaction.

"All right. Round up the others." Lanning's other self beckoned him. He disengaged himself from Lethonee and his other self put a hand on his arm and pulled him close. "One other thing," he said in a low voice. "Lose the self-pity. Most people would have killed for the things you were given. Jonbar owed you everything, except for happiness. That you had to find for yourself. No one else could do it for you, not even Lethonee. If you couldn't find it, it was no one's fault but yours."

Lanning opened his mouth to argue, but could find no words. He was right. Again.

"Good luck," the other said. "And goodbye. I doubt we'll meet again."

Lanning shook hands with himself. His doppelganger looked at Lethonee and for the first time Lanning could see tears in the other's eyes. He looked as if he wanted to go to her and take her in his arms, but in the end he just nodded and strode after Lao, leaving them alone.

"I love you," Lanning said.

"I know."

They embraced again and he held her tightly until his fingers sank into what had become of the flesh of her back. Even then he tried to pull her to him, but soon realized it was easier to hold on to dreams than mist. She faded away to nothing, vanishing finally with his name sighing from her spectral lips.

After a while he went up on deck.

viii

Six of them were in sick bay, five of them wounded, Israel Enders and Lao Meng Shan the worst. Isaac was tending them as best he could, but there was little he could do for Lao and his brother.

The others were on the bridge, in the crystal dome in the middle of the deck. Lanning had powered the *Chronion*. So far everything seemed to be working. They watched in silent awe as Under Jonbar dissolved around them. It faded slowly, like a ghost in the light, until they were enveloped in a blue, flickering abyss of nothingness and everything, the chasm of probability from which flowed the geodesics.

Lanning suddenly remembered something Lethonee had once told him.

"There is a flow from probability to certainty," she'd said. "Probabilities are infinite, but there is only one reality. Many conflicting futures are possible, but the past is certain and complete. The flow of realization must always take one branch and obliterate the rest."

He turned back to the control panel and set their course, putting the tracer to follow the strongest geodesic running toward the future.

"What's to become of us, Captain?" Jean Querard asked.

Lanning shook his head. "I don't know. The other Lanning said there was a chance."

"A chance for what?" Halloran asked.

Lanning shrugged.

"I'd settle for just a hard rock and a bit of sun," Courtney-Pharr said.

Lanning said nothing.

Hours passed in the non-time of the geodesics, maybe days. There was no way to tell. They waited on the bridge, staring ahead, until suddenly there was a world before them.

It was a green world, and the city they approached had soaring towers and pylons that reached to the skies. Hope clutched at Lanning so hard it made his gut ache. They glided toward one of the silver spires set on a hillside. A vast doorway opened and the *Chronion* slipped into a huge hangar. He gingerly steered into an open area and set it down with only a bounce or two.

"Ach," Emil Schorn said. "It's Jonbar again." He sounded almost disappointed.

It was, Lanning thought wildly. It was. If his other self—his future self—hadn't lied, he hadn't exactly told the whole truth either. Just like himself, he thought, to make it hard on himself.

Lanning turned to the Prussian. "It looks like we have a second chance, which is a lot more than most get." He gripped Schorn's massive forearm and stared straight into the Prussian's hard gray eyes, but his words were for everyone. "We have another shot at happiness, but it's up to us to make it work. They can't do it for us. We have to find it ourselves. We have to make our own place in the world."

Emil Schorn nodded slowly. Lanning smiled to himself. It was a good line. He'd have to remember to tell it to himself when they met again.

They left the crystal bubble of the bridge. A crowd was running toward the *Chronion*. Some were carrying stretchers.

First up the ladder and onto the deck was the most beautiful woman Lanning had ever seen. She ran into his arms and he hugged her fiercely, never wanting to let her go.

"Denny, Denny, Denny," Lethonee murmured into his ear. "You made it. You've come back to me."

Lanning looked around himself as the Jonbarians swarmed over the deck. Some had gone immediately to the sick bay and were already bringing out the wounded.

It felt good to hold Lethonee in his arms, but most of all it felt good to be home.

Afterword

Sitting on the desk next to me as I write this is an old paperback called *The Legion of Time* (Pyramid Science Fiction X-1586. Cost: sixty cents). I bought it in 1967, the Golden Age of science fiction. I was thirteen. Pyramid was reprinting a slew of Jack's books with wonderful Jack Gaughan covers, and I was buying, reading, and enjoying them all, but *The Legion of Time* struck a chord that remained vivid in my memory for nearly thirty years.

Now I'm almost three decades past thirteen and you can't find a paperback for anything near sixty cents. When Roger asked me if I would like to contribute to this volume I immediately thought of *The Legion of Time*, remembering that this ninety-some page novella has more potent ideas, colorful characters, and exotic locales than most novels five times its length. When I reread it I was pleased, but not surprised, to discover that although nearly sixty years has passed since it was first published it's still both thought-provoking and entertaining.

I hope that "Worlds That Never Were" does it some small justice.

Thanks, Jack, for almost seventy years' worth of wonderful stories.

—John J. Miller

About the Contributors

Poul Anderson has been a popular and critically acclaimed author of science fiction and fantasy for over forty years. His works have garnered seven Hugo and three Nebula Awards. Equally at home in hard science fiction, light adventure, and fantasy, Anderson has written over a hundred short stories and dozens of novels, including such critically acclaimed novels as *Brain Wave*, the Nicholas van Rijn books, *Tau Zero*, and *The Boat of a Million Years*. He and his wife, Karen, live in the San Francisco Bay area.

Ben Bova is a writer of hard science and adventure science fiction novels and short stories. He is perhaps best known for *Mars*,

The Kinsman Saga, Death Dreams, and the *Orion* series, among more than three dozen novels. Bova has also worked as an editor in science fiction, most notably for his tenure at *Analog,* which earned him the Hugo Award six times in seven years. Later he was also fiction editor of *OMNI,* and then executive editor. Bova has served as President of the Science Fiction Writers of America. He has also done a considerable amount of nonfiction writing about science and high technology. He and his wife, literary agent and author Barbara Bova, live in Florida.

Jeff Bredenberg has had several science fiction novels published, *The Dream Compass, The Dream Vessel,* and *The Man in the Moon Must Die,* as well as a few short stories, including a couple in *The Magazine of Fantasy & Science Fiction,* and one in the anthology *Wheel of Fortune.* He lives with his wife and children near Philadelphia, Pennsylvania.

David Brin has won both Hugo and Nebula Awards for his novels *Startide Rising* and *The Uplift War.* Other science fiction novels include *The Postman,* a post-holocaust tapestry, the epic *Earth,* and *The Glory Season.* In these and other novels he combines hard science and great storytelling to produce compulsively readable science fiction. He has also written fantasy, including the novel *The Practice Effect.* He edited an anthology, with Arthur C. Clarke, about solar-sail technology, *Project Solar Sail.* Since he began publishing in 1980, he has become one of today's most popular science fiction writers. He and his family live in Southern California.

John Brunner was a major British science fiction and fantasy writer. Known for his politically astute and well-written novels and shorter works that dealt with issues both sociopolitical and at times darkly psychological, he is best known for his novel *Stand on Zanzibar*, which won the Hugo Award, the British Science Fiction Award, and the Prix Apollo. Groundbreaking in technique and brilliant in execution, this novel stunned the science fiction world. Other well known works include *The Whole Man*, *The Sheep Look Up*, *The Squares of the City*, *Shockwave Rider*, and *The Jagged Orbit*. Brunner is also known for his dark, existential fantasy cycle, *The Compleat Traveller in Black*. Brunner also wrote a number of adventurous science fiction novels, and also wrote mainstream fiction and poetry. An eloquent and persuasive public speaker, he was known for his passionate commitment to issues of social justice and anti-war causes. Brunner died in 1995.

Paul Dellinger is the author of a number of short stories, including science fiction, fantasy, and mysteries, along with two plays and a comedy-adventure radio series. He lives in Virginia.

Scott E. Green has been a poet in the science fiction, fantasy, and horror genres for many years. His work has appeared in numerous magazines and anthologies, including *Asimov's Science Fiction*, *Amazing Stories*, and *Aboriginal SF*. He has had reference books published, and wrote the entry on poetry for *The New Encyclopedia of Science Fiction*, edited by James Gunn. He lives in New Hampshire.

Jane Lindskold has been writing science fiction and fantasy since the early 1990s. Her published works include the novels *Brother to*

Dragons, Companion to Owls, Marks of our Brothers, Pipes of Orpheus, and *Smoke and Mirrors.* In addition, she has had short fiction published in various anthologies and magazines. She lives in Albuquerque, New Mexico.

John J. Miller has had a number of stories published in George R. R. Martin's *Wild Cards* series. He has also had five science fiction novels published, including two *Ray Bradbury's Dinosaur World* novels, most notably *Dinosaur Empire.* On a completely different note, he has written a number of articles about the history of baseball. He lives in Albuquerque, New Mexico.

Pati Nagle has been selling fiction for a short time, and already has had science fiction and fantasy stories published in *The Magazine of Fantasy & Science Fiction* and in various science fiction anthologies. She lives in Albuquerque, New Mexico.

Andre Norton is one of the most popular and celebrated writers in both the science fiction and fantasy fields. Honored as a Grand Master by the Science Fiction Writers of America and recipient of the World Fantasy Award for Life Achievement, she has written well over one hundred novels of adventure and magic, spanning both fields and other genres as well. Her work is invariably marked by a sense of adventure and a vivid imagination. Her *Witch World* novels have been her most popular works worldwide; in these and other works she has displayed versatile and compelling narrative gifts. Her work spans seven decades, and is notable for her treatment of issues not generally explored by science fiction in its early days, including the use of protagonists who, either by being women, or by belonging to an ethnic minority, broke the mold of the "Golden Age Science Fiction" white male–dominated space adventure genre. Other well-known series by Norton include the *Time Traders* books, the *Solar Queen* books, the *Forerunner* books, and the *Hosteen Storm* books, among others. She has also edited anthologies, including the *Tales of the Witch World* series. In these books, and in other ways, Norton has been a powerful friend to new and talented writers, inviting them to contribute to her anthologies, and encouraging their writing on a personal level. She truly deserves the title bestowed on her by *Life Magazine*: "the Grande Dame of Science Fiction."

Frederik Pohl has done just about everything one can do in the science fiction field. A multiple Hugo and Nebula Award–winning author, his most famous work is undoubtedly the novel *Gateway*, which won the Hugo, Nebula, and John W. Campbell Memorial awards for Best Science Fiction Novel. *Man Plus* won the Nebula Award. His mature work is marked by a serious intellectual agenda and strongly held sociopolitical beliefs, without any sacrifice of narrative drive. In addition to his solo fiction, Pohl has collaborated successfully with a number of writers, including C. M. Kornbluth and Jack Williamson. The Pohl/Kornbluth collaboration, *The Space Merchants*, is a longtime classic of satiric science fiction. *The Starchild Trilogy* with Williamson is one of the more notable collaborations in the field. Pohl has been a magazine editor in the field since he was very young, piloting *Worlds of If* to three successive Hugos for Best Magazine. As an editor, he pioneered original-story anthologies, editing the *Star* series in the early 1950s. He has also at various times acted as a literary agent, edited several science fiction lines, and been President of the Science Fiction Writers of America. For a number of years he has been active in the World Science Fiction movement. He and his wife, Elizabeth Anne Hull, a prominent academic active in the Science Fiction Research Association, live outside Chicago, Illinois.

Mike Resnick has written more than three dozen science fiction and fantasy novels, including *Santiago*, perhaps his best known work. He has also written a number of short science fiction stories, several of which have won Hugo or Nebula Awards, most recently "Seven Views of Mt. Olduvai," which won both awards. He has also edited a number of anthologies of original stories, including the offbeat "Alternate" series, most astonishingly *Alternate Kennedys*. Resnick's science fiction is well written and frequently adventurous in content. In recent years, his own work has become increasingly serious in its agenda, often focusing on Africa and various issues associated with the exploitation of the natural world. He and his wife live in southern Ohio.

Fred Saberhagen has been writing science fiction and fantasy for more than thirty years. He first made a mark with his "Berserker" stories, but has penned several dozen entertaining novels and stories of quite varied content, including horror, adventure, magical, and Arthurian fantasy, as well as science fiction of various types, including such outstanding works as *The Veils of Azlaroc*. His *Swords* series has been especially popular; so have his Dracula books. If he can be said to have a flaw it could only be that he is so versatile. But that is only a flaw if one wants to put a label on the creativity of a multi-talented author. He and his wife live in Albuquerque, New Mexico.

David Weber has in just a few years established a reputation as one of the best young writers of military science fiction. Especially notable are six novels about the career of Honor Harrington, including *Field of Dishonor*. Of his six other novels so far in print, most notable is *Path of the Fury*. He has also contributed to the anthology *Bolos 3: The Triumphant*, and has also collaborated with Steven White. Mr. Weber seems unlikely to slow down anytime soon. He lives in South Carolina.

Connie Willis is one of the most accomplished and versatile science fiction and fantasy writers to have begun in the 1970s. A prolific short story writer, she has won Hugo and Nebula awards for her short work, including "Fire Watch." She also won both Hugo and Nebula Awards for her novel *Doomsday Book*. Another novel, *Lincoln's Dreams*, is a thoughtful, powerful novel of the Civil War. One of the qualities that distinguishes her work is her extremely wide range of tone and subject, ranging from light farce to satire to realistic slice-of-life, to serious and emotionally powerful drama. Her most recent book is a short novel, *Remake*. She has also collaborated with Cynthia Felice on two novels, *Water Witch* and *Light Raid*. She lives in Colorado.